OTHER BOOKS BY THIS AUTHOR

Something in the Wine
Backwards to Oregon
Beyond the Trail
Hidden Truths
Second Nature
Natural Family Disasters
True Nature

CONFLICT OF INTEREST

A ROMANTIC SUSPENSE NOVEL

JAE

ACKNOWLEDGMENTS

As always, it took a village to produce a book. I would like to thank all the people who helped make this second edition of *Conflict of Interest* what it is today.

First and foremost, thanks to my valued beta readers, Alison Grey and Erin, for your support, your time, and your feedback. I can't express with words how grateful I am.

Thank you also to Sue, Angie, and Henriette, who test-read the novel.

Another thank-you goes to Nikki Busch. This was the first time I worked with her, and I can highly recommend her as an editor.

And since people do judge a book by its cover, I also want to thank Glendon for making a shiny, new cover for *Conflict of Interest.*

Last but not least, thanks to everyone who helped with the first edition—Pam, Margot, Rayne, KC, Kristin, Lori, Jonel, Lena, and Michelle.

DEDICATION

For all survivors.

CHAPTER 1

"I'M GOING TO THROW UP," Dawn Kinsley said, rubbing her nervous stomach.

"No, you won't." Her friend and colleague Ally just grinned. "Come on, you're a therapist. You're used to talking to people."

"Not to one hundred cops who would rather be elsewhere and who won't give me the time of day." Dawn knew what the police officers sitting on the other side of the curtain were thinking. Most of them would view her lecture as a waste of time.

Ally rolled her eyes. "A psychologist with glossophobia. I wonder what the APA would say about that."

"I'm sure the American Psychological Association would be much more concerned about a psychologist with your lack of compassion," Dawn answered, now with a grin of her own. Usually, she didn't have a problem with public speaking. She had held her own in front of gum-chewing high school kids, earnest college students, and renowned psychologists twice her age, but cops were a special audience for her. It was almost as if she was expecting to see her father sitting in one of the rows and was trying to impress him. *Oh, come on. This is not the time to start analyzing yourself.*

"Touché," Ally said.

Both of them had to chuckle, and Dawn felt herself relax.

"There are a few techniques that can help in these situations, you know," Ally said.

"Let me guess—picturing everyone in the audience naked?"

Dawn grinned at her friend. "And how would that help with my nervousness?"

Ally shrugged. "Well, maybe it won't." She peeked out from behind the curtain, letting her appreciative gaze wander over the men in the first few rows. "But it might be nice nonetheless."

"Maybe for you, but how would it be nice for me to picture a room full of naked men? Hello?" Dawn gave a little wave. "Did you miss the office memo informing everyone about my sexual orientation?"

"Office memo? Is that what they call it nowadays when spotted kissing your girlfriend in the office parking lot?"

"What?" Dawn sputtered. "I never did that!"

Ally rubbed her forehead and pretended to think about it. "No? Must have been Charlie, then." She pushed the curtain aside to glance at the audience again. "There are also a few female officers down there. You could look at them."

"All two of them?" Dawn joked but stepped closer to follow Ally's gaze. There were more than two female cops in the audience—but not that many more.

"Pick one," Ally said.

Dawn nudged her with an elbow. "I'm here to give a lecture, not to pick up women, Ally."

Ally ignored her protests. "Pick one and concentrate on her during your lecture. Ignore the rest of the crowd. It'll help with the nervousness. So?" She pointed to the seated police officers.

Well, it can't hurt. Dawn craned her neck and peeked past the taller Ally. Her gaze wandered from woman to woman, never stopping for long until... "Her!" she said, pointing decisively.

In the very last row, between a tall African American man in his forties and a younger man whose posture screamed "rookie," a female plainclothes detective was just taking her seat. She had short, jet-black hair, and a leather jacket covered what Dawn could see of her tall, athletic frame.

"Ooh!" Ally whistled quietly. "Nice choice! Didn't know you liked them a little on the butch side, though. Maggie isn't nearly—"

"Compared to Maggie, even you look butch," Dawn said.

"Dr. Kinsley?"

Dawn looked away from the detective and turned around. "Yes?"

One of the seminar organizers stepped up to them. "Here are your handouts." He handed her a stack of paper. "Are you ready to begin?"

Dawn clutched the handouts and swallowed. "Yes."

"Good luck," Ally said. Behind the seminar organizer's back, she mouthed, "Remember to picture her naked."

How's that supposed to calm my racing heart? Dawn stepped out from behind the curtain and made her way over to the microphone with a confidence she didn't really feel.

Aiden slumped into a seat between her partner and Ruben Cartwright. The chair next to Ruben was suspiciously empty. "Where's your partner? Terminal back pain again?" If she had to be at this stupid seminar, so did everyone else, even hypochondriacs like Jeff Okada.

Ruben looked up from the paper airplane that had once been his seminar brochure. He shoved a strand of brown hair out of his boyishly handsome face and glanced from Aiden to her partner. "Uh, what?"

Ray leaned over to him with a grin. "There's one thing you have to know about your new partner, rookie. His back acts up every time a seminar comes along."

"It acts up whenever I have to sit in one of these seats designed for first graders," Jeff Okada said as he walked up to them. Gingerly, he eased himself down next to his rookie partner.

Aiden sighed and glanced at her watch. She had a stack of unfinished reports on her desk, and their thirty open cases didn't get any closer to being solved while she sat here. The seminar also stopped her from spending her lunch hour in the courtroom's gallery, watching her favorite deputy district attorney at work. Maybe she would have even worked up the courage to ask Kade to lunch today.

Sighing again, she wrestled herself into a standing position and pointed to the back of the conference room. "I'm going for coffee."

"If you want to live long enough to enjoy your hard-earned pension, I'd advise against that, my friend." Okada raised his index finger in warning. "In more than twenty-five years on the job, I've never been to a law enforcement seminar with even halfway decent coffee."

Ray smirked. "In twenty-five years on the job, you've never been to a law enforcement seminar, period."

Over the top of his sunglasses, Okada directed a withering glance at Ray before he turned back to Aiden. "The lack of drinkable coffee is obviously a nationwide conspiracy from law enforcement brass to make sure nothing distracts their officers from the lectures. For the same reason, you'll never encounter donuts or attractive female lecturers at a law enforcement seminar."

"Or comfortable chairs," Ray said.

Okada threw up his hands. "Now you're starting to get it."

Aiden sank back into her chair. Giving up on her caffeine fix, she pulled the now crushed seminar program out from under her. The wrinkled paper announced the title of the first lecture: Special Needs and Issues of Male and GLBT Survivors of Rape and Sexual Abuse. The speaker was some PhD named D. Kinsley.

"Great," Aiden murmured. They hadn't even hired a cop or someone who knew the reality of handling sex crimes to give the lecture. Instead, some antiquated Freudian in a stiff suit would bore them to tears with his academic theories.

A young woman carrying a stack of handouts stepped out from behind a curtain and crossed the podium—probably the Freudian's assistant or the poor soul who had the questionable honor of introducing the speaker. The woman tapped the microphone to test its volume and nodded. "Good morning, ladies and gentlemen. I'm Dawn Kinsley, your lecturer for the first part of the seminar."

Aiden's head jerked up. That was D. Kinsley?

Nothing reminded Aiden of the academic Freudian she had imagined except the glasses on the freckled nose. Instead of a suit and tie, slacks and a tight, sleeveless blouse covered a body that was petite, yet not frail. The strawberry blonde hair wasn't pulled back into an old-fashioned bun, but cascaded in curls halfway down to softly curved hips.

Seems she's the PhD, not the assistant. That's what I get for stereotyping. Of course, looking at her instead of an old man is not exactly a punishment. However boring the lecture might be, at least she would have something captivating to look at.

The lecture began, and to her surprise, Aiden found herself looking away from the pretty speaker to jot down interesting details about dealing with male rape victims. The lecture turned out to be informative, practice-oriented, and witty. She even caught Okada bending his aching back to take notes. The psychologist spoke with passion and sensitivity, never even glancing down at her notes.

Instead, Aiden felt as if the psychologist was looking right at her, focusing on her as if there were no one else in the room. *Oh, come on. Stop dreaming. There are a few other people in the room, you know?* Aiden listened with rapt attention to the rest of the lecture.

Forty-five minutes passed almost too soon.

"I knew I should have tried the coffee," Ruben mumbled when they began to file out of the room with the last of the seminar participants. "If there's an attractive female lecturer, there's a chance the rest of your seminar conspiracy theory is bull too."

Okada stretched and shook his head. "I wouldn't bet your meager paycheck on it, partner. Some government employee obviously failed to check the lecturer's picture, but there's no way they would overlook a bill for Blue Hawaiian beans at forty dollars per pound."

Someone chuckled behind them.

Aiden turned and looked into the twinkling gray-green eyes of Dawn Kinsley, their lecturer. The faint laugh lines at their corners indicated that the psychologist was closer to thirty than to twenty as Aiden had first assumed.

"Sorry," Aiden said, pointing at Okada and Ruben. "They're not used to being out and about. We normally keep them chained to their desks."

Dawn didn't seem offended. Her full lips curved into an easy smile that dimpled her cheeks and crinkled the skin at the bridge of her slightly upturned nose, which made the freckles dusting the fair skin seem to dance. "Don't worry, Detective, I've been called worse things than attractive."

Aiden tilted her head. "How do you know I'm a detective?"

"Oh, I don't know, could it be the fact that we're at a law enforcement conference?" Okada said.

Dawn smiled at him, but she spoke to Aiden. "The way you stand, walk, and talk pretty much screams 'cop' in capital letters. And the way you dress suggests you're a detective. Sex crimes unit?"

Aiden nodded. "Aiden Carlisle." She extended her hand.

"Dawn Kinsley, but I guess you already knew that." The psychologist nodded down at her name tag. Her handshake was as genuine and warm as her smile.

"Hey, Aiden." Ray, already halfway out the door, waved her over. "We're gonna make a run for the nearest coffee shop before the next lecture starts. You up for it?"

Forty-five minutes ago, Aiden would have jumped at the chance to leave the seminar room, but now she found herself hesitating. "Um, sure." She glanced at Dawn. "Would you like to come with us?"

"I don't drink coffee." The psychologist laughed at the look on Aiden's face. "Don't look so shocked, Detective. I'm a tea drinker, and I'd love to accompany four of Portland's finest, but regrettably, I've got an appointment."

"Maybe next time, then," Aiden said, knowing they would likely never see each other again. Not as eager to get a caffeine fix as before, she said good-bye and followed her colleagues out of the conference room.

CHAPTER 2

AIDEN RAPPED HER KNUCKLES AGAINST the shiny surface of a watermelon, testing its ripeness. Then she decided that a whole melon would only spoil in her single-person household and reached for a banana instead.

When a young man entered her personal space, she looked up from the fruit, immediately aware of anyone violating a ten-foot zone around her. His gaze met hers, and he backed away. Scowling, Aiden watched him as he walked toward another shopper, who was putting apples into a shopping basket.

Hey! That's the psychologist from last week. Buying fruit like the rest of us mere mortals—in my grocery store. Aiden forgot about the strange young man as she studied Dawn Kinsley. Wearing faded blue jeans and a white button-down shirt, Dawn looked at least as good as she had in the neatly pressed slacks and blouse she'd worn at the seminar. Aiden tilted her head and watched as Dawn pushed back stubborn blonde strands that had escaped from her ponytail. *Should I say hello? Would she even remember me?*

She hadn't made a decision yet when the young man reached into Dawn's purse and fled down the aisle.

Dawn seemed to comprehend what had happened almost immediately. She sprinted after him at a speed that would have done any street cop proud and grabbed his shirt before he could reach the door.

The thief whirled around, towering over the small woman, and raised a threatening fist.

Uh-oh! Aiden sprinted toward them before the situation could escalate further. She grabbed the raised fist and turned the man's arm behind his back in one smooth movement. "That was really dumb, Dr. Kinsley," she said to the staring woman. "Brave, but dumb. You shouldn't grab someone who outweighs you by at least forty pounds—without even knowing if he's armed."

Dawn looked steadily back at her. "He outweighs you too."

Aiden straightened to her full height. "But I am armed and a trained police officer."

"Oh, shit!" At the mention of her occupation, the captured thief started to struggle in Aiden's grip.

The shop owner hurried down the aisle. "Thank you, thank you, Detective!" He wanted to shake her hands, but they were full of struggling thief, so he turned to Dawn. "I'm very sorry, Dr. Kinsley. That never happened in my store before. Would you accept some more fruit as a compensation for the scare?"

"No, thank you. What I have is enough, really." Dawn lifted her shopping basket with two apples and a banana.

The shop owner sighed. "She's another one of those one-banana buyers," he said to Aiden.

She's single. Aiden put the brakes on her hopeful thoughts. *Yeah, and probably as straight as they come.*

"I might only take one banana, but I buy two packets of cookies every time I come in here," Dawn said, smiling.

The shop owner called the police. Once two uniformed officers had taken the thief off her hands and she and Dawn had given their statements, Aiden allowed herself to focus on Dawn. "So, do you come here often?" She winced when she realized it sounded like a lame pick-up line.

"Often enough to get a reputation as a one-banana buyer, it would seem." Dawn winked.

Aiden had to smile. She liked Dawn's wit. "Been there, done that."

"I live just down the street. Do you want to come with me and have the cup of coffee I had to decline last week?" Dawn tilted her head and looked up at Aiden.

"I thought you didn't drink coffee?"

"I don't, but I make a mean cup. Just the way you cops like it—strong enough to be considered black paint in every other occupation."

Aiden laughed. "Now, that's an offer I can't resist." *Asking me to come home with her... Is she flirting?* She shook her head at herself. *You wish.* Dawn was obviously comfortable around people and friendly to everyone she met.

Side by side, they climbed the stairs to Dawn's second-floor apartment. "Make yourself comfortable," Dawn called over her shoulder, already heading for the kitchen.

Aiden lifted a brow. Cop or not, she wouldn't have left a stranger unsupervised in her living room. Hesitantly, she stepped across a colorful rug, past potted plants, overflowing bookcases, and shelves full of framed pictures. Orange curtains suffused the living room in a golden light. In the corner was a desk piled high with books, files, and magazines. Above it, a chaotic arrangement of drawings and colorful postcards fought for space with a shelf full of seashells, a piggy bank, and stuffed animals. A recliner, a rocking chair, and two mismatched chairs completed the furnishings.

It was a bit chaotic, in a charming and almost soothing way. Aiden thought about her own apartment, which was neat and nearly void of any personal knickknacks. Dawn's apartment wasn't overly tidy; it had a cozy, lived-in feel. It felt like a home, not just a place to eat and sleep.

I like it. Aiden sank onto the couch and studied the oil painting of a long-haired cat on the opposite wall. The cat's nose was a bit crooked as if the artist hadn't gotten it quite right, but otherwise it looked very lifelike. Had Dawn painted it?

Within minutes, her hostess returned with a tray bearing coffee, tea, and cookies, and placed it on the coffee table. “Black, without sugar, right?” Dawn sat in a rocking chair across from Aiden and nodded toward her mug.

“Right.” Aiden didn’t ask how Dawn knew her coffee preferences. She seemed to have some sort of sixth sense concerning police officers.

“So, have you recovered from all those attempts to bore you to death?” Dawn looked at her over the rim of her mug, a smile in her eyes.

“Huh?”

Dawn shook a finger at her. “Oh, come on, Detective. I’m well aware how ‘eager’ most cops are to sit in a chair all day and listen to some academics tell them how to do their jobs.”

“Yeah, we just love it,” Aiden said with a grin. “But actually, your lecture wasn’t half bad. You’re not just an academic, are you?”

“No. Maybe I’ll go into teaching someday, but for now, I’m pretty happy with what I do.”

“Which is?”

“I counsel survivors of rape and sexual abuse,” Dawn said.

Aiden looked down into her mug. “That has to be tough.”

Dawn shrugged. “As tough as being a sex crimes detective, I would imagine. But sometimes I feel that I really make a difference for some of my patients, and that makes it worthwhile.”

Aiden nodded. Their jobs had a lot in common. Silence grew between them, but Aiden didn’t find it uncomfortable.

“I have to admit that I didn’t invite you up without an ulterior motive, Detective.” Dawn didn’t beat around the bush.

Aiden swallowed. “And what motive might that be?”

“I know we hardly know each other,” Dawn said, “and I normally wouldn’t do this, but...”

Aiden’s eyes widened. Was this a come-on?

“I have a favor to ask,” Dawn finally said.

Okay, so it's not a come-on. Aiden laughed at herself. *Sleeping with a woman like Dawn couldn't be considered doing her a favor.*

"I've searched for someone who could speak to my group, and it seems I've found the ideal person for the job." Dawn looked at her expectantly.

"Your group?"

Dawn nodded. "It's a support group for survivors who've gotten pregnant by rape."

Suddenly, the coffee left a bitter taste in her mouth. For once, she had been relaxed, not thinking about anything job related, and the question caught her off guard. "I'm in no way ideal for the job."

"Of course you are." Dawn rocked forward and touched Aiden's hand.

Aiden flinched and pulled her hand away. She didn't know how, but Dawn must have found out the circumstances of her conception. The thought did not sit well with her. "No. I can't give advice to women in that situation. I...I just can't, okay?"

"Okay." Dawn blinked but didn't try to pressure Aiden into changing her mind.

Aiden shoved back her only half-empty cup of coffee. "I have to go."

Dawn rose with her. Her smooth brow furrowed as she followed Aiden to the door. "If I insulted you in any—"

"No," Aiden held up her hand, "you didn't. It's just... You haven't insulted me."

"All right." For the first time, it seemed as if Dawn didn't know what to say.

Aiden slipped past her, not allowing herself to look back. The sound of the door closing behind her echoed in her mind for the rest of the day.

CHAPTER 3

AIDEN FUMBLED WITH THE KEY for a few moments, stiff hands and tired eyes refusing to work together. When she finally managed to unlock the door and entered her apartment, everything was dark and silent. Only a wave of stale air, a pile of bills and junk mail, and two parched potted plants greeted her.

For the last three days, she had slept on one of the precinct's cots, tucked away in the "dungeon," the tiny spare room that looked more like a storage closet than a comfortable place to rest. Today, their hard work had finally paid off. Portland had one less child molester to worry about.

Exhausted but content, she threw the mail onto the coffee table and glanced at the answering machine. No blinking red light, which meant she had no messages—not that she had expected any. She didn't have many friends outside of the squad.

Since it was four in the morning, she ignored the coffee pot and headed for the fridge instead. She skipped using a glass and drank directly from the orange juice container. *One of the many advantages of being single.* She tried not to think about how nice it would be to come home to a sympathetic ear and a warm body in her bed.

On the way to the bathroom, she kicked off her shoes and yanked her shirt over her head. Leaning against the sink, she splashed water onto her face and rubbed burning eyes. The mirror above the sink showed disheveled black hair and lines of fatigue on her face. Her amber eyes were bloodshot. Running her tongue over her teeth and tasting three days' worth of coffee and Chinese takeout, she decided a shower could wait and grabbed her toothbrush.

The sound of water dripping from the faucet accentuated the silence in her apartment. Out of habit, she reached up to the place where other people might store their bath radio and turned on her police scanner. She was so used to listening to the radio transmissions of the Portland Police Bureau that it became a soothing background noise while she brushed her teeth. She barely registered a domestic violence callout and two DUIs.

The scanner crackled. "...at 228 Northwest Everett Street."

That caught Aiden's attention. Not only was the address in her immediate neighborhood, but it also sounded oddly familiar. Convinced that her tired mind was playing tricks on her, she returned to her brushing and gargling.

The dispatcher's voice came through the scanner again. "I repeat: We have a 10-31 at 228 Northwest Everett Street. Unclear if suspect is still on scene. Respond code two."

She spat a mouthful of toothpaste across the sink and mirror as she recognized the address. Someone had been assaulted—or possibly raped—in Dawn Kinsley's apartment building. A sudden surge of adrenaline banished her tiredness. She tried to tell herself that there were dozens of other women living at the same address, that it probably wasn't even a rape, that she wasn't on call, but a quivering deep in her gut made her abandon her toothbrush and grab her wrinkled clothes again.

"Dispatch, this is unit one-eighteen," a patrol unit responded via radio. "That's 10-44. I'm en route. ETA two minutes."

Even knowing help was on the way, Aiden didn't stop. She had learned long ago not to question her instincts. She dressed with the automatic movements of someone who had been called out at unholy hours of the night a thousand times. Within minutes, she was on her way.

Blue and red lights colored the night when Aiden pulled her car into a parking space beside the squad car.

A uniformed police officer stopped her before she reached the door to the apartment building. "Sorry, ma'am." He blocked the entrance. "Do you live here? Do you have any identification?"

She silenced him by shoving her badge in his face. "Detective Carlisle, Sexual Assault Detail."

"Wow, you guys are really fast tonight. I'm Officer Trent, patrol district eight-twelve."

Aiden wasn't in the mood to exchange any chitchat or to explain her fast arrival at the scene. "You responded to a 10-31. It was a sexual assault?"

"Yeah." The officer nodded. "It—"

"Which apartment?"

"2B. My partner's up there."

Aiden clenched her hands into helpless fists. It was Dawn's apartment. She didn't wait for the elevator and took the steps two at a time. In front of the door to 2B, she slid to a stop and braced herself, afraid of what she might find on the other side.

A loud knock brought her face-to-face with another uniformed officer staring blankly at her.

"Carlisle, SAD."

"That was fast," the young officer said and stepped aside to allow her entry. Aiden could see his relief at not having to deal with the victim himself. Patrol officers had little, if any, training in dealing with rape survivors. He followed her back in and glanced at the notebook in his hand. "The victim's name is—"

"I know her name." Aiden took a second to compose herself before she looked around.

The half-open bedroom door showed crumpled sheets, a knocked-over lamp, and random objects scattered across the floor. The detective in Aiden began to process the crime scene automatically, but when she entered the living room and saw Dawn, her professionalism wavered.

Dawn sat on the couch, where she had shared coffee and tea with Aiden just six days ago.

Aiden almost didn't recognize her. Dawn huddled on the couch, one hand clinging to the blanket someone had wrapped around her to hide the torn clothing, the other fluttering across the side of her swollen face. Her naturally fair complexion appeared even paler in contrast to the bruises on her cheek.

Aiden cleared her throat to announce her presence and perched on the edge of the couch, careful not to sit too close and make Dawn feel threatened. "Hello, Dr. Kinsley... Dawn." She made her voice as gentle as she could.

Dawn's head shot up. "H-hi. I'd say it's nice to see you again, but under these circumstances..." She looked away, wiping at the tears in her eyes.

Aiden swallowed. She had the sudden urge to hold Dawn's hand or wrap her arms around her, but she kept her distance, knowing it could do more harm than good at this point. "Can you tell me what happened?"

"Someone broke into my apartment. A...a man." Dawn pressed her lips together. "He had a weapon, and...he hit me." Her fingers traced the marks on her right cheek.

Aiden nodded encouragingly but didn't interrupt.

"He...threw me down...onto the bed, and then he..." Dawn squeezed her eyes shut. "He raped me," she whispered. She looked stunned, as if only now realizing what had happened. "Detective, he...he..."

"I know," Aiden murmured. She moved a little closer but not yet close enough to touch. "Did you know him?"

Dawn shook her head.

"Okay. Can you describe him?" Aiden knew she had to

maintain a professional distance and ask the standard questions, but it was hard.

"He was tall and muscular and...heavy," Dawn said. Her voice shook. "Black hair. Angry, blue eyes."

"Good, that'll help us look for him." She lightly touched Dawn's forearm. "I'll take you to the hospital in a second, okay? Can I get you anything or do anything for you before we go? Should I call anyone?"

"No." Dawn shook her head.

"Are you sure?" Aiden didn't like the thought of no one being there for Dawn. Of course she would try to make the rape kit procedure at the hospital as easy as possible for Dawn, but her primary role was that of a detective, not that of a friend.

"I don't want my mother to see me like this, and I'd rather tell her in person than scare her with a call," Dawn said quietly. "There have been too many of those calls in our family."

Aiden nodded but asked no questions. She didn't want to invade Dawn's privacy any further.

"I'd like to change." Dawn looked down at her torn T-shirt.

Aiden sighed. "You can't, at least not yet. I'm sorry, but it's evidence. How about taking a new set of clothing with you to the hospital so you can change after your examination?"

"I...I can't go in there." Dawn pointed a trembling finger at the bedroom.

"It's all right. I'll do it." Aiden stepped over a fallen chair, shattered ceramic figurines, and books and a sketchpad with torn-out pages, careful not to touch anything that might be evidence. Dawn's glasses lay on the bedroom floor, the frame broken and one lens shattered.

Aiden picked out a comfortable-looking sweatshirt, loose-fitting pants, and a pair of warm socks. Adding panties and a bra, she bitterly shook her head. She had fleetingly fantasized about seeing Dawn's underwear—but these definitely weren't the circumstances she had imagined. Even harmless flirting with Dawn was no longer an option. Everything had changed tonight.

She returned to the living room with the bundle of clothes under her arm. Her heart lurched at the sight of Dawn fumbling with her shoes, her fingers trembling too much to manage the laces. She put down the clothes, knelt in front of Dawn, and tied the laces. "Anything else?"

"Can I brush my teeth?"

Aiden bit her lip. "No, sorry. That could destroy evidence. I have to talk to the officer for a minute, okay? It won't take long."

The cop, who had retreated to the kitchen, looked up as she entered. "She give a description?"

"Tall, muscular, black hair, blue eyes. I'll have her work with a sketch artist later, but for now give out a BOLO for a suspect fitting that description to all precincts."

The officer nodded and took a few notes.

"Are there any witnesses, or is Dr. Kinsley the one who called us?" Aiden looked back to the couch to make sure Dawn was still okay on her own.

"A neighbor called it in," the officer answered. "He saw her lean out of the open window and thought she was suicidal. Turns out she wanted to retrieve her cell phone. The perp threw it out the window. It's dangling from the fire escape."

Aiden's brow furrowed. Breaking into the apartment, ripping out the phone line, throwing away the only other means to call for help—that sounded like a planned attack, but the destruction in the bedroom didn't speak of a controlled offender. *Time to think about that later. Dawn's the top priority right now.* "Secure the premises and take the neighbor's statement," she said. "I'm taking her to the hospital."

She crossed the room toward Dawn, making some noise as she approached to avoid startling her. "Are you ready?"

Dawn struggled to her feet without answering.

Aiden sat next to Dawn in a curtained emergency room cubicle at Portland General Hospital, which was busy even at five a.m. The emergency personnel hadn't tried to make them wait in the corridor when they saw the gold shield clipped to Aiden's belt and the grim expression on her face.

"I guess I was really lucky that you were on call tonight," Dawn said after the nurse left in search of a doctor.

As a rape counselor, she probably knew that many victims without life-threatening injuries had to wait for treatment and were often questioned about the rape in the middle of the corridor while nurses and doctors rushed injured patients past them and worried family members paced nearby.

Aiden tilted her head in a vague nod. She didn't want to discuss why she had caught this case, preferring to let Dawn believe she had been on call tonight and was here for strictly professional reasons. "I know it's hard to talk about, but..." She found herself uncharacteristically reluctant to question Dawn about something that would be painful for her. "I have to ask you some specific questions about the attack so the doctor will know what kind of evidence to look for. Let's start with the easy part. I know you didn't shower, brush your teeth, or change your clothes after the attack, right?"

Dawn nodded.

"Did he penetrate you?" Aiden asked quietly.

Another nod. "Vaginally, nothing else, but he kept trying to kiss me. I don't think he wore a condom."

Aiden's stomach twisted at the clinical response. It seemed as if Dawn was trying to get through this by acting as if she were talking about one of her patients and not about herself.

The nurse returned to their curtained-off cubicle. She handed Dawn a blue hospital gown. "Please stand on this sheet of paper," she pointed to the floor, "while you undress. Put your clothes into the paper bag on the table."

Dawn sighed. "I know the routine," she said, still looking at Aiden. She seemed almost afraid to let Aiden out of her sight.

"I'll be right here, outside the curtain, waiting for you, okay?" Aiden stepped back but kept eye contact.

Dawn exhaled and closed the curtain behind her.

Aiden turned her back to the cubicle and bobbed up and down on the balls of her feet in an effort to avoid pacing back and forth. She heard the rustling of paper and then, just for a second, quiet sobs. Helplessly, she pressed her lips together.

After a minute, Dawn reappeared, looking even more fragile in the blue paper gown than she had before.

Aiden gazed into her stormy gray eyes. "You okay?"

Dawn nodded.

The nurse guided Dawn to the examination table.

Silently, Aiden took up position beside her.

A doctor with a clipboard came in and started asking questions while the nurse took photographs of the bruises on Dawn's face and body. "When did you have your last period, Ms. Kinsley?"

"Uh, I'm not sure. Maybe two weeks ago. It could be three. I'm really not sure." Dawn shrugged.

"Have you had recent sexual intercourse?" the doctor asked.

Dawn laughed bitterly. "That's why I'm here, isn't it?"

Aiden touched Dawn's hand with a single finger. "He means voluntary sexual intercourse."

"No." Dawn bit her lip. "No, I haven't."

The doctor scribbled some notes on his clipboard. "What form of birth control do you normally use?"

Once again, the camera flashed, and Dawn closed her eyes. "I don't use any."

At the defensive tone of voice, Aiden took Dawn's hand in hers and squeezed it soothingly. The matter-of-fact question must have felt like an accusation, as if Dawn hadn't properly "prepared" for the eventuality of a rape.

"We need two oral swabs for a DNA sample," Aiden said. "Do you want to do it yourself?" Many victims experienced the rape kit examination like a second violation. Their bodies still didn't belong to them; instead, each body was viewed as a crime scene, a piece of evidence. Aiden tried to give victims as much control over the examination as she possibly could.

Dawn took the swabs from the doctor and rubbed them across the inside of her mouth. She handed them back to Aiden, who sealed them into an envelope.

When the doctor took Dawn's hand, she flinched.

Aiden stepped closer, both for comfort and to hold a sheet of paper under her hand while the doctor scraped underneath Dawn's fingernails and then cut them. Her gaze still on Dawn, Aiden put the clippings and scrapings into another envelope and sealed it.

"Okay. Could you lie back and spread your legs a little, please?" The doctor placed a towel under Dawn's buttocks and combed through her pubic hair, searching for foreign hairs. "It will hurt for a second—I need to pull some of your pubic hair as a control sample."

Soon, another envelope was sealed and labeled.

The physician took two more swabs and stepped between Dawn's bent legs.

Dawn jerked.

Aiden enclosed Dawn's trembling fingers gently in both of her larger hands. She kept her gaze on Dawn's face, not looking down to watch what the doctor did.

Dawn squeezed her eyes shut and moaned. "I can't believe this is happening to me," she whispered.

"Just a little longer. It's almost over." Aiden rubbed Dawn's hand. With relief, she watched the doctor step back and make a smear on a glass slide.

The doctor turned off the light. "I need you to open the gown a little bit, please."

Dawn wrestled with the laces that held the gown closed.

"Need help?" Aiden asked. She didn't move until Dawn nodded. Gently, she untied the laces and stepped back. Instead of looking at Dawn's half-naked body, she kept her gaze on Dawn's face and her upset gray eyes.

The doctor turned on the UV light and moved it above Dawn's abdomen and thighs, showing bright blue fluorescent spots.

Dawn looked down at her bruised body. "Is that...?"

"Seminal fluid," the doctor said and rubbed over some of the stains with a cotton pad.

Dawn groaned.

The doctor turned the light back on and waited for Aiden to help Dawn close her hospital gown. "Are you allergic to anything?"

Dawn shook her head.

He handed her two white pills and a small plastic cup of water. "That's Plan B, an emergency contraceptive pill. You have to take them in two doses—one pill now and one more in twelve hours. You might have some nausea or dizziness after taking them. If you want, I can prescribe you some Dramamine to help with that."

Dawn took the first pill and swallowed it without comment.

"The nurse will be in shortly," the doctor said. "She'll give you antibiotics to prevent sexually transmitted diseases and get blood drawn to test for STDs and HIV. The test results will be back within twenty-four hours. You should be retested in three and six months just to make sure that everything is all right."

Visibly shaking, Dawn nodded.

"The nurse will also take you to get your hand X-rayed," the doctor said, pointing at the nurse who had been taking the photos during the examination.

Aiden immediately let go of Dawn's hand. "Her hand is broken?"

Dawn looked down at her left, then at her right hand as if she hadn't noticed anything wrong with them either.

"Her right index finger might be broken," the doctor answered. "It's hard to tell with all the swelling, so I'd like to do an X-ray."

The nurse helped Dawn into a wheelchair—standard hospital procedure—and took her to radiology, leaving Aiden alone with the ER doctor. "What does the evidence tell you?" Aiden asked when Dawn was out of earshot.

The doctor locked the envelopes in the rape kit box, sealed it, and handed it to Aiden. "Bruise marks on her arms and thighs, which might be consistent with restraint, and about the pelvic and pubic area. Teeth marks on her breasts. Evidence of penetration and seminal fluids."

Classic signs of rape. Aiden swallowed. She left the rape kit with the uniformed officer who had been waiting outside, giving him strict orders to take it directly to the medical examiner, and went searching for radiology.

CHAPTER 4

"MORNING, AIDEN," RAY SAID AS he entered the squad room on the twelfth floor of Portland's Justice Center.

At her partner's greeting, Aiden looked up from the selection of tea bags. "Morning, Ray. Sorry for calling you in on your day off. I hope you're not in the doghouse with Susan for working this weekend?"

"No, that's okay. She wanted to take the girls shopping anyway. Now, tell me why I had to miss four whining kids begging me for 150-dollar shoes or a navel piercing." Ray walked over and poured himself a cup of coffee. "Why did you catch a case when we weren't on call last night?"

"I heard it on the police scanner when I came home," Aiden said.

Ray lifted a brow. "And because you didn't have anything more important to do, like sleep after three 20-hour shifts, you thought you'd help out our brothers in uniform? Did they start a bonus program for catching two rapists in one night?"

Aiden didn't laugh. "Ray, it was Dawn."

"Dawn?" He frowned.

For the first time, Aiden noticed that she had thought of the psychologist as "Dawn," not "Ms. Kinsley," since she had found her on the couch three hours ago. *Three hours. An eternity.* "Dawn Kinsley—the rape counselor from the seminar last week."

"The vic's one of her patients?" Ray asked.

Aiden pressed her lips together. "She's the victim. Someone broke into her apartment last night and raped her."

"Oh. I'm sorry." Ray turned toward her, his coffee mug in his hands. "Did you call Okada and Ruben? I'm sure Ruben wouldn't mind coming in on a Saturday for the woman who proved one of Okada's conspiracy theories wrong."

"They were here, finishing the paperwork on Barclay, when I came in. I told them we'd meet them at Dawn's apartment...at the crime scene once we'd gotten a formal statement." Aiden headed toward one of the interview rooms with Ray in tow.

Dawn still sat where Aiden had left her five minutes ago—on the edge of the chair, her hands, with one splinted finger, in her lap.

Ray kept a respectful distance. "Hello, Dr. Kinsley. I'm Detective Raymond Bennet."

"Hello, Detective." Dawn spared him a quick glance before her eyes immediately searched for Aiden. Her tense posture relaxed when Aiden entered the room behind her partner.

Aiden set the cup of tea in front of Dawn. "Tea, not coffee," she said with a small smile. "I hope you like it with a little sugar."

Dawn nodded, wrapping her uninjured hand around the mug. She inhaled the comforting scent of peppermint but didn't drink; she just held on to the mug as if it were a lifeline.

Aiden perched on the corner of the table and studied Dawn. She looked as exhausted as Aiden felt. "We don't have to do this right now. There'd still be time to take your formal statement after you've slept for a few hours."

"No, that's okay." Dawn shook her head. "I doubt that I'd be able to sleep, anyway."

Aiden sat down and scooted her chair a little closer to Dawn while Ray chose a chair at the end of the table. "I know we've been through some of this before, but I need you to tell me what happened from the beginning," Aiden said.

"Okay. I had just fallen asleep—I think it was around three o'clock—when a noise from somewhere in the apartment woke me. I went to investigate, thinking maybe the cat had knocked something over."

Aiden nodded but didn't interrupt to ask more questions while Ray, probably sensing that the victim was more at ease with Aiden than with him, kept silent and took notes.

"There was a man in my living room," Dawn said, her voice breathless and alarmed as if she was reliving the scary moment. "I opened my mouth to scream, but he pressed me against the wall with his forearm across my throat. He held a gun to my head and told me he'd kill me if I called for help or tried to escape." Dawn shivered violently.

"It's okay. You're here now, safe," Aiden said, trying to bring her back to the present. She waited a few moments. "What happened next?"

"He dragged me back to the bedroom. On the way, he ripped the phone cord from the wall and threw my cell phone out of the window. Then he...he pushed me down onto the bed." Dawn bit her lip. "He was really tall and strong, and he had a weapon—I knew I stood no chance to fight him off."

Aiden swallowed hard. A week ago, she had told Dawn how dangerous it could be to pick a fight with someone who outweighed you and might be armed. Had she robbed Dawn of a chance to get away unharmed by telling her that trying to fight was dumb? Her hands trembled as she lifted her paper cup and tried to wash down the lump of emotions in her throat with a mouthful of lukewarm coffee.

"I knew I couldn't hurt him badly enough to stop him. Maybe I should have tried. If I..." Dawn stopped herself and rubbed her red-rimmed eyes. "I can't count how often I told a patient not to blame herself for any aspect of her rape, and now I..." She stopped and sighed. "Anyway, I decided struggling was useless and tried to talk my way out of the situation. After all, that's what I do for a living—talk." She smiled bitterly.

"What did you say?" Aiden asked.

"I told him he didn't need to do this, because he was handsome, and there should be a lot of women willing to sleep with him. I offered him money. I said everything I could think of. I even told him I had a contagious disease." Dawn looked away from Aiden and stared at the table. "His answer was to unzip his pants, force my legs apart, and rape me."

For a second, everything was quiet in the room, even Ray's pen ceased to scratch over the notepad.

"He held me down with one hand while the other kept pressing the gun against my temple." Dawn tapped her unsplinted index finger against the side of her head. "I squeezed my eyes shut and tried to turn my head so he couldn't kiss me, but he slapped me every time I looked away or closed my eyes. He wanted me to see who was doing this to me. I think that's the reason why he didn't wear a mask. After a while, I had the feeling of leaving my body as if I was looking down at a stranger being raped—I dissociated."

It was a strange experience for Aiden to talk to a victim who used the jargon of a sex crimes expert. She wanted to comfort Dawn, but she didn't dare to use the soothing words that worked with most victims, knowing Dawn herself had said them hundreds of times to her patients. Now that Dawn was the victim, Aiden couldn't think of anything to say.

"What happened then?" Ray asked, covering his partner's silence.

Dawn cleared her throat. "He had problems...finishing. Of course, he blamed it on me 'lying there like a dead fish.' He shoved the gun under my chin and told me to stop acting as if I wasn't enjoying it. He told me to moan and act excited." She closed her eyes, a few silent tears escaping from under her lids. "I know that many rapists who have trouble ejaculating blame their victims and kill them, so I...I did what he told me to do."

Oh, God! Aiden wanted to close her eyes, she wanted to scream or run out of the room, but most of all she wanted to shoot the monster who had done this to Dawn. She had heard a lot of awful stories in her seven years with the Sexual Assault Detail, but for some reason this one was affecting her on another level.

"Finally, he finished, but even that didn't seem to satisfy him," Dawn said. She seemed to be on automatic pilot. "He slapped me one more time and then went berserk on my bedroom furniture. His eyes..." She shuddered. "He trampled on my photos and threw my books across the room. He was so full of anger and hate that I thought for sure he would kill me. But he didn't." She didn't sound relieved.

Tears burned in Aiden's eyes. "What did he do next?" she asked as professionally as she could.

"He kicked a chair out of the way and disappeared through the bedroom door." Dawn exhaled and took the first sip of her tea, which was probably cold by now.

Aiden exchanged a glance with Ray. "We have to ask you some detailed questions now. Can we get you anything before we start? Something to eat?"

Dawn shook her head.

Rising from her chair, Aiden reached for Dawn's mug. "Another tea, then?"

"No, I..." Dawn clung to the handle of the mug. "I don't need anything, really."

Ray looked from Dawn to Aiden. "I'll go."

Without further protest, Dawn handed him the mug.

As Aiden watched the door close, she realized that Dawn simply hadn't wanted her to leave the room.

"Sorry," Dawn whispered. "I don't want your partner to think

I mistrust him. It's just that I don't know him, and I feel like I know you even when I don't."

"It's okay," Aiden said with a smile. "Ray makes much better tea than I do, anyway."

Soon, Ray returned with tea and coffee, and the interview continued.

"You said he didn't wear a mask, so you did see his face?" Aiden asked.

Dawn nodded. "Yes. I had the feeling he wanted me to. He turned on the lamp on my bedside table. I think he broke my finger when I tried to lay a hand over my eyes."

Aiden didn't question it. She trusted the psychologist's assessment. "Could you describe him to a police sketch artist?"

A nod from Dawn.

"And how confident are you that you could identify him in a lineup?"

"I'd know him, anytime, anywhere," Dawn said without the slightest hesitation. "I'll never forget that face."

"You said he was tall. How tall is that, exactly?" Aiden asked.

For the first time, Dawn looked directly at Ray. "What are you, six feet?" she asked, indicating his tall, lanky frame.

"And half an inch." Ray smiled gently.

"I'd say he was a bit taller than that. Maybe six-two or six-three." Dawn hesitated. "I could be wrong, though. I know victims often overestimate the size of their attackers."

Aiden knew she was right. Still, it made her sad to hear Dawn talk about herself in such a distanced way. "Anything else you remember about his face? Did he have a beard, for example?"

Dawn shook her head. "No beard, just some stubble. He had a small scar on his chin, right there," she pointed to her own face, "and another one above his right eyebrow. Given his aggressiveness, I wouldn't be surprised if he had a criminal record with assault and battery."

"We'll look into it," Aiden said. Their work would be easier because their victim already understood how the police worked. "Did he smell of anything in particular? An aftershave or—?"

"He smelled of sweat and cigarette smoke. And I could smell alcohol on his breath." Dawn shivered as if she could smell him right now, right there in the interview room.

Aiden rested one elbow on the table and fiddled with the unused pen in her hand. "What about his clothes? You remember what he wore?"

"Nothing extravagant. Just a white, sleeveless T-shirt, showing off his muscled arms." She rolled her eyes. "His pants were black, I think. I know they were dark."

"Did he speak with an accent?" Aiden continued with her endless list of questions.

"No accent," Dawn answered. "He used a bit of slang. He's street smart, but not a college graduate, I'd say."

Aiden nodded. "What about his age?"

"A little younger than me. Mid-twenties, I would guess."

Fairly young. Maybe he's just starting out? "Did he seem insecure or nervous?"

"Not in the least." Dawn vehemently shook her head. "He was cold-blooded and fully convinced that he had every right to do what he did. There was no room for nervousness or scruples. I wouldn't be surprised if he has raped before."

Aiden glanced at Ray to make sure he had written down that information. "You said you didn't know him, but did he say or do anything that indicated that he knew you or knew who you are?"

Dawn hesitated.

Aiden looked into the cloudy gray eyes. Dawn had answered every other question without delay. What was it about this particular question that made her think twice?

"He didn't say anything like that, and I don't know why, but somehow, I got the feeling that he didn't break into my apartment by chance." The fingers of Dawn's uninjured hand fiddled with her mug. "Maybe I'm just paranoid."

Aiden shook her head. "Never doubt your instincts, Doctor. At this point, even a paranoid feeling could turn out to be a valuable lead."

Dawn smiled timidly. "Thanks."

"Did anything unusual happen in the last few days?" Aiden asked.

"Unusual?" Another almost-smile from Dawn. "I'm a psychologist, Detective. Unusual things happen in my life every day. But if you mean did I notice any strangers lingering around the building or receive any hang-up calls, then no, there wasn't anything unusual."

"Does your building have a doorman?" Aiden asked.

"Yes, but he leaves at midnight." Dawn grimaced. "Cost-saving measures."

Aiden crushed the empty paper cup in her hand. "You said you had just gone to sleep when you heard him. Had you been out or did you stay home the whole evening?"

"I'd been out with some friends. I came in pretty late and just fell into bed." Dawn bit her lip as if her decision to go out that night had somehow led to the rape.

"Did anything unusual happen while you were out? A particularly persistent guy hitting on you or anything like that?"

A ghost of a smile flitted across Dawn's face. "No, nothing like that happened. I didn't talk to anyone but my friends the whole night, and I'm sure no one followed me home."

"Did anything look out of place when you came home?" Aiden asked.

"I don't think so, but I'm not sure," Dawn said. "I was so tired when I came home that I really didn't look around."

"Okay." Aiden rubbed the back of her neck. "You said something, some kind of noise, woke you up. Any guesses to what it might have been? Was it a door opening or the shattering of glass or...?"

Dawn shrugged. "I don't know. Nothing as loud as the shattering of glass, though."

"Did you lock the door when you came home?" Aiden asked.

A determined nod came from Dawn. "I always do."

"What about the windows?"

"God!" Dawn moaned and buried her face in her hands. "I opened the damn window! I let him in! I always leave one window open when I go to bed, if my cat's not home. I practically invited him in!"

"Hey." Very gently, Aiden touched her shoulder. "You didn't invite him in. Unless you gave him a written invitation, he had no business coming into your apartment, even if every door and every window would have been wide-open."

"Still..." A dozen what-ifs lingered between them.

Aiden sighed and decided to break the awkward silence with the next question. "Did he take anything with him? A necklace, a bracelet, rings...anything?"

"He wasn't interested in jewelry or money, Detective. This was no burglar who came across a sleeping woman by chance and took the opportunity." Dawn's voice got louder.

Aiden raised a calming hand. Like many rape victims, Dawn seemed to shift between blaming herself and being angry with the world and its unfairness. "Most rapists take something with them that belonged to the victim. For the most part, it's not financially motivated, but—"

"A trophy," Dawn said, a lot calmer now.

"Yes."

Dawn pressed her uninjured fingers against the bridge of her nose. "I didn't notice anything missing, but it's hard to say with all the destruction in my bedroom."

"And did he leave anything behind?" Aiden asked.

"Like what?"

Aiden shrugged. "A piece of clothing, a tool, a weapon..."

"No. He didn't undress, and he took the gun with him when he left."

The gun. Aiden knew how difficult it was to get a reliable, detailed description of weapons from a civilian but decided to try anyway. "Can you describe the gun? Was it a revolver?"

"No, it wasn't," Dawn answered without a trace of hesitation. "He had a Glock 17."

Ray and Aiden exchanged incredulous glances.

"How can you be so sure?"

"I come from a family of cops," Dawn said with a small but affectionate smile. "My father and my older brother were on the job and some of my friends still are. Most of them had Glocks, so I grew up around them."

Were on the job? Aiden noticed her use of the past tense but decided not to ask. Dawn had enough sadness to deal with for the moment.

With a glance at her watch, which read ten a.m., Aiden asked a few more questions about Dawn's daily routine: Which restaurants, gyms, and clubs did she frequent? Where did she buy her groceries? Which pharmacy and Laundromat did she use? They would compare her answers to those of other rape victims. If they were lucky, there might be a connection, a common place where the rapist first noticed his victims.

Finally, Aiden stretched and looked over at Dawn, who was yawning.

Ray closed his notepad and threw down the pen. "We'll have the written statement for you by this afternoon. You should read it carefully to make sure everything's accurate and then sign it."

Dawn nodded.

"Do you live with anyone?" Ray asked, and when Dawn shook

her head, he said, "Do you have family or friends you could stay with for a few days?"

"I think I'll stay with my mother for a while," Dawn answered.

Ray nodded. "Good. We can have a unit drive you there."

Aiden stood and rounded the table. "I'll drive her home, Ray."

"That's not necessary, Detective. I can take a cab," Dawn said, though it was easy to see that she wasn't looking forward to driving anywhere with a male stranger.

"It's no problem," Aiden said. "I really don't mind."

Her partner studied Aiden for a few seconds before he nodded. "Okay. Meet us at the cr... at Dr. Kinsley's apartment when you're finished."

Aiden parked her car in front of Grace Kinsley's house and turned off the ignition. She got out of the car and waited until Dawn had done the same. "A locksmith is going to change the locks in your apartment," she said, silently wondering how often she had told other rape victims the exact same thing, "and a psychologist will call you to make..." She stopped when she remembered that Dawn was a psychologist too.

"An appointment," Dawn finished for her. "Standard procedure, right?"

Aiden shook her head. Nothing about this case was "standard"—not for her and certainly not for Dawn. When they stopped in front of the house, Aiden took one of her cards, wrote something on the back, and handed it to Dawn. "Those are the numbers you can reach me at—the precinct, my cell phone, and my home number. Don't hesitate to call me—anytime, day or night, okay?"

Dawn looked at the card, then at Aiden. "Thank you. For everything." She took a deep breath and turned to look at her mother's house, clearly afraid to go in and tell her family what had happened.

"I could come with you and talk to your family if you want me to," Aiden said.

"No, thanks, I'll manage," Dawn said but didn't sound convincing.

Before Dawn could reach the door, it swung open. "Dawn!" An older, heavier version of Dawn stood in the doorway. "Where have you been? I've been trying to reach you the whole..." The woman's gray eyes widened when she looked at her daughter and saw the bruises on her face. "Oh, my God, what happened?"

Dawn stared at her, a mixture of emotions written all over her face. She probably wanted to be left alone so she could pretend nothing had happened, but at the same time, she longed to be held in her mother's arms. A tear rolled down her cheek.

When Dawn didn't answer, her panicked mother turned to Aiden. "What happened, Detective?"

Another Kinsley woman with built-in copdar. Aiden said nothing, waiting for Dawn to find her voice. She knew how important it was for Dawn, for any rape victim, to say the words on her own. She rested a supporting hand on Dawn's elbow and waited.

"Mom," Dawn said, her voice a rough whisper. "I was raped last night."

Mrs. Kinsley blanched. "What? Oh dear God!" She reached for her daughter.

Dawn's controlled façade crumbled. Sobbing loudly, she sank into her mother's embrace.

Feeling like an intruder, Aiden stepped back. She wanted to turn her head and give them some privacy but found that she couldn't look away from the comforting caresses and the consoling whispers. Aiden had loved her mother, and she was sure that her mother had loved her in her own way, but she had never known the level of motherly comfort that she was witnessing now. It was a healing experience, yet hard to look at, at the same time. With one last glance, she turned and walked toward her car.

Aiden ducked under the yellow crime scene tape. She looked around Dawn's apartment, where a crime scene specialist and her fellow detectives were already hard at work. It didn't appear to be the same cozy apartment where she'd had coffee with Dawn just a week ago. The warmth and innocence had been destroyed. She crossed the living room and tried to slip on her detective persona along with her latex gloves. "Any luck with prints?"

The crime scene technician looked up from his work. "I've lifted a few from the bedroom door, the phone, and the window. Could belong to the victim, though."

"You should check for prints on the cell phone," Aiden said. "The perp threw it out of the window, so we know he had it in his hands."

"Will do." The crime scene tech continued his dusting.

Aiden entered the bedroom, where Ray was busy sealing evidence bags. "Hey, Ray. Found anything?"

"The usual—semen stains, hairs, and fibers on the bed. Already photographed and bagged everything." Ray sighed. "Doesn't look like he left anything else behind, not even a condom wrapper. No signs of a struggle or forced entry in the living room. Dr. Kinsley was right—the window seems to be the point of entry."

They walked through the apartment to reconstruct the sequence of events. "He must have climbed up the fire escape, found the half-open window, and climbed in. I think in the darkness, he crashed into the side table." Ray pointed to the piece of furniture that stood partially in front of the window. "That's probably what woke the victim up."

"Dr. Kinsley," Aiden said. She barely knew Dawn, but she couldn't think of her as just another nameless victim.

Ray nodded. His nostrils quivered as he suppressed a yawn. "Right. So, I'm thinking he's someone who didn't have access to the building and who'd never been to the apartment before, otherwise he would've known the layout of the furniture and wouldn't have bumped into it."

"Hey, boys and girls," Okada said as he entered the apartment with his partner.

"Neighbors were a complete waste of time—no one saw anything." Ruben shook his head.

"Except for Mr. Bundy, the one who called us," Okada said.

Ray looked up. "His name's really Bundy?"

Ruben shrugged his slim shoulders. "Yeah. Not everyone's entitled to a nice unique name like Bennet. Some have to share a name with a mass murderer or a shoe salesman."

"Did Mr. Bundy tell you anything other than his name?" Aiden interrupted their joking. She had no patience for it at the moment.

Okada raised his eyebrows. "Someone is missing her beauty sleep."

"We could all use a few hours of sleep," Ray said before Aiden could answer. "So let's get this over with, okay?"

"Mr. Bundy was walking around the block with man's best friend at about four a.m.," Okada said. "When Fifi started barking, he looked up and saw Dr. Kinsley hanging halfway out of the window. He begged her not to jump." Okada curved his lips into one of his cynical half smiles. "Little did he know she didn't want to end her life but her phoneless state—"

"Until she called down to him to call 911 because she'd been assaulted," Ruben said.

Aiden rubbed her neck. Her muscles felt like steel ropes. "He didn't see our perp?"

Okada shook his head. "Neither hide nor hair."

"Speaking of hairs..." Ray brushed his hand over the legs of his pants. "There has to be a feline roommate hiding somewhere around here—there are cat hairs everywhere, and I found a litter box in the bathroom."

"Okay, guys, why don't you head on home?" Aiden said. "There's nothing we can do until we have some lab results."

While Okada and Ruben headed for the door without hesitation, Ray didn't move. "And what are you gonna do?"

Aiden stripped off her latex gloves with tired movements. "I'm going to catch a few hours too."

"A few hours?" Ray raised a mocking brow. "You look like you could use a three-month hibernation, not just a few hours of tossing and turning."

"I could." Aiden sighed. "But I'm not going to get three days, much less three months, so I'll take a nap and then head back to the station to let Dr. Kinsley sign her statement."

Ray studied her. "I get the feeling this one's personal for you."

"Yeah. I guess it is." Aiden shrugged and looked around the apartment as if in search of an explanation. "She works with sex crimes too, Ray. She's almost one of us. She didn't deserve this."

Ray nodded. "No one does."

Side by side, they trudged down the stairs.

CHAPTER 5

"Detective? Detective Carlisle!"

Dazed, Aiden rolled around and lifted herself up on one elbow. She blinked at the sudden brightness and peered through sleep-swollen eyes at the young officer standing before her cot.

"There are two women in the squad room asking for you," he said.

Aiden rubbed her eyes and swung her legs off the cot. A quick glance at her wristwatch indicated that she had slept for four hours. Trotting over to the squad room, she clipped her holster back onto her belt and finger-combed her short hair into some semblance of order.

Dawn and her mother sat in front of her desk, two paper cups of tea in front of them.

"Da... Dr. Kinsley, ma'am." Aiden nodded at the two women as she eased herself into her desk chair.

"Dawn's okay, Detective," Dawn said. "You've helped me through situations that surely warrant a first-name basis."

Aiden inclined her head and studied Dawn. The bruises on her face and around her throat were more prominent now, and she looked as if she hadn't slept for even a minute. Sitting with her back to the noisy squad room full of strangers seemed to make her jumpy. "Here's your written statement." Aiden handed her the document. "Please read it thoroughly, and don't hesitate to tell me if there's something wrong or missing in there, okay?"

While Dawn read, Aiden's gaze met Mrs. Kinsley's over the bowed head of her daughter. Her eyes leaned more toward gray than Dawn's, and her hair was a little darker, but the family resemblance couldn't be denied. Neither could the look of sad helplessness in those gray eyes.

Aiden had to look away, and she was glad when Dawn finished reading.

"Everything's correct." Dawn took the pen Aiden held out for her and signed the document. "What else?"

"Nothing, for the moment," Aiden said. "We have no eyewitnesses, so our hope is on forensics coming up with something that will help us ID and apprehend the perpetrator. If that happens, we'll need you to identify him in a lineup."

Dawn fidgeted, unable to sit still and do nothing while her rapist was free to roam the streets.

"We'll need your help when the police sketch artist comes in," Aiden said. "Is there anything we can do for you until then? Are you okay at your mother's for now?"

"She can stay for as long as she wants to," Mrs. Kinsley said.

"Do you need anything from your apartment?" Aiden asked.

Dawn bit her lip. "Actually, my cat is still in the apartment."

"I offered to go and get it," Grace Kinsley said. "But Dawn doesn't want me to see, and she also doesn't want to ask Del, our oldest friend."

Dawn snorted. "Del's a lieutenant with the police department. You know how overprotective she is. If we ask her for help, she'll want to take over the investigation. I don't think Detective Carlisle would like that."

Her mother directed a pleading gaze at Aiden. "Could you get the cat? Dawn can't go back there, not so soon after..."

"I understand." Aiden looked at Dawn, who glanced down. "I could retrieve the cat for you."

"I don't want to bother—"

"It's no trouble, really. I have to go home to change clothes anyway, so it's not a detour."

Dawn lifted one eyebrow. "Do you have any experience with cats?"

Aiden shrugged. "I don't want to marry it. I'm just going to put it into a pet carrier. How hard can that be?"

Dawn smiled genuinely for the first time all day. "Famous last words, Detective."

"Hey, I'm a police officer." Aiden grinned. She was glad that Dawn was smiling again and wanted to keep the lighter mood for as long as possible. "If it resists arrest, I'll convince it to comply with my gun."

The smile disappeared, and Dawn blanched.

Aiden wanted to slap herself. *God! You idiot! You don't joke about that with a woman who has been threatened by a rapist's gun just a few hours ago!* "I'm sorry. That was really thoughtless of me. I should know better." She glanced from Dawn to her uncomfortable-looking mother. *Nice first impression, genius.*

"It's okay, really." Dawn extended her splinted hand in Aiden's direction. "I don't want you to treat me like...just another rape victim."

"Okay." Aiden inhaled and exhaled deeply. "So, any last-minute advice about handling that tiger of yours?"

Dawn visibly relaxed. "She's a tigress, and she's probably hiding under the bed." She covered her eyes with one hand. "Oh, God. Why didn't I try that? I could have hidden. Maybe he wouldn't have found me."

Helplessly, Aiden searched for words. "There's no way you could have—"

One of the officers walked up to Aiden's desk and cleared his throat, interrupting her.

Dawn jumped when he stepped up behind her.

"Picasso's here now," he said.

Aiden nodded. "That's our sketch artist. He'll work with you to create a sketch of the perp so we can send it out to all precincts."

"If you'd follow me, please." The officer gestured in the direction of a small interview room.

Dawn rose but looked back at Aiden.

"I'll be there in a minute," Aiden said. "I just have to look through the stuff in my in-box real fast."

Reassured, Dawn followed the officer across the squad room.

Mrs. Kinsley stayed behind for a moment. "Thank you."

Aiden looked up from her in-box, embarrassed by the gratitude in the gray eyes. "Just doing my job, ma'am."

"I know, but she feels safe with you—and that's worth a lot at a time like this, when she doesn't even feel save in her mother's home." Before Aiden could think of an answer, Mrs. Kinsley hurried after her daughter.

The yellow tape had been removed, but Dawn's apartment still felt like a crime scene. Aiden closed the door behind her and wiped her hands on her pants to get rid of the fingerprint powder lingering everywhere.

A lump formed in her throat as she crossed the hall. *Get yourself together. You've been here before.* But last time, she had managed to hide behind her professional distance. Without that protective shield, she found herself hesitating to enter the bedroom, the place where Dawn had lived through such terror. Images of Dawn crying out in pain flashed through her mind. She roughly shook her head to chase away the images. After staring at the bed for a few seconds longer, she squared her shoulders and stepped over tattered books. Pieces of glass crunched beneath her shoes. Cautiously, she knelt and peered under the bed.

Two yellow-green eyes looked back unblinkingly.

"Okay." Aiden rubbed her hands together and remembered

that she had forgotten to get the cat's name from Dawn. "Hey, kitty-kitty, come here."

The cat didn't move an inch.

Aiden tried again, this time in her gentlest voice, the one that worked with even the most frightened children.

Now the cat moved—but in the opposite direction, hiding even deeper under the bed.

"Great!" At a loss, Aiden went in search of the cat food. The cat hadn't been fed in almost twenty-four hours, so she hoped that it might succumb to the smell of food if not her charming personality.

Aiden shifted her weight from foot to foot, causing the pet carrier she held to tilt and the captured cat to let out a long hiss. "Shush, quiet. Do you want them to think I'm torturing you?" She fell silent when Mrs. Kinsley opened the door.

"Oh, Detective. You're bringing the cat already? That'll cheer her up. Come in, come in." Grace Kinsley ushered Aiden and her living cargo into the house.

Mrs. Kinsley's home had large windows. A sliding glass door led to the deck and the backyard. Aiden could understand why Dawn didn't feel safe in her mother's home. Of course, Dawn wouldn't feel safe anywhere at the moment, but being in a house with so many unsecured entry points only added to the feeling of being in danger.

"Go on in, Detective," Mrs. Kinsley said. "Dawn's is the second door on the left."

Aiden knocked softly. "Dawn? It's Detective Carlisle."

The door inched open, and Dawn's pale face peered out. When she saw Aiden, the pet carrier with the cat in one hand and a bloody scratch on the other, she swung the door open.

Aiden entered the room in which Dawn had apparently lived

as a teenager. Posters of movie and pop stars were still plastered to the walls, but other than that, it was furnished in the same chaotic-cozy style that dominated Dawn's apartment.

She set down the pet carrier next to a bright red desk. "Please don't say 'I told you so,'" she said with a lopsided grin.

Dawn laughed, a wonderful sound in Aiden's ears. "Didn't cross my mind. I was too worried to be a smart-ass."

Embarrassed, Aiden rubbed her scratched hand. "Ah, don't worry, it's nothing." It burned like hell, but it was inconceivable that one of Portland's finest would whine about a tiny little scratch.

"I was worried about my cat," Dawn said and smiled.

Aiden couldn't help answering the smile with one of her own. Sometimes, it was hard to remember that she was dealing with a rape victim. She sensed an inner strength and a unique sense of humor in Dawn that was shaken but not broken.

"Where was she hiding?" Dawn opened the pet carrier.

They watched as the cat shook its long-haired coat, stretched its pale body, and strode majestically away from its prison. A bushy, chocolate-colored tail twitched, and sapphire eyes glowered at Aiden. The cat let out a complaining "Mrrrow!" and circled Dawn's legs once before disappearing under the bed.

"She was under the bed, just like you said."

At the mention of her bed, Dawn swallowed audibly, but then she put on a brave face. "You didn't try to wrestle her out from under there, did you?" She nodded down at Aiden's hand.

Aiden snorted. "Oh, no. Even I know enough about those furry demons not to try that. It all started out pretty promising. We had a nice bonding moment over a can of cat food, but the harmony was destroyed when I tried to put her into the pet carrier. That's when I became closely acquainted with those three-inch claws."

Dawn smiled for a moment before she sobered and pointed

to the still lightly bleeding scratch across the back of Aiden's hand. "Did you wash that out?"

"No." Aiden waved dismissively. "Like I said, it's just a scratch."

Dawn shot her an exasperated glare. "A scratch that could become infected like any other untreated wound. It's not like Kia sterilized her claws because she knew a police officer would come and try to put her behind bars." She left the room and returned with the first aid kit, taking out a wad of cotton and soaking it in hydrogen peroxide.

Aiden grimaced.

"What? Don't tell me you're squeamish, Detective."

"I'm not." Aiden let Dawn take her scratched hand. The fingers cradling her own were soft and warm. The touch sent a tingle through Aiden, and she jerked back.

"Sorry," Dawn whispered, obviously thinking her careful treatment of the scratch had caused the twitching.

Aiden shook her head. "It wasn't you. Must be the loss of blood making me weak in the knees."

The comment enticed another smile from Dawn, who looked as though she was ready to say something, but then thought better of it.

A knock on the door interrupted them, and Mrs. Kinsley peered around the doorway. A surprised but pleased expression appeared on her face when she saw the smile curving her daughter's lips. "Can I interest you in a cup of coffee, Detective?"

Aiden hesitated. Normally, she would politely decline anything a victim's family offered, preferring to draw a clear line between her professional and her personal life. *Come on. It's a cup of coffee, not a marriage proposal. It's well within the bounds of professionalism.* Officially, she wasn't even on duty, and the lab results wouldn't be back until the next day, so she finally nodded.

"Black, no sugar?" Mrs. Kinsley asked.

Aiden nodded again and followed Dawn into the living room. "So, you got it from your mother, then? Correctly guessing people's coffee preferences, I mean."

"Maybe," Dawn gave her a mysterious smile, "or maybe we're both just too stingy to offer our guests sugar and milk."

Aiden grinned and then studied Dawn closely. Behind the thin layer of joking and smiles, Aiden could sense constant pain and fear. She knew the rape was ever-present in Dawn's mind, playing itself over and over again. "We'll get him."

Dawn pressed her lips together. "Don't make promises you can't keep, Detective." Her troubled gray eyes gazed directly into Aiden's. "It's not that I don't trust you or the police in general, but I know the statistics. Most rapists never spend even a single day of their lives in prison."

Aiden couldn't argue with that. She looked into the depths of the black coffee that Mrs. Kinsley set down in front of her. "Then I'll simply promise that we'll do the best we can." She could only hope that it would be enough.

CHAPTER 6

AIDEN LOOKED UP FROM HER computer screen and rubbed her burning eyes when Ruben strode into the squad room. "Rape kit findings finally in?"

A few rebellious strands of brown hair fell into Ruben's eyes as he shook his head. "The lab is backed up from here to Afghanistan. DNA tech said results won't be in until tomorrow."

"Great." Aiden grimaced and went back to comparing the police sketch of Dawn's rapist with photos of registered sex offenders. She knew it was a rather hopeless attempt, but with no other leads, she was determined to try anyway.

"Hey, Aiden, check this out." Ray pointed to his computer screen. He had accessed the sex offender database to make the same comparisons. "This one seems like a perfect match. Ross Wade. Caucasian, six-three, muscular build, black hair, blue eyes. Even the scars on his chin and forehead are mentioned."

Aiden rounded her partner's desk and glanced at Ray's screen. Cold blue eyes seemed to look back at her. He resembled the man in the police artist's sketch. Was this the one who had raped Dawn?

"The MO's similar too," Ray said. "He broke into apartments at night, but he usually wore a condom."

"He could still be our guy. The smart ones change MO just to throw us off stride," Aiden said.

Ray grinned. "I haven't told you the best thing yet. He's out on probation, so it won't be difficult to bring him in for a lineup."

"Do we have a current address for him?" Aiden asked.

Ray scribbled something on his notepad. "Yeah."

"Let's go." Aiden took her service weapon from a desk drawer and clipped it to her belt.

Ruben reached for the phone. "I'll call DDA Matheson and the victim down for a lineup."

Ray and Aiden took positions to the right and left of Ross Wade's apartment door and exchanged a quick glance.

"Mr. Wade?" Ray shouted. He raised his fist and knocked on the door. "This is the police. Answer the door!"

Every muscle in Aiden's body tensed as steps neared the door.

The door opened slightly, and a tall man peeked out. "What do ya want?"

Aiden forced herself to remain polite. She tried not to think about the fact that she might be face-to-face with Dawn's rapist. "Would you mind telling us where you were Saturday night between three and four a.m.?"

"Why are you cops harassing me?" Ross Wade folded his muscular arms across his chest.

"You call it harassment. We call it investigation. There's been a rape in your old hunting grounds. So, where were you Saturday night?" Ray asked.

"In bed, asleep. I didn't rape nobody, man!" Ross Wade began to move back into the apartment.

Aiden slapped her hand against the door to prevent him from closing it. "Right, you're the picture of innocence. Then I'm sure you won't mind accompanying us to the station for a lineup, would you?"

Ross Wade smirked. "Right after I call my lawyer."

Aiden stood at Dawn's side, their shoulders almost touching. They were looking through the one-way mirror into a still-empty room. "Are you ready?" Aiden ignored the other people in the small observation room with them, concentrating only on Dawn.

Dawn tightened her shoulders. "As ready as I'll ever be."

When the door opened, Aiden looked up, frowning. She knew how emotionally draining the confrontation with her possible rapist was for Dawn, and she didn't want to drag it out unnecessarily. Her annoyance vanished when Kade Matheson entered. She hadn't seen the deputy district attorney all week.

Aiden stepped forward, meeting Kade halfway, and gestured back to Dawn. "Dawn Kinsley, this is Kadence Matheson, our DDA." She watched as the two women shook hands and couldn't help comparing them to each other.

Dawn was at least four inches shorter and more curvaceous than the slender attorney whose regal bearing often made her appear taller than her five foot eight inches. Dawn's blonde locks were in disarray because she kept running her hands through them while Kade's straight red hair fell to her slender shoulders in perfect order. Dawn didn't appear as calm and collected as Kade—which wasn't surprising considering it wasn't Kade's rapist who may very well be waiting in the next room. Under these circumstances, you would have expected Dawn to look small and insecure next to the confident DDA, but she didn't. In Aiden's eyes, Dawn possessed an inner strength that didn't resemble Kade's cool confidence in the least. Somehow, Dawn appeared more down-to-earth, more approachable, more real than Kade.

Flanked by Kade and Aiden, Dawn stepped back to the window.

"We'll bring them in now, okay? You just identify him by number," Aiden said.

Dawn nodded. She sucked in a breath when a cop opened the

door and six men walked into the adjacent room in a single-file line.

Aiden turned to face her, blocking Dawn from the one-way glass and the men behind it for a moment. "Don't be afraid. They can't see you. Just take your time." She moved back to stand beside Dawn. "Do you recognize anyone?"

"Move away from the witness, Detective," Wade's defense lawyer said.

Aiden held up her hands and took another step back.

Visibly upset about the sudden distance between them, Dawn turned to look at her.

Aiden nodded at the window, gently bringing Dawn's attention back to it. "Do you recognize anyone?"

Dawn exhaled and stepped forward. She still avoided touching the glass and kept a careful distance. Her gaze flitted from face to face. "He's not in there." She let out a trembling breath.

"Are you sure?" Aiden's tired mind wandered back to countless other rape victims who, like Dawn, had been so sure that they would know their rapist anytime and anywhere, but when confronted with a lineup, they hadn't been able to identify him.

"Yes. Yes, I'm sure." Dawn's voice was a little shaky, but she met Aiden's gaze steadily. "He's not here." Relief and disappointment were warring with each other on the pale face. Finally, fear won out. "Which means he's still out there, free to roam the streets and rape anyone he wants."

Aiden stepped back to her side. "We'll get him when the lab report comes in. He can't get to you again," she said fiercely. Just the thought of someone hurting Dawn made her blood boil. She hid any trace of her anger behind a calm expression, knowing that open displays of violent emotions would scare Dawn even further. She followed a triumphant defense attorney out of the room, making sure to stay close to Dawn as they walked across the busy squad room. Aiden searched the room for Mrs. Kinsley's friendly face but came up empty. "Your mother's not here?"

"No. I have some errands to run after this. Buying new glasses," Dawn pointed to the empty place at the bridge of her nose, "going to the hospital for my HIV and STD test results, and making an appointment with Victim Services."

Aiden lifted her brows. "You have to do all this on your own? Can I drive you anywhere?"

"No, thanks. My mother and a few close friends have been very supportive, but..." Dawn stepped a little closer to Aiden when two detectives dragged a cuffed and swearing suspect through the squad room. "To tell you the truth, they're not really helping so much as trying to take over. I know they mean well and want to spare me from dealing with all this stuff, but by making my decisions, they're taking control away from me, and I can't stand that right now."

Aiden nodded. She admired Dawn for knowing her own needs and feelings so well. Was it Dawn's professional background that made her so insightful, or was it her introspective nature that had made her choose her profession? She rolled her eyes at herself. *Philosophical thoughts before lunch? You'd better get back to work, Carlisle!*

"Aiden?" Ray called from across the room. "Ruben and Okada are about to make an arrest in the Perez/Munos case, and they want us for backup. You coming?"

Aiden reached for the leather jacket that hung over the back of her desk chair. Grabbing her keys, she looked back at Dawn, a question in her eyes.

"I'm fine," Dawn said, reading the question as clearly as if she had asked it out loud. "Go on, Detective, serve and protect." She forced a smile onto her lips.

It wasn't Juanita Perez she wanted to serve, and it wasn't Angela Munos she wanted to protect right this moment, but Aiden was a professional. She squared her shoulders and walked out the door without looking back.

CHAPTER 7

Aiden looked up from the report on her desk when Ray returned from the crime lab.

"Forensics confirmed the presence of fluids," Ray said. "They also found prints that didn't belong to the vic or her family."

"Who do they belong to?" Aiden steepled her fingers to avoid strangling her partner in her impatience.

Ray sat at his desk. "They ran the prints and DNA through every available database, but they don't match anyone in the system. Our perp has no prior criminal record."

Ruben wandered over with a cup of coffee. "So he's a first-time offender? Someone completely new in the business?"

"Hard to believe, if you ask me. Dr. Kinsley got the distinct feeling that he had done it before." Ray looked at the notes he had taken during Dawn's formal statement.

Aiden shrugged. "Maybe Dawn's just the first victim willing to press charges. You know how many rapes go unreported."

"Or he changed MO," Ruben said. "Maybe he used gloves and a condom before, but now he got overconfident, thinking we couldn't get him even with DNA evidence."

Aiden's teeth ground against each other. "If that's what he thought, then it seems like he was right on target. We have nothing on him, not a single lead."

Ray tapped some words on his notepad. "Dawn said he smelled of smoke and booze—maybe he had himself a little liquid courage in one of the neighborhood bars?"

Ruben shook his head. "Nope, already checked. We've shown the police sketch around the neighborhood, including bars. No luck so far. No one remembers seeing a guy like him."

"Same with the tapes from security cameras around the neighborhood," Aiden said. "They didn't show anything related to the rape. Did Okada have any luck with cross-checking Dawn's personal information before he took off for court?"

"We cross-checked every rape victim who used the same hair salon, dry cleaner, grocery story, or whatever," Ruben answered. "Some of them had one or two places in common with Dawn Kinsley, but their rapists are either still in prison or had a completely different MO."

Ray looked at the lab reports. "The fibers CSU found on the sheets and Dawn's clothing were white cotton, which tells us a whole lot of nothing. Seems we're totally out of leads."

Aiden leaned her elbow on the table and rested her chin in her hand. "Why didn't the bastard use a condom? Why did he leave such a ridiculously large amount of evidence behind? I mean, come on, guys! Every first grader in the country knows to wear gloves and not spread around his DNA like free candy."

"Good old plain stupidity?" Ruben shrugged. "Not every perp's a criminal mastermind, Aiden."

Aiden shook her head. "No, there's something more behind it. Dawn said he wasn't exactly Einstein, but he seemed street-smart."

"Why don't you ask our resident shrink if he agrees with the assessment of his esteemed colleague?" Lt. Astrid Swenson, leader of Portland's Sexual Assault Detail, said as she entered the squad room.

Dr. Albert Renshaw followed closely behind the stocky lieutenant. The bearded psychiatrist looked at the file in his hands. "Are you sure that the perpetrator is a stranger who just chose his victim by chance? He literally attacked not only the victim but also her bedroom furniture, her books, her sketches, and other personal belongings. He seems to harbor some kind of personal anger toward her."

"Dawn Kinsley, the victim, clearly stated that she didn't know him," Aiden said. "And he bumped into furniture and didn't seem to be familiar with the layout of the apartment."

"Okay, so we can rule out old boyfriends, but what about a fleeting acquaintance or a neighbor she doesn't remember?" Renshaw took off his reading glasses and glanced at each detective. "Or he's the rapist of one of her clients. If he followed his victim, he might know she's seeing a therapist."

Aiden shrugged. "I'll ask her about it when I call to update her on the investigation."

Aiden turned her desk chair for a little privacy, sitting with her back to the rest of the squad room. She pressed the phone to her ear and dialed the number she already knew by heart.

She wasn't surprised when she heard Grace Kinsley's voice at the other end of the line instead of her daughter's. Dawn seemed to avoid answering the phone or opening the door. "Hello, Mrs. Kinsley. It's Detective Carlisle. Could I talk to your daughter, please?"

"Oh, sorry, you just missed her, Detective," Grace Kinsley answered. "She went out, trying to buy a new bed and to find someone willing to take the old one off her hands."

Aiden lifted her brows. It had been three days since the rape, and Dawn was already throwing herself into solving the practical problems the assault had caused. Aiden could understand Dawn's need to distract herself from constant thoughts of the rape and to try to "get on with her life," but she knew that it was just a temporary solution.

"Her childhood bed is too small if you have to sleep in it for more than a night, and she said she couldn't even close her eyes in the bed from her apartment anymore." Mrs. Kinsley sighed. "I worry when she leaves the house on her own, and I know she's afraid all the time, but she's too stubborn to accept any help. I think she wants to protect me from the reality of her...attack."

"Most women in her situation feel the need to make their own decisions and get some control back," Aiden said and then, without knowing why, asked, "Did she take a car?"

"Yes. She hasn't used the MAX or the bus since the attack."

Despite being afraid, Dawn had forced herself to leave the security of her mother's home. Aiden couldn't help admiring her. She said good-bye to Mrs. Kinsley with the promise to call back later. A glance at her watch made her decide to clock out and head home. With no new leads, there was no need for overtime.

She turned up the collar of her leather jacket when a light rain began to fall. Settling herself into the driver's seat of her car, she stared out the windshield. She jingled the key, finally stuck it into the ignition, and started the car. But instead of leaving the parking lot, she sat with the engine idling. She longed to head home and catch some much-needed sleep, but she knew she would find no peace until she had checked on Dawn. *You're a cop, not a babysitter. You're responsible for catching her rapist, not for holding her hand. Nothing good will come of it if you keep crossing that line.* As much as she wanted to be Dawn's friend, she was the detective investigating her case, first and foremost.

The rain outside was getting heavier now, drumming against the windshield. Across the street from the station, a lone woman was trying to heave a large TV set out of a moving van and to reach the safety of an open front door.

A picture of Dawn flashed through her—Dawn crying alone in her bedroom, trying to take down the bed with trembling hands, and then dragging a bloodstained mattress across the yard while rain drenched her clothes and mingled with her tears.

Aiden pressed her lips together and put the car in drive.

Aiden hadn't been sure if she would end up in front of Dawn's apartment building or her own until she parked the car. *Five minutes, one short look around to make sure everything's all right, then it's back to your own place.*

She was halfway across the street when she discovered Dawn sitting in a small car parked in front of the building, staring at the front entrance as if it were her mortal enemy.

As Aiden came closer, she saw dark shadows under Dawn's eyes, evidence that she probably hadn't slept well in days. She clung to the steering wheel with shaking hands. Twice she reached for the driver's door as if to open it, but each time she hesitated at the last second.

No considerations of professionalism could hold Aiden back now. She bridged the remaining space between them in two long strides and knocked softly on the driver's side window.

Dawn jumped and shrank back from the window. Visibly shaken, she rolled it down but stayed in the safety of the car. "Detective Carlisle."

Aiden found herself searching for words. "Sorry for scaring you."

Dawn didn't try to claim Aiden hadn't. "I've been sitting here for an hour. Ten minutes ago, I had almost talked myself into going in when I saw a tall man with black hair walking down the street. I couldn't leave the car." She pinched the bridge of her nose. "Is there anything new in my...case?"

Aiden looked into Dawn's hopeful gray-green eyes and bit her lip. "Sorry, no good news. DNA didn't match anyone with a prior criminal record, but we're not giving up."

Dawn was silent for a moment. "Thanks for telling me in person." She obviously believed Aiden had come to tell her the bad news.

Aiden bounced on the balls of her feet in front of the car.

This is your chance to say "You're welcome" and leave. You certainly fulfilled your duties as a cop. But, truth be told, she wasn't here as a cop. Dawn was still staring at her apartment building, clearly intimidated by it. She would probably sit in her car and fight her fears until the sun went down. Only then would she leave, too afraid of the darkness and what it might bring to stay any longer. Could Aiden turn her back and leave the scared woman behind like this, just because she was a police officer? Didn't she have duties beyond that of a cop—the duties of a human being providing simple comfort to a scared soul?

Hesitantly, she cleared her throat. "I'm not trying to take over your life or make your decisions for you, but I heard you were going bed hunting, and I thought you could use some company in your quest for a new bed."

Dawn stared at her.

"You're free to tell me to go to hell, you know," Aiden said when Dawn remained silent.

That shook Dawn out of her paralysis. "No," she said quickly. "No, I don't want that. I'd really like to have some company."

"Okay." Aiden found herself smiling at Dawn. "How about a trip to a furniture store? I think we should leave removing your old bed for another day." *Here you go again, Carlisle. That was practically an offer to help her again. What happened to "one short look around, then back to your own place"?* But then she looked at Dawn's trembling hands. It wasn't safe to let her drive through the city on her own. "Why don't I drive? I've got the bigger car."

With obvious relief, Dawn reached out to open the car door—only to be met with resistance. Blushing, she unlocked the door.

Aiden didn't comment. She could only imagine how frightening even everyday things suddenly were for Dawn. She led her to her car and opened the passenger side door for her.

"So, where to?" She would be careful to let Dawn make all the decisions.

Dawn gave directions to a furniture store but otherwise remained silent during the short trip.

Half an hour later, they were strolling along rows of beds. Dawn kept her shopping restricted to the part of the store that presented the single beds, obviously not intending to share her bed with anyone in the foreseeable future. She sat down on the edge of a bed, carefully testing its mattress. "What do you think?" She looked up at Aiden.

Aiden smiled at the softly bouncing woman and shrugged. "Shopping advice isn't really my forte. The decision is all yours."

"Really helpful, Detective." Dawn bounced some more in her attempt to test the mattress.

A young furniture salesman approached.

Aiden assessed him with a trained glance. With his confident stride and rakish grin, he was well aware of his effect on women and not afraid to use it. *God, I hope he doesn't try to come on to Dawn.* Dawn would most likely be overwhelmed even with light flirting from this stranger.

"We have some newer models in the back," the salesclerk said. He tried to take Dawn by the elbow to lead her to another part of the store, but she sidestepped his grip and took refuge in Aiden's closeness.

The salesclerk blinked and seemed to notice Aiden for the first time, now looking her up and down. "Ah." He pointed at the bed next to them. "I don't think that's what you're looking for. If you would follow me, please." He kept a respectful distance as he led them away from the single bed and stopped in front of a king-sized one. "That," he pointed back to the row of single beds and winked at Dawn, "may be long enough for a small thing like you, but I doubt it would be very comfortable for her." He nodded his head in Aiden's direction, then at the larger bed in front of them. "This is more like it."

Jesus! He thinks we're a couple buying a bed together. Aiden held back a sharp reprimand, waiting for Dawn's reaction instead.

Dawn, however, seemed blissfully unaware of the clerk's assumption. "Oh, no, no, it's not for her, I'm the one who's buying the bed."

"Oh, sorry." The salesclerk looked at his shoes. "I thought... So the bed's just for you?"

Dawn looked up. Her gaze wandered from the salesman to Aiden. She laughed, a surprised but not shocked sound. "Yes, I'm the one who will be sleeping in the bed. The only one. She's just along to do the heavy lifting."

So, whatever Dawn Kinsley is, Aiden thought while Dawn decided on one of the single beds, *she's not a homophobe. Not that it matters for the investigation.*

Neither of them commented on the salesclerk's assumption as they left the furniture store.

"Have you eaten yet?" Dawn asked.

Aiden busied herself with looking into the rearview mirror before pulling out into traffic. She hadn't taken the time to eat, but going to dinner with a victim in one of her cases was a line she didn't want to cross.

"I'd really like it if you would accept an invitation to dinner as a thank-you for your help," Dawn said before Aiden could answer.

Aiden started to shake her head when the faint rumbling of Dawn's stomach interrupted her. "Sounds like I'm not the only one who hasn't eaten yet."

"I haven't had much of an appetite lately," Dawn said quietly.

God! Aiden groaned inwardly. *How can I say no now?* A quick glance to her right showed Dawn's hopeful gaze directed at her. It was obvious that Dawn felt safe in her company and wasn't ready to let go of that safety line and return home alone yet. *It would be a business dinner. You could ask her about Renshaw's theory.* "Dinner it is, then."

"It's not much," Aiden said, shifting the pizza box into her left hand so that she could open the door to her apartment, "but I'm rarely home, so it's enough for me." Since Dawn probably wouldn't feel at ease in a public place like a restaurant and she didn't want to question Dawn about her rapist in front of her mother, she had decided on takeout in her own apartment. Hastily, she cleared a few files from the coffee table. "Have a seat, please. You want something to drink?" She looked into her almost empty refrigerator. "Orange juice, mineral water, beer. I think we should avoid the milk, though."

"Orange juice, please."

Aiden took the juice container and reached for a bottle of beer before stopping herself. *Not a good idea. She said she smelled alcohol on the perp's breath. You don't want her to have a flashback, do you? And besides, this is business, remember, so no drinking.*

"How long have you lived here?" Dawn asked, taking the glass Aiden handed her.

Aiden sighed inwardly. So now the personal questions would start. "A while."

Dawn continued looking around the apartment. She pointed at the sculpture next to the couch and at the painting above it. "Are you a fan of Robyn Carlisle? You're not related to her, are you?"

Keeping this at a strictly professional level seemed to be impossible. Aiden gave a short nod. "She was my mother," she said, hoping to leave it at that. She put a slice of veggie pizza on Dawn's plate.

Instead of eating, Dawn studied Aiden's face. "Are you uncomfortable with my being here?"

Why did I think dinner with a psychologist was a good idea? Aiden felt as if Dawn could look right through her and read her like a picture book—a feeling she didn't like. "It's not that."

"But?"

"This is business." *At least, it should be.* "There are a few questions I have to ask you."

"Okay." Dawn pushed back her plate, obviously no longer hungry.

A sharp stab of guilt shot through Aiden. *You have to be professional, but do you also have to be an asshole?* In her attempt to draw a clear line between her job and her private life, she had denied Dawn a rare opportunity to relax and not think about the rape. "I'm sorry." She rubbed her temples, feeling the onset of a headache. This was clearly a catch-22 situation.

"Don't apologize for doing your job." Dawn sounded sincere, but there was an emotional distance between them that hurt.

"I'm not." Aiden had been the one trying to stake out the boundaries of this acquaintance, and now she was the one who couldn't stand them. "It's just—"

"Detective, if anyone can understand the need to separate the job from...friendships, it's me. In my profession, meeting a patient in a nontherapeutic context is a big no-no."

"I'm not your therapist," Aiden said.

Dawn tilted her head in agreement. "No, you're not. You're a detective and a good one at that. I grew up surrounded by cops, so I know the requirements of the job. I apologize if I made it difficult for you."

Aiden had a sudden urge to bang her head against the coffee table. She felt like an insensitive bastard trying to reduce a wonderful and complex woman to the role of a rape victim. She couldn't find the words to make Dawn—or herself—feel better. If she tried to speak the comforting words of a friend, this whole conversation would be in vain. *Damn, what a mess.*

"Hey." For a second, Dawn put her hand on top of Aiden's. "What was it you wanted to ask me?"

Aiden put the uneaten pizza back into its box. She couldn't help admiring the woman across from her. *I should be the one to make her feel better, not the other way around.* "My colleagues and I are working with Dr. Albert Renshaw, a forensic psychiatrist," she said, trying hard to hold on to her professional role. "He thinks your attacker might be someone you know, a passing acquaintance or something."

"Because of the way he wrecked my apartment?"

"Yes. Dr. Renshaw thinks it might be something personal he held against you. Are you sure you don't know him?"

Dawn tugged at her lower lip with her teeth. "I had the feeling he knew me better than the other way around—or at least he thinks he does. If I have seen him before, I'm sure it was as nothing more than a stranger on the street, a cabbie who drove me home once, or a cashier who wrapped up my tomatoes or bananas for me."

"Banana," Aiden mumbled before she could stop herself.

Their conversation in the grocery store seemed to have happened in another life, to another person. And perhaps it had. No rape victim would ever be the same again, and at the moment, Aiden felt as if she wouldn't either. She sighed. "Come on, I'll wrap up the pizza and drive you home."

Dawn stood without hesitation and followed Aiden to the door.

CHAPTER 8

RAY GLANCED AWAY FROM THE heavy traffic for a moment, looking at Aiden in the passenger seat of the unmarked car. Something was going on with his partner. Aiden had been silent for the whole drive uptown. Not that she was a regular chatterbox otherwise, but she seemed to be downright moody today. He was sure that every single sex crimes detective had heaved a sigh of relief when they had left the station to visit Dawn Kinsley's office.

Determined to find out what troubled his partner, Ray tried to bring her out of her shell with their usual teasing. "You're really slipping in your old age, partner."

"I forgot, okay?" Aiden stopped and rubbed her neck.

Ray didn't believe it for a second. It was unlike Aiden to forget asking a witness a question that could be essential to solving the case. He lifted both hands in a calming gesture before gripping the steering wheel again. "Don't take my head off. It's no big deal. Since we can't find Dr. Kinsley for the moment, we'll just ask one of her partners if they remember any cases with similar rapes, all right?"

Aiden didn't answer. She stared out the window.

Was there a connection between her bad mood and her sudden forgetfulness? Ray knew Aiden had met with their victim last night, and she had asked Dawn about some of Renshaw's questions—but then had supposedly forgotten to ask her if the perp could be the rapist of one of her patients. Ray would have simply attributed it to stress, but why had Aiden balked at calling

Dawn for further questions? "Did something happen between you and Dawn?" he asked as casually as possible.

Aiden's head jerked around. Her amber eyes flashed. "What are you getting at? There's nothing between Dawn and me!"

Ah! Things were becoming clearer now. *That's what got her undies in a bunch. I knew she liked that little shrink.* He abstained from grinning. "I'm not implying that. I just thought... You seemed to have a really good rapport with her. What happened?"

"The job, what else?" Aiden sighed. "She's a victim and the key witness in one of our cases, Ray."

"And that means you can't interact with her?" Ray kept his tone neutral.

Aiden shot him a sharp glance. "Not in anything other than a professional manner. It could hurt the case, you know that."

Who's she trying to convince—me or herself? Aiden was usually reluctant to let people get close to her. Finding herself becoming friends with a shrink—and a victim in one of their cases—had to have her running for cover. Or was it more than friendship? Ray eyed his partner. He had known for years that Aiden was gay, but they had never talked about it. It didn't matter between them. She was his partner, and that was all he needed to know to support her. *Hell, it would cause more of a problem between us if she ogled Ruben's ass.* Even he, a married man, could understand her sneaking a peek at Kade Matheson's long legs.

He cleared his throat. "Pulling away from her like she has a contagious disease or bad breath could hurt the case too. Dawn is our key witness, but now you're reluctant to talk to her, and she's not picking up her phone. This can't go on."

"I know, I know." Aiden rubbed her eyes. "I'm sending her mixed messages, and it's confusing her. Hell, it confuses me."

Ray gave her a side-glance. "Mixed messages?"

"Yeah. One minute, I'm telling her she can call me day and

night, and I'll be there for her, and when she takes me up on it, I play the it's-just-the-job card."

"No one says you can't get to know her," Ray said, allowing himself a grin, "as long as it's not in the biblical sense." He dodged the punch Aiden threw at him. "Okay, okay, just kidding. I know she's not up for anything like that. You should be okay as long as you keep it on a friendly, supportive basis, at least till the investigation is over. That doesn't mean you have to play the emotionless detective. You're a human being, Aiden, not Robocop."

That finally got him a laugh. "Thanks, Ray."

Ray waved her away. "Hey, maybe I should ask those shrinks what the usual fee is for such great advice." Not waiting for an answer, he pulled into a parking space in front of Dawn's office and got out of the car.

Next to a student union office from the nearby Portland State University, a discreet sign announced the joint practice of A. Barry, PhD; C. Rosenbloom, MD; and D. Kinsley, PhD.

"Normally, wild horses couldn't make me go in there." Ray shuddered dramatically but then opened the door.

The reception area of the psychologists' office looked like every other doctor's office Aiden had seen. Tasteful watercolors and landscape photographs hung on white walls. An open door led to a waiting room with a pink plastic table and toys in one corner and a rack with magazines in the other.

On closer inspection, Aiden detected what she believed to be Dawn's touch on the room: A group of crooked Play-Dough animals was proudly displayed on the reception desk. Colorful cartoons and psychologist jokes adorned one wall, and instead of a coatrack, patients could hang their jackets on a wooden cactus next to the door. It was exactly the bizarrely creative but cozy jigsaw puzzle style Aiden had come to associate with Dawn.

"How may I help you?" A gray-haired secretary looked up from her computer.

Ray stepped toward the reception desk. "Are any of the doctors in?"

The secretary nodded. "They're all in today. But I suppose you're the police, wanting to talk to Doc Kinsley and not a couple here for marriage counseling, are you?"

"Are we, darling?" Ray's shining white teeth flashed against his dark skin as he shot a grin at Aiden.

"We're not." Aiden flashed her badge instead of a smile. She wasn't in the mood for jokes, too occupied with staring at the secretary. Dawn was already back at the office, counseling rape victims, when it hadn't even been a week since she herself had been raped? Aiden didn't need to have a PhD in psychology to know that Dawn was either punishing herself for any self-perceived contribution to her rape or in deep denial, trying to forget about her own problems by dealing with someone else's. Aiden knew all about that—firsthand.

"I can't comprehend how someone could do something so terrible to someone as sweet as Doc Kinsley." The secretary leaned across her desk and looked right and left as if to make sure no one could overhear her words. "I work for all three of the doctors, but she's my favorite. Don't tell the others, though. Psychologists' egos, you know?"

One of the doors leading to the psychologists' offices opened, and a visibly upset woman stepped out, only stopping at the reception desk to make a new appointment with Dr. Kinsley.

A minute later, the door opened a second time, admitting Dawn, who looked only marginally better than her patient. Her blonde hair was tousled as if she had run her hands through it, and the dark circles under her eyes had become even more pronounced.

Aiden couldn't help wondering—would Dawn have fared as

badly if she had not cut her last safety line by trying to distance herself from the situation?"

The smile that appeared on Dawn's face when she saw Aiden almost reached her eyes.

Aiden found herself walking toward Dawn without conscious thought. "Hi," she said, not knowing what else to say after their less than spectacular last meeting.

"Hi." This time, Dawn didn't help her out by filling the awkward silence.

Aiden shifted her weight. "I tried to call you at home. I didn't know you were already back at the office, treating patients." She was careful to keep any form of judgment from her voice.

Dawn shrugged. "I'm not treating patients per se. I just came in to finish some reports, but a client called for an emergency appointment. Her rapist is up for parole, and she wanted some support before the parole hearing."

Aiden nodded. She respected and admired Dawn for her professionalism and her willingness to help her patients, but that didn't keep her from worrying. *Who counsels the counselor? Who's there for her?* "It's good to have someone who supports you in situations like that." She stepped closer so no one would overhear her. "Have you thought about seeing a therapist?"

Dawn smiled. "I am a therapist."

"Yes, of course, but you're also human. When it concerns ourselves, our professional experience becomes meaningless. Even if you know all the symptoms, you can't prevent them. We react like any other victim." Aiden was speaking from experience. She couldn't think about her mother's rape like a detective.

"I'll think about it." Dawn squared her shoulders. "Now, what brings you to my humble workplace?" She opened the door to her office and beckoned them to follow her.

It didn't resemble the austere doctors' offices Aiden had seen in the past. Behind a desk, where a small toy served as a paperweight for a pile of folders, Dawn's diploma hung side by side with a photograph showing two men in the uniforms of the Portland Police Bureau.

Aiden circled two yellow beanbags and stepped closer to study the photograph. The older man seemed to look back at her with calm, gray-green eyes. His tanned face held a serious expression, but there were deep laugh lines around his eyes and mouth. The family resemblance to Dawn couldn't be missed. The younger man beside him grinned rakishly, one hand proudly resting on his duty belt. *A rookie, still thinking that nothing could ever hurt him as long as he wears that uniform.* But obviously, something or someone had, since Dawn had spoken of her father and brother only in the past tense.

Aiden turned back around and sank onto one of the chairs in front of the desk when Dawn gestured toward them.

Ray took the chair beside her, resting one foot on the edge of a beanbag. He made no move to take over the questioning.

"I forgot to ask you something concerning Dr. Renshaw's theory," Aiden finally said.

"That would be the theory about him...the rapist...being someone I've met before?"

Aiden nodded. "Could he possibly be the rapist of one of your clients?"

"I don't think so," Dawn said. "Most of my patients do one-on-one and group counseling with me at least once or twice a week, often for years at a time. I spend a lot of time with these women, and I care about them. I wouldn't forget the face of one of their rapists if I saw it."

"I wasn't thinking about one that got caught," Aiden said. "If that was the case, we'd have his DNA and would have gotten a match. Maybe one of your patients' rapists followed her after the rape, basking in his power to destroy her life. He could have followed her to her appointments with you. Did any of your patients ever describe a similar rape? A rapist who broke into the apartment at night and..." She stopped and bit her lip. Dawn didn't need to be reminded of the details.

Dawn shook her head.

"No? Think about it carefully," Aiden said. Their investigation was at a dead end, and this was the only possible lead they had.

"Even if I could remember a similar case, I wouldn't tell you." Dawn held Aiden's gaze, even when Aiden stared at her. "I want to catch the bastard as much as you do—probably more, but I can't disclose anything a patient might have told me in a session. You know that."

So, there's steel under all that velvet if need be. Aiden wanted to be annoyed with her, but she couldn't. She was frustrated and disappointed, but she couldn't help admiring Dawn's determination to protect her patients no matter what it would cost her. "We're at a dead end."

"I know."

Dawn seemed to accept it calmly, but Aiden could see the shadows darting across her eyes, making them appear like gray rain clouds. She couldn't leave Dawn like that. Not again. "Do you need a ride home?"

"I have my car." Dawn said it almost regretfully.

Aiden grinned. "That little sardine can?"

Dawn shrugged. "You know what my colleagues say about people who drive big cars?"

"Please, come in, my fee is three hundred dollars an hour?" Aiden said.

Dawn laughed, her eyes now appearing more green than gray. "That they feel the need to compensate for something."

Ray was still laughing when they left the building. "You're good for her." He studied her over the roof of their car. "You can make her laugh even when she feels like her whole world is crumbling. Don't give that up. At least not totally, okay?"

Aiden looked back at the small car parked in front of the psychologists' office. "I'll try."

CHAPTER 9

AIDEN PUSHED THROUGH THE DOUBLE doors leading to the courtroom. She was early. The judge hadn't taken his seat on the bench yet, and the two attorneys were just unpacking their briefcases.

Kade seemed to sense Aiden's gaze on her. She looked up from her pretrial rituals and smiled at her before putting on her courtroom poker face again.

Aiden swallowed the last bite of the sandwich she had wolfed down on her way to the courtroom. The gallery was still relatively empty, so she had her choice of seats. She sat on the prosecution's side of the courtroom. This way, she could show her support for the People and had a better view of Kade when she sat down at her table. She leaned back in anticipation of the Kade Matheson show. *Some popcorn and a cold pop, and this would be perfect.*

Someone sat down in the seat next to her, annoying Aiden because there were still a lot of other unoccupied seats. She was here to watch Kade at work, not for small talk with whoever had just sought out her company.

"Hello, Detective Carlisle."

Aiden's annoyance vanished when she looked up. "Dawn! Have you been looking for me?" Her heart pounded. "Did something happen?"

"No, nothing happened." Dawn calmed her worries with a quick smile. "I wasn't looking for you, but I'll surely be glad for the company in a few minutes. I'm here for the trial."

Aiden attempted to remember which case was being tried today. She wasn't particular when it came to her Kade fix, so she hadn't kept track of the court's docket. *Wasn't it that pizza boy raping three women? Or is that tomorrow's case?* When she couldn't come up with the right case, she studied Dawn. She looked better. Shadows still lurked under her eyes, but the bruises on her cheek and throat were fading. Dawn had traded the jeans she had worn the week before in favor of a dark gray pantsuit, the matching blazer folded over her lap. A silver silk blouse, buttoned to the very last button, made her eyes appear more gray than green.

Aiden suspected that this was not Dawn's usual style. She remembered a vivacious psychologist at the seminar, her charmingly freckled collarbone exposed by two undone buttons. *Being raped changes everything, even the way you dress.*

"Are you here supporting a patient?" Aiden asked.

Dawn nodded. "I promised I'd watch at least the opening statements for her. Was this one of your cases?"

"No," Aiden said and searched for an answer that was a little more appropriate than admitting that she was here to ogle their deputy district attorney. She gestured to the cuffed defendant sitting behind his table. "Just showing a little police presence to make sure he doesn't try anything stupid."

Dawn's gaze never moved away from the rapist. "Good idea."

They both fell silent when the judge took his place and the trial began.

Kade rose to give her opening statement, patiently walking the jurors through the timeline of events.

Dawn watched for a while and then leaned toward Aiden, who had to hold herself back from breathing in Dawn's enticing scent. "She's good, isn't she?" Dawn whispered.

Aiden couldn't stop her proud grin. "Yes, she is." Kade was confident without appearing arrogant, cool without being uncaring, yet today, she failed to capture Aiden's attention and pull it away from the woman next to her. She blinked and cleared her throat. "Uh, do you know a lot about law, or how do you know she's any good?"

"I know a lot about body language." Dawn leaned toward Aiden again as she spoke, making Aiden want to loosen her collar because of the sudden rise in her body temperature.

You wanted to keep your distance, remember? Seems like you managed to do the complete opposite.

Thankfully, Dawn seemed to be unaware of Aiden's internal debate and her bodily reaction to Dawn's nearness. "She makes constant eye contact with the jurors, and she chose the perfect distance to the jury box—close enough to draw them in but not so close that she would be encroaching on the jury's comfort zone."

"Trials by jury have a lot to do with psychology," Aiden said, glad to be in control of herself once again.

Dawn nodded toward Kade, who sat back down when the defense attorney began his opening statement. "See how she isn't even fidgeting when opposing counsel points out the weaknesses of her case?"

"After two years with the Sexual Assault Detail, I'm sure she could listen to the graphic biography of a serial killer without fidgeting," Aiden said.

Kade leaned back as if she didn't have a care in the world, almost bored with the defense attorney's opening statement.

Dawn inclined her head. "She learned it earlier than that. I think she had the kind of mother who had her sit down with the grown-ups at boring dinner parties. I'm sure building paper planes out of a napkin wasn't very popular with Mrs. Matheson. I can practically hear her: 'Stop fidgeting! You are making a nuisance of yourself, young lady!'"

Aiden's eyes widened. She had met Kade's mother once and could hear her say the same thing. "Do you know Mrs. Matheson?"

"I know body language," Dawn repeated with a smile.

Aiden looked down at herself, wondering what her body language might tell Dawn. She sat still for a minute, folding her hands on her knees, before she realized that trying not to have any body language was impossible. The stiff posture resulting from her attempt spoke loud and clear. She leaned toward Dawn so she would understand her against the background of defense counsel's opening statement. "So, what would your mother have said to you building paper airplanes out of napkins?"

Dawn smiled. "There weren't any napkins at our dinner table. My mother was happy if she could get us to keep still long enough to eat dinner while sitting down. My family was never big on formalities."

"Growing up free and unrestricted, huh?"

"Unrestricted?" Dawn opened her gray-green eyes comically wide. "Are you kidding? My dad was a cop. We had to play by the rules, believe me."

Aiden thought back to the last Thanksgiving dinner she had spent with Ray and his family. His kids were free to express their opinions with the adults, but there were unspoken boundaries they weren't allowed to cross.

"What about your family? Were you the napkin-at-dinner kind?" Dawn asked.

Defense counsel's opening statement had ended by now, and the courtroom was almost silent for a few moments while he sat down. Judge Gilmartin's annoyed glance in their direction saved Aiden from telling Dawn that her family dinners had consisted of vodka for her mom and cornflakes for Aiden. With a quick glance at her wristwatch, Aiden gestured to Dawn that she had to go and slipped out of the courtroom.

Dawn followed. "I don't think I'm quite ready to listen to the detailed description of another rape."

Aiden turned up her jacket's collar when they left the building, eyeing Dawn's thin blazer, which couldn't protect her from the cool October wind. *You're not her mother or her lover. It's not your business to make sure she doesn't get cold.*

They stood facing each other on the steps of the courthouse.

"So, are you off to serve and protect, or is this your day off?" Dawn stopped two steps above Aiden so they could talk face-to-face.

"It's back to work." Aiden stuffed her hands into the pockets of her coat. "And you? Going back home?"

Dawn nodded. "When you get back to the precinct, maybe you could take care of something for me."

Anything. For a moment, Aiden wasn't sure if she had said it out loud. "Yes?"

"My address is going to change soon. I will call you later to let you know. You should probably make a note in your records or something."

"You're moving out of your old apartment." It didn't come as a surprise for Aiden.

A curt nod from Dawn. "It doesn't feel like a home anymore, and I don't want to stay at my mother's for much longer. I love her, but I'm twenty-eight, and I don't want to live with her for more than a few weeks. I'm looking at some apartments this afternoon."

Another crossroad opened up in front of Aiden. Should she just nod and promise to write down the change of address once Dawn knew it or offer to help her find a new home where she could feel safe? *Are you out of your damn mind? You want to go apartment hunting with her? What's next, wanting to move in with her?* After a few seconds of hesitation, she allowed herself to compromise. "Listen. I'm not sure if your old apartment has been released yet or if it's still taped off as a crime scene. If you need any help with that or you want someone to go with you when you go to the old apartment to get some of the furniture..." It would only be for security reasons, she told herself. Sometimes, offenders came back to the crime scene, after all.

"Detective, I don't expect you to—"

"Please do," Aiden said before she could talk herself out of it. "Please expect me to be there for you." A part of her was glad that she had said it, another part wanted to take it back immediately.

For a long time, Dawn looked at her without saying anything. Perhaps she sensed Aiden's conflicting emotions, because she appeared to be equally hesitant to accept the offer. Then she drew her blazer more tightly around her small shoulders and nodded. "Thank you."

CHAPTER 10

"Hello. Please come in, Detective." Grace Kinsley opened the door wider. "Dawn's still on the phone with the electric company."

As Aiden entered, she wondered what Dawn's mother might think about her continuing visits to her home. Did she find it odd that a Portland police detective was helping her daughter move into her new apartment? Did she sense Aiden's attraction to Dawn just as she had immediately known Aiden was a cop?

Without many words, Mrs. Kinsley led her into the kitchen, handed her a cup of black, unsweetened coffee, and leaned against the kitchen counter, studying her.

"How did you immediately recognize me as a cop when you first saw me?" Aiden asked to distract her from her scrutiny.

"I was married to a cop for almost twenty years," Mrs. Kinsley said, smiling wistfully. "I should know a cop when I see one."

Aiden kept her questioning gaze directed at her.

Grace shrugged. "It's the body language."

"Body language?" Aiden snorted into her coffee. *What is it with those Kinsley women and body language?*

"Yes." Dawn's mother stared into her own cup of coffee. "I think my husband used to call it command presence. You walk with a purposeful stride, your head held high, always aware of your surroundings. And, when you're knocking, you always stand to the side of the door to be safe from any bullets that might be fired at you from inside the house."

Aiden stared at her. "I do that?"

"You do." Grace smiled and gestured toward Aiden. "Even now, you stand facing the door to get a good view of the dangerous criminals that might invade my home."

"Sorry," Aiden said.

Grace shook her head. "Don't apologize. It's what keeps you alive while on the job."

Twenty years of marriage had taught Mrs. Kinsley a lot about police officers and the dangers they faced, and Aiden was sure that she would never want to see her daughter in a relationship with a cop.

"Hey." Dawn entered and laid the cordless phone on the kitchen table. She smiled at Aiden. "You're very punctual, Detective."

Aiden almost told Dawn to call her by her given name but held herself back from crossing that line.

The doorbell rang, making Dawn jerk. She didn't move to open the door but let her mother do it.

Grace came back with a short-haired Latina in her forties. As the stranger strode into the room, her gaze took in Aiden, then immediately went to Dawn.

Aiden knew without asking that she was dealing with a fellow police officer. The stranger definitely had what Grace had called "command presence." *And if my gaydar isn't totally off, she's also a fellow lesbian.*

The woman went straight to Dawn and pulled her into a tight embrace. Neither of them said a word, but Dawn clung to the stranger as if she were a lifeline.

Aiden couldn't help frowning. Who was this woman? A friend? Or was there more between them?

When the embrace ended, the stranger cradled Dawn's cheek in one hand. "Hey there, grasshopper. How are you doing?"

"I'm fine, considering the circumstances. I'll be better when this day is over and I never have to see that apartment again." Dawn wasn't afraid to express her feelings, and Aiden admired her for that. "Oh, Del, this is Detective Aiden Carlisle. Detective, this is Lieutenant Delicia Vasquez Montero. She offered to help me move too."

So I was right. She is on the job.

"Don't call me that, grasshopper. I have a reputation to uphold. Besides, what do you mean...offered?" The lieutenant raised a brow and grinned at Dawn. "More like I was being roped into helping by the promise of a thank-you dinner. You know I can't resist your cooking." She turned to Aiden. "She can cook like a goddess."

"Goddesses don't cook," Dawn said, returning the grin. "They have their people do it for them."

"Carlisle..." Lieutenant Vasquez stepped closer and looked Aiden straight in the eye. They were about the same height. "You're with the Sexual Assault Detail, right? Are you the detective investigating Dawn's case?"

"Yes, ma'am."

"God, don't ma'am me." Del groaned. "Bad enough that the grasshopper here told you my dreadful first name." She scrutinized Aiden closely, looking her up and down like a parent checking out her daughter's prom date. "Did I miss the memo about the Portland Police Bureau offering moving services now?"

Aiden tried not to fidget. "No, I..." *Yeah, you what? She's got you there.*

"Leave the poor woman alone, and come help me in the kitchen." Grace pulled Lieutenant Vasquez away.

When they disappeared in the kitchen, Dawn turned to Aiden. "Sorry about that. Sometimes, my aunt can be a bit overprotective."

Aiden stared at her. "Lieutenant Vasquez is your aunt? Excuse me if I sound politically incorrect, but you don't look like a Latin girl to me."

"What, you mean I don't have that kind of exotic, vivacious sex appeal?" Dawn pretended to pout.

"Uh..." *You'd better plead the Fifth. Telling her what you think about her sex appeal would definitely cross the line.*

Dawn laughed. "I'm just kidding. Del is my adopted aunt. She was my dad's partner."

So she was practically a member of the family, not a lover or an ex. That made Aiden like Lieutenant Vasquez much better than before. "It's good that you have her."

"Yeah." Dawn nodded. "We almost lost her once. After Dad died, Del stopped coming around. She felt guilty that she hadn't been able to save him. She felt like she had failed us."

Aiden nodded. "I wouldn't know how to face Susan and the kids if anything should ever happen to Ray."

"One day, Mom had enough of Del avoiding us," Dawn said. "There was some shouting and screaming from Mom, some tears from both of them, and Del has been coming to see us at least once a week since then."

The ringing doorbell interrupted them.

Again, it was Grace who opened the door. She returned with a slightly overweight woman and a thin man with a receding hairline.

"Hey, girl." The woman headed for Dawn and gave her a short hug while the man gently squeezed Dawn's shoulder. "How are you?"

Aiden—and any other cop—would have answered with a joke about writing the answer to that question down on a big piece of paper so she wouldn't have to repeat herself, but Dawn answered with the same honesty as before.

"Ally, Charlie, this is Detective Carlisle. Detective, these are Allison Barry and Charles Rosenbloom, the colleagues I'm sharing my office with."

Aiden shook their hands with increasing discomfort.

Loaded down with thermoses of coffee and tea, Del Vasquez came out of the kitchen and nudged Aiden. "Looks like we're going to spend the day with three psychologists. Carlisle, we're doomed."

Yep. Aiden had thought the same thing.

"Hey, we psychologists can be perfectly nice." Dawn pinched her.

Del rubbed her arm. "Said the psychologist who attacked the defenseless police officer."

"All right, let's get started." Grace handed out work gloves and herded the helpers out the door.

When Aiden wanted to head to her car, Del held her back. "You're driving over with me. No sense in taking all the cars."

"Christ, Del." Dawn shook her head. "You sure have gotten used to ordering cops around since your promotion."

Del grinned. "One of the perks of my job. Come on, Carlisle."

They got into the car and followed Dawn's colleague, who was driving the moving van. Del stopped at a red light, but still she said nothing.

Oldest trick in the book. I'm not falling for that. Aiden did the same with suspects. Let them sweat and wait for them to blurt stuff out, just because they couldn't stand the silence any longer.

Finally, Del glanced over. "Does your lieutenant know you're here?"

Aiden tried in vain not to become defensive. "No reason why I should tell her. It's my day off."

"And you chose to spend it helping out a victim in one of your cases?"

"I chose to spend it helping out Dawn." Her answer was out before Aiden could think about it.

Del was silent as she steered the car through yet another intersection.

"Listen," Aiden said and then berated herself. Now she had fallen for the oldest trick in the book. "I know how this must look to you."

"Yeah?"

Aiden ignored her. "I want to help. That's all. I don't have any ulterior motives. Dawn didn't deserve what happened to her."

"No," Del finally said. "She sure didn't. I won't let anyone else take advantage of her."

"I'm not trying to do that."

"Good."

They spent the rest of the drive uptown in silence.

The joking and teasing from before stopped and they all grew quiet as they got out of the cars and walked up to Dawn's old apartment building. Aiden and Del lengthened their strides so they would be next to Dawn when she reached the front door.

Pale and visibly trembling, Dawn rummaged in her purse for the key.

Aiden stepped closer and leaned down so that no one but Dawn could hear. "Do you want to stay outside, maybe drive to the new apartment while we—"

"No," Dawn said. "It's kind of you to offer, but this is something I need to do. If I dodge the last opportunity to enter the apartment, I'll never know if I could have done it."

Aiden nodded and wanted to step back, but Dawn's fingers closed around her wrist. "Stay close, please?"

After one quick glance at Del, who didn't look happy to relinquish her role as Dawn's protector, Aiden nodded. "I'm right beside you." She practically plastered herself against Dawn's back while Dawn opened the door.

No one spoke as they climbed the stairs.

Dawn squared her shoulders, opened the apartment door, and strode inside. In the middle of the living room, her steps faltered and her glance wandered to the bedroom door.

"Okay." Del slapped her work gloves against her thigh. "How about you and Grace pack the dishes and the other household stuff, and your colleagues take care of the living room while Carlisle and I dismantle the bedroom furniture?"

Good. Aiden gave Del an appreciative nod. That way, Dawn didn't need to enter the bedroom.

A hard, impatient knock on the front door made Dawn jump and take a step back.

"Do you expect anyone else trying to earn one of your home-cooked meals?" Aiden asked.

Dawn shook her head. She nervously eyed the door.

Aiden stepped past her and nearly collided with Del, who had moved toward the door too. They exchanged a quick gaze, then, after an unspoken communication, Aiden moved left and Del moved right until they stood on either side of the door. Aiden reached for the gun on her hip, only to find it missing. Of course, she hadn't been carrying, since it was her day off. She gestured for Dawn and her colleagues to move back before she opened the door.

A tall man with windblown brown hair glared at her. "Who the hell are you? Where's Dawn?"

Aiden kept blocking the door, never moving an inch. "Who are you?"

"I'm her husband."

Husband? Dawn is married? Aiden could only stare at the stranger.

"Ex-husband," Del said. "What do you want, Caleb?"

Caleb groaned. "Del. Great. Of course you'd be here."

"Yeah, I'm trying to be there for Dawn, not that you'd know anything about it."

"How can I be there for her if no one tells me anything?" His voice rose. "I had to hear it through the precinct grapevine. I'll kill the goddamn bastard who did this to her!"

Dawn took a step back.

Aiden glared at Dawn's ex-husband. "Can I talk to you for a minute? Outside."

"Who is she?" He pointed a finger at her.

Aiden stretched herself to her full five foot ten inches. Her leather jacket creaked as she squared her shoulders. *Down, girl. This is not a pissing contest. This is about Dawn—or at least it should be.*

"This is Detective Carlisle," Dawn said before Aiden could answer. "A friend of mine."

Aiden was proud to be called friend by a woman like Dawn, but at the same time, those words started the guilty internal debate about acceptable professional behavior again.

"What's going on in here?" He peeked into the apartment.

"I'm moving into a new apartment," Dawn said.

"Hmm." Caleb eyed the five women and the skinny Charlie Rosenbloom. "Looks like you could use a little help."

"Sure, we could use the help," Dawn answered, looking him right in the eye, "but we can do without the patronizing comments."

Damn, I like this woman. She doesn't take shit from anyone. Aiden bit her lip to keep from laughing. She exchanged a quick glance with Del, stepped aside, and let him enter.

Caleb picked up one of the screwdrivers lying around and looked at Aiden. "Bedroom, you and me?"

"Ha! In your dreams," Aiden said but followed him to the bedroom. This way, she could at least talk to him without Dawn overhearing.

Del stayed back to help Dawn's colleagues with the large bookcase in the living room.

Caleb took in the room where his ex-wife had been raped. Clenching his jaw, he threw off the mattress and started to take down the bed's headboard. His movements were angry and uncontrolled, making the screwdriver scratch over the wood.

"She lived through enough violence that night," Aiden said softly but with a steely resolve. "Don't scare her any further, okay? She doesn't need your anger or your hateful tirades of revenge. She needs your support."

Caleb looked up from his work. "Are you with the Sexual Assault Detail or something, Carlisle?"

Aiden nodded and held his gaze. "You have something against that?"

"No. We can't all be real cops." His grin took the sting out of the words.

"Not only a real cop but a real comedian too, huh?" Aiden took off her leather jacket and pushed up the sleeves of her old PPB sweatshirt. She started loosening the screws on the other side of the headboard.

"So..." Caleb leaned over the headboard so he could see the screw heads. "How do you know Dawn?"

Was that his way of asking whether Aiden was sleeping with his ex-wife? "I met her at a seminar a few weeks ago."

"I see."

"My partner and I are also investigating her rape case." She was hesitant to admit it but didn't want to lie.

Caleb straightened and looked at her with an incredulous expression. "You're the investigator in her case, and you offered to help her move into a new apartment? Wow! Me and my colleagues, we wouldn't help a lady we're busting for speeding buy a new car."

Now it was Aiden who found herself becoming angry. "Your

lead-footed ladies are breaking the law, but Dawn's not a perp. She's the victim. Don't you think she deserves a little help?"

"Okay, maybe it's not the best analogy I could have chosen." Caleb shrugged.

"No, it sure isn't."

They each grabbed a side of the headboard and lifted it clear of the rest of the bed. It banged against the slatted frame already lying on the floor.

"No need to be careful with the bed," Aiden said. "I don't think she cares or even wants to know what happens with it."

"Goddammit! How could this happen to Dawn?" Caleb kicked out at the half-dismantled bed. "Do you know who...?"

Aiden held up her hands. "I can't talk about an ongoing investigation. You know that." She might have crossed a few lines of professionalism to help Dawn deal with the aftermath of her rape, but she wasn't willing to break the rules for anyone else.

"Get him!" He pointed his index finger at Aiden. "We may be divorced, but I still care for her."

Aiden wondered why they had divorced—and why they had gotten married in the first place. Once he calmed down, he was probably a decent guy, but he didn't seem like a perfect match for Dawn. *Oh, yeah? And who would this perfect match be—you?*

Caleb moved to one of the bookcases and grunted when he tried to push it to the side. "Three damn shrinks in the house, you'd think one of them could shrink all this heavy furniture into a more maneuverable size."

Laughing, Aiden went to help him with the bookcase.

Aiden stood next to Dawn in front of her old apartment building. The muscles in her arms and back protested the heavy lifting she had done all day long—not that she would ever admit it. They had just carried down the last of the packed boxes while the rest of the moving team took another trip to Dawn's new apartment.

Del and Aiden had checked out Dawn's new home thoroughly, testing out the two locks on the door and experimentally shaking the bars in front of the windows before declaring it safe. The fifth-floor apartment had recently been renovated and was up to the newest security standards. It also didn't hurt that the new apartment was close to the Justice Center, which housed the Portland Police Bureau headquarters, the central precinct, and some offices of the district attorney, ensuring a constant police presence in the neighborhood.

Dawn slid the last of the boxes into the back of her mother's car. "I'm sorry about Cal trying to back you into a corner when he first arrived."

"Hey, it's all right. I think we've come to an understanding." Aiden studied Dawn's tired face. "I just didn't know you'd been married."

Dawn shrugged. "Not for very long. It didn't work out between us, so we got a divorce after less than two years."

"Yeah, old story. We cops don't make the best spouses, being married to our jobs and all." It was one of many reasons why Aiden wasn't searching for a relationship.

"That may have been part of our problems, but mainly, it wasn't him, it was me. I..." Dawn sighed and kicked the heap of dismantled bed parts they had stacked on the sidewalk. "He was an old friend of Brian, my brother. I'd known him for years, but there was never anything but friendship between us. Then Brian died, not long after my father did, and I thought I had come to love Cal, but I guess I just needed someone to hold on to. Should have known myself better than that."

"You know now," Aiden said.

Dawn snorted. Tears gleamed in her eyes. "A little late for that insight. I'm not exactly good relationship material now." She looked at the bed lying in ruins at her feet—the bed she had been raped in. Silent sobs shook her.

Aiden had wondered whether something like this would happen at some point. Dawn had thrown herself into taking care of the practical things, making calls, looking at apartments, trying to resume a somewhat normal life. She had kept herself too busy to think about what had happened.

Now that the moving out of and into apartments had almost been completed and there was nothing else to do, everything caught up with her, the dam broke, and tears began to fall.

Aiden wished Dawn's psychologist friends or her mother were here, but they weren't. It was up to her to comfort Dawn or just stand there and let Dawn cry her eyes out, just because she had to remain professional.

When Dawn hastily tried to dry her tears and hide them behind her sleeve, Aiden finally stepped forward and wrapped her in a gentle embrace. Hot breath danced across the skin of her neck when Dawn let out a shaky breath, immediately accepting the embrace and burrowing herself deeper into Aiden's arms.

"I'm sorry," Dawn said after a minute. "It's just that I feel like he took everything from me and left no part of my life unsullied."

Aiden let her talk it out, not offering advice or asking any questions. She kept one arm around Dawn's trembling shoulders when Dawn took a step back.

"I can't look at any male stranger without wondering whether he's a rapist. My family and friends can't look at me without pity or sadness. I even lost some friends who told me to just get over it."

"Excuse me? What kind of friends are those?" Aiden shook her head.

"Not really close ones, but it hurt nonetheless," Dawn answered. "I don't need other people to make me feel guilty or doubt myself. I do that well enough on my own. He took my self-confidence, my trust in people, my friends, and my job. I don't know if I can ever work with victims of sexual assault again. I have to pay attention to them and not to my own feelings. What if I keep having flashbacks when one of them tells me about her rape?"

"Don't stress yourself out." Aiden caressed Dawn's heaving shoulder. "You'll cross that bridge when you come to it. It's too soon to be thinking about going back to work. Even if you can never work with rape victims again—and we don't know that yet—I'm sure there are a lot of people out there who need your help. I bet you'd be good with children, family therapy, maybe."

Dawn looked up, blinking back tears with her long, blonde lashes. "Have you ever considered a change of careers for yourself? You should be a therapist." A small smile trembled on her lips.

Aiden's ears started to burn under Dawn's grateful gaze. "I'm quite happy with the job I have, thank you very much."

"I'm also quite happy that you have this job," Dawn said.

Aiden bit her lip, unable to come up with an appropriate response.

"Come on." It was Dawn who finally broke the awkward silence. "Let's hurry up before the others start gorging themselves on pizza or Chinese takeout without us."

When Aiden arrived for the thank-you dinner the next day, it was once again Grace Kinsley who opened the door and walked her into Dawn's new apartment. "Hello, Detective. You're the last one in. All the other helpers are already waiting impatiently for you—or rather for the entrée Dawn refused to serve before your arrival."

"Sorry." Aiden took off her jacket and hung it on the coatrack she had assembled yesterday. "Ray, my partner, kept pushing unfinished reports onto my desk."

"Yeah, the dangers of being a desk jockey," Caleb said from his place at the dining table.

Aiden stopped in front of him. "Do I sense some deep-rooted jealousy, here?" She wasn't sure whether he was jealous of her career or because he suspected her sometimes more than friendly feelings toward his ex-wife. "We can't all be detectives, pal." Not waiting for an answer, she rounded the table and greeted the other guests.

"Dawn's still slaving over the stove," Grace said.

Being familiar with the layout of the apartment, Aiden went in search of their hostess. "Hi," she said from the doorway, careful not to startle Dawn. "Thanks again for the invitation. It smells really nice in here. Anything I can help with?"

"Hi." Dawn's smile lit up the kitchen. She appeared to be a lot better than the day before. "I still haven't found the serving tray."

"Ah." Aiden entered the small but functional kitchen. "I think we put it somewhere on the highest shelf." A quick glance told her that Dawn wouldn't be able to reach it, so she stretched her body and reached over her for the serving tray. For a second, she breathed in the scent of honey and almonds from Dawn's hair when their bodies came into close proximity, then she hastily stepped back and handed Dawn the tray.

Dawn smiled. "Thank you, Detective."

Aiden was glad that Dawn accepted her boundaries, never once trying to call her by her given name. *Speaking of names...* "When I was searching for a parking space, I noticed the name of the street you're now living on."

"Great name, huh?" Dawn grinned.

Aiden shook her head. "I've lived in Portland my whole life, but I never knew there's a Carlisle Street."

"Do you think it was named after one of your ancestors?" Dawn asked. "Maybe they rendered outstanding services to the city too."

Aiden stared at her. Had Dawn forgotten for a moment that Aiden had been fathered by a rapist? But now was not the time to think about that. She helped Dawn carry salad, bread, and spinach soufflé to the table. When she sat on the only unoccupied chair, right beside Dawn's, she took the time to look around the spacious living room.

The setting sun was filtering in through orange curtains, giving the room a soothing quality. Where just the bare furniture had stood only yesterday, signs of the Dawn Kinsley decorative style were now evident to Aiden. She found herself surrounded by small trinkets, stuffed animals, colorful drawings, and photos—memories of people and events Dawn obviously held dear.

"Help yourself." Dawn gestured toward the soufflé. "Like I said, we're not very big on formality."

Aiden pointed to the place next to her plate. "But you do have napkins."

Dawn inclined her head and smiled. "My one concession to a house full of guests."

Aiden waited until the others had filled their plates and then took her first bite. She loved leaf spinach, but with her limited cooking talents she had never tried a spinach soufflé. Her eyes widened, and she licked her lips. She held back a joking "Marry me!" and instead said, "It's really delicious."

"I told you she can cook like a goddess," Del said.

"Have a little white wine with it." Grace extended the wine bottle in Aiden's direction.

With a glance at the clear liquid in Dawn's glass, Aiden shook her head. "Water's fine, thank you."

Dawn set down her fork. "You're not on call, are you?"

"No, I'm not." Aiden would have liked a glass of wine but preferred red wine anyway, and she was determined to avoid any alcohol as long as Dawn still couldn't stand the smell of it. "Even if I was, I'm not sure I could leave while there is still food on the table. It's not often that I get to eat like this. I'm not much of a cook, myself."

"Donuts don't need any cooking," Allison said.

Del set down her glass, and Aiden realized that she was sticking to water too. "Hey, no donut cop jokes, please," Del said. "Us law enforcement personnel are very sensitive when it comes to our main food group."

Not bothering to ask in the relaxed, informal atmosphere, Aiden served herself a second helping of the soufflé. "Actually, I can't stand the stuff."

Grace poked her in the shoulder with the blunt end of her fork. "I'm sure you didn't admit that in your entrance interview with the police academy."

"Dad didn't like donuts, either," Dawn said with an affectionate smile. "He always said that white-powdered donuts and blue uniform shirts are not a good combination."

Aiden wanted to know more about Dawn's father and what had happened to him, but she didn't want to introduce a sad topic into an otherwise relaxed evening.

"He died in a traffic stop ten years ago," Dawn said as if sensing the unasked question. "He stopped a car because of a busted headlight, and the driver, a man with an active warrant out on him, panicked and pulled the trigger."

"I'm sorry." Aiden looked from Dawn to her mother, not sure what else to say.

Del stopped eating and clenched her hand around the fork, staring down at her plate.

Grace put her hand on Del's arm before she reached out and patted Aiden's shoulder. "It's an honorable but dangerous profession. I knew that when I married Jim. I just never thought I'd lose one of my kids to it too."

Aiden couldn't maintain eye contact, almost feeling guilty just because she was a police officer.

Dawn cleared her throat and lifted her glass of water. "To Portland's finest. May they all be safe tonight."

The toast was echoed all around the table.

That woman's really got style. Aiden sipped from her water glass. When she had first met Dawn, she had admired her good looks, her charm, and her easy way of relating to people. Now that she knew Dawn better, she found that she wasn't just attracted to Dawn physically; she liked her as a person too.

She spent her first relaxed evening in what seemed like forever, in the company of Dawn and her family and friends. The three psychologists were not at all as she had expected. Not once did she feel as if she were under constant scrutiny, the object of appraisal and analysis. *Their job is hard enough. Why would they want to do it in their free time too?* Even Del and Caleb seemed to warm up to her after a while.

Finally, every last bite of the meal had been eaten, and the dishes had been done. One after the other, the guests said goodnight and left. When only Dawn, her mother, and Del remained, Aiden stood and reached for her jacket. "Thank you for a very nice evening and a wonderful meal. I haven't eaten so well since my partner had to take me to a five-star restaurant on a lost bet."

"Has the Portland Police Bureau added another zero to our generous cop paychecks while I wasn't looking?" Del asked. "My colleagues and I only ever bet a hot dog and a coffee to go."

Aiden laughed. "No sudden enlightenment on part of the PPB, I'm afraid. We usually bet for hot dogs too, but this one was a bet we both were really confident we'd win."

Del chuckled. "Do I even want to know?"

"No, you don't. I have a certain image to uphold, ma'am," Aiden said with a dignified expression. She slipped on her jacket and turned to go.

"I told you, don't ma'am me," Del said, rolling her eyes.

"How about you call her Del?" Grace said. "You're both not on duty, after all."

Hesitating, Aiden glanced at Del.

Finally, Del relented. "All right, call me Del."

"Aiden." She put on her jacket, while Del and Grace did the same. Together, they walked toward the door.

"Detective?" Dawn's voice made her turn around. "Could you stay for a few minutes longer? I'd like to talk to you about something."

Aiden nodded and swallowed, almost afraid of what Dawn might want to talk about. She slipped off her jacket while Grace and Del said goodnight and hugged Dawn. Watching the warm family interaction always left Aiden with a vague feeling of longing.

Del threw one last, warning glance back over her shoulder before she followed Grace out the door.

"Let's try out the new couch," Dawn said once they were alone. She had given away her old one, probably not wanting to be reminded of the devastation she had felt sitting on it just after the rape. Dawn brought coffee and tea, and they sat down. Dawn put one socked foot onto the coffee table while the other rested on the couch, both arms wrapped around her knee.

Dawn's cat, which hadn't made an appearance all evening, strolled into the living room and sniffed on every chair leg that had come into contact with the strangers invading her territory. She stopped in front of the couch. The slanted pupils of her sapphire eyes widened when she spotted Aiden. Promptly, the cat sat down and ignored the humans. She licked her bushy tail and used her paw to wash behind chocolate-tipped ears. When she looked up after a minute and the stranger still sat on the couch, she let out a complaining "Meow!"

Aiden looked down at the cat, feeling decidedly unwelcome. "Am I sitting in her favorite spot?"

"She's a cat—every spot in the apartment is hers, and the one place she can't have because it's occupied is always her favorite," Dawn said.

"Cat psychology, huh?" Aiden shifted to the side when the cat hopped up onto the couch and eased her body into a sphinxlike position between them. Aiden reached out a single finger and scratched the cat behind one ear. "What kind of cat is she?" she asked, reasonably sure that there were different breeds of cats.

Dawn rubbed the cat's belly, making her purr and lie down more fully. "Kia's a Balinese, a long-haired version of the Siamese. Remember when you said you didn't want to marry her? What changed your mind?"

"Huh?"

"You told me you didn't want to marry my cat when you had to put her into a pet carrier, but yesterday you were the one who carried Kia over the threshold. Guess you're a closeted romantic, huh?" Dawn grinned.

Aiden laughed and leaned back against the soft cushions, sipping her coffee. *This is nice.* She usually spent her days in the company of men and had few, if any, close female friends. Her relationships with women were usually one-night stands or short flings. It was safer that way. Her male friends didn't expect her to give them insight into her heart and soul. With women, Aiden was afraid to feel too much and lose control. She was convinced that it would be just a matter of time before she would hurt her girlfriend. It was in her genes. So she hid behind secret attractions that couldn't go anywhere—the object of her admiration was straight, unavailable, totally unaware of Aiden's feelings, or all three. That way, she could be sure nothing of any significance could ever happen between them.

She had put Dawn firmly into the straight/unavailable/unaware category. Most of the time, she didn't even think about sharing anything more with Dawn and was content with being friends at best. Sometimes she even thought that it was only Dawn's unavailability that made her so attractive for Aiden. If Dawn hadn't been raped, if she had been gay and interested in a relationship, Aiden would have run the other way as fast as she could.

"So," Aiden interrupted her own dangerously introspective thoughts, "what did you want to talk about?"

Dawn moved the cat into her lap and turned to face Aiden. "Well, now that I moved into a new apartment and live all alone again, I want to do everything I can to make myself feel safer."

"Okay. How can I help?"

Dawn shrugged. "I thought about buying a gun."

"A gun." Aiden rubbed her neck.

"Not a good idea?" Dawn watched Aiden's reaction closely.

"No, I didn't necessarily say that. It just depends. A weapon doesn't always keep you safe. If you depend on an external object for your protection, it could be taken away and used against you." Aiden studied the gentle woman next to her. "And a gun won't do you any good if you don't use it. Are you sure you could aim it at a human being and pull the trigger?" Twice she had shot someone in the line of duty, and she knew that it came with a price.

Dawn looked down at her hands. "I always thought that I could never kill anyone, but that night, I think I could have."

Aiden was still ambivalent about the thought of Dawn owning a weapon. "What about enrolling in a self-defense course? That doesn't have to mean we're completely ruling out the possibility of buying a gun."

Dawn frowned. "I'm not terribly coordinated."

"We're talking about a poke in the eye or a kick to the groin, not about Hollywood kung fu," Aiden said. "Learning how to defend yourself is as much about empowerment as it is about technique."

"I know. Maybe you're right." Dawn turned to face Aiden more fully. "Do you teach self-defense?"

In her mind's eye, Aiden already saw herself instructing Dawn in self-defense, wrapping her arms around her and pressing her body against Dawn's from behind as she simulated an attack. "I know someone who does," she said. "I'll give you his number."

"His?" Dawn's brow wrinkled.

"Who better than a man to teach you how to hurt a man?" Aiden said. "He's the best, and I promise you'll like him. And he works with a female partner."

Finally, Dawn nodded. "Okay, I'll try it out. Can't hurt, right?"

"Not if you follow instructions and don't try a 360-degree spin kick." Aiden rose and walked toward the door. "Thanks again for the invitation."

"No, thank you," Dawn said. "I know lugging furniture around is not part of a detective's job description."

Aiden said nothing.

"Wait a minute." Dawn disappeared into the kitchen and came back with a small plastic container, which she handed Aiden. "Here. That's some leftover coconut chicken and rice. I would have given you the recipe, but you said you don't have the time to cook."

"Or the talent," Aiden said. She stared at the plastic container, feeling like a husband who was being handed his lovingly prepared lunch at the door before being kissed good-bye. She shook her head at the thought and turned to go. "Thanks. Goodnight."

Ray leaned back, put his feet up onto the corner of his desk, and took a bite of his tuna sandwich. "And then this guy looks down and says..." He paused to swallow and to keep his listeners in suspense for a moment longer.

"Uh-huh," Aiden mumbled.

Irritated, Ray gazed across the desk at his partner. She was sitting behind her own desk, shoveling food into her mouth with one hand while thumbing through a stack of reports with the other. This had been the third time that she had mm-hm'ed or uh-huh'ed at the wrong point of his tale. "Are you even listening to me?"

Aiden didn't look up from her food or her reports. "Yeah."

"Okay, so they're chasing him up the stairs, and when he has nowhere else to go, he looks down at them and says..."

"Mm-hm."

Ray folded his arms across his chest. "You didn't hear a word I said, Aiden Carlisle."

"Sure I did."

"So, you did hear that I told you Okada is going to get married again?" Ray asked.

Aiden nodded, head still bent over the reports and her lunch.

"To Kade Matheson," Ray said.

The dark head lifted. "What?"

"Ah, that finally woke you up, didn't it?" Ray threw his crumbled sandwich paper at her.

"Sorry, Ray, it's just..." Aiden gestured down at her desk.

Ray craned his neck, trying to glance into the bowl she had brought to lunch. "What's this?"

"I think I should give our friends from narcotics a call because you're practically inhaling that stuff, whatever it is," Ruben said from his desk.

Okada walked over. "I think our dear colleague is holding out on us, my friends. She won't even share a small sample of her lunch with us."

"It's 'serve and protect,' not 'share and protect,' guys," Aiden mumbled around a mouthful of rice and chicken.

Ruben peeked into Aiden's bowl on his way to the coffeepot. "Is that home-cooked? Are you dating a chef or something?"

Ray knew that there was no chef in the picture. "Aiden..." He directed a concerned glance at her. Aiden had been interested in only two women lately, and both were completely inappropriate partners. Having an affair with either a victim or their deputy DA could be devastating for Aiden's career. He looked around and lowered his voice, making sure that their conversation couldn't be overheard. "Is there any chance that this lovingly prepared meal was cooked by someone you really shouldn't exchange recipes or anything else with?"

Finally, Aiden set down the empty bowl. "It's not what you think. This was just leftovers from a thank-you dinner."

"Okay." Ray trusted his partner's word. "But if you ever want to talk about it..."

Aiden nodded and stood, grabbing a stack of files. "I'll know where to find you."

CHAPTER 11

Dawn's index finger hovered over her phone before she reluctantly pressed the button for the last digit. Holding her breath, she listened to the phone ring. *Maybe I should wait until Monday. I bet she works too much as it is. She doesn't need me to interrupt her at home on the weekend.* She lifted the phone away from her ear to end the call, but before she could do it, Aiden's indistinct voice came from the receiver. The phone almost slipped from her hand before she held it to her ear again.

"Hello?" Aiden's voice came again.

There was no way back now. "Hi, Detective. It's Dawn Kinsley."

"Hey, Dawn. What can I do for you?"

Dawn took a deep breath. *I can't do this over the phone. This was a bad idea.* "Um..."

"Dawn? Everything all right?" Aiden's tone went from surprised to concerned.

"I'm fine," Dawn said. "I just... There's something I need to tell you."

"Yes?"

"Could we meet on Monday? I don't want to discuss this on the phone."

Aiden was silent for a moment. "Do you want me to come over?"

"No, Monday is fine," Dawn said. "I don't want to interrupt your weekend."

"Dawn, you wouldn't have called if this wasn't important. You're not interrupting anything of importance. I'm just lazing around, reading a little. I can leave anytime. Or you could come to my place."

Dawn hesitated for a few more seconds. If she was honest, she didn't want to wait until Monday to get this off her chest. "If you're sure."

"I am."

"Then I'll come over." Dawn didn't want to interrupt Aiden's weekend any more than necessary by having her drive halfway across the city.

"Do you still remember where I live, or do you need directions?" Aiden asked.

"I'll find it."

"Then I'll see you soon." Aiden ended the phone call before Dawn could change her mind.

Half an hour later, Dawn parked her car in Aiden's neighborhood. While she got out of the car and walked up to Aiden's apartment building, she searched for the right words. She stopped in front of the building and, after a quick glance back over her shoulder, started searching for the right buzzer. She lifted her index finger but hesitated one last time.

The door to the apartment building opened, making Dawn jump. An older man exited and held the door open for her.

Trying to calm her racing heartbeat, Dawn hurried past the man and climbed the stairs. After a few seconds of yet another internal debate, she finally knocked on the door, which swung open without delay.

"Hi." Aiden smiled at her.

"Uh, your neighbor let me in." Dawn gestured back over her shoulder.

Aiden stepped back. "Come in."

Dawn followed her into the apartment. She looked around,

glad to postpone an explanation for another minute or two. The apartment was as neat as it had been the last time she had seen it. To Dawn, it was obvious that this was the home of a workaholic. Except for a few books, there was no sign of any hobby, and the only personal object was a framed photograph of Aiden with an older woman. With her blonde hair, blue eyes, and fragile features, the woman didn't resemble Aiden at all, but Dawn had a feeling that this was Aiden's mother. Aiden probably looked like her father, but there was no photo of him.

Aiden threw the Afghan off the couch and gestured for Dawn to sit down. She was barefoot and held a book in her hand.

Dawn tilted Aiden's hand to read the title and then raised an eyebrow. "Not getting enough crime at work, Detective?"

Aiden shrugged. "Well, I can't relate to romance novels, and this one is very well written. Can I offer you a cup of tea?"

"No, thanks. I don't want to interrupt you for long."

"So what is it that you didn't want to discuss on the phone?" Aiden asked, sitting down in an easy chair across from Dawn.

"I've been keeping myself busy cleaning my office while I can't see patients and... Maybe I'm paranoid and just imagining things, but..." Dawn took a deep breath. "I came across a file of a patient whose story resembles mine."

"Resembles it how?" Aiden's gaze was now fixed on Dawn. "I know you said that you wouldn't disclose patient confidentialities, but—"

"It's okay, Detective. I talked to that particular patient, and she released me from my duty to maintain confidentiality."

Aiden nodded. "Good. So, what are the parallels between her case and yours?"

Dawn hesitated.

"I know it can be hard to talk about the details of—"

"It's not that," Dawn said. What she had to tell Aiden had nothing to do with the details of her rape. She had trusted Aiden from the very first moment and still did, even when her trust in other people had been thoroughly shaken. She didn't fear Aiden's reaction; she had a feeling that Aiden would understand. But her revelation would change their status quo. "Detective...Aiden... Perhaps I should have told you before, but I didn't think that it had any bearing on the case."

"What?" Aiden slid onto the edge of her easy chair. "Just tell me, please."

Dawn took a deep breath. "I'm gay."

Aiden blinked.

Dawn stared at her. Had she misjudged Aiden so badly?

"You...You're gay?" Aiden's voice sounded an octave higher than usual. "Are you sure?"

Dawn laughed. "Yes, Detective, I am sure. Trust me."

"But you..." Aiden gestured wildly.

"I know, I know. I've been married, right? But that's not a guarantee of heterosexuality, is it? It was one of the many problems in our marriage."

Aiden nodded and leaned back in the easy chair.

"So, you're okay with it?" Dawn asked.

"Of course." A tiny grin curled Aiden's lips. "It would be pretty hypocritical of me if I wasn't."

Dawn had suspected that Aiden might be gay when they first met but had immediately reprimanded herself for the assumption. Being a confident woman with short hair, a purposeful stride, and a successful career in a typically male job didn't necessarily make Aiden a lesbian. But the subtle impression had stayed with Dawn when she had met her again in the small grocery store. Then she had been raped and Aiden had become her lifeline, the one thing linking her to reality in her state of numbness and chaos. All thoughts about Aiden's sexual orientation—or her own—were gone. All that mattered were Aiden's compassion and the aura of calm and safety she projected.

Aiden didn't say anything more on the subject, but it was clear enough to Dawn that she was a lesbian too. Dawn was curious. She wanted to know how her private and her professional lives mixed and how a lesbian police officer was treated by her peers, but she decided not to ask. Like most cops, Aiden was clearly uncomfortable discussing herself, and she was the detective investigating her case, so Dawn had to accept the limits that Aiden had set for their acquaintance.

Aiden cleared her throat. "Okay, now that we've got that cleared up, how does it relate to the case?"

"I'm not sure. Sometimes everything I see and hear seems to be connected to the rape. Every little noise in the apartment sounds like someone trying to break in, and every stranger in the street looks like him." Dawn swallowed against a dry throat and rubbed her clammy hands on her jeans. "I'm not sure if I can trust my own judgment, but I'd rather sound like a paranoid fool than risk him getting away because I was too proud or too scared."

Aiden leaned forward, her amber eyes sincere. "Just tell me. I promise I won't think you're a fool."

"He...he told her...he told that patient of mine..." Dawn's hands started to shake, and she wrapped her arms around herself to hide it. "He hit her and said she shouldn't just lie there and act as if...as if she didn't enjoy...being fucked by a real man." She was fighting for breath now, feeling as if she couldn't get enough air. For a few seconds, she was back in her old apartment and his weight pressed her into the mattress.

Then she felt a strong, warm hand take her own—a touch so gentle that her body couldn't mistake it for that of the rapist. Finally, she looked up into Aiden's compassionate eyes.

"You okay now? Do you want a glass of water?" Aiden asked.

Dawn shook her head. Her mouth was dry, but she didn't want to lose the safe feeling of Aiden by her side, and she still needed to finish telling her about the parallels between the two cases. "He told me the same thing when he raped me. This patient is a lesbian, and so am I. Do you think that's a coincidence?"

Aiden studied her. "I don't want to make rash assumptions, but this could very well turn out to be our first solid lead. Thank you for trusting me enough to tell me. I know most gay rape survivors never out themselves to the detectives investigating their case, and I understand why."

Dawn had heard enough stories from some of her lesbian patients. Some of the police officers hadn't exactly busted a gut trying to solve the case after finding out the victim was gay. Dawn was sure that she didn't need to fear that.

Aiden gently squeezed Dawn's hand once more before letting go. "I'll need the name and the address of that patient. Did she file charges?"

"No, she never even told anyone but me and her partner," Dawn said.

"Do you think you can get her to talk to us?"

Dawn shrugged. "Maybe, but it's been six years since her rape. The statute of limitations has run out, and I don't want to make her go through this again if you can't use it in court anyway."

"We have to catch him before we can go to court," Aiden said, "and that's what your patient can help us with. If this rapist really is targeting lesbians, we need to investigate how he finds out about their sexual orientation. I don't know your patient, but you, for one, are not exactly a leather-clad dyke with a rainbow bracelet."

"You're not stereotyping, are you, Detective?"

Aiden rubbed her neck. "No, I don't mean to, but I'm asking myself how he could have known. He couldn't tell just by looking at you."

"Are you sure?" Dawn had asked herself that question repeatedly since finding the file of her lesbian patient. If she had to think that every stranger in the street could pick her out as a lesbian and attack her because of it, she would never feel safe again. It was easier to think that her attacker had just picked the first open window he had come to. Windows and doors could be locked to make sure that no one else came in. It was the feeling of being targeted that she couldn't stand.

"Even I couldn't tell that you're a lesbian, and I'm supposed to have gaydar," Aiden said. "How well-known is your sexual orientation?"

"I haven't made a public announcement or anything, but it's not a big secret. My mother, my colleagues, and most of my friends know. My ex-husband knows but prefers to ignore it. I'm sure that none of them would discuss my sexual orientation with a stranger." Everyone Dawn knew accepted her sexual orientation or at least would never hurt her because of it.

"I'll look into some of our old cases tomorrow," Aiden said. "Maybe there are other rape survivors who have been targeted because of their sexual orientation."

"Tomorrow's Sunday," Dawn said.

Aiden shrugged. "Justice doesn't observe Sundays."

"Don't I know that." Dawn sighed and smiled at the same time as she remembered her childhood. "Sometimes I didn't get to see my father all week. With night shifts, overtime, and interrupted holidays, my mom was practically a single mother."

"I always wondered how Ray, my partner, makes it work," Aiden said. "He's married with four kids."

Dawn tilted her head. She could see Detective Bennet as a family man. "He must have found a way to make the time they spend together count. Maybe he's good at sharing his work experiences, not excluding his wife from this important part of his life like most cops do."

Aiden shook her head but didn't say anything, clearly unwilling to discuss relationships and what made them work with Dawn.

Yawning, Dawn stood. "I should go now." Then her gaze fell on the window behind the couch, and she noticed with a sudden start that it had gotten dark outside. She swallowed and bit her lip when she remembered how far away she'd had to park. Now she would have to walk back alone in the dark.

"You look really tired." Aiden stood up from the couch.

That was the understatement of the century. "I haven't slept much, and I'm in a constant state of alert throughout the day. It's exhausting." She felt as if she could be honest and vulnerable with Aiden and didn't need to put on a show.

"Want me to drive you home?" Aiden asked.

"No, thank you." While she would have loved for Aiden to deliver her safely to her doorstep, she knew how difficult the situation was for Aiden. As much as Aiden wanted to help, she couldn't do it without risking her objectivity as a police officer. "I think I'll drive downtown and wake up my mother. I don't think I can be alone tonight." Perhaps it didn't make sense, but now that they had a possible lead, the rapist appeared to be a more substantial threat than before.

Aiden lingered between Dawn and the front door. She chewed her lip and then said, "Stay here tonight."

Dawn stared at her.

"It doesn't make sense for you to drive all the way downtown while you're this exhausted," Aiden said. "I might think of more questions you need to clarify before I go through old case files tomorrow, and I would hate to wake up your mom by calling early, so you sleeping on my couch would be the logical choice."

Aiden sounded as if she was reasoning more with herself than with Dawn. After one glance at the darkness outside, Dawn finally nodded. "Thank you. I'll stay if it really doesn't bother you."

Aiden shook her head. "I'll lay out something for you to sleep in. Pajamas okay?"

Dawn nodded. The thought of Detective Aiden Carlisle in her nightclothes seemed almost surreal. *Look behind the gold shield.* Of course Aiden needed to sleep just like any other human.

Aiden gave her a pair of pajamas that looked brand new and pointed her to the bathroom. "There should be a spare toothbrush somewhere in the cupboard."

Closing the door behind her, Dawn debated with herself whether to lock the door or not. Finally, she left it unlocked. Aiden wouldn't come in unannounced, and she would protect her from any intruder. The pajamas were a little too big on her, and with her splinted right index finger, she fumbled with the buttons.

By the time she left the bathroom, Aiden had already moved the coffee table out of the way and made up the couch for her. Aiden, now wearing sweatpants and a tank top, handed her a glass of water. "Do you need anything else?"

Dawn swallowed her pride. "Can we leave one of the lights on?"

"Sure." Aiden turned on a lamp sitting at one end of the couch. "Is this one enough?"

Dawn nodded and slipped under the covers. "Goodnight. And thanks."

"Goodnight." With one last glance over her shoulder, Aiden walked into the bedroom and left the door ajar.

Dawn lay with her eyes open, listening to the little noises in the apartment: the creaking of bed springs, the jingling of some coins when something metallic—Aiden's watch, Dawn imagined—was dropped on top of them. In her own apartment, every sound tended to scare her, but the sounds here had a soothing quality.

For a while, Dawn thought she could sleep tonight, but the position of the couch made her nervous. Above her, at the head end of the couch, was a window, and her feet were pointing in the direction of the front door. She was trapped between two possible entryways into the apartment.

Trying to distract herself, she reached for the book Aiden had forgotten on the coffee table. She knew the book, had read it a month before and knew it was good, but it couldn't capture her attention now. She didn't feel like the woman who had read the book just four weeks ago.

"Hey, everything okay?" Aiden called from the bedroom. "Can't sleep?"

Dawn sat up. "Maybe I should just drive home."

"What?" A few seconds later, Aiden was kneeling down in the space between the coffee table and the couch. "Why? Aren't you comfortable here?"

"No. Yes. It's..." Dawn pointed between the door and the window at either end of the couch.

"Ah." Aiden rubbed her neck. "Why don't you sleep in the bed? I'll take the couch, and believe me, I won't even let a housefly pass through to the bedroom."

Dawn shook her head. "I can't make you sleep on the couch."

"Most nights I crash on the couch, anyway. I've slept out here hundreds of times before," Aiden said. "Come on."

Reluctantly, Dawn rose, followed her into the bedroom, and took in the punching bag in one corner and the two portraits over the bed, one showing a baby and the other a teenager with rebellious amber eyes. "Is that you?"

Aiden gave the painting on the right a fleeting glance before taking the cordless and her cell phone from the nightstand. "Yes. Do you want fresh linens?"

Dawn shook her head and wished her a good night again. After slipping under the still warm covers, she exhaled and relaxed. The bed was in the corner of the room that was farthest away from the front door, which Aiden was blocking from any intruders. A small bedside lamp lit up the room around her. The pillow she laid her head on was obviously Aiden's own, and she inhaled the soothing scent. For the first time in three weeks, she felt safe enough to close her eyes without sheer exhaustion forcing her.

Aiden lay in the semi-darkness of her living room, listening to the deep breathing of her guest. Earlier, she had berated herself for inviting Dawn to sleep over. She could only imagine what Ray or the rest of her colleagues would say when she told them that a victim had stayed at her apartment overnight. But while she listened to Dawn's peaceful breathing, knowing it was the first good night's sleep she had gotten in weeks, it was hard to regret her decision.

So Aiden was lying awake, scolding herself, and watching over Dawn's sleeping form. She tried to keep her thoughts on the investigative steps she would take tomorrow, but her mind kept wandering back to Dawn's revelation. She still couldn't believe that Dawn was gay. It didn't change anything, of course. Dawn needed the professional Detective Carlisle, not the infatuated Aiden.

A scream from the bedroom interrupted her thoughts. With a curse, Aiden threw off the covers and raced to Dawn's side.

The blankets were twisted around Dawn, practically tying her to the bed. She tossed around and woke with a cry. Tears ran down her cheeks as she blinked up at Aiden. Her breath was coming way too fast, and her pulse hammered in the carotid artery at the side of her neck. She looked around like a scared animal, as if needing a few seconds to remember where she was.

"Hey, it's just me. No one's going to hurt you here." Aiden sat on the side of the bed, careful to leave some space between herself and her panicked guest. "Were you dreaming?"

"Nightmare," Dawn rasped.

Aiden longed to hold her and comfort her, but she didn't want to frighten her with an unexpected touch. "Do you want...?" She cleared her throat. "A hug?"

Dawn didn't answer, at least not verbally. Her silent tears turned into sobs as she threw her arms around Aiden and buried her face against her neck.

Aiden held her carefully as though she would hurt her by holding on more tightly.

"I can't stop thinking about it," Dawn whispered against Aiden's skin. "My thoughts are going in circles even when I sleep."

"It's okay." Aiden stroked her blonde hair. "Just relax and breathe. Nothing can hurt you here."

Finally, Dawn's sobs quieted. "Sorry." She moved away from Aiden's embrace but kept one hand on Aiden's arm. "I didn't mean to go all weepy on you again."

"You're allowed to 'get weepy,'" Aiden said. "Don't be so hard on yourself. You wouldn't think of a crying client as weepy, would you?"

"Of course not."

"Then why do you hold yourself to a different standard?"

Dawn sniffled. "Maybe I'm just not ready to think of myself as a victim."

"Then think of yourself as a survivor," Aiden said.

"You're really, really good at your job. Has anyone ever told you that?" Dawn dabbed at her eyes with the sleeve of her pajamas.

"Sure, my partner tells me every time he wants me to question a suspect he can't stand," Aiden said. But all joking aside, being here with Dawn was not just a job for her. "Do you want to stay up for a while or try to go back to sleep?"

Dawn brushed a few damp strands of hair from her face and looked up at Aiden. "Well, that depends."

Aiden swallowed hard. *Oh, please, please, please, don't let her ask me to sleep in the bed with her to keep the nightmares away.* She wanted to help Dawn, but she really couldn't do that. She braced herself and asked, "Depends on what?"

"On whether or not you have ice cream in your freezer."

And that was how Aiden found herself sitting on her couch, eating ice cream at three a.m.

Aiden tiptoed into the bedroom. She smiled and leaned against one wall, watching Dawn sleep.

Dawn was sprawled across the length of her bed, not rolled up into a frightened little ball as she had been last night. Sunlight danced across her creamy skin and blonde hair, making it shine like gold. For the first time in weeks, Dawn looked totally at peace.

It had been years since Aiden had watched another person sleep. She hadn't been celibate by any means, but she never stayed in bed long enough to watch her bed partners sleep. Usually, she preferred to slip out of bed and out of their lives as soon as possible. Now, although she had shared nothing but a pint of ice cream with Dawn, she wanted to stay and make her breakfast.

She had decided that she would forgo her usual Sunday morning run because she didn't want Dawn to wake up alone in the unfamiliar apartment. So, bringing back pastries, croissants, and rolls from the bakery down the street was out of the question. After brushing her teeth, Aiden tiptoed into the kitchen and searched her cupboards and the fridge for breakfast ingredients.

"Morning."

Aiden jumped and slammed her head against the refrigerator door. Rubbing her head, she turned and regarded Dawn, who had changed into the pair of snug-fitting low-rise jeans from last night. Aiden had secretly decided that she liked seeing Dawn in jeans even more than seeing her in elegant skirt suits. "Hey, up already? I hope I didn't wake you?"

"Not at all. I'm surprised I slept as long as I did. Sorry for surprising you," Dawn said, indicating Aiden's head.

Aiden gave her a grin. "No harm done. Ray always says my head's the thickest part of me."

Dawn smiled and studied the things Aiden had arranged on a tray. "Are you making breakfast?"

"Don't sound so skeptical, please. I'll let you know I can make breakfast with the best of them. It's not considered cooking, so you're in no danger of food poisoning."

Laughing, Dawn helped her set the table. "You're an only child, aren't you?"

Aiden blinked. "You know that from the way I like my eggs or what?"

"No, I know it from the way you set down the cornflakes within easy reach of me," Dawn said. "When I grew up, I had to grab the cereals first or risk having to watch my brother eating the last of them. To this day, I tend to keep the cereal box on my side of the table."

Growing up without sisters or brothers, Aiden had never really understood sibling rivalry. She had often regretted not having a sibling. *But who knows, maybe I just don't know about them. There could be a litter of offspring that bastard fathered somewhere out there.* "You and your brother, were you close?"

"Brian was five years older than me, so I got on his last nerve when he was a teenager and I would follow him around like a puppy, but other than that, we were close, yes." Dawn sighed. "Sometimes, I'd give everything to be able to see him now, to see the man he would have become. He was only twenty-three when he died and in some respects still very much a kid."

Aiden counted quickly. *God, she lost her father and her brother within one or two years.* "Did he...?" She stopped and stared into the pan in which their scrambled eggs were frying.

"He was shot when he and his partner ran after some drug

dealers. Brian loved being a cop. Even after Dad's death, he never considered that he could die doing his job too. It was very hard on my mom."

And on you. Aiden didn't know what to say. She sprinkled a little salt and pepper across the eggs and put equal parts of them onto the two plates.

Dawn put the orange juice back into the refrigerator before they both sat down.

Aiden had never liked sharing her morning routine with anyone. Except for Ray, she hadn't looked across a breakfast table at another person in years, but now she found that she didn't mind Dawn's presence in her home in the least.

Despite telling her about her brother's death, Dawn was smiling this morning, obviously not one of those people who wouldn't even exchange a halfway polite greeting before their second cup of coffee. Nothing reminded Aiden of the sobbing woman who had clung to her last night. In the light of day, Dawn appeared to be strong and full of life.

The smile vanished from Dawn's face when Aiden set a plate with eggs, bacon, and toast in front of her. She stumbled from the table and disappeared into the bathroom.

Aiden squinted down at the scrambled eggs. "They're not that bad."

From behind the bathroom door came the sounds of gagging and retching.

Abandoning her own food, Aiden jumped up and crossed the room to lean against the bathroom door. "Dawn? Are you sick?"

It took a few moments for Dawn to answer. "I...I'll be out in a second." Her voice sounded shaky.

Aiden waited a second, then a minute. Still, Dawn was in the bathroom, not saying a word. Only occasional gagging and heaving could be heard. "Dawn?" Aiden knocked on the door to announce herself. "I'm coming in, okay?"

"No! Stay out there. I'll be fine in a second."

"Dawn." Aiden pressed her hands against the closed door separating them. "Cut the macho superhero routine, please. It's reserved strictly for cops."

"I don't want you to see me like this," Dawn said.

Aiden hesitated. She wanted to respect Dawn's privacy, but when another round of retching started behind the bathroom door, she couldn't stand it any longer and opened the door.

Dawn was kneeling on the bathroom tiles, holding on to the toilet with trembling hands. Her skin was ghostly pale and glistened with cold sweat.

Aiden ran water over a washcloth and handed it to Dawn while she gently brushed back limp strands of hair from her face. "Why didn't you tell me sooner that you didn't feel well?"

Dawn shuddered and clutched the toilet bowl. "I was perfectly fine until I smelled the food." She wiped her mouth and stood.

Concerned, Aiden watched as she stood on shaky legs. Not wanting to take the risk of Dawn falling and hitting her head in the small bathroom, she wrapped a supporting arm around her and tried to lead her out of the bathroom.

"Wait," Dawn said. "I'd like to brush my teeth first."

"Oh. Of course. Want me to wait outside?"

"If you don't mind. I promise I'll be fine on my own."

Aiden stepped outside and waited right next to the door. When Dawn emerged from the bathroom, she led her to the couch, away from the smell of food. She spread the Afghan across Dawn's lap and retrieved her cup of tea for her. "Better now?"

"Yes, thank you." Dawn leaned back, still a little pale.

"Do you think you could eat a little?" Aiden asked. "I can make you something else if you want."

Dawn swallowed. "No. I think my stomach is too upset right now. But you should have breakfast." She pointed to the table where Aiden's breakfast was getting cold.

"Later." Aiden studied her. "Seems like all those stressful things we talked about last night and this morning were a little too much for your stomach."

"Maybe," Dawn said but didn't sound as if she believed it.

What is it, then? Can't be my cooking. No one's ever gotten sick before taking a bite of it. Her eyes widened when another common cause of queasiness and throwing up occurred to her. "Dawn..."

Dawn bit her lip. Tears shone in her eyes, but she refused to let them fall. "I don't know how it's possible. Well, I know how... but you know what I mean. I think I might be pregnant."

Aiden took a deep breath. She forced down her personal feelings and hid behind her cop persona. "Pregnancy in spite of taking emergency contraceptives is not very likely, but it's still possible. Did you do a pregnancy test?"

Dawn shook her head. "When I missed my period, I didn't have the courage to do the test. I don't know what I would do if I'm really pregnant." She looked at Aiden as if searching for an answer.

A dull throb started in Aiden's temples, and she pinched the bridge of her nose in a futile attempt to ward it off. This was quickly becoming more than she could handle, and she could only imagine what it must be like for Dawn. She was determined to make things easier for Dawn, but this was one decision she couldn't make for her. "I told you before. I'm not the best person to ask. No one who was conceived through rape can ever be objective when it comes to such a decision."

"What?" Dawn sat up on the couch.

"I said no one who was—"

Dawn shook her head. "I heard you the first time. Do you mean to say that you're...your mother was raped and..."

Aiden furrowed her brow. "You didn't know?"

"No!"

"But you asked me to speak to your group, remember? The one with the women who've gotten pregnant through rape."

"I asked you to speak to the group because you're one of the few women working with the Sexual Assault Detail," Dawn said. "I knew the women in the group would feel more comfortable talking with you than with your male colleagues. I wanted them to meet someone who has to deal with rape every day of her life and can still relate to people with compassion."

Aiden rubbed the back of her neck. "I thought you knew."

Dawn rolled her eyes. "I don't know why people always think psychologists are mind readers. How could I have known such a personal thing about you?"

Now that Aiden thought about it, it was a really stupid assumption, but when confronted with this particular issue, she tended not to think, too busy building walls to protect herself. "You wouldn't have told me about your possible pregnancy if you'd known about...about the way I was conceived, would you?"

"I don't know. I didn't plan on telling anyone until I'd made a decision." Dawn pinched the bridge of her nose, unconsciously mirroring Aiden's earlier action, and looked down at the carpet. "I love kids, and I've always known that I'd have at least one someday, but I imagined having a loving co-parent and not... this...this whole situation." She closed her eyes.

Aiden knelt next to the couch to be at eye level with Dawn. "I can't make that decision for you, but I'll support you, no matter what you decide to do."

Dawn's gray-green eyes searched Aiden's own. "You'd hold my hand in the waiting room of an abortion clinic if that's what I wanted?"

"Of course," Aiden said. "Just because I was conceived through rape doesn't necessarily mean that I'd make the same decision my mother made all those years ago. I don't know what I'd decide. I know how hard it can be to bring up a child, being aware every day that it was his or her father who brutally raped you. I saw the effect it had on my mother."

They looked at each other in silence. Finally, Aiden sighed and glanced at her watch. "You are welcome to stay here a little longer, but I want to head over to the precinct and look at some old files."

Dawn set down her empty cup. "I'll just go home."

"If you want to talk to someone, you can call me any time, okay?"

Dawn just nodded without saying anything.

Aiden rose and went to the bedroom to retrieve her gun and badge.

Dawn watched as Aiden prepared for her unofficial shift. As she buckled on the holster with her duty weapon and clipped her gold shield to her belt, the soft, almost vulnerable side she had shown Dawn earlier seemed to disappear. The detective's face was a picture of concentration, as if she was already planning her investigations.

Aiden crossed the room with a confident stride, one strong hand reaching for her car keys while the other grabbed the ever-present leather jacket.

There was no doubt in Dawn's mind that Aiden Carlisle was a good detective, a wonderful friend, and an amazing person. How could any mother not be proud and love a child like her, regardless of how she came to be? Then she shook her head, reprimanding herself for judging Aiden's mother. *Tell me you won't feel conflicted if you have a child who grows up to be the spitting image of his or her father. How would you handle seeing the face of a man you hate on your own child every day?* Still deep in thought, she followed Aiden to the door. But on the other hand, how could she have an abortion, violate her body again, and kill an innocent child? A child who might have the potential to grow up into a person as wonderful as Aiden Carlisle.

Aiden held the door open for her. Side by side, they made their way to the elevator. "I'll give you a lift to your car," Aiden said when they left the apartment building. "Where did you park?"

Dawn slipped into the passenger seat and gave her directions, glad not to be left alone with her thoughts for another few minutes. She knew she'd have a lot of thinking to do in the very near future.

"There it is." Aiden stopped next to Dawn's car and turned off her ignition.

Dawn turned to her, reluctant to just say good-bye and slip out of the car after everything Aiden had done for her. She had intended for it to be just a quick hug good-bye, a little squeeze around the shoulders to show how grateful she was. But when she wrapped her arms around Aiden and smelled the mixture of leather and Aiden's perfume, a scent she had come to associate with comfort and safety, the embrace lasted longer than appropriate between mere acquaintances. After a few moments, Dawn felt the strong muscles of Aiden's shoulders move uncomfortably beneath her hands. She pulled back and reached for the door. "Be careful," she said and got out of the car. When she closed the door behind her, it occurred to her that there was now another cop in her life that she had to worry about.

CHAPTER 12

When Ray entered the squad room on Monday morning, an unexpected sight greeted him. "I could have sworn it was a stack of unfinished reports I left on my desk Saturday, but now it seems to have morphed into my sleeping partner."

"It will take you months to get the drool marks off of your desk," Okada said.

Ruben looked down at their colleague, who was sprawled across the files, reports, and photos she had laid out on Ray's desk while her own desk was covered with crime scene photos. "What's she doing here this early?"

"I assume she's indulging in every detective's favorite hobby—becoming overly involved in one of our cases," Okada said.

Ruben walked over, cradling a mug of coffee. "Wanna bet she spent the weekend scaring the cleaning ladies when they came in to clean up the donut crumbs around your desk, Jeff?"

"They're not just donut crumbs, my friend. They're directional devices I use to find my way back to my apartment after our marathon shifts."

Ray studied his sleeping partner. "She tried to call me yesterday and left a message on my answering machine that we may have a break in the Kinsley case, but it was already too late to call her back when we returned from visiting the in-laws."

"She really is throwing herself into that case," Okada said.

Ray shrugged. Okada was right, but he didn't want to betray his partner's confidence. "Oh, come on, this is Aiden we're talking about. It's almost normal for her. I'd start to worry if she didn't become overly involved in one of her cases every now and then. We all do." Only this time, it wasn't just the case Aiden was becoming overly involved with.

Aiden stirred and rubbed her eyes as she sat up. She blinked in the bright lights of the squad room. "What time is it?"

"It's seven thirty." Ray sat at Aiden's desk and swung his feet up onto the corner. "I didn't get your message until midnight. There's a break in the case? A DNA match on another rape?"

"No." Aiden stretched, combing through her short hair with one hand while organizing the stacks of files on the desk with the other. "I don't think this is as random as we first thought. I think we're dealing with a hate crime here."

"Hate crime?" Ray rolled up his shirt sleeves and picked up some of the files.

Aiden nodded. "He picks his victims because they're gay."

Ray raised an eyebrow at his partner. Was Dawn really gay, or was it just wishful thinking on Aiden's part?

"Dawn pointed out the parallels between her case and that of a patient. They're both lesbians, and the perp told them not to, and I quote, 'act as if they didn't enjoy being fucked by a real man.'"

"And you think there are more than just those two cases, or is this an early spring cleaning?" Okada asked, pointing to all the files.

Aiden massaged the back of her neck. "I've searched for lesbian rape victims, but that's not as easy as it sounds. Many of them never call 911, and even if they do, they're hesitant to come out to the detectives working the case."

"So we'll never know if there might be other victims with the same MO," Okada said.

"You really think I'd spend the whole night in here only to come up empty?" Aiden shook her head. "I had to dig through a whole lot of reports, and I went through hundreds of crime scene photos, but I eventually found two other women who are either lesbians or have very eclectic reading interests." She pointed to pictures of chaotic crime scenes. Books, magazines, and other objects were scattered across the floor just as they had been in Dawn's apartment.

Ray studied the photos. "Could be the same MO, but what makes you so sure the victims are lesbians?"

"This," Aiden held up a crime scene photo and pointed to one of the objects on the floor, "is a lesbian magazine. And this victim," she lifted the other file, "had three dozen books in her bookcase that you would never find in your grandmother's collection, including *The Joys of Lesbian Sex*."

Ray clapped her on the back. "Well done, partner."

"So we have a total of four cases with a number of similarities." Aiden looked at her notepad. "One, the victim's a lesbian or bisexual and in her twenties or early thirties. Two, the perp breaks into the apartment at night, always between three and four a.m. Three, the perp is always described as tall, dark-haired, and muscular. And four, he never wears a condom."

"What about DNA evidence?" Ray asked. "We could at least prove that these cases are linked to each other."

Aiden sighed. "No, we can't. Dawn's patient never reported the rape, and the statute of limitations ran out last year. Victim number two, Melanie Riggs, hesitated a week before calling us, and Jayne Matthews took a shower, so no DNA evidence from any of them."

Dr. Albert Renshaw entered the squad room and headed directly toward the detectives. "You left me a message about a case?"

"Yes." Aiden handed the files to the forensic psychiatrist. "I think you should have a look at these. We've discovered three other cases that seem to be connected to Dawn Kinsley's."

Renshaw skimmed through the files for a few minutes before he looked up. "Seems like you found the reason why his attacks appeared somehow personal. We're dealing with a rapist who's expressing his hatred against lesbians through this kind of violence. That's why he never uses a condom. He wants them to experience his masculinity. In his mind, he's showing them how good 'sex' is with a man so that they can understand what they really need and repent their 'unnatural ways.'" He tapped the files he still held. "You're searching for a man who has been abandoned or rejected by a lesbian."

"Maybe a former girlfriend left him for a woman?" Ray said.

Renshaw tilted his head. "That's a possibility, but if that was the case, he'd be more likely to simply take his anger out on that specific woman instead of transferring it to other lesbians, unless she humiliated him in public."

Ruben grinned. "By standing him up at the altar or something like that?"

"Perhaps." Renshaw shrugged. "But maybe we're looking at something deeper here. It's more likely that he faced repeated or more profound rejection in some form. Something happened that made him hate lesbians. He's hunting these women." He studied the files again and scratched his beard. "Were all the victims single?"

Ray looked at his partner.

"Uh, Dawn...Dr. Kinsley is," Aiden said. "I'm not sure about the others. Does it matter?"

"It might," Renshaw said. "I think he might be targeting single, white lesbians in their twenties and thirties."

"Why singles? Does he fantasize about starting a relationship with them?" Ray asked.

Renshaw shook his head. "To him, a single lesbian is a threat, more likely than a lesbian couple to take something away from him. He's clearly a power-reassurance rapist—he rapes to assert power over his victims and to reassure himself of his masculinity."

"So he is likely to rape again?" Aiden asked.

Renshaw nodded and handed her the files. "Yes. And he will escalate if we don't stop him. If the rape doesn't live up to his fantasies, he'll get frustrated. He'll get more violent. Sooner or later, he could end up killing someone, especially if the victim tries to resist."

Aiden's grip around the files tightened. What if Dawn had tried to fight him off?

"Any suggestions how we can find this nutcase?" Okada asked. "We can't very well question every man who's ever been given the old heave-ho because of another woman."

"He probably committed some minor hate crimes—spraying homophobic slogans on front doors, harassment, assault—before he advanced to rape," Renshaw said.

Ray shook his head. "Even if he did, it's next to impossible to find him that way. Most victims of hate crimes never file charges."

"He exploits that," Renshaw said. "That's why he can take the chance and leave his DNA behind."

"How do we find him?" Aiden asked.

"You need to find his hunting grounds," Renshaw said. "None of the victims remembers meeting him before. There has to be a place where he sees them and can determine their sexual orientation just from them being there. Maybe a lesbian club, bar, or bookstore."

Ray scratched the back of his neck. "That's a lot of places. We can't put them all under surveillance."

"Then start with the clubs and bars," Renshaw said. "Bookstores don't give him the time or opportunity to observe the victims and their interaction with other women. It's either a mixed gay/straight place, or he works there. Otherwise his presence would raise some red flags."

Aiden twirled her pen through her fingers. "Dawn said in her formal statement that she had come home late that night. Maybe she went to a lesbian nightclub."

"Call her," Ray said while he picked up the phone to call the other victims.

Grace didn't ask why Aiden was calling or how she had known that she would find Dawn in her mother's home.

"Could I talk to Dawn, or is she lying down?" Aiden asked, careful not to reveal how sick Dawn had been Sunday morning, in case she hadn't told her mother about her possible pregnancy.

"Lying down?" Grace laughed. "No, she's up and running around my kitchen like a whirling dervish. She finally got some sleep the last few nights."

Aiden held her breath, waiting for further comments, but they didn't come. Apparently, Dawn hadn't told her mother where she had slept Saturday night.

"Here she is now." Grace handed over the phone.

"Detective?" Dawn sounded out of breath.

"Hi," Aiden said, hesitant to interrupt Dawn's good mood. "How are you?"

"A lot better," Dawn said. It sounded sincere. "And officially not pregnant. My doctor said it was probably just the stress and the emergency contraceptives that threw off my cycle and upset my stomach."

Aiden almost dropped the phone. "Wow! That's good news, isn't it?"

"Yes." Dawn's voice was a whisper. "I think it is. It spared me from having to make a decision that I really didn't feel up to making."

Aiden cleared her throat, not knowing what else to say. "Listen, there's something I need to ask you. You said that you had been out and came home late that Saturday night. Was it by any chance a lesbian club or bar you'd been to?"

"Yes. How did you know? Do you have a new lead? Do you know who...?"

"Calm down," Aiden said, not unsympathetic to Dawn's excitement. Her own adrenaline rose at the thought of catching the perp. "You know I can't talk to you about the specifics of the case. We'll tell you when we know for sure, okay? Now, can you give me the address of that club?"

Aiden leaned back in the passenger seat of the unmarked police car, sipping her coffee and watching the club's entrance.

"How are we going to play this?" Ray asked from the driver's seat. "Looks like it's not a mixed gay/straight club, so I can't go in undercover. Or do you think I could pass as a lesbian?" Grinning, he fluffed his short, frizzy hair.

Aiden backhanded him across the chest. "No, you can't, smart-ass. But maybe I could if I try hard enough, huh?" She winked.

Ray laughed. "Who's the smart-ass now?"

"How about you flash the badge at the back door and ask to talk to the manager while I stand in line like a good little lesbian and keep an eye on any man I encounter in there?"

Ray hesitated. "I don't like this, Aiden. If you go in there as a customer, you could become a target."

"If I go in there as a cop, we won't get the answers we're after," Aiden said. "Besides, if he comes after me, it might be a good thing. At least it'll give us a reason to arrest him without a warrant."

"Okay." Ray sighed and checked his weapon one last time. "We'll do it your way."

Aiden waited until he had crossed the parking lot and

disappeared behind the building before she got out of the car. She strolled toward the front door and joined the line. She looked around as she waited, pressing her right elbow against the gun hidden under her half-open leather jacket so no one in the waiting crowd could see it. Through the open door, she caught glimpses of the club. The strobe lights flashing across the dance floor and a thick wall of smoke made it hard to see, but she could tell that it was already crowded inside.

She was almost sure now that the rapist had spotted Dawn and the other victims here. The smoke and alcohol Dawn had smelled on him indicated that he had been in the club, perhaps as one of the male bartenders behind the three bars covering the walls.

After a few minutes, she reached the front of the line, but the bouncer kept blocking the entrance. "ID, please."

"Oh, come on." She hadn't gotten carded in many years. No one could mistake her for a twenty-year-old.

"You're holding up the line, lady," the bouncer said.

Aiden took a better look at him and froze.

In front of her stood the man who had raped Dawn and at least three other women. There was no doubt in Aiden's mind. The police sketch artist couldn't have gotten his picture any better if he had sat for his portrait. *The bouncer! Of course!* He probably carded the women to get their addresses. That way, he didn't even have to follow them but could wait until the club closed and his shift ended.

He glared at her. "If you don't want in, step aside!"

Aiden would have liked nothing better than to cuff him right then and there, but she didn't have an arrest warrant. "Sorry. I'll get my ID from the car."

Ray joined her in the car a few minutes later. "Why aren't you inside? I thought you wanted to look around?"

"One look was all I needed. We have the bastard, Ray!" She pointed to the only male figure in front of the club.

"The bouncer?" Ray's eyes widened. He looked down at the papers in his hands. "When I told the manager we could come back with a bunch of uniformed officers to search her club, she gave me a list of her employees. The bouncer's name is Gary Ballard."

Aiden reached for her cell phone and pressed the speed dial for Kade Matheson's home. "Kade? Hi, it's Aiden. Sorry to interrupt you at home, but we need an arrest warrant."

"When?"

"Right now would be great."

"On whom?" Kade asked.

Aiden looked at the club's payroll Ray held out for her. "One Gary—or Garett—Ballard. He's the man who raped Dawn Kinsley and three other women, probably more."

"Allegedly raped," Kade said.

Aiden was not in the mood for political correctness. "Yes, he allegedly broke into their homes, allegedly held them down at gun point, and allegedly raped them. Come on, Kade. I know he did it. I'm looking at him right now. He matches the police sketch to a T, and he works as a bouncer in the club all the victims frequented, so he had easy access to their addresses."

"Okay. I'll go and make myself unpopular with one of the judges and then meet you at that club."

Relieved, Aiden gave her the address. "Kade is on her way with a warrant," she said when she put down her cell phone.

They sat in the car without speaking, never letting the suspect out of their sight. It was a very long hour until Kade arrived and handed Aiden the folded blue document.

Trading one last quick glance with her partner, Aiden put her hand on her holster and strode toward the club's entrance again, this time without patiently standing in line.

When Ballard saw her coming, he smirked. "Finally found the ID?"

"Yes, in fact I did. Good enough for you?" With a sneer that matched his, Aiden flipped back her leather jacket to reveal the gold shield now clipped to her belt. "Garett Ballard, you are under arrest for—"

"Bitch!" He hit her in the face with his fist.

Pain rushed through Aiden.

"Hey!" Ray sprang forward, drawing his gun. "Don't move! Hands above your head! Aiden, you okay?"

"Yeah." Aiden regained her balance and pulled her gun from its holster. For a second, she almost wished he would attack her again and give her a reason to use it.

"Put your hands on the wall." Ray patted him down and drew a gun from the back of Ballard's jeans.

"A Glock?" Aiden asked, touching the left side of her face. It hurt, but she was determined not to give Ballard the satisfaction of letting it show.

Ray shook his head and pocketed the weapon. "SIG Sauer." He snapped his handcuffs around Ballard's wrists.

Ballard continued to struggle.

Grunting, Ray tightened the cuffs and grabbed Ballard's arms to hold him still. "Wanna try again for the Miranda, now that we have Mr. Ballard's undivided attention?"

Aiden nodded. Her jaw hurt, but she wouldn't miss this for all the pain in the world. "Garett Ballard, you are under arrest for the rape of Dawn Kinsley, Melanie Riggs, and Jayne Matthews. You have the right to remain silent. Anything you say can and will be used against you in a court of law. You have the right to speak to an attorney and to have that attorney present during any questioning. If you cannot afford an attorney, one will be provided for you. Do you understand these rights?"

Ballard spat in her direction.

"I think that's a yes." Ray dragged him to the car.

Aiden sat on the steps leading to the Portland Community College's sports hall, waiting for Dawn's self-defense course to wrap up.

Finally, the door opened and a stream of women filed out of the building. Dawn was the last one out. She held on to the strap of her backpack with one hand, while gesticulating to the two women she was talking to with the other. When she saw Aiden, she quickly said good-bye and walked over. "Hi. Are you waiting for me?" She sat on the steps next to Aiden.

Aiden nodded. "Your mother said I'd find you here. How's the self-defense class going?"

"Great. It's really helping. I've even forced myself to leave the house after dark. It's—" Dawn stopped when she got her first good look at Aiden's face. "Oh my God! What happened to you? Maybe you should go right in and sign up for a refresher course." The teasing couldn't hide the concern in her eyes. Her gaze wandered up and down Aiden's body as if searching for more injuries. She reached out to touch Aiden's face, which was swollen and discolored around the left side of her jaw.

Before Dawn could touch her, Aiden gently grabbed her hand, held it for a few moments, and then awkwardly let go. She wasn't sure how she'd react to Dawn's touch, and this was not the time to find out. "It's nothing."

Dawn rolled her eyes. "Standard police answer for everything from a paper cut to a chest wound."

Aiden smiled even though it hurt. "I'm fine, really." She was silent for a few moments, not knowing how to start. "Dawn, we arrested someone tonight."

"What?" Dawn grabbed Aiden's forearm. "You caught him? Are you sure it's him?"

"Easy, easy." Gently, Aiden pried Dawn's fingers from her arm, surprised by her unexpected strength. "I can't tell you that. You have to tell us. If I influenced you in any way, the lineup would be inadmissible in court."

"Another lineup." Dawn bit her lip.

"Yes."

Dawn looked up at her. "For the last time?"

Aiden laughed. "Don't think I didn't notice you asking me if it's him only in different words."

Dawn smiled and stood. "I can't get anything past you, can I? Okay, let's get it over with."

Ray leaned against the edge of the table, crossing his arms as he waited for the six men in the lineup to be led into the adjoining room. Normally, he would have stepped up to the one-way mirror to flank Dawn on the side his partner didn't occupy, but Dawn was clearly more comfortable with just Aiden by her side—or at least as comfortable as she could be one room away from the man suspected of raping her.

Aiden hovered next to her in a protective stance.

What is it between those two? Ray had seen his partner show a total disinterest in women who had been more attractive, wealthier, and a whole lot less complicated than Dawn Kinsley.

His thoughts were interrupted when a police officer opened the door to the adjoining room and six men filed in.

"Do you recognize any of these men?" Aiden asked.

Dawn didn't even hesitate for a second. "Number four."

Bingo! Ray directed a triumphant smile at the defense attorney Ballard had immediately hired. How on earth Ballard could afford to hire Victor D'Aquino, one of the best defense attorneys in the city, on a bouncer's salary was beyond Ray.

"Where do you recognize him from?" Aiden asked.

"He's the man who broke into my apartment and raped me." Dawn's voice shook, but her gaze never wavered, never turned away from the one-way glass.

While the other two victims hadn't been as sure, this positive identification was above reproach.

Kade nodded in the direction of Dawn and the detectives before she turned on her heels and strode out of the room, tossing a "See you at the arraignment, Mr. D'Aquino" over her shoulder.

The defense lawyer grimaced and followed her out of the room.

Dawn turned away from the one-way glass. "I picked the right one, didn't I? It's him."

Aiden nodded.

Dawn sank onto the edge of the table. "What now?" She looked at them, her eyes holding equal parts relief and fear.

"Now you go home and let us worry about burying him in evidence." Aiden directed her to the door with one hand lightly resting on her elbow. "You can sleep tonight, knowing that he's enjoying our hospitality."

CHAPTER 13

AIDEN STARED AT THE MAN sitting at the small table across from her. They had been at this for hours, but still no confession from Gary Ballard. His lawyer was earning his money by sitting there and studying the interrogation room's walls with feigned interest.

"So, let me sum up the vast information your client has given us in the last four hours: he's as innocent as a newborn babe," Aiden said.

"Got that right, Officer." Ballard flashed a smile.

Ray, who had leaned against the wall behind Ballard, stepped forward. "It's Detective, but I guess that's really hard for you to remember with your little memory problem."

"What memory problem?"

"Well, you didn't remember meeting Dawn Kinsley, Melanie Riggs, or Jayne Matthews. Maybe the results of the DNA test we're running on your blood sample will refresh your memory."

Ballard shrugged. "Maybe I met them, but I never heard their names. You know how it is with one-night stands. You don't stay around long enough to learn the life story."

One-night stands? You sorry excuse for a human being! For a few seconds, the blood rushing through Aiden's ears drowned out Ballard's voice. She clenched her teeth until her jaw began to hurt again.

In the adjacent observation room, Dr. Albert Renshaw stepped back from the one-way mirror and shook his head. "He's not going to give us anything. Not like this."

Kade, who was watching the interview next to him, nodded. It didn't take a degree in psychology to see that the interrogation was going nowhere. "Should I tell my detectives not to waste their time with him?"

"No." Renshaw turned and looked into Kade's eyes.

It always amused her a little that he had to look up to do so, and she wondered if there was a Freudian complex that matched the situation.

"I want you to go in there," Renshaw said.

"Me? If two experienced detectives can't get him to agree on the time of day, I hardly think that I'll scare him into talking."

Renshaw just smiled. "It's not fear I'm after. It's anger and hate, which seem to be his most dominant emotions. He's confident and cocky, but he's not dumb. He won't give us anything as long as he's able to control his anger. We know it's there. Just think about the way he hit his victims and destroyed every symbol of lesbianism in sight. His anger is always lurking just beneath the surface. We only have to trigger it and get him to lash out, like he did at Detective Carlisle when she arrested him."

Kade had to admit that it sounded reasonable. If Ballard lost his cool, maybe he would let some details slip that she could use against him in court. "How do we do that? Short of going in there and slapping him in the face, what can I do to provoke his anger?"

A grim smile formed on the psychiatrist's lips. "You have to grab him by the balls."

"I hope you mean that in a figurative sense," Kade murmured.

"You have to hit him in his weak spot and reject his masculinity," Renshaw said. "His motive, the whole reason why he commits those rapes, is the urgent need to validate his masculinity."

Kade shrugged. "Why is that so urgent for him?"

"Not only does he hate lesbians, I suspect that deep inside, he fears that he might have inherited the 'gay gene' from his mother," Renshaw said.

"His mother?" What was he talking about?

Dr. Renshaw handed over a slim file.

Kade opened it and skimmed the report. "His mother is a lesbian?"

Renshaw nodded. "Yes, but for a long time, she didn't live openly gay, so Ballard might secretly be afraid that there's latent homosexuality in him too. He has to have total control over a woman, a homosexual woman, to counter these fears. If you take away that control, he has to do something to reestablish it."

"How do I do that?"

Renshaw ticked it off on his fingers. "First, you send Ray out of the room—and don't be nice about it. Order him around as though men are inferior."

Kade grinned. "No problem. I can do that. What's next?"

"You ignore Ballard for as long as you can get away with it," Renshaw said.

Kade raised an eyebrow. "What do I do instead? There aren't exactly a lot of distractions in there." She pointed to the bare, sterile interrogation room.

"Detective Carlisle is in there," Renshaw said, his baby blue eyes twinkling over the rim of his glasses. "You pay attention to her—only her. Look at her. Smile at her. Touch her. Give Ballard the impression that you're more than colleagues. If you ignore him in favor of a woman, especially a woman he thinks might be a lesbian, he has to do something to get your attention."

Kade stared at him for a moment, but she had to admit that his plan seemed logical. "Shouldn't we explain the plan to Detective Carlisle first if we expect her to play the role of my lesbian lover?"

Renshaw grinned. "No, that would grant Ballard a breather that we don't want to give him. I'm sure Detective Carlisle is experienced enough to play the game and improvise if you give her the right cues."

"Okay, let's do it." Kade squared her shoulders and strode out of the room.

Aiden glanced up when the door opened and Kade entered without knocking.

The DDA didn't look at Ballard or his lawyer. She gave Ray a curt nod. "You're needed elsewhere, Detective," she told him in the condescending tone that was normally reserved for low-life criminals. "Doing something more important than this." She pointed at Ballard, and her facial expression seemed to add, "Like scraping chewing gum off the underside of your desk."

Ray lived with five females, so Aiden figured he knew when it was safer to leave the room.

Wow. What put her in such a bad mood?

Kade turned to her. A warm smile lit up her features. "Hi, Aiden." Her voice was an intimate purr, and she threw back her red hair in a gesture that was pure seduction.

Aiden? Something was up. Kade rarely called her by her first name.

Kade perched on the edge of the table directly in front of her, turning her back on Ballard and his lawyer.

When the suit skirt slid up, Aiden's gaze was drawn to the long, slender legs.

Instead of addressing Ballard, Kade leaned forward, her body almost touching Aiden's, and began to chat. "So, Aiden, how have you been since this morning?"

Since this morning? They hadn't seen each other that morning.

What the hell is going on here, Kade? When her gaze fell on Ballard, she realized what Kade was trying to do.

For the first time since his arrest, Ballard's face showed something other than cool arrogance. His eyes were glowing with an almost unnatural rage.

"Sadly, the day didn't continue as exciting as it began, Counselor," Aiden answered. She let her voice caress the last word, making it sound like a lover's pet name. "Just sitting around, wasting my time listening to a bragging liar."

Kade turned toward Ballard as if noticing him for the first time. Her cool gaze slid up and down his body before she turned back to Aiden, dismissing him. "What's he lying about?"

"He's claiming to have slept with three lesbians."

Again, Kade turned. She looked at Ballard with a pitying smile. "I can hardly believe he slept with three women in his life, much less three lesbians."

Ballard jumped up. His chair clattered to the floor. "You fucking dykes! I should—"

Aiden started to rise, but Victor D'Aquino, his lawyer, was already dragging Ballard back from the table and the two women who sat behind it.

"Get your hands off me!" Ballard glared at him. "I'm going to show—"

"Garett! Don't say another word! Sit down, and don't open your mouth again, no matter what they say. They're trying to provoke you." The lawyer straightened the chair and sat the red-faced, glowering Ballard onto it.

Shit! Aiden traded disappointed glances with Kade. They wouldn't get anything else out of Ballard now. It might not have been a total waste, though. There was still the trial to think about, and if Ballard could be provoked once, they could do it again.

Aiden pushed her chair back from the table, signaling Kade to leave the room with her. Out in the hallway, she drew a few deep breaths and waved at one of the uniformed officers. "We're finished here."

Okada joined them. "Mr. Ballard still exercising his Fifth Amendment rights?"

"For the most part." Aiden clenched her teeth, then stopped when her jaw began to hurt. "The little bastard admits a remote possibility that they may have been one-night stands, just in case DNA results come back positive. Got anything from the lab?"

"Fresh from the press." Okada handed her a piece of paper as they headed toward the squad room. "Ballard's blood sample is a perfect match to the semen from the rape kit done on Dawn Kinsley. And the prints found in her apartment are his too."

"Good." While that didn't disprove his allegations of a one-night stand, it was a start, making it impossible for him to deny any knowledge of the victims. "Anything on the Glock? Does he have a concealed handgun permit for it?"

"No permit, no signs of the Glock," Okada said.

"No Glock? Damn."

"No worries, Detectives." Kade showed them her sharklike lawyer smile. "That'll give us a reason to search for it in his apartment."

Aiden looked up from the lab report. "We have enough for a search warrant, right?"

"With the DNA match, a positive identification in a lineup, plus motive and access, we have enough for Judge Gilmartin to offer to search the apartment himself."

Aiden smiled. "No, thanks, I think I'd rather do it myself. His signature will suffice."

Ray looked up from his desk when they reached the squad room. "Did he cop to anything?"

"No," Aiden said. "But Kade can get us a warrant for his apartment."

"Can I talk to you for a second?" Ray dragged her over to a quieter corner, where they would have more privacy.

Aiden frowned, impatient to get going and search Ballard's apartment. "What is it?"

"Why don't you take a nap in the dungeon and let Okada and Ruben search Ballard's apartment?" Ray nodded toward the small room that they sometimes used to catch an hour of sleep during long shifts.

"What?" Aiden turned so she was facing him fully, going into confrontation mode. "What is this crap, Ray? I don't need a nap, not when we're this close to—"

"What you're this close to is either a breakdown or a complaint in your personnel file." Ray stared at her. "You haven't really slept since Sunday, and it's not only the lack of sleep that's affecting you. You're emotionally involved in this case."

Aiden fixed him with an angry glare. "Now wait a minute, Bennet! If memory serves me correctly, it was you who told me just a few weeks ago that it was okay if I got to know Dawn. It was you who told me not to give it up."

Ray nodded. "I did tell you that because I could see that you're the only one who could help Dawn through this, but you're not the only one who can search Ballard's apartment."

Aiden ground her teeth. He was right, but she was loath to admit it and to leave this case in anyone else's hands.

"Aiden," Ray said, a lot gentler now. "I know you never behaved improperly toward Dawn, but you and she... You've become friends, and if the defense attorney finds out, he'll try to use it against us. Even the appearance of impropriety could hurt the case, you know that."

"Okay, okay." Aiden rubbed her neck and sighed. "I'll stay out of it."

Ray clapped her on the shoulder and turned to walk away.

"Ray?" Aiden called. "Thanks for looking out for me."

He smiled. "Hey, that's what partners are for: reminding you to sleep, eat your vegetables, and keep a healthy emotional distance."

"Well," Aiden returned the smile and caught up with him, "two out of three ain't bad."

CHAPTER 14

"NEXT CASE."

Aiden slipped into the courtroom where the arraignments were held just as Judge Stenton banged his gavel. Dawn's case was number fifteen on today's docket, and Aiden had timed it so that she arrived just before the case was called. She headed toward one of the free seats in the back, where Del Vasquez was already sitting, but Kade waved her over. After a quick nod to Del, Aiden walked up to Kade.

"Sit in the first row, please," Kade said. "Can't hurt for Judge Stenton to see the gigantic bruise on your jaw."

Aiden grimaced but then had to smile. "Thanks a lot for the compassion, Counselor."

Kade shrugged. "I've got no choice but to use what I have."

"Bad news?" Aiden furrowed her brow.

"Okada did a background check on Ballard. His grandparents are quite wealthy. If I can't get Stenton to decide on remand, he'll be out before lunch. Unfortunately, Stenton likes to release defendants on their own recognizance or set minimum bail."

Shit. Aiden turned her head, pointing her colorful jaw in the judge's direction. "Why are the grandparents supporting this asshole?"

"Looks like they took him in when their daughter moved in with her female lover and the family broke apart," Kade said.

Aiden raised a brow. "So, Renshaw was right, at least in part. It wasn't a girlfriend but his mother who left him for a woman."

"Docket number 79608, the People versus Garett Ballard," the bailiff called out. "The charges are three counts rape in the first degree, three counts burglary, three counts possession of stolen property, one count unlawful possession of a firearm, one count resisting arrest, and two counts of assaulting a public safety officer."

So Kade was going after him with both barrels. Aiden smiled. The search of Ballard's apartment had brought to light not only a Glock 17 but also various bracelets, key-ring pendants, and pins with symbols of lesbianism that Ballard had taken away from his victims as trophies.

"Victor D'Aquino for the defense, Your Honor," the defense attorney said.

Kade stood when an officer led Ballard in front of the judge. "Kadence Matheson, representing the People."

"Is the defendant ready to enter a plea?" Judge Stenton asked.

Ballard's lawyer nodded. "Yes. Not guilty on all counts, Your Honor."

The judge turned toward Kade. "Recommendations on bail, Ms. Matheson?"

"Your Honor, the People request remand," Kade said with a stern expression. "The defendant has no significant ties to the community, and we just learned that he has the financial means to flee the jurisdiction of this court. The risk of flight is blatant."

"If it pleases the court, we ask that the defendant be released on his own recognizance," Victor D'Aquino said. "My client has no prior criminal convictions. He's lived in the area for the last six years and holds down a steady job. He's not a flight risk."

"A job which provides him with continuing access to his victims," Kade said.

The defense attorney raised his index finger. "Alleged victims. Your Honor, my client has a spotless record, not even a traffic ticket!"

"Your client isn't charged with a parking offense," Kade said. "The defendant has brutally raped and beaten at least three women."

"My client is a first-time offender. Remand is ridiculous."

Judge Stenton nodded. "Hold your horses, Mr. D'Aquino. While I'm loath to order remand on all cases other than homicides, I must agree with Ms. Matheson that the defendant does pose a flight risk. Bail is set at two hundred thousand dollars, payable in cash or bond." He raised his gavel.

"Your Honor!" Kade stepped forward. "The People request no contact as a condition of bail."

Stenton looked at his files. "So ordered. Mr. Ballard, you cannot have any form of contact with Ms. Riggs, Ms. Matthews, or Dr. Kinsley. That includes in person, by phone, by letter, or through a third party. In addition, for the duration of this trial, you will no longer be an employee of the Rainbows club. If you violate this order, I'll be very happy to revoke your bail. Is that understood?"

While Ballard just shrugged, his lawyer answered for him, "Yes, Your Honor."

"Next case." The gavel banged.

Aiden slipped from the room and waited outside until Kade had shouldered her briefcase.

"Sorry," Kade said when she caught up with her. "I had a feeling Stenton would deny remand. At least we've gotten him away from the club, so he can't scout for new victims there."

Aiden suppressed a sigh. She wasn't looking forward to telling Dawn that her rapist had been set free for the time being. "Good thinking on the no-contact order." Not that it would do much good. A man who had brutally raped women wasn't likely to be impressed by a simple court order. *Maybe I can get the lieutenant to assign a protective detail to Dawn and the others.*

"Ms. Matheson?" Victor D'Aquino, the defense attorney,

called from behind them. "One minute of your time, please. I'd like to discuss a deal."

Kade stepped away from her and toward Ballard's lawyer.

A deal? Kade, no! No deal for this bastard! Aiden strained her ears to listen in on the conversation.

"I'm not interested in a plea bargain, Mr. D'Aquino," Kade said.

Yes! Aiden resisted the urge to stick out her tongue at the defense attorney.

"Come on, Counselor, spare the taxpayers the expense of a trial, yourself the public humiliation of a loss, and the alleged victims the cross-exam. It's a he said/she said on the rapes, and you know I'll take them apart on the stand," D'Aquino said. "You've got no eyewitnesses, no prior record, and no confession. You've got nothing."

Aiden's throat constricted at the thought of Dawn being mercilessly questioned on the witness stand, having to relive the rape. Maybe a deal wasn't such a bad idea after all.

"I wouldn't call DNA evidence 'nothing,' Mr. D'Aquino," Kade said coolly.

The defense attorney shrugged. "My client admits he had sexual relations with Ms. Kinsley—it was consensual. So, how about a deal?"

Consensual? Yeah, right. Lying bastard! Aiden changed her mind about a deal again.

"You want a deal, Mr. D'Aquino? Here's a deal for you," Kade said. "He pleads to the rapes and the assault, and I'll drop the other charges."

D'Aquino shook his head. "That's laughable, Ms. Matheson. The other charges are mere misdemeanors. Take the felonies off the table."

Kade held his gaze. "I could charge your client with a

hate crime since he selected his victims based on their sexual orientation. That would add another five years to his sentence."

D'Aquino hesitated. "Sexual misconduct. He does six months."

"Sexual misconduct? You mean he's admitting he did something wrong? No deal, Mr. D'Aquino. Garett Ballard is a menace to this city, and I'm going to put him behind bars. See you in court." Kade gave Aiden a curt nod. "Later, Detective." She strode away without another word.

Aiden grinned and watched Kade's retreating back. *I think that was the Kade Matheson version of "Kiss my ass!"*

Just as Aiden walked out the front entrance, Ray climbed the stairs to the court building. "Arraignment over already? How'd it go?"

"Stenton was handling arraignments today," Aiden answered.

They began to make their way back to the Justice Center, walking the two blocks side by side. "Damn. That means Ballard's out on bail, doesn't it?"

Aiden nodded. "Afraid so. The judge issued a no-contact order, but we all know that this won't impress Ballard."

Ray stopped for a moment and studied her. "You're worried about Dawn, huh?"

"I'm worried about all of them," Aiden said, "Ms. Matthews and Ms. Riggs too."

Ray smiled. "Don't bother hiding it. I know that you worry about Dawn most of all."

"She's most endangered since she's the only one we have any DNA on," Aiden said, in an attempt to make her worries sound professional and logical. "If Ballard can prevent her from testifying and we have to rely on the others, the case will be pretty shaky."

"So, what are we gonna do?"

Aiden smiled, grateful for the support the simple "we" showed.

"Maybe we can get the lieutenant to detail a few uniforms or two detectives to watch Dawn's building at night."

"Forget it," Astrid Swenson said. The stocky blonde leaned back in her desk chair and looked at her detectives with a steely expression.

Ray had expected this answer, but his partner didn't seem ready to give up.

She stepped closer to Swenson's desk. "But Lieutenant, Dr. Kinsley—"

"I know that she would sleep better at night if she had a unit at her front door; we all would, but I can't spare the people," the lieutenant said. "Most of my people are already doing maximum overtime—including you."

"If we could put just one unit on her for a few nights..."

Lieutenant Swenson shook her head. "Dr. Kinsley is in no concrete danger. Ballard didn't threaten her in any way. He doesn't even know her new address." She looked back and forth between them and then fixed her gaze on Aiden. "Is there something going on here that I'm not aware of? What's so special about this case when you have three dozen others on your desk? Dr. Kinsley isn't a friend of yours or something, is she?"

Aiden's shoulders drooped. "No, not really."

Ray mentally shook his head. It wasn't a lie, but it sure as hell wasn't the truth either.

Swenson's gaze drilled through Aiden. "I don't want anything to compromise this case. There can be no conflicts of interest. I like for my detectives to show some zeal and compassion for the victims, but if you become emotionally involved, you hurt your credibility."

"I know," Aiden said, staring at a point somewhere above the lieutenant's shoulder.

"I met Dr. Kinsley. I'm sure she would make a good friend," Swenson said. "But there are plenty of other fish in the sea."

Yes, there are. Problem is, she likes this little goldfish, not some other scaly creature.

Aiden pressed her lips together. "Come on, Ray, let's go back to work. There are three dozen other cases waiting."

"Want me to call her?" Ray asked.

Aiden looked away from the phone on her desk. She knew exactly whom her partner meant. "Nice of you to offer, but I think I'll do it myself."

"Okay." Ray wandered off in the direction of the coffee pot.

Aiden glanced at her watch. *She should be back from having lunch with her mother, and it's still two hours until self-defense class starts.* She grabbed the phone and then stopped and shook her head at herself when she realized that she knew Dawn's daily routine by heart. Shoving the unwelcome revelation back into the deepest recesses of her mind, she dialed Dawn's new home number. "Hey, Dawn, it's—"

"I know your voice by now, Detective," Dawn said. From the sound of her voice, Aiden could tell that she was smiling. "How are you?"

"Um..." Aiden was thrown off balance by Dawn's friendliness, not prepared for the simple question when all she was thinking about was how she could tell Dawn that her rapist was free again without scaring her to death. "I'm fine," she finally managed to say. "How are you?"

"Hanging in there, telling myself that it'll all be over soon—at least the trial part of it," Dawn answered.

"Yeah. About that..." Aiden rubbed the back of her neck. "Ballard was arraigned this morning."

Dawn exhaled. It sounded like a sigh of relief. "Good."

"Not entirely, I'm afraid." Aiden hated to burst her bubble. "There are enough charges to put him away for a long, long time if we win, but we had a little bad luck with the arraignment judge. He set him free on bail."

"He's free?" Disbelief colored Dawn's voice.

Aiden had to clear her throat. "Yes."

"But he's the right one this time. I'm sure of it. I'll swear on a stack of Bibles that he's the one who raped me."

"I know. No one is doubting your identification," Aiden said. "The judge at arraignment doesn't decide over guilt or innocence. He just makes the decision about bail. Listen, why don't you think about leaving the city until the trial starts?"

There was a moment of silence at the other end of the line. "No. I won't run away. Ballard has already taken away enough of my life. I won't let him interrupt it again."

Aiden could understand that. "Okay, but how about moving in with your mother for a few days?"

"No."

Aiden sighed. "Dawn, we don't have the resources to protect you should he try to find you."

"I suppose I could stay at my mother's for a while, but she won't even be home until the day after tomorrow," Dawn said. "She and Del are in Spokane because my grandmother's in the hospital."

"Oh. I'm sorry." Aiden didn't know what to say. She never had to deal with family emergencies, because it had always been just her mother and her.

"It's nothing too bad," Dawn said. "She'll be back at her beloved poker night in no time."

Aiden had to smile as a picture of an older version of Dawn appeared before her mind's eye. "I don't suppose you'd consider staying with your ex for a few days?" He was a police officer too, and one that wasn't expected to keep an emotional distance.

"Which one?" Dawn asked.

"Huh?"

"Which ex?"

Aiden waited a few moments until she was sure she could answer without stuttering. She didn't want to think about Dawn with any other man—or woman. "Your ex-husband. You've only got one of those, haven't you?"

"One's more than enough, thank you very much, and no, I won't stay with him. I still haven't recovered from living under the same roof with him when we were married," Dawn said. "Don't worry, Detective. I'll be fine on my own."

Aiden had no choice but to give up. It seemed they were evenly matched with regard to their stubbornness. "All right, but promise that you'll call me immediately if you get scared or see something suspicious."

"I will. Thank you."

Aiden said good-bye and hung up.

Ray handed her a cup of coffee. "How is she?"

"Stubborn and trying to be brave, but I think she's pretty scared."

"The chances that he'll find her—if he even tries to—are very slim," Ray said.

Aiden bit her lip. "Any chance at all, even if it's slim, is too much."

Aiden shivered and wrapped her hands more tightly around her cup of coffee. The warmth in her car had dissipated long ago, and she didn't want to call attention to herself by letting the engine run, but at least everything was quiet in Dawn's neighborhood.

When a tall figure appeared at the end of the street, Aiden put the paper cup down. She rested her right hand on her gun holster as the stranger walked toward her. She couldn't see his face in the darkness, but something about the way he moved seemed familiar. She shifted a little so that the steering wheel wouldn't get in the way if she had to draw her gun. Finally, the man stepped under a streetlight, and she could see his face. "Ray!" She let go of her gun and opened the door on the passenger side. "What are you doing here?"

Ray slid into the passenger seat. "Same as you, it would seem."

"Let me guess. You were in the neighborhood and decided to enjoy the view from this lovely little street for a while?" Aiden raised an eyebrow at him.

"Actually, I stopped by to remind you of rule number one." Ray set a thermos on the dashboard.

"And that would be?"

"No surveillance without backup," Ray said. "You're a cop, not a one-woman army."

Aiden studied the steering wheel. "I didn't want to drag you into this. You won't get paid for it, and if the lieutenant gets wind of this, she'll probably make us walk the beat and write up parking tickets for the rest of the year."

The chirping sound of Aiden's cell phone interrupted whatever Ray was about to say. Giving him a quick glance, she pulled the cell phone from her belt. "Carlisle."

"Detective? Hi, it's Dawn Kinsley. I'm really sorry to disturb you, but..."

"Dawn, hi." Aiden looked up at the brightly lit window on the fifth floor of the building. "Is everything all right?"

"I'm probably just being paranoid, but there's a car parked in front of my apartment building. It's been there for hours. It's too dark to really see, but I think there's someone sitting in it, watching the building," Dawn said, her hastily spoken words betraying her fear.

Aiden looked around. There was no one sitting in a car, except for her and Ray. "God, I'm sorry." She groaned. Instead of protecting Dawn, she had scared her even further. "Dawn, you don't have to be afraid. That's me."

"You?"

A figure appeared in the fifth-floor window, and Aiden turned on the light in the car and waved.

"What are you doing in front of my apartment at ten p.m.?" Dawn asked.

Aiden tugged at her bottom lip. "I was in the neighborhood and thought I'd drive by and make sure everything's all right."

"So, you've been 'driving by' for two hours, with your engine turned off?"

"Well, with the price of gas, I decided to do a poor man's drive-by instead," Aiden said, glad that Dawn couldn't see her blush.

Ray laughed and began to cough when she shot him a glare.

"Come on up," Dawn said.

Aiden shook her head even though Dawn couldn't see it. "No."

"Come on up, Detective."

"No, really, we're quite comfortable down here. We even have coffee." Aiden had bargained with herself to sit in front of Dawn's apartment building so she could protect her and still keep the emotional distance that was expected of her.

But Dawn was relentless. "I don't care if you have a whole coffee shop in the car. I want you to come up."

"Dawn..." Aiden pinched the bridge of her nose.

Ray laughed again. "God, the woman's more stubborn than my mother-in-law. Can you imagine being married to her?"

Aiden could, and that was the problem. She felt so drawn to Dawn that she was in a constant internal debate. She knew she wouldn't cross the line and become involved with Dawn while her case was still open, but sometimes she found herself thinking about the time after the trial was over—and that scared her because she had never planned for the future in any of her relationships with another woman.

"You're here to keep me safe and make me feel better, right?" Dawn said when Aiden kept silent.

Aiden slumped against the back of the driver's seat. She couldn't deny the obvious. "Yes."

"Well, I would be safe and I would feel better if you came up instead of freezing your stubborn ass off down there in the car," Dawn said.

Aiden sighed in defeat. "I'm not alone. Ray's here too."

"The more the merrier. Come on up," Dawn said one last time before hanging up.

Ray grabbed his thermos. "If you're going up, I think I'll go home to my own stubborn woman."

"She's not my stubborn anything."

Ray shrugged. "You won't need backup while you're drinking coffee with her, will you?"

Aiden wasn't sure if he was talking about backup or a chaperone. She rubbed her eyes. "I think I can handle it. Give my best to Susan and the girls."

"Will do." Ray got out of the car and disappeared into the night.

Hesitantly, Aiden locked the car and crossed the street. When she pressed the buzzer for apartment 5D, Dawn immediately let her in.

Dawn greeted her at the door. "Come in and thaw out. You must be half-frozen."

"It's not that bad," Aiden said, rubbing her cold hands as she followed Dawn into the apartment.

A woman was sitting on Dawn's new couch.

Aiden stopped and looked from Dawn to the stranger. "Uh, sorry to interrupt. I didn't know you had company."

"Introduce yourselves while I make coffee," Dawn said and left them alone.

Aiden had seen her fair share of beautiful women, but this stranger definitely made the top five, maybe even topping them all. The woman had arranged her slender body into a pose of casual elegance on the couch, one long leg crossed over the other. Ebony hair contrasted with startling blue eyes and flowed in carefully coifed waves down to her narrow waist. The stranger was stylishly dressed in a designer skirt suit that must have cost more than Aiden's entire wardrobe put together.

The woman practically screamed money, style, and Ivy League education. Aiden had spent enough time around Kade to recognize the signs. She instantly felt inferior. *Stop it. This is not a beauty contest. You're here to protect Dawn.*

The stranger stood with graceful movements, extending a hand in Aiden's direction. "Hello, I'm Maggie Forsyth." Her voice was soft, almost sensual.

Aiden shook the offered hand, careful not to grip it too hard. "Aiden Carlisle."

"Carlisle? You're not by any chance related to Robyn Carlisle, the artist?"

The question made Aiden even more uncomfortable, but she didn't want to be impolite to Dawn's guest, so she answered, "I'm her daughter."

Maggie's eyes lit up. "I know you're a detective, but do you paint too?"

"No. Drawing crime scene sketches is as far as my artistic talent goes."

"Oh." Maggie seemed almost disappointed.

Yeah, well, she's not the first. Her lack of artistic talent had disappointed her mother.

"So, you're the stalker who just scared us to death," Maggie said with a smile.

"Sorry about that." Aiden willed herself not to blush.

"Oh, I don't mind," Maggie said. "It's not like I had a reputation as a fearless protector to lose. Dawn called me to keep her company, but I doubt very much that she expected me to be able to protect her in hand-to-hand combat."

Kia, Dawn's Balinese cat, strolled into the living room and circled Aiden's legs with a welcoming "Mrrrrow" before disappearing into the kitchen.

Aiden stared after her.

"Looks like you know each other rather well," Maggie said.

Aiden looked up sharply, not sure if Maggie was talking about the cat or its owner. She mentally rolled her eyes. *Great. Now she thinks there's something going on between Dawn and me because the cat suddenly acts like I'm her long lost mouse-hunting buddy.* "She never did that before. The only two times I saw her, she scratched my hand and then proceeded to treat me like an intruder into her territory."

Maggie smiled. "Cats and women, the two last unsolved mysteries in the universe."

So she's gay? No woman who didn't have to live with one ever thought women were anything but perfectly logical and understandable creatures. *Is she Dawn's girlfriend or something? Not that I'd care. Yeah, right, Carlisle.*

Dawn returned from the kitchen, a cup of coffee in her hands and the cat in tow. "Please, have a seat, Detective." She handed Aiden the coffee and sat down in her rocking chair, leaving Aiden to sit next to Maggie. Dawn studied Aiden over the rim of her mug. "Didn't you tell me that your department doesn't have the resources to have a protective detail watch my apartment?"

Aiden shrugged as casually as possible. "Some last-minute resource distributions made it possible."

"Resource distribution?" Dawn lifted one brow. "If your

precinct is anything like my dad's, that means you distributed your time from your private life to more overtime."

"No overtime." Aiden didn't even have to lie.

Maggie rose from the couch, smoothing invisible wrinkles out of her skirt. "I think I'll take my leave, now that you have a more suitable protector. Detective." She nodded at Aiden, who merely nodded back.

Dawn stood and followed her to the door.

The front door lay in full view of the couch, and Aiden couldn't help watching them say good-bye.

"Will I see you at our exhibit next week?" Maggie asked, one hand resting on Dawn's arm.

"I'll be there." Dawn leaned over to give Maggie a hug and a kiss on the cheek. "Goodnight."

Aiden quickly looked away when Dawn returned to the living room.

"That," Dawn said, pointing over her shoulder, "was the other ex I mentioned this afternoon."

Her ex comes over to keep her company? When a man and a woman break up, they usually hate each other's guts and never want to see each other again. When two women end their relationship, they become part of the big ex-girlfriends network.

"Very lesbian of us, isn't it?" Dawn laughed as if guessing Aiden's thoughts.

It almost scared Aiden how easily Dawn could read her. "She seems great." Maggie Forsyth was elegant, sophisticated, rich, and completely untouched by all the things that made Aiden lie awake at night. She was everything Aiden was not.

"She is great," Dawn said. "But we're better off as friends. We've always lived in different worlds. Maggie couldn't relate to my life. She never understood the things that are most important to me."

Aiden wanted to know about the things that were important to Dawn but was reluctant to ask.

"Maggie didn't share my love for kids. She always made herself scarce when I was babysitting. And she never understood my job." Dawn shrugged. "I understand how irritating it can be to have a romantic evening interrupted by the call of an upset patient, but like it or not, that is—or was—a part of my job, a part of my life."

Aiden could empathize. Many of her dates had been interrupted, never to be picked up again, when she had been called away to a case. Finally, here was a woman who could understand, and she wasn't allowed to befriend her, much less anything more.

"I liked sharing art, literature, wine tastings, and haute cuisine with Maggie, but I also like having a hot dog at a baseball game or a beer in the cozy little bar around the corner, and I like ice-skating or romping around the park with my niece." Dawn shrugged. "Nothing special, I know, but I like the simple things in life."

Sounds like the perfect woman. Aiden shoved the thought away. "You have a niece? I thought your brother...?"

"Jamie, my niece, was just a baby when Brian died. Now she's almost ten, going on thirty." Dawn smiled affectionately. "Brian and Eliza, Jamie's mom, were never married."

"Jamie... She's named after your father, right?"

Dawn nodded. "I always planned to name my first child after Dad, but Brian was faster. Now I think I'll name the first one after my brother—Brian for a boy and Brianna for a girl."

"Sounds good." Aiden didn't know what else to say. Dawn's openness regarding her private life astonished her, and she wondered whether Dawn was always so open and willing to share information about herself or whether she had somehow earned a special trust.

"Have you ever thought about having kids?" With unerring

precision, Dawn found one of the topics that made Aiden most uncomfortable.

"Not really."

Dawn's eyebrows lifted. "No? Something about you tells me you'd be great with kids."

"Being good with children is part of my job," Aiden said.

"I'm not talking about the job."

Finally, Aiden relented. "I like kids, and under the right circumstances I could see myself living with a child or maybe even more than one."

"You would like to live with a child but not have one."

Aiden shrugged. "I don't need to give birth to a child to be able to love it."

Dawn looked at her with her open, attentive gaze.

"I don't think having a child that's biologically mine, passing on my genes, is a good idea," Aiden finally said.

"Why's that?" Dawn looked her up and down. "From what I can see, your genes are working perfectly fine. No club foot, no hunchback, and no overbite."

"You know what I mean."

"I do. I once had a patient exactly like you."

"Exactly like me?" Except for the odd suspect here and there, she had never before met anyone else who had been conceived through rape. She had never really wanted to, but now she felt a spark of curiosity.

Dawn smiled a little. "Well, maybe not exactly like you. You're a pretty unique individual, Detective. I can't go into detail, but the issue of having children has been the same for him. He didn't want to pass on the genes of a violent rapist."

"Dawn..." Aiden sighed, not wanting to wade deeper into that emotionally turbulent topic. "I'm sure you're a wonderful psychotherapist, but I'm not searching for one, and I don't see why we should talk about any of this."

Dawn regarded her calmly, but for a moment Aiden thought she could see the hurt in her gray-green eyes. "I'm not offering therapy," Dawn said quietly. "I'm offering friendship."

And I can't accept the offer. At least not until after the trial. And even then... Aiden had always kept a safe distance from women she found not only physically attractive but who appealed to her on an emotional and intellectual level too. Dawn was getting maximum points in all three departments, so she normally would have stayed away from her anyway.

Dawn bit her lip when Aiden didn't answer. "I apologize if I went too far and—"

"No," Aiden said. As uncomfortable as she was, she didn't want Dawn to apologize. "No apology necessary. I just don't like to talk about this and feel like I shouldn't talk about it with you, anyway."

"You don't want me to know about your father because I've been raped? Do you think I can't separate the way you were conceived from you as a person?"

Some days, even Aiden couldn't think about herself independently from the circumstances of her conception. But she didn't want to talk about it with a psychologist, not even this psychologist.

"You're nothing like Gary Ballard, and I'm sure you're nothing like the man who raped your mother."

The conviction in Dawn's voice, the sureness in her eyes astonished Aiden. Her mind was reeling. "That's not the reason why I can't talk to you about any of this. I'm the detective working your case."

"And that means I'm not allowed to see the person behind the badge?" Dawn asked. "I'm not allowed to be a little curious about her...to like her?"

Do you? Do you like the person behind the badge? She wanted to ask but didn't. "You're allowed to."

"But you aren't," Dawn voiced what Aiden hadn't said. "You're not allowed to see me as anything other than a victim...a witness for the prosecution."

Aiden studied the fine features. She couldn't shake the feeling that this conversation was like an iceberg—just the tip of it was visible, but there was an enormous subtext lurking just beneath the surface. Was Dawn asking her if she would ever be interested in her when she wasn't a witness any longer? Or were they still just talking about the possibilities of a friendship?

Angry voices from the staircase interrupted the moment. Aiden stood and crossed the living room, reaching for the gun at her side.

Dawn followed her but stayed back.

Aiden glanced through the peephole and listened for a while. "Just your neighbor and his loving wife exchanging some pleasantries."

"They do this every day. Maybe I should offer them some marriage counseling so I can finally have some peace and quiet."

Aiden smiled, glad that Dawn was allowing her to change the subject. "Or maybe you could just sic the cops on them."

"Speaking of cops, where has your partner disappeared to?" When they returned to the living room, Dawn sat in the rocking chair and gestured toward the couch for Aiden to sit too. "Don't tell me you left him in the car."

"I even cracked a window," Aiden said.

Dawn laughed. "I'm sure he'd appreciate that—if he were a dog."

"Okay, okay, he went home to spend some quality time with the family."

Dawn studied her. "He's a good man and a good partner, isn't he?"

Aiden thought about the way Ray had shown up in front of Dawn's apartment building tonight without her even telling him that she planned to watch over it. He'd known the only thing it could earn him was a reprimand from their lieutenant and Aiden's gratitude, but he'd packed a thermos and driven downtown anyway. "He's the best I ever worked with."

"I bet you could tell a lot of stories. There are still some cops who don't react kindly to being partnered with a woman."

Aiden nodded. "True. But most of the detectives with the Sexual Assault Detail know that there are some things a female officer is better equipped to handle than a male one. If you're good at your job, you get the respect you deserve." She leaned back against the couch, more relaxed now that they were back on the safe topic of her work.

"The Sexual Assault Detail is, well, special," Dawn said. "I, for one, was very glad that it was you who held my hand during the exam in the hospital and not one of your male colleagues."

Aiden inclined her head. She understood the sentiment but didn't want to bring the conversation back to a more personal level.

"When my father was first partnered with Del, I think my mother had some doubts about him spending so much time with a female partner," Dawn said, going back to the original topic as if sensing Aiden's unease. "But after Dad invited her home for dinner a few times and she saw that they interacted more like siblings, Mom was okay with it."

Aiden thought back to the first dinner she had shared with the Bennets. She had sensed Susan's gaze resting on her all the way from the entree to dessert. Slowly, they had gotten to know each other, and now Susan respected her and trusted her to keep her husband safe. From time to time, Aiden still sensed some jealousy from Susan, not because she suspected them of having an affair but because Ray refused to talk about his job with his family and talked about it with Aiden instead.

"Now Del is part of the family," Dawn said. "She was my

maid of honor when I married Caleb and the first person I came out to."

Aiden wanted to ask a thousand questions, curious about Dawn's friendship with Del, her marriage, and her coming out, but once again she held herself back. "I think I'll go now," she said with a glance at her watch.

Dawn rocked forward in her chair, directing a piercing glance at her. "So you can sit down there in the car for the rest of the night?" She shook her head. "There's no sense in that when I have a perfectly fine couch here. Or is there some rule demanding a police officer has to be cold and uncomfortable during surveillance?"

"Not that I know of," Aiden said.

"Okay, it's settled, then. You sleep on the couch." Dawn's tone left no room for objections. She measured the couch, then Aiden with a long gaze. "Unless you'd be more comfortable in the bed?"

"No!" Aiden said so quickly that she almost choked on her own tongue. "No, the couch will be fine, thanks."

Dawn stood. "The couch it is, then. I'll see if I can find you something to sleep in."

Sleep sounded really good to Aiden because she hadn't gotten much since the break in the case. Without further protest, she took the pillow and the blanket Dawn handed her. She heard Dawn rummage around in her closet while she made her bed on the couch. Like the week before, when Dawn had stayed at her apartment, she found that she liked Dawn's presence, liked hearing her in the background while she did everyday things. *You're here to protect her, not to play house with her.*

"This okay?" Dawn had returned from the bedroom, holding out an oversized T-shirt and a pair of sweatpants. She had changed into a pair of pajamas. Two of the buttons were done incorrectly, showing a hint of skin.

Aiden bit her lip, hesitant to point it out to Dawn.

"Something wrong with my choice of nightclothes?" Dawn asked.

Aiden quickly looked up, not wanting her to think that she had been staring at her chest. "No, no. It's just..." She gestured in the general direction of the pajama top. "You left a button out."

Dawn looked down. "Oh. That happens frequently since... since I had my finger broken." She reached up and clumsily started to undo the buttons without the use of her splinted index finger.

Without thought, Aiden stepped closer to help, then stopped when she noticed what she was doing. "Sorry."

"It's okay," Dawn said. "I'm not too proud to accept a little help."

Aiden had no other choice now. She took another step toward Dawn and reached out her hands, willing them not to tremble. This close, she couldn't help noticing the elegant curve of Dawn's collarbone and the charming freckles that dusted the fair skin until they disappeared under the pajama top.

Dawn stood still. She looked down and watched Aiden's fingers button the shirt properly.

Aiden had undressed her fair share of attractive women in her life, but somehow the innocent buttoning of a pajama shirt was the most erotic thing she had experienced in some time. "There," she finally said, her voice rough and uneven in her own ears, "all done."

"Thanks." Dawn licked her lips and stepped back, looking a little flustered herself.

No more sleepovers with this woman. Aiden distracted herself by checking the door and the windows. *If I have to do this again, I'll park the car a few buildings away.*

A small sound woke Aiden, but she kept her eyes closed, orienting herself to her surroundings by sound alone at first. The quiet breathing of another human being told her that she was not alone in the room. When she felt the warmth and the subtle movements of another body against her abdomen, she quickly opened her eyes, almost afraid of what she would find.

She exhaled sharply. It was only the cat that had joined her on the couch sometime during the night.

"I hope she didn't disturb you?" Dawn's voice came from behind her.

Aiden sat up, one hand making sure that the cat wouldn't fall off.

Dawn was leaning next to the window behind the couch, already dressed in a sweatshirt that didn't require buttoning. Her hair, still damp from her shower, was combed back and accentuated the attractive angles of her face.

How long has she been standing there? Aiden was surprised that her finely honed senses hadn't alerted her to Dawn's presence in the room but blamed it on her exhaustion. "Um, no, she didn't," Aiden answered belatedly, giving herself a mental slap to the back of her head. "I'm a little surprised because I had the impression she couldn't stand me." She stroked the lazily stretching cat, glad to have an excuse to look away from its owner.

"Well, you didn't leave a stellar first impression when you put her into the hated pet carrier, but once she gets to know you, Kia tends to be a certified cuddleholic," Dawn said.

Aiden climbed out from under the purring cat and gathered her clothes. When she came back from the bathroom, Dawn was still standing next to the window, but there was a cup of what Aiden suspected to be tea in one hand and a second cup in the other.

Aiden stepped next to her and silently accepted the mug of coffee Dawn held out for her. Taking careful sips of the hot liquid, Aiden looked out of the window. It was dawning outside, the light not yet reaching the small street.

Aiden found herself thinking about Dawn—not the one lighting up the streets of Portland but the woman carrying the same name, standing beside her at the window. Their shoulders were touching, but Aiden was hesitant to step back, afraid that this would draw unnecessary attention to the innocent touch. "I have to get going," she finally said when her cup was almost empty. "I have to be in court at nine."

Dawn turned away from the window to face her. "How long until I have to be there? In court?"

"Last I heard from Kade, probably not before the end of next week. She will call you for trial preparation."

Dawn nodded. "She'll handle my case, won't she?"

"Yes, she will."

"Good," Dawn said. "I like her, and I think I'll feel comfortable with her."

Aiden lifted her head to study Dawn. Was it the competent lawyer Dawn admired or the woman behind it? *Jealous, Carlisle?* She smirked at herself but didn't want to take a closer look and discover who it was she might be jealous of, Kade or Dawn.

"She has this air of confidence," Dawn said, "like nothing can touch her. I'd like to have that for myself." She looked down into her cup.

Aiden admired Kade's regal bearing too, but it was Dawn's openness, her easy, approachable way, and the hint of vulnerability underneath her strength that she valued most about her. "Nothing can touch you," she said. "Kade, Ray, and I will be there to make sure of that."

"Have I ever really thanked you for—?"

"No." Aiden didn't want to hear the words of gratitude. "You don't need to. I'm just—"

Dawn lifted one hand. "If this is going to be the just-doing-my-job-ma'am speech, you can save it for the next victim. I know for sure that hand-holding and tear-drying are not in your job description, Detective."

"They are," Aiden said. "Right there on page ninety-seven, somewhere between paper-pushing and political ass-kissing."

"Ah." Dawn chuckled. "So I'm one of the highlights of your day, huh?"

Starting the day to the sound of Dawn's voice and the smell of coffee that someone else had prepared for her had been a highlight, but she would never admit that to Dawn, so she just smiled and carried her empty cup to the kitchen. Not wanting to take the risk of being hugged again, she slipped out of the door with a quick good-bye.

CHAPTER 15

At first sight, this case seemed to be a pretty ordinary one. A man breaking into apartments at night and raping women in their own bedrooms was something Kade Matheson had seen before in her two years with the sex crimes unit. But whenever she entered the squad room, she got the feeling that the Kinsley case was somehow personal for the SAD detectives. Kade had to admit that she was beginning to take it personally too—she didn't take kindly to suspects hitting one of her detectives.

Murphy's Law dictated that they had to draw Judge Ruth Linehan, the strictest judge in the city, as the one who would hear the case. Knowing Linehan wouldn't let her get away with anything, she hoped that the evidence they had would prove to be solid and that no witnesses would begin to waver. On the plus side, Linehan wasn't likely to go easy on her opposing counsel either.

"Mr. D'Aquino, Kadence." Judge Linehan nodded as they entered her chambers for the motions hearing.

Only her mother and Ruth Linehan ever called Kade by her full first name—and she didn't particularly like it from either one of them. She said nothing, preferring not to alienate the judge who would soon decide what evidence she would be taking into trial.

Linehan leaned back in her chair and motioned for them to take a seat in front of her desk. She pointed to the pile of written motions the defense attorney had submitted. "I hope this is not just your contribution to deforestation, Mr. D'Aquino."

Kade suppressed a smirk.

"No, Your Honor, it's more than that." D'Aquino was experienced enough not to let the comment fluster him. "Defense moves for a dismissal of all charges."

Dismissal? Kade snorted. She had won cases with less evidence. When Linehan sent her a warning glance, she pretended to study her nails.

"On what grounds?" Linehan asked.

"The warrants to arrest my client and to search his home were obtained based on information that had been received in violation of patient-doctor confidentiality," D'Aquino said. "Any evidence obtained thereafter is fruit from the forbidden tree and has to be excluded, leaving the DA's office with nothing to link my client to any crime."

Linehan turned to look at Kade, a stern expression on her face. "Ms. Matheson?"

"That's a clear misinterpretation on Mr. D'Aquino's part, Your Honor," Kade answered. "Dr. Kinsley, one of the victims and a rape counselor, noticed the resemblance of her own case to that of one of her patients, but she obtained a waiver of client-doctor confidentiality before she approached the detectives. Here's her affidavit and that of her patient confirming it." She handed the papers across the table.

Linehan scanned the documents. "The motion is denied."

"Then I move to dismiss the charges for failure to properly Mirandize my client," D'Aquino said.

"Did the arresting officers read Mr. Ballard his rights, Ms. Matheson?"

Kade nodded. "I was there when they arrested him. I assure you, the reading of his Miranda rights was by the book—except for the interruption caused by the defendant's assault on Detective

Carlisle. You're not trying to blame the detectives for that, are you?" She directed a sharp gaze at the defense attorney.

"Why don't you let me ask the questions?" Linehan said. It wasn't a suggestion.

Kade bit her lip and nodded.

"The arresting officers are experienced detectives, and I believe them when they say that they resumed the reading of his rights as soon as they had Mr. Ballard under control." The judge tapped the arresting reports Kade had provided. "You'll have a chance to question them about the arrest during cross. The motion is dismissed. I trust that you have a motion of some value, Mr. D'Aquino, and are not just wasting my time."

"Of course, Your Honor. Defense moves to suppress the bracelets, pins, and key-ring pendants found in my client's apartment," D'Aquino said. "They weren't in the scope of the search warrant."

Kade mentally rolled her eyes. "They were in plain view, Your Honor. No warrant needed."

The defense attorney laughed. "Plain view? You want me to believe your detectives have X-ray vision? They unlawfully removed the objects from a box in my client's closet."

"Is that true, Ms. Matheson?" Linehan's piercing brown eyes looked at Kade over the rim of her glasses.

"The items could have been wrapped in a blanket and shoved into a drawer; it still wouldn't have mattered. Mr. Ballard is facing multiple rape charges and has been positively identified by the victims. As such, the police were well within their rights to search his home for any evidence linking him to the crimes, as stated in the warrant signed by Judge Gilmartin."

"Alleged crimes," D'Aquino said.

Linehan read through a copy of the search warrant and shook her head. "Mr. D'Aquino, this is not the time for semantics. I find that the detectives were justified in searching for any personal items of the previous victims. The motion to suppress the objects in question is denied."

"Then I move to dismiss the—"

Linehan held up her hand. "Mr. D'Aquino, so far we've gone through three motions that have clearly been without merit, so let me make this short. Your remaining motions are denied. However, I am dismissing the second count of assaulting a public safety officer."

Kade leaned forward. "Your Honor, with all due respect—"

"Ms. Matheson, while I concede that Mr. Ballard did assault Detective Carlisle, Detective Bennet didn't sustain any injury. Now, is there anything else?"

Kade shook her head.

"All right. Jury selection in my courtroom, tomorrow morning at nine," Linehan said, dismissing them.

Sparing D'Aquino a cool glance, Kade strode past him and left Linehan's chambers.

"Kade!"

When Kade recognized Aiden's voice, she slowed her stride. "Loitering in the courthouse hallways, Detective?"

Aiden grinned. "Not with criminal intent. I just wanted to see how the motion hearing on Ballard went."

Kade didn't ask how Aiden knew when the hearing had been scheduled. She had learned long ago that rumors traveled faster than a patrol car with lights and sirens. "You came over just to ask me that? Don't you trust me to do my job?"

"Of course I do. It's just that..."

Kade had to smile at the awkward shrug, reminding her of the teenager the confident detective must have once been. "You want to keep tabs on the man who graced you with that lovely bruise?" She pointed at the fading marks on Aiden's jaw.

Aiden rubbed her jaw. "Um, yes, something like that. So?"

Kade resumed her fast clip, her high heels echoing down the

hallway. "We're going to trial. Linehan denied the motion for dismissal."

"Good."

"It's a start," Kade said. "My favorite judge also threw out the second assault charge on Ray."

"But the charge for assaulting me is solid, right?" Aiden asked, pointing to her jaw.

Kade nodded. "If I can prove that Ballard knew you were a police officer on duty when he hit you. That knowledge is a condition of the 'assaulting a public safety officer' charge."

"He knew who I was and why I was there."

"You know that and I know that, but my job is to make sure the jury knows it too," Kade said. "I'm sure his lawyer will come up with an idiotic, but plausible-sounding explanation."

Aiden frowned. "And that would be?"

"You were standing in line in front of a lesbian club, and excuse me for saying so, but you don't exactly look out of place." She directed a rare full-blown Kade Matheson smile at Aiden.

Aiden stared at her.

Kade suppressed another smile. Just because they had never discussed Aiden's sexual orientation didn't mean she was unaware of it.

"Are you saying I look butch?" Aiden asked after a few seconds of silence.

"Are you saying you don't?"

Aiden laughed. "I shouldn't try to argue with a woman who does it for a living." Then her expression turned serious again. "Are you worried about the case?"

Kade shrugged and then reached up to stop her briefcase from slipping off her shoulder. "I want to nail this guy for everything I possibly can. We have a pretty solid case if the witnesses hold up. D'Aquino has already filed motion after motion. He's going to do whatever he can to stall us so he can buy himself more time to dig up dirt on our victims."

Aiden grimaced and held the courthouse door open for Kade.

Kade stepped outside and smiled at Aiden's gentlemanly gesture. "Are you going back to the precinct?"

"Yeah."

"Do me a favor and see if you can find someone to bring Dr. Kinsley a copy of her written statement. She needs to review it today so I can meet with her for trial prep tomorrow."

Aiden nodded. "Consider it done."

Aiden rang the doorbell for the fifth time, bouncing on the balls of her feet when once again no one opened the door. She knew Dawn was home. She had seen the lights in the apartment before she had slipped into the building with one of Dawn's neighbors.

Increasingly concerned, she reached for the cell phone clipped to her belt. She almost dropped it when the door was cracked open, the chain latch still in place.

Instead of Dawn, a girl of maybe nine or ten peeked at her through the small gap between the door and the doorframe. What was visible of the child—red-blonde hair, light skin, and sparkling green eyes—made Aiden think that she was face to face—or rather face to belly—with Dawn's niece.

"Hi. You must be Jamie, right?"

The girl stared at her through the narrow gap and nodded. "And who are you?" she asked, one tiny fist on her hip.

Aiden bit her lip to hide her amusement. She could see the resemblance to Jamie's feisty aunt. "My name is Aiden. I'm a police officer."

"Really?" The girl looked interested but still didn't open the door. “My dad and my grandpa Jim were police officers too. Did you work with them?”

“No, I didn’t, but I know your aunt.” Aiden tried to get a peek into the apartment, hoping to see Dawn and be let in, but she could only see the empty hallway behind Jamie.

The girl hesitated. “Do you have a gold shield?”

Aiden handed over her badge through the narrow gap. “Can I come in now?”

After a thorough examination of the gold shield, Jamie lifted herself up onto her tiptoes and pulled the chain back from the door.

There was still no sign of Dawn as Aiden entered the apartment. “Where’s your aunt?”

Jamie shrugged. “Don’t know.”

“You don’t know where she is?” Aiden frowned. She was sure that Dawn would never leave a child alone in her apartment without an emergency.

“We’re playing hide and seek,” Jamie said. “You can help me find her if you want.”

Aiden smiled down at the girl. “Thanks, I’d love that.” She wanted to find Dawn, if only to make sure that everything was all right and to give her the formal statement she had promised to deliver.

“I already searched the living room, and now I’ll go check out the bathroom. Maybe Auntie Dawn is hiding behind the shower curtain again.” Jamie ran down the hall.

As soon as she had closed the bathroom door behind her, Aiden moved to the bedroom. “Dawn?” she called through the closed door.

A whimper came from the bedroom.

Without further hesitation, Aiden entered.

Dawn was sitting on the floor, her back against the wall and her head between her knees.

Aiden could hear her desperate panting from five steps away. She quickly closed the door behind her and crossed the room to kneel beside Dawn. "Dawn, hey. It's Detective Carlisle...Aiden." She hesitated to touch the trembling woman, but then the urge to see her face, her eyes, to make a connection and find out what was wrong was too strong. Gently, she touched her shoulder, noticing that the shirt was wet with perspiration. "Dawn?"

Finally, Dawn lifted her head and looked up at her with wide eyes. Beads of sweat were running down her pale cheeks.

"Easy, easy." Aiden tried for her most soothing voice. "What's wrong?"

"P-p..." Dawn gasped for breath. "Panic attack."

"What can I do?"

"H-hold me."

Aiden sank onto the floor. She wrapped her arms around Dawn and drew her against her body. When Dawn's trembling stopped, she whispered, "What happened?"

"I was playing with my niece," Dawn said, her voice rough and shaky. "I had the glorious idea of hiding under the covers... where I had a flashback." She tensed in Aiden's arms. "My niece! God! Can you make sure she's okay?"

"She's fine," Aiden said. "She probably thinks you found the world's best hiding place."

"Would you go and look after her, please?"

Aiden hesitated. She didn't want to leave Dawn.

"I'm okay now. I'll be out in a minute. I just need to change my shirt." Dawn tugged at the damp garment. "Please, I don't want my niece to see me like this."

After one last squeeze, Aiden let go and stood. "Are you sure you're okay?"

"Yeah. It just took me by surprise. I thought the worst of the flashbacks were behind me. But I'll be fine."

Aiden stepped backward, not taking her gaze off Dawn. Just

when she reached for the doorknob, the door began to move. She quickly prevented it from opening fully and slipped outside, blocking Dawn's niece from entering the bedroom.

"I can't find her anywhere. Is Aunt Dawn in there?"

Aiden nodded. "Yes, I found her."

"Is she okay?" The girl stared up at Aiden with wide eyes.

Her compassion and the intuitive understanding that something wasn't quite right with her aunt reminded Aiden once again of Dawn. "Yes, she is. She's just a little tired from all the hiding and seeking. She'll join us as soon as she's rested for a bit, okay? How about we set up the Parcheesi board so we can play when she comes out?" She had seen the game board on the table when she came in.

Jamie hesitated to leave her place next to the bedroom door. "Auntie Dawn isn't very good at that."

Aiden grinned. "All the better for us, don't you think?"

The girl giggled and joined Aiden at the table. "Do you know how to play?"

"I used to, but it's been a long time," Aiden answered, trying to keep the bedroom door within her sight without Jamie noticing. "You may have to remind me about the rules."

"I can do that," Jamie said. "I'll take the red ones. You can have green or yellow."

"What about blue? Why can't I have those?"

"Because they're mine," Dawn said from the doorway.

"Aunt Dawn!" Jamie jumped up from the table, raced across the room, and hugged her aunt around the waist. "Are you sad again?"

Dawn caressed the red-blonde hair. "How can I be sad when my favorite niece is here? Although I won't be very happy if I lose at Parcheesi again." She smiled at Aiden over her niece's head.

Aiden admired her self-control. If she hadn't seen her

trembling and hyperventilating just minutes before, she wouldn't have believed that this was the same woman.

"What are you doing here?" Dawn asked while she took the blue pawns. "And how did you get in?"

"Kade wanted me to bring you a copy of your statement. Your niece let me in," Aiden said, very aware that the girl was listening to every word she said.

Dawn directed a reproachful glance at Jamie. "We talked about this before. Letting strangers in can be dangerous even if they look nice."

"But, Auntie Dawn, she had a gold shield."

"Which could be fake," Dawn said.

Jamie stared at Aiden. "Is it?"

"No. It's real, but your aunt is right."

"Okay. Next time, I won't let her in," Jamie said.

Dawn gave her a gentle nudge to the chin. "You can let Aiden in since she's not a stranger anymore. Everyone else has to stay outside and wait until an adult lets her or him in, okay?"

Jamie nodded. "Can we play now?"

Half an hour later, Aiden watched as Jamie walked her fourth and last piece around the game board. "Do something, Dawn. Your niece is about to win my paycheck."

"We're not playing for money," Dawn said. "Even if we were, I can't influence how the dice fall. My field of expertise is psychology, not telekinesis." The doorbell interrupted before she could throw the dice.

"Uh-oh!" Jamie looked back and forth between her aunt and the door.

Dawn nodded. "I think that's your mom, rug rat."

"Can't I stay just a little longer? I was winnin'!"

"You can beat us again next time, okay?" Dawn got up and opened the door, apparently unaware that she had included Aiden in her plans for future Parcheesi games.

Aiden cleared the game board, one eye on the two women hugging each other in the hallway.

Jamie's mother was a tall brunette with a warm smile. The baby on her hip, who Aiden guessed to be less than a year old, held his little arms out in Dawn's direction.

Dawn took him from his mother and cuddled him against her body as she walked back into the living room. "This is Eliza, the little cheater's mother."

Jamie giggled. "I didn't cheat, Aunt Dawn."

"Yeah, yeah." Dawn laughed. "Eliza, this is Detective Aiden Carlisle."

"Ah." Eliza stepped past Dawn. "Very pleased to finally meet you."

Aiden shook her hand, wondering what Dawn had told her almost sister-in-law about her.

"And this little guy here is Tim, my nephew." Dawn leaned down to press a soft kiss against the baby's head.

So Eliza has a new partner and a new baby—and Dawn accepted both willingly into the family. Amazing.

Eliza studied the woman bouncing her son. "Are you okay? You're looking a little—"

"I'm fine," Dawn said. "Your daughter just ran her favorite aunt a little ragged, that's all."

"Her only aunt," Eliza said.

"Details, details."

Eliza stepped forward and touched Dawn's arm. "Thanks for babysitting her."

"Mom!" Jamie stomped her foot. "I'm not a baby."

Her mother smiled. "Oh, sorry, your ladyship. Must've been momentary confusion on my part."

Jamie nodded. "I'm almost a teenager now."

Eliza crossed herself. "Yeah, God help me. Maybe your aunt

can keep you a little longer." She looked at Dawn. "Until she's, say, eighteen or nineteen."

Aiden had to laugh. In moments like this, she regretted having no family.

Dawn handed over Jamie's backpack but kept the baby until the very last second. It was easy to see that she loved him as much as she loved her niece, even though he wasn't related to her by blood. "Listen, if you and Rick want me to take the kids overnight, just give me a call."

"Like you don't already have enough on your plate without a nine-month-old and a nine-year-old vying for your attention."

"My plate will never be too full for them," Dawn said.

Eliza nodded. "You'll call us when you know the court date, right? We want to come."

Dawn hesitated, playing with her nephew's tiny foot. "I'm not sure about that."

"About the date?"

"About you coming to watch the trial."

"All these years you've been so supportive of us," Eliza said. "Now let us support you for a change."

Dawn sighed, but there was a smile on her lips. "Guess I can't stop you, huh?"

"No, you can't." Eliza hugged Dawn again and took her son from her.

Jamie hugged and kissed her aunt. To Aiden's surprise, the girl turned and hugged her too before she followed her mother out the door.

"Friendly girl, your niece," Aiden said to Dawn when they were alone.

"Yes, she is." Dawn smiled. She walked to the door and locked it. "If she likes you, that is. She can be a little devil if she can't stand someone, though. I think Maggie would rather wrestle a cobra than stay in the same room with Jamie ever again."

Aiden studied her. "Are you okay after that flashback?"

"I'm all right now."

"Really?" Aiden didn't want Dawn to put up a strong front.

Dawn squeezed Aiden's arm. "Yes, really." This time, she looked her in the eyes, and Aiden believed her. "Sometimes, I'm pretty out of it for hours or even days afterward, but being with somebody always helps me to quickly orient myself to the here and now."

"You have those flashbacks often?" Aiden asked.

"No, just sometimes, mostly when I'm under a lot of stress and a situation reminds me of that night. Trying to hide under the covers was stupid. Suddenly, I was back in my old apartment, with him." Dawn closed her eyes, her breath once again becoming fast and shaky.

Aiden covered Dawn's hand with her own, rubbing her thumb over the clammy fingers. "You're not," she said softly. "You're here." *With me.*

Dawn opened her eyes and looked into Aiden's.

Aiden cleared her throat and handed her the statement. "Kade wants you to read this and refresh your memory before you meet with her tomorrow."

"I can do that."

"Okay." Aiden moved toward the door, in a hurry to get far away from Dawn and her growing feelings for her.

"Why don't you stay a little longer?" Dawn asked. "The apartment always seems so empty after the children are gone."

Aiden shook her head. The more time she spent with Dawn, the more fascinating she found her, and that was dangerous. "I can't. I still have to review my reports on your case." It was a lie. She would look through the reports and statements again tonight, but she already knew them by heart.

Dawn nodded. "Will I see you before the trial?"

"Sure. We'll see each other in the witness room. I have to

testify too, remember?" After answering, she realized that Dawn had probably meant to ask whether she would see her in more private surroundings.

"Do you think you'll have to testify before I have to?"

Aiden nodded. "I'm pretty sure that Kade will call me as her second or third witness. She likes to keep a somewhat chronological order of witnesses to avoid confusing the jury. And she usually saves her strongest witness for last."

Dawn swallowed audibly. "And that would be me?"

"Kade believes in you. And so do I."

"I'm scared," Dawn said.

Aiden was tempted to pull her into an embrace but held herself back. "It will be over before you know it."

"You're not scared or nervous at all, are you?"

"It's not the same for me. I'm just the detective working the case, not the victim here." Actually, Aiden was nervous, not so much about her own testimony but about Dawn's and what effect it could have on her. Having to face her rapist and the defense attorney's questions had reduced many rape survivors to tears on the stand. She pushed back the intense wave of protectiveness flooding her. "I have to go." She walked to the door and opened it. "Keep your chin up, okay?"

"I'll try to," Dawn murmured.

Aiden left, dissatisfied with herself and the situation.

CHAPTER 16

"THAT'S IT." KADE LEANED BACK in her desk chair and nodded at the woman across from her. It had taken only two repetitions of the questions-and-answers game until she was confident that Dawn could handle herself on the witness stand. If only she had witnesses like that in all of her cases—a woman who was confident enough to look the jury in the eyes while she explained what had happened to her, yet who also possessed a trace of vulnerability that resonated with many jurors. It also didn't hurt her credibility that she was a psychologist and a rape counselor.

"It was okay like that?" Dawn asked.

"Absolutely," Kade said. "Just look at me and answer as directly and with as many details as you can. You'll be fine."

Dawn nodded. "I heard jury selection was this morning. Do you have a good feeling about the group?"

Kade raised her brows. "You have an inside source somewhere?"

"No, I was a little early for our appointment, and I heard two of the people you had excused from jury duty talk about it."

"It was the most extensive jury selection I've had in quite some time."

"Why's that?" Dawn asked.

"I tried to unearth prejudices against lesbians and exclude the homophobes while the defense attorney sought to keep them in the panel because he hopes they'll sympathize with his client. D'Aquino tried to use his peremptory challenges to exclude everyone he suspected to be gay or have gay friends or family members."

Dawn's eyes widened. "He can do that?"

"Theoretically, no. The law prohibits exclusions of jurors based upon their sexual orientation," Kade said. "But if he can give a group-neutral explanation for his challenge and I can't prove that it was not the real reason for excluding that juror, the judge has to overrule my objection."

Dawn rubbed her forehead, sighing. "Was I too naïve in thinking that my sexual orientation wouldn't be an issue in this trial?"

"Not naïve, no. The defense attorney is not allowed to bring up your sexual history, but in this case, I think we should."

"Is that really necessary?"

"Yes," Kade said. "If you testify that you identify as a lesbian, it contradicts Ballard's claim that you consented to have sex with him."

"What are our chances for a conviction?"

That was the million-dollar question. Kade shrugged. "Normally, I would say they're more than good—we have DNA evidence, a solid identification in a lineup, and the Glock we found in his apartment."

"But?"

With any other victim, Kade would have left it at the more optimistic assessment, but she knew that Dawn didn't want to be spared from the truth. "With the evidence we have, Ballard and D'Aquino are up to their necks, and a desperate lawyer is a dangerous lawyer. He'll use whatever he can get his hands on, and he'll try to discredit every single witness I call. If he can get enough jurors to buy Ballard's ridiculous story, we might be in trouble."

A rapid knock on the door interrupted them.

"Yes?" Kade called. A quick glance at her watch showed that

it was already time for her appointment with the next victim. Lunch would have to wait. Her mother and whatever man would accompany her to the next fund-raiser would be thankful for it, but her stomach, at the moment, wasn't.

The door swung open, revealing Aiden, who led a fidgeting Melanie Riggs into the office. The young woman had been raped six months before and still couldn't leave the house on her own, so Kade had asked Aiden to drive her to the trial prep appointment.

"Hi, Kade, Dawn." Aiden guided Ms. Riggs to the chair next to Dawn.

Dawn turned and directed a few encouraging words toward the pale woman, getting her to relax a little.

Aiden set something on Kade's desk. Instead of the stack of reports Kade had expected, it was a salad and a sandwich.

Furrowing her brow, Kade looked up at Aiden. "For me?"

Aiden nodded. "With jury selection and trial prep, I figured you probably hadn't eaten yet."

"Thanks." Kade picked a piece of tomato out of her salad and chewed it. "That was really nice of you."

"Yeah, well, we can't have our DDA wasting away. Would be too much trouble to break in a new one just when we finally have the old one housebroken."

Kade waved her fork at Aiden. "I think that's your cue to leave before I decide that I need a search warrant executed at two a.m. tonight."

"I'm not on call tonight," Aiden said, grinning.

Kade smiled. "You would be, on my special request. After all, why should I work with another detective when I finally have the old ones housebroken?"

Aiden laughed and held up her hands. "Touché, Counselor. Back to work, it is."

Dawn stood. She leaned down to Melanie Riggs and squeezed her hand. "You'll be just fine. You're working with the best deputy district attorney in the city." She smiled at Kade and nodded her good-bye.

Dawn closed the door to Kade Matheson's office behind her and strolled down the hallway, noticing how Aiden slowed her strides and matched them to her own shorter ones.

"Maybe I should have complimented her like you did instead of calling her housebroken, huh?" Aiden pointed back to the DDA's office.

Dawn studied her. "You like her."

"Kade? Yeah, of course. She's easy to work with."

Dawn could have predicted that Aiden would say something like that. She should have just nodded and let her get away with it, but it was getting more and more difficult to think of Aiden Carlisle as just the detective working her case. It seemed like such a waste when the woman behind the badge was so much more fascinating. "That's not what I meant, and you know it."

Aiden glanced at her. "She's a nice person."

"Ah, ah, ah!" Dawn waggled her finger at Aiden. "That's not what I meant either. I was speaking of another kind of like."

"And what kind of like would that be?" Aiden asked.

"The 'I'd like to kiss her senseless at that two a.m. search warrant execution or any other time' kind of like." A mental image of Aiden and Kade in a passionate embrace flashed through Dawn's mind, and although she had to admit that the two would make a striking couple, she found the picture strangely disturbing. She forced down her feelings of jealousy. Even if Aiden were interested in her, Dawn knew she wasn't ready to start a relationship. After what had happened, she couldn't give a woman like Aiden what she needed.

Aiden opened the entrance door for Dawn and waited until they had both reached the parking lot before she spoke. "Well, that's not exactly what I was thinking, but yeah, she's pretty attractive. I mean, come on, anyone with a pulse would notice Kadence Matheson. I admire her. That's all."

"No, it's not."

"Okay." Aiden threw up her hands in surrender. "So maybe it's more than just pure, innocent admiration. A bit of good old-fashioned lusting may be thrown in too."

But once again, Dawn wasn't satisfied with the answer. "Why do you always play down your feelings?"

"I don't do that!" Aiden's voice rumbled like a warning peal of thunder.

Since the rape, Dawn had shrunk back from people displaying signs of anger, but she wasn't afraid now. She knew instinctively that she had nothing to fear from Aiden. "Yes, you do. You can admit professional respect and even lust but no deeper feelings. You pretend that your job and sex are all that's connecting you to people." It made her sad that a woman as wonderful as Aiden robbed herself of any meaningful relationship in life.

Aiden whirled around. Her amber eyes hurled angry flashes at Dawn. "Stop playing the psychologist with me!"

Dawn bit her lip. "I don't play the psychologist. I am a psychologist." She looked down at her hands and added in a whisper, "But not when I'm with you."

Aiden froze. Her hands fell limply back to her sides, and her gaze softened. "Dawn..." She breathed deeply. "Can we agree not to discuss things like that again, please?"

Dawn knew that Aiden wasn't willing or able to discuss her private life with her, but it still felt like a rejection. "Okay," was all she could say through a constricting throat.

"At least until the trial is over," Aiden added in a low voice.

Dawn lifted her head, but Aiden was looking anywhere but at her. *Does that mean...?* She searched Aiden's face. The detective mask was firmly in place, not revealing any feelings. "Okay," Dawn said again.

"Come on." Aiden led her toward the parking lot. "Let's get out of here."

Kade threw her pen onto the legal pad and leaned back with a groan. It had been a long day, and now all she wanted was a nice glass of chardonnay, a bath with four inches of bubbles, and eight hours of sleep. *Come on, Matheson. One more trial prep and you can go home. At least this time, it's Aiden and not a victim. She knows the drill, and you'll be out of here in half an hour.*

A knock on the door interrupted her momentary daydreams. "Yes?"

Aiden's head appeared in the doorway, the black hair ruffled. "Hey, you all right? You look kind of beat."

After dealing with three rape victims in a row, Kade felt beat. Interacting with victims had never come as naturally to her as it did to Aiden. "Nothing a glass of wine and a hot bath wouldn't cure."

Aiden stepped into the office and closed the door behind her.

Is that a blush I see on her cheeks? Kade held back a chuckle. *She investigates horrible sex crimes for a living but blushes when I mention a bubble bath?* Mercifully, she chose not to comment on it. She had dealt with the innocent and not-so-innocent crushes of coworkers and detectives before. While not exactly used to the admiring glances from a woman, Kade didn't feel uncomfortable or threatened by them. Whatever Aiden felt for her, she was a dedicated police officer and a professional first and foremost—and someone Kade had come to think of as a friend.

"I'd suggest we take a rain check and do the prep another time, but seeing as the trial starts tomorrow..." Aiden shrugged.

Kade rounded her desk and sank onto the small couch she

had in her office. With a relieved sigh, she slipped out of her high heels. "It won't take long. You already know most of the questions I'll ask you on the stand. 'Detective Carlisle, you were called in by the responding unit on the night in question, correct?' et cetera, et cetera. We can skip the standard questions for now."

Aiden cleared her throat, intently studying the floor. "I should probably tell you that those questions aren't as standard as usual."

"What's that supposed to mean?" Kade gestured for Aiden to sit.

"I wasn't called in by the responding unit," Aiden said. "I heard dispatch report a 10-31 in my immediate neighborhood and decided to drive over."

Kade stared at her. "You listen to your police scanner at three a.m.?" *You really need to get a life, my friend. And so do I.*

"It was the night of the Henderson arrest. I'd just come in from the precinct, and I was wide-awake."

"A 10-31..." Kade took off her glasses and rubbed her eyes. "Correct me if I'm wrong, but that doesn't necessarily mean a sexual assault occurred, does it? It could have been something a SAD detective wasn't needed for."

Aiden tilted her head. "Could have, but I had this feeling. And I recognized the address."

Kade sat up. "What's going on here, Aiden? You knew the victim before this whole case started? Ever heard of conflict of interest?" She glared at Aiden. "You should have excused yourself from the investigation. God, D'Aquino will rip us apart on cross!"

"Oh, come on, Kade." Aiden stood and began to pace in the small space between the couch and the door. "I spent a total of twenty minutes in her company before she was raped. It's not like we were best buddies. I went to a lecture she gave, and when I met her the week after, she invited me to her apartment because she wanted me to talk to her support group—that's all. Do you really expect me to turn my back on a rape victim just because I'd seen her before?"

Kade sighed. "No, of course I don't. But I expected you to tell me."

"I'm telling you now."

"Not that it does me any good." Kade looked at the ceiling, shaking her head. "I already turned in my witness list, and you're on it. I can't call Ray to the stand instead of you."

Aiden stopped pacing and looked at her. "What are we gonna do?"

Kade shrugged. "What we always do: hope for the best and prepare for the worst."

CHAPTER 17

DAWN LOOKED UP AT THE Multnomah County Courthouse. The huge building occupied the entire block. With its massive Corinthian columns and the somber gray concrete, it intimidated Dawn a little. The steps leading to the large portal seemed endless. With a deep breath, she started toward them, the loyal horde of her companions following silently behind her.

Her mother, Caleb, and Eliza and her husband, Rick, were there. Even her colleagues, Charlie and Ally, had taken the day off to hear the opening statements with her. Dawn was grateful for their company, but as she made her way toward the courthouse entrance, she looked around, wishing for the reassuring presence of a certain detective.

She stepped through the heavy doors, her footfalls on the marbled floor echoing through the columned hall. A familiar, dark-haired figure leaned by the metal detector. It wasn't the police officer Dawn had been on the lookout for, but she would certainly do. "Lieutenant Delicia Vasquez Montero!"

Del turned. Her frown turned into a smile. With three quick steps, she crossed the space between them and engulfed Dawn in a warm embrace. "Don't call me that, grasshopper. You'll ruin my reputation."

At the familiar nickname, Dawn closed her eyes and relaxed into the comfort provided by the only aunt she had ever known. "Hi, Del."

"Hey, sweetie." Del pressed a kiss to the crown of her head. "How are you?"

"Hanging in there." Dawn stepped back to study the woman in front of her. Only a few gray hairs at the temples showed in the short, jet-black hair, but other than that, Del was still the same strong woman Dawn had known growing up.

Del had studied her too, and now she shook her head with a sad but affectionate smile. "You look more like your dad every day."

"I'll take that as a compliment," Dawn said.

"It is a compliment. He was the best damn partner I ever had. The young cops these days..." Del shook her head and trailed off, looking at something to her right. "Speaking of young cops... Your detective friend is staring at us."

Dawn turned.

Aiden was leaning against one of the hall's columns. She was wearing neatly pressed black slacks and a formfitting crème-colored turtleneck. The leather jacket Dawn had come to love had been traded in favor of a more conservative blazer, and the detective's badge dangled proudly from its breast pocket. When she saw Dawn looking at her, Aiden gave a curt nod but didn't smile or move any closer.

Great. Was that the cool, overly professional behavior that she had to look forward to until after the trial, or was Aiden keeping her distance because of Del?

"Is she testifying today, or is she here as your secret admirer?" Del asked from behind her.

Dawn turned back to her. "She's testifying."

Del lifted one brow. "Then why are you blushing?"

Dawn studied her feet. How could she explain what Aiden meant to her when she didn't fully understand it herself? She rubbed her face. "Del, I..."

"It's all right, grasshopper. I didn't mean to give you a hard time. I just don't want you to get hurt."

Aiden approached them. "Lieutenant Vasquez." She nodded at the older officer. "Dawn."

Del nodded back. "Detective."

"Didn't you agree on a first-name basis?" Dawn asked.

"Uh, right, we did." Del and Aiden stared at each other.

Grace, Eliza, Caleb, Rick, and Dawn's colleagues joined them, and the whole group, with Dawn in the middle, started to move toward the courtroom. Del wrapped her arm around Dawn and only let go when they reached the double doors leading to the courtroom.

Dawn took a deep breath before she stepped through the doors and let Del lead her to the prosecution's side of the gallery. She sat between her mother and Del and giggled in spite of her tension when Del used her patented lieutenant wave to get Aiden into the seat next to her. *God, Del, please don't scare her off. The poor woman has to feel like some high school boy meeting the parents of the girl he wants to take to the prom.*

When Garett Ballard was being led to his place behind the defense table, all thoughts of Del and Aiden fled from Dawn's mind. Her heart started to pound, and she forced herself to calm down and look at him as objectively as she could. In the light of day, he appeared human, like someone she could have met in the subway or in a coffee shop. Then he turned his head and looked directly at Dawn. His eyes were cold and without mercy.

Dawn shuddered.

"You okay?" Aiden and Del asked at the same time, looking at her with concern, then at each other. After a second, both leaned back, giving the other precedence to talk to Dawn.

"What is it with those two?" Grace whispered from the other side. "Is there some bad blood between them?"

"No, Mom. Let's talk about it later," Dawn whispered back.

Much later, like never. Her mother, while supportive after her coming out, had never been a big fan of Maggie. After Dawn's first and only relationship with a woman had ended, Grace seemed to prefer thinking that it had been just a phase and Dawn would turn to a man for her next relationship.

"All rise!" the bailiff called out, interrupting any other thoughts. "This court is now in session. The Honorable Judge Ruth Linehan presiding."

The black robe rustled as Judge Linehan took her place behind the bench. "Be seated." The judge was tiny and looked almost dwarfed by her robe and the tall mahogany bench, but from what Aiden and Kade Matheson had told Dawn, she made up for it with a sharp tongue and a huge ego.

The judge instructed the jury, but Dawn was too busy trying to control her churning nerves, so she didn't listen.

Finally, Kade rose to deliver her opening statement. She smoothed her skirt with a practiced gesture, rounded the prosecution's table, and strolled toward the jury box. "Good morning, ladies and gentlemen." She nodded at the jurors as if she knew each and every one of them by name—and perhaps she did. Dawn had heard that good attorneys memorized the jurors' names, and Kade Matheson was certainly impressive. "The case you were chosen to hear is a case about hate. You are here today because of a man's primitive, uncontrolled hate against lesbian women. On the night of October fifth, this man broke into the apartment of Dawn Kinsley." Kade paused and turned toward Dawn, giving the jurors ample opportunity to look into Dawn's face and see the fear in her eyes.

Dawn didn't have to act to give the jury the impression of a frightened victim. As Kade began to describe the circumstances of her rape, images of that night began to flash through Dawn's mind. She dug her nails into her palms in an attempt to anchor herself in the present. She didn't want to have a flashback in front of all these people. Struggling to control her breathing, she pretended they were talking about someone else.

"He ripped her phone line out and threw away her cell phone, leaving her without any chance to call for help. He pressed a gun against her head." Kade held her index finger against her temple and let her gaze wander over the rows of jurors while she did so. "He threatened and hit her, and then he brutally raped her in her own bed." Her voice was clear and confident, painting a vivid picture for the jurors.

Dawn distracted herself by gazing around the room, looking at anything but Garett Ballard or the prosecutor telling the story of her rape. She glanced to her right, where Del and Aiden sat side by side, both looking calm and collected but with an intense, righteous anger in their eyes. Dawn looked down at their hands, the strong, competent hands of trained protectors, which rested in the exact same positions against their thighs.

"He moved fast. He had a plan, and he acted without any scruples," Kade said. "Dr. Kinsley, who is also a psychologist and rape counselor, will testify that he wasn't nervous at all—because, as the police later discovered, he had committed this heinous crime before. The same man had raped Melanie Riggs and Jayne Matthews. The People will prove during this trial that it was this man," Kade extended her slender arm, pointing at the man sitting next to the defense attorney, "the defendant, Garett Ballard, who brutally raped these women. You will hear not only how the victims identified Mr. Ballard in a lineup, but you'll also see DNA evidence that will prove, beyond a reasonable doubt, that no other man could have committed the crime."

Ballard didn't even wince or blink an eye.

"The defense will try to tell you that the defendant's semen was found on Dr. Kinsley because they had unprotected consensual sex. But that's not what the ER physician or Dr. Kinsley will testify to, and I want you to ask yourselves: Why would she lie?" Kade looked at the jurors. "Because she hates Mr. Ballard? Because she wanted revenge? For what? Keep in mind, before that night, she had never seen Mr. Ballard before nor had Ms. Matthews or Ms. Riggs. We have not one but three witnesses, three victims who accuse Garett Ballard of raping them. Why would all of them lie?" Turning toward the gallery for a second, Kade looked at the detectives sitting there. "In addition, police officers will testify how they found the gun used to threaten Dr. Kinsley in the defendant's apartment—a gun he wouldn't have needed for consensual sex, would he?" She shook her head. "The victims didn't harbor plans of hate and revenge. The defendant did. Because his mother left the family for another woman, he developed a pathological hatred of lesbians. He sought employment as a bouncer at a lesbian club for the sole reason of gaining access to the addresses of lesbian women, which he then used to break into their apartments."

As the opening statement went on and on, Dawn struggled to sit still. Her anxiety rose. Had she been sitting next to Aiden, she would have taken her hand to calm herself down even if she wasn't sure how Aiden or anyone else in the courtroom would react to it. Instead, another strong hand, that of Del, covered her own and gave her fingers a soft squeeze. Dawn squeezed back before returning her attention to Kade.

"So, Mr. Ballard has motive, opportunity, and the means to commit these hateful crimes." Kade counted it off on her fingers. "At the conclusion of this case, you will be able to find, beyond any reasonable doubt, that Garett Ballard raped three women. I ask you to weigh all the evidence, without hate and prejudice against the victims or the defendant, and then return with a verdict of guilty. Thank you."

As Kade returned to her table, Dawn took a few deep breaths.

Judge Linehan leaned forward. "The prosecutor has

completed her opening statement. Does defense counsel wish to give his opening statement now?"

"Yes, Your Honor." The defense attorney rose from his seat, buttoning his suit jacket. "Victor D'Aquino representing Mr. Ballard. Your Honor, ladies and gentlemen of the jury, the prosecution wants you to believe this is a case about hate, but it's not. My client is not a hateful man."

Dawn glanced toward Ballard, who sat behind the defense table with his hands folded, looking to the world as if he couldn't hurt a fly.

"Garett Ballard is just a man who supports himself with hard work as a security specialist. In this line of work, he's used to protecting and helping people, to prevent danger and harm, not to cause it."

Dawn scrunched up her face. *He's equating that bastard with honest cops who are out there every day, risking their lives to protect innocent people?*

"Mr. Ballard has no previous criminal record. He never caused anyone any problems, and his employer—a lesbian woman—will testify that he held no ill feelings toward lesbians. So, what this case is about is an innocent man wrongfully accused of crimes he didn't commit." D'Aquino gesticulated as if he had just uncovered a conspiracy against his client. "As Her Honor instructed you, an opening statement is not evidence. The prosecution simply told you their theory about what happened on the night of October fifth, but the problem with the prosecution's case is—they don't have one. There—never—was—a—rape," the defense attorney emphasized every word. "Mr. Ballard had sex with consenting, adult women, which is not a crime. The prosecution has neither eyewitnesses nor substantial pieces of evidence to prove a rape. The only thing they've got is the testimony of the alleged victims—the unverified accusations of women who decided to sleep with my client despite their self-claimed identities as lesbians and then, after the heat and passion of the moment were over, were too embarrassed to admit to a heterosexual affair, claiming it a rape instead."

Dawn stared at him. *Since when is it embarrassing to be straight?*

"The prosecution will tell you Mr. Ballard allegedly tried to resist arrest," D'Aquino said. "But he was just doing his job. On the evening of his arrest, two plainclothes detectives—not uniformed police officers—came up to my client at the front door of the club he had been assigned to watch over. He didn't recognize them as police officers but thought of them as troublemakers trying to get into the club, and he acted accordingly."

Troublemakers? Dawn looked at Aiden, then at Ray Bennet, who sat somewhere behind his partner in the second row of the gallery. Every inch of them spoke of dedicated police officers. No one could mistake them for troublemakers trying to get into the club without paying.

Victor D'Aquino held up his index finger. "Remember, my client is presumed innocent until proven otherwise. I am confident that, after hearing all the evidence and testimony in this case, you'll agree with me that the prosecution has not been able to prove Mr. Ballard's guilt beyond a reasonable doubt, and you'll find him not guilty. Thank you."

Judge Linehan lifted her gavel. "Before we hear the case for the prosecution, we'll take a ten minute recess so that all witnesses who will be called later can leave the courtroom."

Dawn stood, glad to leave the courtroom and the whole trial behind her for as long as she could.

Ruth Linehan waved to her clerk. "Bring in the jury, please." She waited until all the jurors had taken their places and then nodded at Kade. "Call your first witness."

Kade rose, glancing back toward the double doors. "The People call Officer Jonathan Riley to the stand."

The young officer walked toward the witness stand.

His more experienced partner, Officer Trent, was out with the flu, leaving Kade with the rookie at the last minute. She wasn't looking forward to his cross-exam by D'Aquino, but there was nothing she could do about it now.

Once Riley had been sworn in, she rounded the prosecution's table and stepped in front of the witness-box. "Officer Riley, you are a police officer with the central precinct, responsible for the area Dr. Kinsley lived in, is that correct?"

Riley fiddled with the tie of his uniform, making Kade want to slap his hand. "Yes, that's correct."

"On the night of Saturday, October fifth, you and your partner, Officer Trent, responded to a call at 228 Northwest Everett Street, did you not?"

"Yes, ma'am, we did. The call came over the radio at approximately three thirty-five. Dispatch reported an assault at that location."

Kade nodded. "When you arrived at the crime scene—"

"Objection, Your Honor!" The defense attorney sprang up from his seat before Kade could finish her question. "Assumes facts not in evidence. Ms. Kinsley's apartment is not the scene of any crime that's been proven yet."

Kade looked at him over the rim of her glasses. *Nitpicking and bickering like that won't bring you any points with the jury or with Linehan, you little idiot, so by all means keep it up.* "I'll rephrase, Your Honor," she said before Linehan could rule. "Officer Riley, would you please tell us what you encountered when you arrived at the location in question?"

"The apartment was a mess," Riley said. "Through the bedroom door, I could see a knocked-over chair and a lamp, I think. There were some objects—books, figurines, a pair of broken glasses, and such—scattered across the floor."

Kade turned and lifted a photograph from the prosecution table before carrying it to the witness stand. "I'm showing you what's been marked as People's exhibit one for identification. Can you tell the jury what is pictured in this photograph?"

"It's a photograph of Ms. Kinsley's bedroom. It was taken on the night in question."

Kade carried the photograph to the jury box, letting the jurors see the destruction in Dawn's apartment with their own eyes. "What about Dr. Kinsley? How did she appear?"

Officer Riley fingered his tie again. "Her clothing was torn, and a bruise was forming on her cheek."

Kade held up two transparent evidence bags. "Officer Riley, have you ever seen these exhibits before?" She laid the evidence bags down in front of the young officer.

"Yes. I believe this is the clothing Dr. Kinsley wore that night."

Kade turned, showing the torn T-shirt and panties to the jury members. "What conclusions did you draw from the state Dr. Kinsley and her apartment were in?"

"Objection!" came the expected interruption from the defense table. "Your Honor, she's calling for a conclusion on the part of the witness."

"Overruled," Linehan said as Kade had thought she would. "The witness is a trained police officer. I want to hear his conclusions. Please answer, Officer Riley."

"I thought it likely that an assault had occurred," Riley answered.

Kade nodded. "Thank you, Officer. No further questions." She sat down.

D'Aquino rose for his cross-examination and stepped close to the young cop so he would tower above him. "Officer Riley, how long have you been a police officer?"

Kade had seen it coming. She held back a grimace.

"Since last year," Riley answered.

"Just last year," D'Aquino repeated, in case one of the jurors hadn't caught it the first time. "And how long have you been working in the field?"

Riley blushed. "Two months."

"And in those two months, have you ever been summoned to the site of a sexual assault before?" D'Aquino asked.

"No, sir," Riley said. "This was my first."

D'Aquino nodded. "Have you ever met Ms. Kinsley before that night?"

"No, of course not."

"Is it safe to say, then, Officer Riley, that you have no frame of reference to assess her appearance or her behavior?"

Riley hesitated. "I guess not."

"In your direct examination, you said that you saw the objects on the floor through the open bedroom door, so you weren't actually in the bedroom, were you?"

"Ms. Kinsley didn't want me to," Riley said. "She was pretty shaken, and we were waiting for a female detective—"

"A simple yes or no, please," the defense attorney said. "Were you or were you not in the bedroom?"

The officer's shoulders slumped. "No, I wasn't."

"So, not having seen the evidence at close range, how could you be sure that the objects scattered about the bedroom floor hadn't simply gotten there by two people having passionate sex, tumbling into the apartment, kissing and tearing each other's clothes off?"

"Because...because...it didn't look like that."

"From the distance," D'Aquino muttered.

Kade stood. "Objection! Is there a question?"

"Withdrawn. No further questions." The defense attorney returned to his seat.

The judge looked at Kade. "Redirect, Ms. Matheson?"

"Yes, Your Honor." Kade knew she couldn't leave it like that. D'Aquino had destroyed Riley's credibility. "Officer Riley, how did the living room of Dr. Kinsley's apartment look when you arrived?"

"Tidy, ma'am. No signs of a struggle."

"How would you expect a living room to look if two people having passionate sex, tumbling into the apartment, kissing and tearing each other's clothes off, had stumbled through on their way to the bedroom?" Kade asked, quoting the defense's argument. She hoped that even the inexperienced officer had caught on to what she was trying to get him to say.

"If that was the case, there would have been some scattered objects in the hallway and the living room too," Riley answered.

"Thank you. Nothing further." Kade sat back down.

"I call Detective Aiden Carlisle to the stand."

Aiden strode into the courtroom, careful to hide any trace of her nervousness as she placed her left hand on the Bible the bailiff held out for her. She hadn't been this nervous about testifying since her very first time in court as a rookie fresh from the academy. She swore to tell the truth, the whole truth, and nothing but the truth and took her place on the witness stand.

"Would you please state and spell your name for the record?" the bailiff asked.

"Aiden Carlisle," Aiden said and then spelled it out for the court reporter.

Kade moved closer to the witness-box and gave her a small nod. "Tell the jury your profession, please."

"I'm a detective with the Sexual Assault Detail of the Portland

Police Bureau," Aiden answered, keeping her head up and her shoulders squared.

"How long have you been a police officer, Detective?"

"Nine years," Aiden answered.

"How many of those years have you spent investigating sex crimes?"

"Seven years."

Kade put on an impressed expression, as if she hadn't known that fact before. "For comparison, what is the average time a detective works with the Sexual Assault Detail before transferring out?"

"The average is two years," Aiden answered. *Okay, now everyone should have noticed that I know my stuff.*

"Detective Carlisle, would you please describe for the jury what you found when you arrived at Dr. Kinsley's apartment on the night in question?" Kade asked, purposely leaving out why Aiden had been present at the apartment in the first place.

"Furniture had been knocked over in the bedroom, and a series of broken objects and trampled books were scattered across the floor," Aiden answered. "In the living room, nothing was out of order, except for a wide-open window, a knocked-over table in front of the window, and a ripped-out phone cord."

Kade nodded. "Did you actually enter the bedroom?"

"Yes, I did."

"Where was Dr. Kinsley when you arrived?"

This was her cue to report Dawn's physical and emotional state since Kade couldn't ask directly without drawing an objection from D'Aquino. "She was sitting in the living room, too scared to return to the bedroom."

"How do you know she was scared?" Kade asked.

"She was very pale—except for the bruise on her right cheek—and trembling, obviously in a state of shock." Sometimes, Aiden couldn't get that picture out of her head.

"What did Dr. Kinsley tell you—?"

"Objection, hearsay!" D'Aquino shouted.

Linehan nodded. "Sustained."

Aiden pressed her lips together. The defense had just successfully prevented her from explaining to the jury how Dawn had immediately told her she had been raped.

Kade had no choice but to move on to the next question. "Detective Carlisle, you were the lead investigator in Dr. Kinsley's case, correct?"

"My partner, Detective Bennet, and I, yes."

"Tell us a little about the investigation, please," Kade said.

Aiden looked at the jury members, speaking directly to them. "The first solid lead came when we noticed similarities between the cases of Dr. Kinsley, Ms. Matthews, and Ms. Riggs." She decided to leave out their useless attempts to get a DNA hit in one of their databases because it would draw attention to the fact that Garett Ballard had no previous criminal record. "All of them frequented a lesbian club known as Rainbows."

"And after that discovery, what was the next step in your investigation?"

"We went to the club to show around the sketch our police artist had drawn from Dr. Kinsley's description of her rapist." Aiden fixed a steely gaze at Ballard. "But that didn't prove necessary because before I even reached the front door, I identified the defendant, Mr. Ballard, as the man we were searching for. Dr. Kinsley had described him in detail, right down to the scars on his chin and above one eyebrow."

Kade turned and regarded Ballard for a second, giving the jury the opportunity to do the same, before she held up a sheet of paper. "Is this sketch, which I've filed as People's exhibit four, the sketch you're referring to, Detective?"

"Yes, it is." The resemblance of the portrayed man to Ballard was obvious.

Kade walked the sketch over to the jury for closer inspection. "What happened next?"

"We waited for a warrant, as the law requires, and then went to arrest Mr. Ballard," Aiden said. "As I started to read him his rights, he called me a bitch and hit me in the face with his fist."

Kade handed her a photograph, taken the day after the arrest when the bruise on her jaw had been the most colorful. "I'm showing you what's been marked as People's exhibit five. Detective Carlisle, is this the injury you sustained during the arrest?"

"Yes, it is." Aiden gave back the photograph so Kade could show it to the jury.

"Detective Carlisle, how many suspects have you arrested during your career?"

Aiden shrugged. "I don't know the exact number; must have been hundreds, though."

"And how many times has a suspect hit you during an arrest?" Kade asked.

"Most don't try to resist, but I've been hit, kicked, spat on, and sworn at more times than I can count." Aiden looked across the courtroom at Ballard. *You're nothing special, you bastard.*

Kade stepped closer. "And how often have you been hit, kicked, spat on, or sworn at by a suspect whose innocence was later established?"

D'Aquino shot up from his seat. "Objection!"

"I withdraw, Your Honor," Kade said. The jury had heard what she had meant to imply anyway. "Detective Carlisle, when you and your partner arrested the defendant, did you wear your badge, identifying you as a police officer?"

"Yes, I did. I showed it to Mr. Ballard right before I began to read him his rights," Aiden answered.

Kade looked at the gold shield proudly displayed on Aiden's breast pocket. "So, how likely is it that Mr. Ballard thought you were, as Mr. D'Aquino said in his opening statement, 'troublemakers' who wanted to cheat their way into the club?"

Aiden allowed a sarcastic smile to show on her lips. "Highly unlikely. He knew who we were and why we were there when he hit me."

"Was Mr. Ballard armed when you arrested him?" Kade asked.

"Yes, he was. He had a Sig Sauer tucked in his waistband, covered by his shirt, although he doesn't have the necessary permit to carry a concealed weapon."

"You and your partner, Detective Bennet, were the officers who questioned Mr. Ballard after he was arrested, is that correct?"

"Yes."

Putting one hand onto the witness-box, Kade turned to look at Ballard. "What was the result of that interrogation?"

"Mr. Ballard was not very cooperative. He claimed not to know any of the victims, at least not their names. In the course of the interview, he became increasingly agitated, even aggressive. He jumped up and called me a 'fucking dyke.'" It felt good to finally have an opportunity to portray Ballard as the homophobe he was.

"Detective Carlisle, another question while I have you here as an expert. Your training as a police officer included lessons in officer safety and weaponless self-defense, right?"

"Yes."

"You've also been the academy's kickboxing champion, right?" Kade asked.

Aiden nodded. "That's right. Twice." This was not the time for humbleness.

"And despite all that training, the defendant was able to hit you?"

Aiden gritted her teeth and swallowed her pride, trusting that Kade was aiming at something other than humiliating her in front of her fellow detectives in the gallery. "Yes, he was."

"Then, with firsthand knowledge of the speed and force of his attack, would you expect an untrained woman to be able to defend herself against the defendant?"

Ah, this is where she's going with this. Aiden hid a smile.

"Objection, Your Honor!" The defense attorney jumped up again. "Counsel's asking for an opinion."

"Sit down, Mr. D'Aquino," Judge Linehan said. "As Ms. Matheson established, Detective Carlisle is a trained police officer. The jury is entitled to hear her opinion. Objection overruled."

Kade turned back toward Aiden, giving her a nod.

"No, there's not a doubt in my mind that an untrained woman would have no chance defending herself against him," Aiden answered.

"Thank you, Detective. No further questions at the moment." Kade walked back to her table.

Aiden braced herself as Victor D'Aquino approached the witness stand. "Detective Carlisle, you just told us that you've been hit by a suspect during arrest more times than you can count, correct?"

"Not literally, but it's been a few times, yes." Where was he going with this?

"Has anyone ever tried to draw a weapon and shoot you to resist arrest?" D'Aquino asked.

Aiden nodded. "Once or twice."

"On the evening you arrested him, did Mr. Ballard carry a weapon?"

"Yes, although he—"

"A simple yes or no will suffice, Detective."

Aiden forced herself to answer calmly. "Yes, he did carry a weapon."

"But he didn't try to use that weapon against you, did he?"

"No," Aiden said through gritted teeth.

"Detective Carlisle, you mentioned in your report that you

didn't arrest my client immediately when you saw him at the club, is that correct?" the defense lawyer asked.

Aiden gave a nod. "Yes. After I recognized him, I had to wait for backup and an arrest warrant."

"Is it not true that you came up to Mr. Ballard, not revealing yourself as a police officer but undercover as a customer who wanted to enter the club?" D'Aquino asked.

"I wasn't undercover."

D'Aquino tapped the witness-box in front of Aiden. "But your clothing and your behavior were such that Mr. Ballard could have assumed you were a customer?"

"That's possible the first time I approached him," Aiden said, "but—"

"Thank you, that answer is enough for me." The defense attorney leaned against the witness-box. "Isn't it true that you first arrested another innocent man for the alleged rape before you set your sights on my client?"

Oh, now he's trying to make it sound like we arbitrarily arrested Ballard because we didn't like the color of his socks! Another innocent man? Come on! "We followed a lead and arrested a known sex offender whose description resembled that of Mr. Ballard, that's true, yes." She noticed with satisfaction that D'Aquino wasn't happy with her answer.

"Okay, let's back up a little, Detective. Were you assigned to the case initially?"

Shit! Aiden had hoped it wouldn't come to this. "I was the detective working the case from this first night on, yes."

"And on that evening, were you on duty?"

"No."

"You were called in for backup, then?"

"No." Aiden fought the urge to grind her teeth together.

D'Aquino dramatically raised his eyebrows. "How come you appeared on Dr. Kinsley's doorstep on that night, then?"

"I heard about the assault on my police scanner, and since it was in my immediate neighborhood, I went to see if I could help," Aiden said, hoping he would leave it at that.

D'Aquino, of course, had other plans. "So, your eagerness to respond to that call had nothing to do with the fact that you knew the alleged victim, Ms. Kinsley, before that night?"

A murmur went through the audience.

Aiden forced down a wave of anger and panic. "No, it hadn't. If you had investigated that a little more thoroughly, you would know that dispatch never announces the name of the victim on the radio. I had no way of knowing who the victim was."

"But you did, didn't you?" D'Aquino asked. "You knew Ms. Kinsley before the alleged attack?"

"I heard Dr. Kinsley's lecture at a law enforcement seminar the week before her rape, just like every other SAD detective." Aiden hoped the defense didn't know about their chance meeting at the grocery store or her short visit in Dawn's apartment.

D'Aquino nodded. "So Ms. Kinsley gave a lecture about rape?"

Aiden's brow furrowed. *Where is he going with this?* It looked as if D'Aquino had given up on making her look biased and was now trying to impeach Dawn's credibility. "Yes, she did."

"She makes her living dealing with rape?"

Aiden clenched her hands into fists behind the witness-box. *Are you accusing her of anything here, you bastard?* "So do I, Counselor," she said, trying to draw his attack away from Dawn.

"You do." Thoughtfully, the defense attorney tapped his finger against his chin as if he had just now remembered that he was questioning a sex crimes expert. "Then, with a professional background like yours—or that of Ms. Kinsley—you'd know what kind of behavior to look for in a rape victim?"

"Yes, I do know that—it was exactly the kind of behavior Dr. Kinsley showed when I found her in her apartment that Saturday night." Aiden knew now what he was trying to do—implying that Dawn had faked the "symptoms" of a rape victim.

"And Ms. Kinsley also knows what kind of behavior a sex crimes detective would expect her to display if she had been raped, correct?"

"Objection!" Kade threw her pen onto the table and jumped up. "Defense counsel is trying to put the victim on trial, here. Your Honor, I respectfully request that you admonish Mr. D'Aquino for this behavior."

Aiden hid a smile. Kade looked like an avenging angel, glaring at D'Aquino.

"Approach the bench." Linehan clicked off her microphone so the jury couldn't hear what she said to the attorneys.

With various degrees of enthusiasm, Kade and D'Aquino made their ways toward the front of the courtroom.

Aiden let her gaze wander around the courtroom while she waited. Dawn's mother still sat in the first row, her face pale and her hand clamped around Del's. Aiden was glad that Dawn hadn't had to witness D'Aquino's accusations.

Finally, D'Aquino returned to the witness stand. "Detective Carlisle, you testified that you heard Ms. Kinsley give a lecture, right?"

"Right." What was he trying now?

"A lecture you were impressed with?" D'Aquino asked.

"Yes. Dr. Kinsley seemed very competent in her field of work." Aiden knew he wouldn't dare to pick up his line of questioning about Dawn's professional knowledge again after Linehan's admonition.

D'Aquino nodded. "So already knowing Ms. Kinsley and being impressed with her, wouldn't you say you were predisposed to believe her accusations against Mr. Ballard?"

Kade shifted onto the edge of her chair, as if ready to jump up and object again should the opportunity arise.

"I would say that I'm predisposed to believe every woman who sits there trembling and beaten and tells me she has been raped."

"What happened to innocent until proven otherwise?" D'Aquino muttered, loud enough for the jury to hear.

"Objection!" Kade stood, one hand on her hip. "Is there a question for this witness, or is defense counsel already delivering his closing argument?"

"Withdrawn. No further questions, Your Honor."

Kade rose. "Redirect, Your Honor?"

The judge nodded.

"Detective Carlisle, as defense counsel just pointed out, you saw Dr. Kinsley before the night of October fifth, correct?" Kade laid her hand onto the witness-box.

Aiden stared at her. Why was Kade drawing attention to that fact? But she trusted Kade and her abilities as an attorney, so she nodded. "Yes."

"Then unlike Officer Riley, who had never met Dr. Kinsley before and therefore had no frame of reference, as defense counsel pointed out, how would you describe your ability to assess Dr. Kinsley's appearance or behavior?" Kade asked.

Ah. Brilliant, Kade. Beating D'Aquino with his own weapons. Aiden suppressed a grin. "I would say that I should be able to assess her behavior fairly well."

"And compared to that first meeting, how did she behave on the night of October fifth?"

"Completely different," Aiden said. "Her confidence and her sense of humor were gone. Something had scared and upset her deeply."

The defense attorney rose from his table. "Objection, speculation, Your Honor! I move to strike. The witness has no personal knowledge of whatever did or did not happen that night."

Kade turned toward the judge. "The People are not attempting to show precisely what transpired that night, Your Honor, but merely to determine that, in Detective Carlisle's expert opinion, something occurred which had a negative effect on Dr. Kinsley."

"Overruled. You may proceed, Counselor," Linehan said.

"Thank you, Your Honor. Detective, it has been stated that you did not reveal yourself as a police officer on your first meeting with Mr. Ballard. Is that correct?"

"Yes."

"Was it your intention to arrest him on this occasion?" Kade asked.

Aiden shook her head. "No. I was merely attempting to gain access to the nightclub as part of an ongoing investigation."

"I see. And, on the second occasion, when you were actually attempting to arrest him, did you reveal yourself as a police officer?"

"Yes, I showed him my badge and the arrest warrant and proceeded to inform him that he was under arrest," Aiden said.

Kade nodded. "And it was at this point that he hit you?"

"That's right."

"Detective Carlisle," Kade paused for a second, letting the jury know with a meaningful glance that one last, important question was to follow, "having made, in your own words, 'hundreds of arrests,' do you believe that there is any way Mr. Ballard would not have known you were a police officer at the time of his arrest?"

"No, I don't see how."

With a brief nod, Kade stepped back from the witness stand. "No further questions, Your Honor."

"Thank you, Detective, you are excused," Linehan said.

On legs that felt wobbly, Aiden stood and walked out of the courtroom.

CHAPTER 18

"DETECTIVE CARLISLE?" STEPS ECHOED ACROSS the marble floor as Del and Grace caught up with Aiden.

She scanned the courthouse hallway behind the two women to see if Dawn was with them. While keeping her distance from Dawn might have been good for her job and her sanity, she wondered how Dawn was doing. "Lieutenant, Mrs. Kinsley."

"How is it going in your opinion?" Grace asked, pointing in the direction of the courtroom.

Aiden rubbed the back of her neck. "Well, Officer Riley didn't help our case—D'Aquino made him look like a greenhorn. Detective Okada's testimony about the execution of the search warrant guarantees us a conviction on the possession of stolen property charge but doesn't help much with the other charges."

"What about the DNA analyst and the fingerprint expert? Their testimony was good for us, right?" Grace fixed a hopeful gaze on Aiden.

"Not really. Ballard's fingerprints and his semen don't rule out consensual sex, and that's what Ballard claims."

"What about the other two girls?" Grace asked.

"We have no DNA evidence on them, and their lineup identification of Ballard was a little shaky, but the fact that there are two other women who accuse Ballard makes the defense's theory that the victims are just too ashamed to admit to an affair with him a little less likely."

Del nodded grimly. "So, a lot will depend on Dawn."

Grace sighed. "When Dawn decided not to become a cop, I thought that at least my daughter would be safe from this kind of crime."

Del, who had silently taken position behind her, squeezed her shoulder.

Another deep sigh, and then Grace straightened and smiled at Aiden. "At least she was lucky having you as the detective working her case...and as a friend. I know how comforting having one of those strong cop shoulders to cry on can be." She patted the hand resting on her shoulder.

"Oh, yes, that's us boys and girls in blue, always ready to lend a hand or a shoulder." Del grinned.

Grace turned so she was facing her. "Well, I'm glad that this time it was a girl in blue offering her shoulder. The last thing Dawn needs now is to fall in love with another cop. It would break her heart to lose another loved one to this job, to worry every time he goes to work, to jump every time the phone rings when he's out in the field. I wouldn't wish that for her." Her eyes clouded over as if she were remembering her own pain.

Aiden bowed her head. She understood Grace's sorrows. What she didn't understand was why Grace excluded her as a possible love interest for Dawn. Either she wasn't as aware of her daughter's sexual orientation as Dawn thought, or she was deeply in denial. *Or she just knows that you're so not the woman for Dawn and is trying to warn you off.*

Her cell phone chirped, announcing a text message. She looked at the display. It was a message from Ray, telling her that they finally had the warrant on McPherson. "I have to go." She hesitated for a second and then added, "Give my best to Dawn."

Kade rounded the prosecution table and looked down at the bald man on the witness stand. "Doctor Van Hayden, would you tell us your profession, please?"

"I'm an emergency room physician at Portland General Hospital."

"How long have you been practicing medicine?" Kade asked, determined not to let the defense undermine the credibility of one of her witnesses again.

"It'll be twenty years in December."

Kade paused to give the jurors a moment to let that sink in. "And how many rape survivors have you treated in that time?"

Doctor Van Hayden shrugged. "A lot, but I don't know the exact number."

But Kade did. She looked down at the paper in her hand. "Would it surprise you to hear that you were involved in the treatment of two hundred eight rape victims?"

"Not at all. That sounds about right."

Now that the vast experience of the witness had been established, Kade moved on. "Did you also treat Dr. Kinsley?"

"I did."

"What were the findings of your medical examination?" Kade asked.

"I found bruises on her upper arms, thighs, on the right side of her face, and in the pelvic region," the doctor said. "There were bite marks on her breasts and a hairline fracture on her right index finger."

"Your Honor, I move People's exhibits nine, ten, eleven, and twelve into evidence. Doctor, are these the photographs that were taken during your examination?" Kade laid the pictures out in front of him.

Van Hayden nodded. "Yes, they are."

Kade walked the photographs over to the jury box and handed them to the juror closest to her. She watched the faces of the jury members while they saw Dawn's injuries for the first time. When dealing with a jury, the old saying was true: A picture was worth a thousand words. Finally, she turned back to her witness. "In your professional opinion, Doctor, what has usually been the cause of injuries similar to those you found on Dr. Kinsley?"

"Objection!" D'Aquino jumped up. "Counsel is asking for a personal opinion."

Linehan looked at him like a mother reprimanding her toddler. "Opinion testimony is admissible in the area of specialized knowledge that an expert witness is qualified in. You know that, Mr. D'Aquino. The objection is overruled. Please answer, Doctor Van Hayden."

"The bruises on her arms and thighs are consistent with restraint, and the bruise on her cheek was most likely caused by a backhanded slap to the face," the doctor answered.

"What about the bruises around her neck?" Kade asked.

The doctor looked at the photo Kade held out for him. "The pattern was not consistent with manual strangulation. I think someone pressed down on her throat with a forearm."

"You also did what is called a rape kit or sexual assault evidence collection kit on Dr. Kinsley, is that correct?"

"Yes, I did. The examination revealed seminal fluid and vaginal lacerations at the six o'clock position," Doctor Van Hayden answered.

"When you say six o'clock position, what exactly do you mean?" Kade asked for the sake of the jury. She had to make sure every juror understood the vaginal clock.

The doctor turned toward the diagram they had prepared to help illustrate his testimony. "When we do a rape examination, we mentally divide the vagina into areas. The upper part," he pointed at a certain point of the diagram, "is the twelve o'clock position while the lower part is the six o'clock position and so on."

"And what practical relevance do these positions have?"

"Injuries at the five, six, or seven o'clock position imply rape while small injuries near the twelve o'clock position are generally attributed to rough but consensual sexual activity," the doctor said.

Kade circled the lower part of the diagram. "So your medical findings corroborate that Dr. Kinsley had been raped?"

"Objection, Your Honor, leading," D'Aquino shouted across the courtroom.

Linehan nodded. "Sustained. Rephrase, Ms. Matheson."

"In your professional opinion, what conclusions can be drawn from your examination of Dr. Kinsley?" Kade asked.

"It seems very likely that she's been raped."

"Thank you, Doctor. No further questions."

D'Aquino stood. "Doctor Van Hayden, isn't it true that bruises can be caused by rough, consensual sex too?"

"Yes."

"And isn't it also true that pressure against the throat to cut off the air is sometimes used to enhance sexual pleasure?"

The doctor nodded. "Yes. The lack of oxygen can heighten sexual excitement."

"So, bruises around the throat don't necessarily show intent to kill or seriously hurt someone, do they?"

"Not necessarily, no."

Kade gritted her teeth. The defense attorney was keeping his questions general and wide enough that the doctor had to agree.

"Is it correct that there are other common signs of rape?" D'Aquino looked down at his notes. "For example injuries to the vaginal fourchette and the perineum?"

The doctor inclined his head. "In some cases, yes."

"And did you find lacerations at the fourchette when you examined Ms. Kinsley?"

"No, I didn't."

D'Aquino nodded with a grave expression. "What about injuries to the perineum? Did you find that?"

"No, I didn't," Van Hayden said.

"We heard that you've been a doctor for twenty years," D'Aquino said. "In this time, have you ever encountered injuries you believed to be caused by rough but consensual sex?"

The doctor smiled. "After twenty years in the ER, there's not much I haven't encountered."

"So, that's a yes?"

"It is."

"And did the patients usually tell the truth and give rough sex play as the cause of their injuries?" D'Aquino asked.

"Only when it was so obvious that they couldn't get away with any other explanation."

The defense attorney rubbed his chin. "Other explanations... such as?"

"Falling out of bed or household accidents."

"Did someone ever try to claim she had been raped even though the injuries were caused by rough sex?"

Kade was on her feet in a second. "Objection! Your Honor, this is another attempt to accuse the victims of lying and put them on trial here."

"Sustained," Linehan said. "Mr. D'Aquino, I have spoken to you on this matter already. Cease that line of questioning, or you shall be held in contempt of court. You will have the opportunity to question Dr. Kinsley's credibility when she takes the stand. Do I make myself clear?"

"Yes, Your Honor." D'Aquino straightened his tie and turned back to the witness. "Doctor, did you run a toxicological analysis on the blood sample taken from Ms. Kinsley?"

"No, that's not part of standard procedure. The blood is taken to test for sexually transmitted diseases."

"So there's no way to prove whether Ms. Kinsley had been drinking?" D'Aquino asked.

The doctor furrowed his brow. "I didn't notice—"

"Yes or no, please: can you prove if Ms. Kinsley had been drinking or not?"

"We can't determine the blood alcohol level, no," the doctor said.

"Thank you, nothing further."

Kade rose for her redirect examination. "Doctor Van Hayden, how close did you stand to Dr. Kinsley while you examined her?"

"Objection, relevance?" D'Aquino said without getting up.

"The relevance will become clear with my next question, Your Honor," Kade said.

Linehan fixed her with a strict gaze. "It had better, Counselor. Overruled. Continue, Doctor Van Hayden."

"I had to stand very close to Dr. Kinsley," the doctor answered.

"Close enough to smell alcohol on her breath if she had been drinking heavily?" Kade asked.

This time, D'Aquino stood. "Objection, leading and speculation!"

"Your Honor, we have already established the witness's credibility as a medical practitioner for twenty years. During this time, he has surely dealt with intoxicated patients, and he is experienced enough to recognize such a state."

"Overruled," the judge said. "The witness may answer the question."

Kade gave Dr. Van Hayden an encouraging nod.

"I didn't notice the smell of alcohol on Dr. Kinsley's breath," he said.

"Doctor, is the lack of injuries to the perineum or the fourchette proof in itself that the alleged victim is lying and no rape has occurred?"

"No, not at all. Only some rape victims show injuries to the fourchette, and injuries to the perineum are rather rare," the doctor answered. "The majority of rape victims don't have signs of genital trauma."

"Nothing further, thank you." Kade was glad to sit down. Her feet were starting to hurt after a full court day in high heels.

"Thank you, Doctor Van Hayden. That will complete your testimony. You may step down. I suggest we break for the day and reconvene tomorrow." Linehan raised her gavel. "Court is adjourned."

Across town, Dawn was sitting in the busy waiting area of Portland General Hospital, her back pressed against the uncomfortable plastic chair in an attempt to make herself feel more grounded. She had never liked hospitals, but now the smell of disinfectant made her heart race and her breathing catch. *Get yourself together. You can't have a panic attack. Not here.*

"Hey," a voice said right next to her.

Dawn jerked and glanced up into eyes the color of honey. "Detective Carlisle!" Her voice trembled with relief at having her personal guardian angel show up.

"Hello." Aiden ran her fingers through her unruly black hair before wrapping her hands around the gold shield on her belt. "What are you doing here? Everything all right?"

"Yes," Dawn said. "I'm just here to get this splint removed and my finger X-rayed to see if it's all healed up." She held up her right index finger. "And you? Everything okay?" She let her gaze travel over Aiden's long legs, her trim waist, and up a muscular yet feminine upper body. Aiden certainly seemed to be in perfect health and didn't look as if she needed medical attention.

"I'm here on a case," Aiden said.

"Oh." *What did you expect? That she somehow knew about your appointment and came to hold your hand? To her, you are just a victim in one of her cases—one of many.* She bit her lip. "Then I shouldn't keep you."

Aiden eased her tall frame down onto the plastic chair next to Dawn's. "I have a few minutes."

"Are you sure?" As much as Dawn needed Aiden's company, she knew there was another rape survivor who needed it more. Aiden's presence had been the only thing that had made her rape kit examination halfway bearable, and she didn't want to deprive anyone else of that soothing presence.

Aiden nodded. "I'm sure. The victim..." She hesitated. "She's in a coma, and the doctors aren't sure if she'll ever wake up."

Dawn closed her eyes for a moment. "Maybe," she said when she opened them again, "maybe I've been lucky." She didn't feel lucky, but compared to a woman who might spend the rest of her life in a coma...

Aiden said nothing. She sat next to Dawn, silently keeping her company until a doctor called Dawn into the examination room. Aiden stood too. "Take care."

"You too, Detective." Dawn watched her walk away. When the doctor called her name again, she shook herself out of her daze and stepped into the examination room.

CHAPTER 19

Aiden adjusted the Plexiglas safety glasses and the earmuffs and moved the target back to the twenty-five-yard line. She spread her feet for balance and gripped the butt of her Glock, one hand supporting the other. After pulling the trigger five times, she stepped back and pressed the button to retrieve the target for closer inspection. She smiled with satisfaction. Not only had all five rounds hit the black paper, they had all landed in the target's center and head.

"Would you look at that, boys?" Okada said from behind her. "Is this part of your evil plan to humiliate your colleagues?"

Aiden laughed. "Oh, you don't need me for that. You manage it all on your own."

"Don't listen to Okada," Ray said. "He's just jealous because he wants to have a partner who scores ninety-eight too, instead of one who barely passed the requalification."

"I had something in my eye." Ruben rubbed the eye in question.

"Yes—the female range instructor who stood there, trying not to laugh," Okada said.

Ruben squared his shoulders. "She wasn't laughing. She was ogling me. She even agreed to go out with me." Grinning, he waved a piece of paper with her phone number.

Okada shook his head. "Some women will do anything out of pity."

"If this is how you shoot when you take pity on these guys,

I'd like to see your score when you shoot without mercy," another voice said from behind Aiden.

When Aiden turned and recognized Lieutenant Del Vasquez, she hastily took off her safety glasses.

The three men exchanged glances. "I think we'll try the outdoor range," Ray said. "There's still hope that we can beat you there, Aiden." He dragged his colleagues from the room.

"Do you have a minute, Detective?" Del pointed at the door.

"Sure." While following her outside, Aiden wondered what Del was doing here. The only thing they had in common, other than their work, was Dawn. After what Grace had said about not wanting Dawn to become involved with a cop, Aiden dreaded the conversation Del wanted to have with her.

Once they stepped outside, Del turned toward her. "I'll get straight to the point."

Aiden nodded, preferring not to suffer for long.

Del looked her right in the eyes. "I want you to hook me up with your deputy DA."

Aiden almost swallowed her tongue. Coughing, she stared at Del. *Good to know my gaydar's still in full working order, but...Kade? What the hell?*

Del rolled her eyes and laughed, a dark, husky sound. "Get your mind out of the gutter, Detective. I'm neither straight nor blind, but the hookup I requested was meant in a strictly professional capacity."

"Oh." Aiden rubbed her neck, trying to look as if she had never assumed anything else even for a moment. "Yes, of course. What should I tell Ms. Matheson?"

"I want her to call me to the stand," Del said.

Aiden looked down at her black boots. "Lieutenant, I know you want to help Dawn. We all do. But in a criminal case, character witnesses are usually called only for the defendant, not for the victim."

Del's dark eyes narrowed. "Don't you think I know that? I've been on the job for much longer than you. I don't want Ms. Matheson to call me as a character witness. That Saturday night, I accompanied Dawn to the club."

What? Aiden stared at her. *Why didn't we know that? Shit, we should have investigated Dawn's night out in the club more thoroughly.*

"The club is not really my scene, but Dawn had never been there before, and I knew that those girls she went with would disappear from her side as soon as an attractive butch waved a beer at them, so I went with them."

"You drove her home?" Aiden knew by now how protective the older officer was of Dawn. "Then you can testify that she never took Ballard home with her."

Del's strong jaw clenched. "No. I didn't, and I can't. I left before Dawn did because all those flashing lights and the smoke were giving me a frigging headache." She closed her eyes. "God, I've wished a thousand times that I'd insisted she come with me or talked her out of—"

"It wouldn't have done you any good," Aiden said. "Dawn's too stubborn to be ordered around. And even if you'd taken her home, Ballard knew her address by then. It wouldn't have made a difference."

Del sighed. "What I can testify to is that Dawn never talked to Ballard while I was there."

"I don't want to appear disrespectful, but why didn't you offer to testify before?" Aiden asked.

"I wanted to, but, as you said, Dawn is stubborn, and she vehemently refused my offer. She didn't want to drag me into it when I didn't really see anything. I didn't like Dawn's decision, but I respected it because I know how important it is to give her complete control over her life." Del poked the toes of her boots into the gravel. "But now that it all comes down to whether the jury believes Ballard's story about consensual sex and so much rests on Dawn's shoulders, I want to testify."

"You know this could mean outing yourself in open court—"

Del stopped her with a raised hand. "I've known that girl since she was knee-high to a grasshopper and came to the station with pigtails, begging me to let her ride in a police cruiser. I couldn't love her more if she were my own daughter. If it would help get the bastard who raped her behind bars, I would out myself in front of the police commissioner by propositioning his wife."

Aiden held back a chuckle. *God, I could have used a friend like that when I grew up.* "Understood. I'll tell Kade to expect a call from you."

Del nodded and turned to go.

"So, did she ever get it?" Aiden called after her.

Del turned, raising one black eyebrow. "Did who get what?"

"Dawn," Aiden said. "Did she ever get that ride in a police cruiser that she begged you for?"

Del folded her muscular arms across her chest. "You're not implying that I misused police property for the entertainment of a little girl, are you, Detective?"

Aiden held her gaze. "I'm implying that you would do anything for that girl, Lieutenant."

Gravel crunched under Del's boots as she stepped back toward Aiden. She stopped only one foot away to study Aiden's face.

Aiden stiffened, unsure if this was the calm before the storm and Del would soon explode into a sharp reprimand.

After long moments of scrutiny, the laugh lines around Del's eyes deepened, and she allowed a smile to play around her lips. "You're all right, Detective." She clapped Aiden on the shoulder. "Treat her right, and we won't have a problem with each other."

Aiden stared after her as Del turned again and disappeared around the building. Only then did she remember that Del still hadn't answered her question about Dawn and the ride in the police cruiser.

Ray came strolling along the gravel path. He pointed in the direction in which Del had disappeared. "So, did she give you the good old 'if you hurt her, I'll hunt you down and kill you' speech?"

"I think you've watched *The Godfather* once too often," Aiden mumbled. "Why would Lieutenant Vasquez say something like that?"

Ray only smiled at her attempt to play dumb and innocent. "Because that's what I would do if one of my girls ever came home with a cop."

Aiden shook her head. "For a cop, you don't seem to hold your brothers in blue in very high esteem."

"Oh, I like my brothers in blue just fine," Ray said. "Just not as a son-in-law. Being married to a cop can be hell, and that's not what I'd want for my girls."

Aiden crossed her arms across her chest. "What would you have done if Susan's parents had said the same thing when you asked for her hand?"

"They did," Ray answered. After a second, he smiled. "Not that it was of any use."

"But of course your daughters are so much more obedient than Susan ever was."

Ray snorted. "I can't even get my daughters to keep to their curfews. I can only try to keep them away from the likes of you."

"The likes of me?" Aiden pointed at her chest.

Ray laughed. "Yes, you, Casanova."

"Hey, Aiden Crockett," Okada shouted from the outdoor shooting range. "Want to join us mere mortals and show us how it's done?"

"Only if you guys lay off these historical nicknames," Aiden called back.

Aiden watched as their forensic psychiatrist took his place on the witness stand. Renshaw was wearing his glasses, probably to appear more intelligent to the jury. Kade had once told her that this was the reason why she chose to forgo contact lenses or corrective operations. Aiden could have told her another reason. *Women with glasses are really sexy!* For a moment, she thought about the new turquoise-rimmed glasses Dawn wore before she forced her attention back to the trial.

"Doctor Renshaw, can you tell us about your involvement with the investigation in this case?" Kade asked.

"Detectives Carlisle and Bennet contacted me to look at the crime scene photos," Renshaw said. "I noticed right away that the perpetrator attacked not only the women but also their belongings, as if he harbored personal anger toward them."

Kade tacked enhanced photographs of the chaos in the victims' bedrooms to a board.

"He destroyed books, magazines, and DVDs with lesbian content, but we only discovered that later," Renshaw continued.

"What were your conclusions when you discovered the connection between the cases of Dr. Kinsley, Ms. Riggs, and Ms. Matthews?" Kade asked.

"I came to the conclusion that we were dealing with a rapist who had a homophobic motive. Rape is not about sexual satisfaction. It's about control and power. The perpetrator wanted to exert control over lesbian women. He wanted them to experience and go back to a heterosexual life."

"Why would he want them to do that?" Kade tilted her head and sent him a questioning gaze, as if she didn't already know the answer.

Renshaw looked over at Ballard, who stared at him from the defense table. "Mr. Ballard's mother left the family to live with another woman. He was just eight, so he had no power to prevent it."

"Can you offer an explanation as to why Mr. Ballard didn't use a condom?"

"Objection," D'Aquino called. "Irrelevant and no personal knowledge."

Kade turned toward the judge. "I'm not asking for personal knowledge but for the professional opinion of an expert, Your Honor."

"Overruled," Judge Linehan said. "The jury will keep in mind that this is only one possible explanation, and you'll later have enough opportunities to offer alternative explanations, Mr. D'Aquino." She nodded at Renshaw to answer.

"He wanted these women to experience his masculinity without barriers," Renshaw said. "He wanted them to see how good 'sex' with a man could be. For the same reason, he broke Dr. Kinsley's finger and hit the other women when they tried to look away from him. He wanted them to know that they were with him, a man, not leaving them any room to fantasize about being with a woman."

"That sounds like a man who is blinded by hate. Would you say that the defendant's mind was clear enough to know right from wrong?" Kade asked.

Good. She's covering all the bases. Aiden nodded. Knowing Ballard's weaselly lawyer, he would otherwise try to portray Ballard as a poor man, who, abandoned by his evil lesbian mother, was not to blame for his own behavior.

"He knew what he was doing, and he knew it was wrong," Renshaw said. "Despite his anger and hate, he was clear enough to get a job in a lesbian club, which gave him access to the victims' addresses."

"What about Mr. Ballard's contention that the sex was consensual and the victims are lying?" Kade asked.

"I have had an opportunity to interview the three women, and I highly doubt that they agreed to have sex with Mr. Ballard. The two earlier victims had never been in any form of a relationship with a male before, and while Dr. Kinsley had been married, her relationships since then have been strictly with women. In addition, at least one of the victims was completely in the closet at the time of the attack and would have had no reason to cover up an affair with a man."

"Thank you, Doctor." Kade passed D'Aquino on her way back to her own table. "Your witness."

The defense attorney straightened his tie and looked at the bearded psychiatrist. "How long have you worked with the Sexual Assault Detail?"

"Almost a year now," Renshaw answered.

"Have you written any books or journal articles or done any studies on sex crimes?"

"No, not yet."

Aiden gritted her teeth. D'Aquino had an uncanny talent to make Kade's experts sound like inexperienced bunglers.

"How many diagnostic interviews did you do with my client before forming your theories about the alleged homophobic rape motives?" D'Aquino asked.

"Mr. Ballard refused to talk to me."

D'Aquino rested his hands on the witness-box and leaned forward. "So, that would be zero, right?"

"Yes."

"Thanks, nothing further."

Kade stood. "Redirect, Your Honor?"

"Mr. D'Aquino didn't give you much scope to work within, Ms. Matheson," Linehan said.

"I'll stay within the scope of the cross, Your Honor," Kade said. "I have just one question."

Finally, the judge nodded. "Proceed."

"Doctor Renshaw, how could you form an opinion of Mr. Ballard if you couldn't interview him?" Kade asked.

"Interviews are not the only sources of information for a trained psychologist or psychiatrist," Renshaw answered. "I could rely on observation, physical evidence from the crime scenes, the police report from his interrogation, which I witnessed, and I talked at length with a social worker who had contact with the Ballard family during the divorce of Mr. Ballard's parents. His father and later his grandparents managed to get sole custody, and they prevented any contact with his mother, so the only thing Garett Ballard knows about lesbians is the hate-filled image he learned from his father and his grandparents."

Kade gave a curt nod. "No more questions."

Judge Linehan excused Renshaw. "Are you ready to proceed with your next witness, Ms. Matheson?"

"Yes, Your Honor," Kade said from the prosecution's table. "The People call Lieutenant Delicia Vasquez Montero to the stand."

Aiden, still sitting in the first row of the gallery, held her breath. This late in the trial, Linehan could easily deny Del's testimony.

D'Aquino jumped up from his seat. "The defense objects, Your Honor! Lieutenant Vasquez Montero has never been identified as a possible witness."

"It was only recently brought to my attention that she might have information relevant to this case, Your Honor," Kade said.

Linehan peered at Kade from her place on the bench, like a hawk looking down at a field mouse from its aerie. "Counselor, approach."

Kade stepped to the bench and listened to whatever the judge had to say.

From her place in the gallery, Aiden couldn't make out what Linehan told the DDA, but it was easy to see that the judge wasn't happy about new witnesses appearing out of nowhere and told her so in no uncertain words.

Kade returned to her seat, and Linehan waved to the bailiff. "Lieutenant Vasquez may testify."

D'Aquino didn't sit down. "But, Your Honor…"

"We'll take a recess after the direct examination, leaving you ample time to prepare for your cross-exam," Linehan said.

Del entered and strode toward the witness stand without looking left or right. Her posture and her voice when she swore to tell the truth were confident, and Aiden had to admire her professionalism in this personal situation.

"Lieutenant Vasquez." Kade nodded at her witness, and Aiden remembered her misunderstanding that Del had requested a hookup of the nonprofessional kind with the DDA. Then Kade began her questioning, and all other thoughts disappeared. "You are a decorated police officer, but you're not here in that function today, is that correct?"

"Yes, that's right."

"How do you know Dr. Kinsley?"

For a second, Del's gaze wandered to the gallery, where Grace Kinsley sat. "I was partnered with her father, James Kinsley, for ten years. I've known Dr. Kinsley for twenty years."

"Do you see her a lot?" Kade asked.

"About once a week," Del said. "I'm invited to all of the family dinners."

"And did you see Dr. Kinsley on the evening of October fifth?"

"Yes, I did. I went with her to the club."

"Why did Dr. Kinsley go to the club on this evening?" Kade asked.

"Objection, speculation!" came D'Aquino's protest from the defense table. "The witness is not a mind reader. She can't know Ms. Kinsley's thoughts."

"Withdrawn," Kade said before Linehan could force her to do it. "Why did you go to the club, Lieutenant?"

Del shrugged. "To kick back after an exhausting week, have

a drink, dance, talk to Dr. Kinsley and some other friends—the usual."

"The usual," Kade repeated. "So, picking up men wasn't a part of your plans for the evening?"

"Objection!"

"Overruled," Linehan said before D'Aquino had even finished voicing his objection. "I want to hear this."

An ironic half smile flitted across Del's face. "We wouldn't have gone to a lesbian club if it had been."

"Did Dr. Kinsley talk to a man during the evening?" Kade asked.

"There weren't that many to talk to, and no, she didn't. She never talked to anyone other than me and the two friends who came with us."

"Did she talk to Mr. Ballard when you entered the club?" Kade asked.

Del shook her head. "No. She handed over her ID when he requested it, but she didn't give him a second glance."

"Thank you, Lieutenant. Nothing further." Kade walked away from the witness stand just as Linehan banged her gavel.

The hour of recess Linehan had granted the defense to prepare for Del's cross-examination seemed to drag by slowly. Aiden was glad that she had taken the day off, because otherwise, the unplanned witness would have caused her to miss Dawn's testimony later today.

Finally, sixty long minutes were over, and the bailiff called them back into the courtroom.

D'Aquino took position in front of the witness stand. "On the evening in question, did you leave the club with Ms. Kinsley?"

"No," Del said. "I left an hour or two before she did."

"Oh?" D'Aquino looked at her in fake surprise. "Then it is possible that Ms. Kinsley talked to my client and you just hadn't seen it because you'd already left the club?"

"Objection! Speculation," Kade called. "The witness has no personal knowledge and can't testify to what might or might not have happened during her absence."

"Sustained."

D'Aquino gave up that line of questioning. He had already shown that Del hadn't been a witness to the whole evening. "You said that you've known Ms. Kinsley for twenty years?"

"Yes."

"And in this time, have you ever known Ms. Kinsley to sleep with a man?"

Aiden clenched her hands to fists, and from the tensing in Del's shoulders, it wasn't hard to guess that, hidden by the witness-box, she was doing the same.

"Objection, Your Honor!" Kade leaned across the prosecutor's table to fix D'Aquino with an indignant stare. "Dr. Kinsley's sexual history is inadmissible."

"Your Honor, Ms. Matheson opened the door to the question by asking about Ms. Kinsley's plans to pick up men on the night in question," D'Aquino said.

"The objection is overruled," Linehan said after a moment of hesitation. "The witness will answer the question."

Del took a moment before answering.

Probably to unclench her teeth, Aiden thought grimly.

"She was married, but—"

"A simple yes or no, please," D'Aquino said.

Del's shoulders slumped. "Yes."

The defense attorney smiled. "No further questions."

Kade stood for the redirect before D'Aquino had reached his own table. "Lieutenant Vasquez, to your knowledge, does Dr. Kinsley regularly frequent nightclubs?"

Del shook her head. "Not regularly. Work kept her busy, but she would find the time now and then."

"And how often did you accompany Dr. Kinsley on these evenings out?"

"A fair number of times."

"On those occasions, did you see Dr. Kinsley flirt with any men?" Kade asked.

Aiden relaxed her tense muscles. There was no way that Kade would let D'Aquino get away with manipulating all her witnesses. Kade had to get the jury to see Dawn in a good light since her testimony came next.

"No," Del answered, her voice firm.

"Lieutenant Vasquez, is it safe to assume that you know Dr. Kinsley well?"

"Like my own daughter, yes." Del looked toward the gallery for a moment.

"So it would also be safe to assume that she confides in you?" Kade asked.

"Yes, she does."

"Did she ever confide in you that she brought a man home for the night?"

Aiden didn't like this line of questioning, but she knew that since D'Aquino had poked into Dawn's love life, Kade had to do the same. Still, she was glad that Dawn didn't have to witness this dissection of her private life.

The corner of Del's mouth twitched as if she didn't know whether she should become angry or laugh at the mere suggestion. "No, as far as I know, Dawn has never had a one-night stand with anyone, male or female. It's just not her thing."

Aiden looked away. *Wish I could say that for myself.*

"Then can you tell us about her romantic interests in the last few years?" Kade asked.

Aiden turned her head and looked at Grace, who was sitting two seats down the row. She looked pale, her lips pressed together.

Del looked at Grace for a moment too before she answered.

"She hasn't been in a relationship with a man or shown any interest in men for the last five years."

"Nothing further." Kade sat back down.

Linehan raised her gavel. "We'll break for lunch now and reconvene in two hours. Court is adjourned."

CHAPTER 20

AIDEN LENGTHENED HER STRIDE WHEN she saw Grace Kinsley in the courthouse hallway. She looked around for Dawn but didn't see her anywhere. "Where's Dawn?" Nervousness hummed through Aiden's every vein, and she wasn't sure if she was nervous because Dawn had to testify soon or because this would be the first time in a week she'd see her.

"In there." Grace directed a concerned glance at the door of the ladies' room.

"Is she okay?"

Grace sighed. "She has hardly eaten or slept in two days. I hope it'll all be over soon."

Aiden couldn't agree more. "I'll go and see how she's doing."

When she entered the bathroom, it was empty except for one person. Dawn stood hunched over one of the sinks, leaning heavily on it with both hands. Her head hung down, and when she finally lifted it, drops of water glistened on her pale face. At least Aiden hoped it was water, not tears rolling down her cheeks.

Dawn looked at Aiden in the mirror. "What are you doing here?" she asked without turning around.

Aiden shrugged. "I took the day off to watch the trial and offer a little support."

A small smile formed on Dawn's lips. "That's nice of you. Thank you."

"I built up so much overtime that my lieutenant was breathing down my neck to take some time off anyway." Aiden didn't want

Dawn to think she was behaving unprofessionally and giving her special treatment—even though she was.

"I'm not too proud to admit I need all the support I can get." Dawn exhaled shakily.

Aiden stepped closer and gently touched Dawn's back. "You okay?"

"I'd be in there," Dawn pointed to one of the stalls, "chucking up my lunch if I'd eaten anything. I just hope I don't have a flashback right there on the stand or freeze up and—"

"It'll be all right." Aiden moved her hand in small, soothing circles over Dawn's stiff back. "If you need a break, just ask for one. Linehan will grant it."

Dawn took a deep breath and turned. "Okay." She searched Aiden's face. "Can I have a good-luck hug?"

Without hesitation, Aiden opened her arms. Dawn needed the reassurance, and Aiden didn't care who might walk in on them. She wrapped her arms around Dawn and inhaled deeply. "I'll be right there, sitting in the first row, okay?" she whispered into the blonde hair.

Dawn said nothing. She rested against Aiden for a few seconds before she stepped back and squared her shoulders. "Let's go."

"Dawn?" Aiden said before Dawn could open the door. "Did you ever ride in a police cruiser?"

A small smile formed on Dawn's lips. "Are you asking if I've ever been arrested?"

Aiden returned the smile. "No, that's not why I'm asking."

"Ah, then is it an offer to spring me out of here with lights and sirens?"

Aiden chuckled. "Sorry, no, it's not. I'm just curious."

"Once around the parking lot of patrol district eight-nineteen—without lights and sirens, though," Dawn said, smiling fondly at the memory.

"Did she get into trouble over it?" Aiden asked.

"She?"

"Your driver."

"What makes you think it was a she?" Dawn asked.

Aiden shrugged and grinned. "Let's just call it detective's intuition."

They stepped out into the hallway and joined Grace and Del, who had arrived by now. "Sorry I'm late. I got held up at the station. Are you okay?" Del wrapped one arm around Dawn.

Dawn nodded and started down the hallway. She stopped in front of the dark oak doors separating them from the courtroom.

"Want me to wait with you in the witness room?" Aiden asked, even though that would mean that she wouldn't be able to hear Dawn's testimony.

"No, you three go on in. I'll see you in a few minutes." Dawn hugged her mother and Del and then walked down the hallway toward the witness room.

After watching her for a few seconds, Aiden held open the double doors for Grace and Del and entered behind them.

A court clerk opened the doors for her, and Dawn took her first steps into the courtroom. Her gaze immediately fell onto Garret Ballard, who had turned in his seat and was smirking at her.

Dawn looked away and took another step. Her vision blurred, and a wave of dizziness overcame her. Her steps faltered. She pressed a hand to her heaving chest, afraid that she would faint. Then her vision cleared a little, and she glanced at the gallery, where her friends and family were looking at her with concerned expressions. Forcing a small smile, she nodded at them and resumed her way toward the witness stand.

As she was sworn in, the smooth, cool leather of the Bible

under her palm calmed her, perhaps because it reminded her of Aiden's favorite jacket.

Kade stopped next to the witness-box and set down a glass of water in front of Dawn, who gave her a nod for the thoughtful gesture. "Doctor Kinsley, can you tell us what happened on the night of October fifth?"

Dawn's mouth went dry, and she took a sip of water. "I had been out to a club called Rainbows that evening with three friends. I had come home alone. Around three o'clock, a loud noise woke me up. At first I thought it was my cat, but when I went to investigate, there was a man standing in my living room." She remembered that moment of terror with startling clarity. She had stood there, frozen for a second, not sure if she was awake or still dreaming.

"Go on," Kade said.

"He had a gun. He pressed me against the wall with his forearm across my throat and pointed the gun at my temple. He said he would kill me if I tried to escape or call for help." Dawn looked straight at Kade, avoiding even a fleeting glance at Garret Ballard, afraid that she would lose her composure. "He ripped the phone cord from the wall and threw my cell phone out of the window. Then he dragged me back into the bedroom."

Kade nodded grimly. "What happened in there?"

Dawn took a few careful breaths, trying not to hyperventilate. This time, she avoided looking at the gallery. She hadn't told her mother any details about the rape, and she didn't want to see the expression on her mother's face when she heard them for the first time. "He pushed me down onto the bed and ripped my clothes. He forced my legs apart with one hand while the other kept pressing the gun against my head." She had to force out every word past the lump in her throat, knowing that she needed to paint a detailed picture for the jury. "Then he raped me."

"Did he say anything?" Kade asked.

Dawn's fingers tightened around her water glass. "He told me to look at him—and he hit me anytime I tried to turn my head away. When I covered my eyes with my hand, he broke my finger. He wanted me to see who was doing this to me."

"Did he say anything else?"

"H-he..." Dawn shook her head to clear it when her vision began to blur. "He said I shouldn't just lie there like a dead fish and to stop acting as if I didn't enjoy being fucked by a real man." The words left a bad taste in her mouth, so she emptied her water glass.

Kade waited for a few seconds. "What happened next?"

"When he finally...ejaculated, he backhanded me one last time and then started to throw things from my bookcase around and trample them," Dawn said.

"Can you tell us what things specifically?" Kade asked.

That night, Dawn had lain there, trying to remove her mind from the present and not notice anything he did. But she had looked at photos of her bedroom a few weeks later. "Some books with lesbian characters, a few lesbian movies, the photographs and sketches of my ex-girlfriend, and a few other things that were in the way."

"Doctor Kinsley, had you ever seen the man who raped you before that night?"

"Well..." Dawn cleared her throat. "I thought I hadn't, but it turned out I just hadn't paid him any attention. He was the doorman of the club I went to that evening."

"Did you ever talk to that man before?" Kade asked.

Dawn shook her head emphatically. "No, never."

"Is the man who raped you here in this courtroom today?" Kade stepped to the side so Dawn could get a clear view of the courtroom.

For the first time, Dawn was forced to look directly at Garett

Ballard. She wondered how he could return her gaze so coolly. "Yes."

"Would you point that man out for the jury, please?"

Slowly, Dawn raised her hand and pointed at Ballard. Her fingers were shaking.

"Your Honor, may the record reflect that the witness identified the defendant, Mr. Ballard, as the man who raped her," Kade said.

The judge nodded. "Let the record so indicate."

"Dr. Kinsley, you said the man threatened you with a gun. Could you describe it?"

"It was a Glock 17."

Kade held up a transparent evidence bag with a red seal. "Have you ever seen this weapon, indexed as People's exhibit seven, before?"

Dawn looked at the semiautomatic pistol. "It's the Glock he held to my temple."

"Objection, Your Honor!" D'Aquino's voice boomed through the courtroom, making Dawn jump. "Move to strike. The witness is a psychologist, not a weapons expert. She can't identify individual weapons."

Linehan looked from him to Dawn. "Overruled. You can impeach her ability to identify the weapon in your cross-examination, Counselor."

"Doctor, you were able to help the police with their investigation. How so?" Kade asked.

"I work as a rape counselor, and I noticed the similarities of a patient's case to my own. After the patient agreed to waive patient-doctor confidentiality, I alerted Detective Carlisle to the fact that the rapes might have a homophobic motive," Dawn said, feeling more confident now that her testimony resembled that of an expert witness, not that of a victim.

"And after they arrested Mr. Ballard, did the police ask for your help again?"

Dawn looked over to the gallery and made eye contact with Aiden for a second. "They asked me to come to the station for a lineup."

"What were the results?" Kade asked.

"I was able to identify Mr. Ballard as the man who had raped me."

Kade nodded, looking back over her shoulder at Ballard. "How sure of that identification were you?"

"One hundred percent," Dawn said without hesitation.

"Thank you. No further questions for now, Your Honor."

Dawn pressed her lips together as Kade sat down and the defense attorney approached.

"Ms. Kinsley, do you own a gun?"

"No, I don't." After much consideration, Dawn had decided not to buy a gun after all.

"So, you're not a weapons expert?"

Now Dawn knew what he was trying to achieve with the question. He wanted to poke holes into her identification of Ballard's gun. "Not in the strictest sense of the word, no."

"Did you know that Smith & Wesson is being sued by Glock because Smith & Wesson's Sigma series is very similar to the Glock?" D'Aquino asked.

Dawn pressed her lips together. She had to answer truthfully even though the question had nothing to do with her ability to identify Ballard's weapon. "No, I didn't know that."

The defense attorney held up another evidence bag with a gun in it. It had the same black polymer plastic grip the Glock had. "I submit defense's exhibit one, a pistol produced by Smith & Wesson, into evidence."

"Received."

He turned back to Dawn. "Ms. Kinsley—"

"Doctor," Dawn said. She wouldn't let him get away with his attempts to make her look less than she was.

D'Aquino nodded. "Dr. Kinsley, do you think someone who is not a weapons expert could tell the difference between a Smith & Wesson and a Glock?"

"I can—"

"Answer my question, please," D'Aquino said.

Dawn bit her lip. "Most probably couldn't." She hoped Kade would pick up the question in her re-examination.

D'Aquino stepped closer to Dawn, and she already dreaded his next question. "Dr. Kinsley, you said you'd been out to a club on the night in question?"

"Yes."

"How much did you have to drink?"

Kade's objection saved Dawn from having to answer. "Objection, relevance? Even if Dr. Kinsley had been drunk—which she wasn't—engaging in sexual intercourse with a person who is incapable of consent because of intoxication is still rape."

"Don't lecture me on the law, Ms. Matheson." The judge glared at her. "Overruled. Please answer the question, Doctor Kinsley."

"I had one low-alcohol cocktail, nothing more," Dawn answered.

"Did you limit yourself because you're not used to alcohol?" D'Aquino asked.

Anger began to replace the fear Dawn felt. "I limited myself because I was the designated driver and still had to drive home."

"Still, isn't it true that you don't drink a lot and are not used to alcohol?"

Has that suddenly become a bad thing? Dawn frowned.

"Objection!" Kade stood again. "Already asked and answered. He's badgering the witness."

"Sustained. Move on, Counselor." Linehan waved at the defense attorney.

"You said you are a rape counselor?"

Now that they were back in familiar territory, Dawn could breathe more freely. "Yes. I do one-on-one and group counseling of survivors of rape and sexual abuse. Or rather, that was what I did before I was raped." It hurt to admit that perhaps she would never work with those patients again.

"You only worked with rape victims?" D'Aquino asked.

"There's no 'only' about it, Mr. D'Aquino, but yes, I work...I worked exclusively with rape and sexual abuse victims."

D'Aquino stepped closer. "Are you obsessed with rape, Doctor? Is every man automatically a rapist for you?"

Kade was on her feet before he had uttered the last word. "Objection! Your Honor!"

"That is enough, Mr. D'Aquino." Linehan's voice rose. "You have been warned repeatedly to cease that line of questioning. I am hereby imposing a fine of two hundred dollars for contempt of court. Make one more attempt and you will be enjoying the hospitality of the county tonight. The jury is instructed to disregard Mr. D'Aquino's question, and it shall be stricken from the records."

Breathing heavily, Dawn watched as the defense attorney got an earful from the judge. Linehan had stricken D'Aquino's questions, but the jury had heard them and what they implied. The damage had been done. She looked at Kade and then across the courtroom at Aiden, Del, and her mother. All of them gave her reassuring nods, helping her to regain her composure.

Finally, D'Aquino returned to his position in front of the witness stand. "Ms. Kinsley, when Mr. Ballard took you to the bedroom," he began, choosing words that could imply that she had willingly followed him as easily as they could imply the use of force, "did you do or say anything that he could have misunderstood as a sign of consent?"

"What? No!"

"You didn't compliment him?" D'Aquino rested one hand on the witness-box, leaning toward her.

Dawn wildly shook her head. "I didn't."

"Then it is not true that you told my client that he's handsome?"

Dawn opened her mouth for another vehement "no," but then closed it again. *Oh, dear God! He's trying to use that against me?* She hadn't been prepared for it.

"Ms. Kinsley?"

She bit her lip and laid a hand over her eyes. "I..."

"Your Honor, please instruct the witness to answer the question," D'Aquino said.

"Doctor Kinsley." Linehan's voice was gentle but firm. "You have to answer."

"I told him—"

"A yes or no answer is enough," D'Aquino said.

Dawn clenched her teeth. "Yes."

"And did you not also tell my client you were sure that there were a lot of women who found him attractive and would like to sleep with him?"

Dawn looked down at her hands, aware that her words sounded like the compliments of a lover, even though they had been a victim's desperate attempts to talk her way out of a rape. "Yes, but—"

"And is it not also true that, while you were in bed with Mr. Ballard, you never sounded scared?"

"I tried not to—"

"Yes or no?"

Dawn sighed. "Yes."

"Nothing further."

When the defense attorney moved away from her and sat back down, Dawn heaved a sigh of relief.

Kade looked calm and collected as she stood again. "Doctor

Kinsley, is there a reason why you told Mr. Ballard things that sounded complimentary?"

"Yes!" Now that Dawn could finally say it, the words were practically shooting out of her. "I was trying to talk him out of raping me. I told him he didn't have to resort to violence to get a woman to sleep with him."

"Did you have the impression that he took that to mean you would sleep with him out of your own free will?" Kade asked.

"Objection!" D'Aquino called. "Prosecution is calling for an opinion."

"Your Honor, Doctor Kinsley is not only a victim, she's an experienced psychologist specializing in rape cases," Kade said. "Her opinion is more than the mere speculation of a lay witness."

"Objection overruled," Linehan said. "Doctor Kinsley, please summarize your impression for the jury."

"Mr. Ballard knew I wasn't consenting," Dawn said. "He didn't listen to a word I said. He told me to shut up and hit me. He threatened me with his gun the whole time. I submitted to him because I feared for my life, but that doesn't equal consent."

Kade pointed back toward the defense table. "Mr. D'Aquino mentioned that you didn't sound particularly scared that night. Is there a reason for that?"

"Yes. In my professional experience, begging and crying sends a weak psychological message. Studies have shown that people who sound like victims have a higher probability of becoming victims, so I tried to reason with him instead."

Kade nodded. "One last question. Why is it that you're so sure regarding the weapon Mr. Ballard used during the attack?"

"My father, my older brother, my ex-husband, and several of my friends were or are police officers. I've seen their duty weapons a thousand times, so I could identify a Glock anytime. And," Dawn swallowed, "I'll never forget the weapon I had to stare at for half an hour while I lay there and feared for my life."

Kade returned to her table. "Nothing further, thank you."

"Recross, Your Honor." D'Aquino approached her again. "Ms. Kinsley, is there any possibility that a man, blinded by attraction, could misread signals and misinterpret words as compliments even if the woman didn't mean it like that?"

"Yes, but—"

"Thank you," D'Aquino said. "No further questions."

Long after Linehan had decided to adjourn until the next day, Dawn sat in the witness-box, numbly staring straight ahead while each of D'Aquino's questions still echoed through her head.

CHAPTER 21

Aiden looked up as Dawn slipped into the courtroom a few minutes before the trial was set to continue. She hadn't been sure if Dawn would want to watch her rapist's testimony. Aiden stood and moved down the row, vacating her seat for Dawn so she could sit between her and Del, where she seemed to feel safest.

"Thanks." Dawn's half smile was genuine but tense.

"How are you?" Aiden asked, studying her.

Dawn's gaze flitted from the still-empty witness stand to Aiden's face. "I hate being here and having to listen to all the lies Ballard's going to tell, but I hated the thought of sitting at home and imagining what might go on in here even more."

"Just two or three more days and it'll all be over."

"Not everything will be over." Then Dawn's grim expression gentled, and she squeezed Aiden's forearm. "But I know what you mean, and that'll probably help me get my life back to some level of normalcy."

Aiden gazed down at the clammy hand on her arm. She hesitantly lifted her own hand to cover the smaller fingers, but before she could, the defense attorney called his first witness, and Dawn grabbed the edge of her seat with both hands as Garett Ballard strode toward the witness stand.

Ballard didn't blink an eye when he swore to tell the truth.

Aiden gritted her teeth. *Bastard. Every word out of your mouth will be a damn lie.*

"Garett," Victor D'Aquino used his client's first name to

make him appear more likeable to the jury, "can you tell us where you were on the evenings of June 4th, 2011, and April 21st and October 5th, 2013?"

"At work," Ballard answered, looking very much like the honest, hardworking man he had never been. "I work as a security specialist for a club on Gansevoort Street."

"What kind of club is it exactly?"

Ballard shrugged. "All kinds of people frequent the club, but mostly it's lesbians and bisexual women."

D'Aquino smiled. "So, there's not a lot of workplace romance going on, huh?"

"Oh, I wouldn't say that." Ballard showed pearly white teeth as he grinned. "I've had women come up to me and ask me straight out to come home and have a one-night stand with them."

"Objection, Your Honor!" Kade took off her glasses to look at Ballard and his attorney with unveiled disgust. "Is there any relevance to this line of questioning, or does counsel just want to give his client an opportunity to brag about his alleged conquests?"

Aiden suppressed a grin. *Go get him, Kade!*

A few people in the audience somewhere in the row behind Aiden chuckled, and Linehan sustained the objection, ordering D'Aquino to move on.

"Under what circumstances did you get to know Melanie Riggs, Jayne Matthews, and Dawn Kinsley?" D'Aquino asked.

"I never knew their names, but I knew them in the biblical sense."

Ballard's answer garnered a few laughs.

Aiden didn't find it funny in the least. Gritting her teeth, she looked at Dawn out of the corner of her eye and saw her getting even paler than she had been before.

Judge Linehan fixed the defendant with a disapproving stare, and D'Aquino quickly asked the next question before she could reprimand his client. "How did you meet them?"

"They came to the club and struck up a conversation with me," Ballard said. "They sent me drinks, and when the club finally closed, they asked me to come home with them."

"Why did you accept these invitations if you knew they were lesbians?"

Ballard looked directly at Dawn. "They were attractive, and I knew it would be sex without emotional entanglements. They wanted this one night and nothing else from me, and that was just what I wanted."

He made it sound believable; Aiden had to give him that.

"What happened when you reached the apartments you had been invited to?" D'Aquino asked.

"We usually stumbled straight to the bedroom. The last one," Ballard pointed at Dawn, "even ripped the phone line out to make sure we wouldn't be interrupted."

Aiden clenched her fists and saw Del and Grace on Dawn's other side do the same. Dawn was trembling, but Aiden couldn't tell if it was with fear or anger or maybe a mix of both.

D'Aquino nodded. "And how do you explain the bruises and bite marks the ER doctor described?"

"Some of them were into pretty wild stuff," Ballard said with a grin. "Bondage, domination, sadomasochism, sex games. They told me they liked it rough and demanded that I do it harder and make it hurt. I just went along with what they wanted."

"No," Dawn whispered. "That's not true! I didn't... That bastard!"

"I know." Aiden wanted to reach over and take Dawn's hand, but she knew it was not a good idea. She didn't want the defense attorney to think she was anything but the detective investigating her case to Dawn. "I know he's lying and everyone here is going to know it by the end of the day. Just wait for Kade's cross."

"Can you tell us why you didn't use protection with any of these women?" D'Aquino asked.

Ballard held up his hands. "I had some with me, but they didn't want me to use 'em."

D'Aquino pretended to be puzzled. "Did they tell you why?"

"Oldest story in the book. They're lesbians wanting to get pregnant by having a one-night stand with a good-looking stranger."

Gone were the hateful slurs and derogatory terms he had spouted when Aiden had interrogated him. His lawyer had probably drilled him to appear like a tolerant, lesbian-friendly man who was kind enough to donate his sperm.

"Did any of them indicate that they wanted to stop at any time?"

"No, never," Ballard answered with conviction.

D'Aquino looked at the jury, making sure everyone had heard it. "Why would they file a police report and falsely accuse you of rape, then?"

Ballard shrugged. "I don't know, but I guess their girlfriends must have found out that they had slept with a man and reacted none too pleased, so they tried to save their hides by making it look like an assault."

"Did you clear up that misunderstanding when the police came to the club?" D'Aquino asked.

"Defense is leading his own witness, Your Honor," Kade called from the prosecution table.

"Sustained," Linehan said. "Rephrase that question, Mr. D'Aquino."

"What happened when the police came to the club?"

"I would have tried to clear up the misunderstanding," Ballard said, using his lawyer's words, "but I didn't know they were police officers. The female cop stood in line like every other customer, and when she suddenly stepped close to me, I expected an attack and had to fight back."

D'Aquino nodded at him. "Thank you, Garett. Nothing further for now."

Kade strode toward the witness-box, closing in on Ballard like a tigress going after her prey. "Mr. Ballard, you just mentioned that you had to fight back, implying that Detective Carlisle attacked you. How do you explain the fact that a dozen witnesses, myself included, saw you attack her, not the other way around?"

"I guess it was a misunderstanding. I felt threatened."

Kade raised her brows, silently looking at the big, muscular man. "You also claim you didn't know that Detectives Bennet and Carlisle were police officers even though they testified that they had shown you their badges?"

Ballard smiled coolly. "People say and do all kinds of crazy things to get into the club, claiming they're celebrities, showing fake ID."

"Did anyone ever start to read you your Fifth Amendment rights to get into the club?" Kade asked.

"Uh, no."

Kade wandered over to the jury box, forcing Ballard to half-turn to keep her in his sight. "How do you usually react when someone tries a trick to get into the club?"

"I tell 'em that their trick is old hat and send them on their way," Ballard said with a grin.

"What does 'send them on their way' mean?" Kade asked. "Do you resort to violence?"

Ballard shook his head. "That's usually not necessary."

"So, you don't hit them, spit at them, or call them a bitch like you did with Detective Carlisle?" Now Kade was in her shark-attack mode.

"Objection!" D'Aquino shouted. "My client already explained that he doesn't normally use violence."

"Sustained," Linehan said. "Ms. Matheson."

Kade lifted her hands. "I'll move on. Mr. Ballard, you do know what the word 'lesbian' means, don't you?"

At Kade's condescending tone, Aiden slid to the edge of her seat. Obviously, Kade wanted to have another go at the tactic they had used during the interrogation.

"Yeah," Ballard spat out, but a warning glance from his lawyer prevented him from saying more.

Kade fixed the defendant with her cross-exam stare. "Then you know that the scientific definition is not 'a woman who's never been fucked by a real man' like you told Ms. Riggs, Ms. Matthews, and Dr. Kinsley?"

"Objection! Your Honor, she's badgering the witness," D'Aquino said.

"Counselor." Linehan didn't raise her voice—she didn't need to; one piercing gaze was warning enough.

Kade nodded, silently promising that she would tone it down. "A lesbian is a woman who is physically and emotionally attracted to women, and you are a man, aren't you?"

A vein pounded on Ballard's forehead. Aiden wanted to cheer Kade on and encourage her to further provoke Ballard, but at the same time, she was afraid that Kade would go too far and Ballard would attack her.

This time, D'Aquino didn't even have to object. Linehan spoke before he could. "Drop this attitude right now! Another question like that and I'll hold you in contempt and let you enjoy the hospitality of my holding cell!"

Kade raised a placating hand and took a step back. "How do you explain that three women who identify as lesbians, not as bisexual, allegedly slept with you when they could have picked any of the attractive women from the club?" she asked, a little tamer now.

"There's some things they still need a man for."

"And that is...?" Kade asked as if she truly didn't know why any woman would need a man.

Ballard glared at her, looking as if he would love to show her. "Making babies, for one thing."

Kade tapped her finger against her leg. "You said it was the women's decision not to use a condom?"

"That's right," Ballard said. "They told me they wanted a baby."

Kade raised one eyebrow. "All three of them?"

"Yes."

Aiden grinned. Unless the club put some hormones into the cocktails that activated the need to reproduce, that sounded pretty unlikely.

"And all three of them chose you as the father?"

"Guess they wanted my good looks for their kids."

The corner of Kade's lips twitched as if she barely held back her laughter or a sarcastic comment. "Did you know that according to scientific studies most lesbian couples who want to have a baby choose an anonymous donor from a sperm bank or a donor who is related to one of them?"

Aiden raised a brow. *Seems like our Kade is full of information about lesbians, huh?*

"Not these three," Ballard said.

"Tell me, Mr. Ballard, are you capable of fathering children?"

Ballard flushed. He leaned forward and glared at Kade. "Of course I am!"

"You're sure of that?" Kade had perfected the skeptical glance, looking at Ballard as though he couldn't even manage to raise a pencil, much less anything else.

"Sure I'm sure. There ain't nothing wrong with me!"

"Well, if all of them only slept with you to become pregnant, and there's nothing wrong with you, how do you explain the fact that none of them got pregnant?" Kade asked, moving back to the witness-box to stare down at the defendant.

Ballard shrugged. "I suppose sometimes it takes more than one time."

"And how do you explain the fact that Ms. Matthews and Dr. Kinsley took the morning-after pill when they were treated in the hospital? Why would they do that if they wanted to get pregnant?"

Ballard fingered his tie as if it were choking him. "Maybe they changed their minds."

"Both of them?"

D'Aquino stood. "Objection, Your Honor, asked and answered."

"Sustained," Linehan said.

Kade had already proven what she wanted and moved on. "It's your theory that Ms. Riggs, Ms. Matthews, and Dr. Kinsley accused you of raping them because their girlfriends found out and reacted negatively to their alleged one-night stand with you, is that correct?"

"Exactly."

"Wouldn't you say it disproves your little theory when I tell you that none of them had a partner at the time?" Kade rested both hands on the stand, glowering down at Ballard.

"No!" Ballard's voice was getting louder, less controlled. "Then there must have been other people who would have disapproved of a heterosexual affair. Maybe their lesbian friends."

Kade shook her head. "Why should they try to hide it? If they would have gotten pregnant, surely no one would have believed it was from a lesbian affair."

"That is why they lied and accused me!"

"Why would they choose such a complicated lie, then?" Kade asked. "Why not just tell their families they had gone to a sperm bank and used an anonymous donor?"

Ballard's mouth opened and closed, but he didn't answer.

"Did you understand the question, or do you want me to repeat it, Mr. Ballard?"

Kade's condescending tone made Aiden smile. *Go, Kade! Rip him to shreds!*

Ballard stared at Kade as if he was only seconds away from calling her a bitch too.

Kade didn't move an inch. "You don't want to answer my question, do you?"

"Objection, Your Honor," D'Aquino called. "Mr. Ballard is not a psychologist. He can't answer questions about the motive and reason for these women's behavior."

"Not being a psychologist didn't prevent your client from offering us his theories about why the women allegedly had sex with him," Kade said. "He was not afraid to speculate about reasons and motives then."

Linehan nodded. "The objection is overruled. Mr. Ballard, please answer the People's question."

Ballard glowered at Kade. "What was the question?"

"Why did none of the three women choose a simpler lie to hide their alleged one-night stand with you? Why choose a lie that would result in a police investigation and a trial, where the truth could easily be discovered?" Kade folded her arms and looked down at Ballard along the line of her aristocratic nose.

Ballard hesitated.

Aiden grinned, hoping that it was as obvious to the jury as it was to her that Ballard was running out of feeble excuses.

"I guess they didn't think that far ahead," Ballard finally said.

"You want us to believe that they were intelligent enough to think up an elaborate conspiracy to frame you for three rapes but not clever enough to think about the consequences?" Kade asked, her eyebrows arched. "Not one of them?"

"Objection, my client has already answered that," the defense attorney called.

Linehan spared a glance in the direction of the defense counsel. "He has not. Overruled. Mr. Ballard?"

"Uh, I guess they weren't as smart as they thought."

Kade took a step closer to the witness stand so she could look down at Ballard more effectively. "They weren't or you weren't, Mr. Ballard?"

"Objection, Your Honor! She's badgering my client."

"Withdrawn. No further questions," Kade said and strode away. The jurors had heard her question and would draw their own conclusions.

D'Aquino stood and fiddled with his tie for a few seconds.

Aiden hid a grin. *Does it feel like the noose around your neck is getting a little tight, buddy?*

"Garett, having seen the apartments of Ms. Riggs, Ms. Matthews, and Ms. Kinsley, what assumptions would you make about their finances?" D'Aquino asked.

Kade shot up from her seat. "Objection, Your Honor! The question is exceeding the scope of the cross-examination."

"No, it's not," D'Aquino said. "It is meant to show why some of the women preferred a one-night stand to get pregnant instead of using a sperm bank."

"Overruled—for now," the judge said. "I'll give you a little rope, Mr. D'Aquino. You'd better not hang yourself with it. You may answer the question, Mr. Ballard."

"Well, I guess the first one, Ms. Matthews, I think, was not too well off. She hardly had any furniture, and the whole apartment building was pretty run-down."

You mean easy to break into, you bastard! Aiden gritted her teeth.

"Do you think she could afford to use a sperm bank to get pregnant?" D'Aquino asked.

Visibly relieved at having been shown a possible explanation for his allegations, Ballard shook his head. "Definitely not."

"Garett, do you have any proof that the women slept with you because they wanted to have babies?"

"The strawberry blonde," Ballard pointed to Dawn, making her jerk, "had photos of kids everywhere, like she was obsessed with them."

"Thank you, nothing further."

Kade stood again. "Recross, Your Honor? Just two or three questions."

Linehan nodded.

"Mr. Ballard, would you describe the apartment of 'the strawberry blonde,' as you put it, as being run-down?"

"Well, not really, but—"

"Would you expect a successful psychologist and a history professor to make enough money to afford artificial insemination?" Kade asked.

"I suppose."

"Did you know that the children in the photos in Dr. Kinsley's apartment are her niece and her nephew?"

Ballard began to fidget. "No."

"Would you call it an obsession with babies to have a few pictures of your niece and nephew in your apartment?" Kade asked.

"I don't care what you say," Ballard shouted. "She wanted to have a baby!"

Dawn blanched. "Not with him," she whispered.

"That was not what I asked you, Mr. Ballard," Kade said.

Ballard shrugged. "I guess it's not directly an obsession, but—"

"Thank you, Mr. Ballard. One more thing. You testified that Dr. Kinsley ripped the phone cord out herself even though Mr. Jenkins, the fingerprint expert, testified that your prints were found on the cord?"

"She did," Ballard said, his jaw set.

"How did her cell phone, on which your prints were also found, get tossed out the window? Did she also do that herself?"

"Yes."

"Because she didn't want to be interrupted at three a.m.?" Kade didn't bother to hide the disbelief in her voice.

"Yes."

"Why didn't she just turn it off? Are you saying that she was so overwhelmed by your being a 'real man,'" Kade formed quotation marks with her fingers, only a few inches away from Ballard's face, "that her common sense deserted her and she tried to throw a perfectly good phone down to the street?"

The defense attorney stood again. "Objection! Your Honor, counsel is badgering the witness."

"Withdrawn. No further questions." Kade sat back down with one last, cold stare at Ballard.

The judge looked at D'Aquino. "Do you have any other witnesses?"

"Yes, Your Honor. The defense calls Janice Cahill."

Aiden squinted at the tall, short-haired woman taking the stand. *Who's she? Ballard's character witness?*

"Ms. Cahill, what is your occupation?" D'Aquino asked after the witness had been sworn in.

"I'm the manager and co-owner of a club called Rainbows," the blonde said.

"How long has the defendant been your employee?"

Janice Cahill thought for a few seconds. "Five, almost six years now."

"And during that time, has Mr. Ballard ever acted in a hostile manner toward any of your customers?" D'Aquino asked.

"No, never."

"Did Mr. Ballard ever indicate any negative feelings toward homosexual people?"

The club owner shook her head again. "No."

"Have you ever heard of affairs between members of your male staff and some of the customers?" the defense attorney asked.

"Not often and I certainly don't encourage it, but yes, it has happened before," Janice Cahill said.

D'Aquino turned back toward the defense table with a satisfied smile. "Thank you. That will be all."

Kade got up and paced in front of the witness-box. "Ms. Cahill, tell us what would have happened if you had ever heard derogatory remarks against lesbians from Mr. Ballard or seen him act hostile toward a customer."

Ms. Cahill's expression hardened. "I would have fired him immediately."

Kade stopped her pacing to look into the witness's eyes. "Did Mr. Ballard know what the consequences would be should his homophobic attitudes become apparent?"

"Yes. All employees are informed of the club's policies before their first day at work."

"Mr. Ballard testified that your clientele consists mainly of lesbians and bisexual women. Is that correct?" Kade's voice was not as cold as during Ballard's cross. Her gestures were softer, and she had taken a step back, not encroaching on the witness's personal space as she had done with Ballard.

"Yes, it is," the club owner answered readily, reacting to Kade's friendly approach.

"Generally, how well do you know your customers, Ms. Cahill?"

"I know most of the regulars pretty well."

Where was Kade going with this? Aiden knew that Dawn hadn't been a regular at *Rainbows*, but she trusted Kade's abilities and kept listening in silence.

"These affairs between male staff members and some of your customers, were these women regulars you were familiar with?"

"Yes."

"And did they identify as lesbians?" Kade asked.

The club owner shook her head. "No, they were bisexual."

"Did you ever see a lesbian customer flirt with Mr. Ballard, buy him a drink, or ask him to go home with her?"

Cahill shook her head again. "I never witnessed that, no."

"No further questions, Your Honor." Kade was through with the last witness of the trial.

D'Aquino stood again but didn't make the effort to walk to the witness stand to ask his last question. "Is it possible that Mr. Ballard had affairs with customers without your knowledge?"

"Objection!" Kade obviously didn't want him to have the last word. "That's beyond the personal knowledge of this witness. The answer would be a mere speculation."

Ruth Linehan inclined her head. "Sustained."

"No further questions, Your Honor. The defense rests," D'Aquino said.

"Very well." Linehan excused the witness. "We'll reconvene on Monday morning at nine to hear the closing arguments. Court is adjourned."

The gavel banged, and everyone rose while the jury and the judge filed out the side entrance.

"Is the defense ready to proceed with its closing argument?" Ruth Linehan asked.

"Yes, Your Honor." D'Aquino took position in front of the jury box. "Ladies and gentlemen of the jury, when I stood before you a little over a week ago, I told you this case was about an innocent man who was wrongfully accused of crimes he didn't commit. I still feel that way." He shifted his weight and let his gaze wander along the rows of jurors. "As in every criminal case, the prosecution has the burden of proof, and in the case against

Garett Ballard, they could not keep their promises and prove his guilt beyond a reasonable doubt. During this trial, the prosecution presented no concrete evidence to support their allegations of rape."

No evidence? Aiden snorted. *Give me a break, you jerk!*

"The only evidence they have is circumstantial and can be interpreted in many ways. According to the law, you have to adopt the interpretation in favor of the defendant because he has the presumption of being innocent." D'Aquino raised his index finger and gazed at the jurors with a serious expression. "The prosecution presented an inexperienced police officer who would not know a real crime from a staged one. Next, they called a detective who was predisposed to believe anything the alleged witness said because of their previous acquaintance. Their physical evidence—fibers, semen, and fingerprints—proved nothing more than that my client had been in the apartments and had sex with these women, a fact that he readily admitted to. The People didn't prove a homophobic motive. Just the opposite, in fact: a lesbian woman who worked closely with Mr. Ballard for years told you he has always acted with respect and tolerance toward lesbians."

Someone in the audience noisily cleared his or her throat.

"Even their own expert witness, Doctor Van Hayden, admitted that patients rarely confess that their injuries were caused by rough sex. And that is exactly what happened on the nights in question. Therefore, I ask that you acquit my client and find him not guilty. Thank you."

Linehan scribbled something down on her legal pad. "Are the People ready for their closing argument?"

"Ready, Your Honor."

Aiden's gaze was on Kade as she rose and strode over to the jury box, appearing calm and focused. "Ladies and gentlemen, this is not a case resting on circumstantial evidence as the defense wants you to believe. Every possible testimony you heard in the last week pointed to the fact that three brutal rapes had been committed by the defendant, Garett Ballard. While some of the evidence may blur the line between rough consensual sex and rape, there is more than enough to prove the latter: torn clothing, bruises, broken bones, vaginal tears at a position consistent with rape, a gun that has been found in Mr. Ballard's apartment, his fingerprints on a ripped-out phone line and on a cell phone that had been thrown out of the window." Kade counted it off for the jury with her fingers and then shook her hands to emphasize her next words. "Every single piece of evidence tells us that these three women have been raped, just like they said. Why should they be ashamed of a heterosexual affair when many families of lesbians would throw a victory party should that ever happen?"

Aiden looked at each of the jurors, but their faces gave nothing away. They listened to Kade with rapt attention.

"When Mr. Ballard tried to explain why three women, who had never spoken to him or to each other, should first sleep with him and then accuse him of rape, he got entangled in his own web of lies. All of the testimony—that of an experienced ER doctor and a detective with the Sexual Assault Detail, for example—indicates that Melanie Riggs, Jayne Matthews, and Dawn Kinsley were raped by the defendant, and Dr. Renshaw explained his motive: a pathological hatred against lesbians that the defendant developed after having been left by his lesbian mother and raised by the rest of his homophobic family." Kade half turned toward Ballard, who was staring at her with angry eyes. "The crime, the motive, and the perpetrator have been proven beyond a reasonable doubt. I ask that you seek justice for the victims, make the defendant accountable for his actions, and return a verdict of guilty on all counts." She looked at every juror who would make eye contact. "Thank you."

Linehan instructed the jury and then excused them to the jury room for deliberations. She raised her voice to be heard over the whispered conversations that started in the gallery. "This court is adjourned."

Aiden exhaled and leaned back. She looked at Dawn, who was sitting next to her on the edge of her seat with a pale face and a white-knuckled grip on Del's hand.

"God, I think I need a drink." Dawn groaned and rubbed her face with her free hand.

"Then let's go and have one," Aiden said before she could stop herself. "I'm off duty, and Kade will call me when the jury returns."

Dawn hesitated. She looked to her left, where her mother and Del sat.

"Ah, you go with her, grasshopper," Del said. "Your mom and I can manage to get smashed on our own."

"Del!" Dawn and Grace slapped her on the shoulders from both sides.

Aiden smiled, grateful that Del's comment had lightened the mood and made Dawn laugh. She gave Del a nod while she waited for Dawn's decision.

"Okay, let's go." Dawn rose and followed her out the courtroom's double doors.

Aiden shortened her stride, remaining protectively at Dawn's side. Her warning gaze and the gold shield she wore made sure that no one in the busy hallway strayed too close to Dawn. Soon, they descended the steps leading to the courthouse building. "Where do you want to go?"

"You know what?" Dawn stopped on the step above Aiden so she could gaze into her eyes without looking up. "If you don't mind, I'd rather take a rain check on that drink."

Directly face-to-face now, Aiden studied the other woman. Dawn seemed edgy and exhausted. "You're tired, huh?"

"I'm still not sleeping very well," Dawn said. "The trial brought back a lot of memories. And I don't want to be falling down drunk when the jury comes back with the verdict, no matter what it's going to be."

Aiden pushed back her disappointment about parting ways so soon and nodded. "Kade said it could be a while before the jury gets back, and your place is just around the corner. Why don't you go home and take a nap?"

"I'd like that—but not alone."

She wants to take a nap with me? Aiden nearly tumbled down the rest of the stairs.

Dawn laughed. "I didn't mean it like that. I'd just like some company while we wait for the verdict. All I'm offering is some coffee, nothing more."

Fool! Aiden mentally shook her head at herself. *Sharing a bed with you, even platonically, is probably the last thing on her mind.* "Nothing more? Does that mean I don't get cookies with my coffee this time?"

Dawn smiled. "Hmm, maybe I can scare up a few."

They strolled along the tree-lined Fourth Avenue and finally took the elevator up to Dawn's apartment in companionable silence.

"Is coffee okay?" Dawn asked when they crossed the threshold. "Or do you want something stronger? You can still have a drink."

"No, coffee's good," Aiden said. "I'm off duty, but I promised myself I would never depend on alcohol to make myself feel better or help me forget." The words were out before she could censor herself. *She's just too easy to talk to.*

"Your mother drank?"

Aiden nodded. "My mother and a lot of good cops who end up drunk every night to forget about the evil they've seen that day." She leaned against the doorframe and watched Dawn as she prepared coffee and tea, her small hands moving efficiently, giving the everyday activity of boiling water an easy grace.

When Dawn looked up and glanced at her questioningly,

Aiden let her gaze wander around the rest of the apartment instead and studied the methodically cluttered desk and the watercolor landscapes on the living room wall.

"When did you decide that you wanted to be a cop?" Dawn asked.

Aiden blew out a breath. While she wasn't keen on playing "twenty questions" with a shrink, she couldn't refuse to answer the questions of this particular psychologist. "I don't know. On some level, I think I always knew."

"You never considered other careers?"

"Not really, no."

Dawn leaned up on her tiptoes, reaching for the cookie box on the top shelf, and for a moment, her blouse stretched taut across her breasts, distracting Aiden. "And you always planned to join the Sexual Assault Detail?"

Aiden forced her gaze away from Dawn. "I didn't plan it. That's just the way it happened. Guess it's my fate." Her facial muscles hurt from the effort it took to keep her face calm and expressionless.

Dawn's hands stilled on the cookie box. She turned around and fixed Aiden with an intense gaze. "If you were destined to work with rape survivors, it's because of your strength and compassion, not because you have anything to atone for. The sins of your father are his own, not yours."

Aiden swallowed. A whirlwind of thoughts raced through her mind, and she didn't know what to say. "What about you?" she asked when she couldn't stand the silence any longer. "Why did you become a psychologist instead of following family tradition and becoming a cop?"

"Well, I thought about it when I heard that there are some lesbians who have a thing for women in uniform," Dawn said with a grin. "No, seriously, I considered going into the 'family business' for a while. There are some things about being a cop that really appeal to me."

Aiden took a step forward and leaned against the kitchen cupboard. She didn't want to miss a word that Dawn said. "What things are those? Apart from the attention-getting uniform."

"Helping people. Protecting them." Dawn shrugged. "But I quickly realized that protecting and serving is not really the main focus of police work. Investigations and legal proceedings are about the perpetrators, not about the victims."

"So you became a psychologist," Aiden said. "And you love your job."

Dawn poured hot water into the mug with her tea bag. "Some days I want to chuck everything and move to the Bahamas, but overall, yes, I love my job—even if it's not a chick magnet like yours."

Aiden reached for the tray before Dawn could and carried it into the living room. It surprised her how at home she felt in the cozy apartment. "How did your parents react to your career choice?"

Dawn shoveled sugar into her tea and stirred thoughtfully. "My dad died before I had my degree, but he was always very supportive of me."

"And your mom?"

"My mom was relieved when I chose not to attend the law enforcement academy. She almost burst with pride when I got my PhD. I think she called me 'Doctor' for a week." Dawn chuckled around a mouthful of cookie.

Aiden laughed. She was glad that Dawn had a parent who was not reluctant to show her love and pride.

"At first, she wasn't too keen on my idea to specialize in counseling rape survivors. She wanted me to go into family therapy or any other field of work where I wouldn't be confronted with all the violence and the crimes that my dad and Brian had to deal with on a daily basis."

Aiden shrugged. "She wants to protect you from the ugliness of the world. That's what mothers do."

Dawn studied her over the rim of her mug. "Did yours?"

"Sometimes."

Dawn didn't pressure her to explain, but Aiden felt it wasn't fair to pump Dawn for information about her family and then give her one-word answers in return. "There were times when she just wanted to forget everything that had happened to her, including me." She clenched her fingers around the mug without drinking. There was already a bitter taste in her mouth, even without coffee. "When she was drunk, she didn't care about other people."

Dawn took the mug from Aiden and replaced it with her own hand. She silently squeezed Aiden's fingers.

Not wanting to be pitied, Aiden squared her shoulders but did not dare to break the connection between their hands. "She did care when she wasn't drunk. She was proud when I became a police officer, but she hated that I joined the Sexual Assault Detail. At least once a week, she begged me to transfer to homicide, narcotics, or any other unit."

Dawn closed her other hand around Aiden's and looked down at their tangled fingers. "She hated it because she knew it had the potential to hurt you. But I'm sure she loved you for doing it anyway."

Aiden's gaze followed Dawn's, taking in the contrast of Dawn's fairer, smaller fingers against her own. She noticed that her thumb had been drawing circles over the back of Dawn's hand, and she wasn't sure if the gesture was meant to sooth Dawn or herself.

The beeping of her cell phone made her jerk back from Dawn. Quickly, as if she had been caught doing something forbidden, she disentangled their fingers and grabbed her phone to read the text message. "It's Kade. The jury's back."

CHAPTER 22

DESPITE BEING SURROUNDED BY FAMILY and friends, Dawn was trembling inside when she took her seat in the courtroom's gallery. She clutched the edge of her seat and leaned toward Aiden. "They didn't take long to reach a verdict, did they? Is that a good or a bad sign?"

"Let's hope it means that they saw right through Ballard's feeble defense," Aiden said.

Dawn glanced toward the front of the courtroom, where Garett Ballard sat behind the defense table.

As if feeling her gaze, he turned and stared at her.

Dawn stiffened. Quickly, she turned away and watched Kade, who looked calm and secure behind the prosecution's table, as if any verdict other than "guilty on all counts" was not even a possibility. Once again, Dawn envied her cool confidence.

Judge Ruth Linehan settled her black robe around herself on the bench and looked down at the jurors. "Has the jury reached a verdict?"

The jury foreman stood. "We have, Your Honor."

Dawn watched anxiously as the bailiff walked a folded piece of paper over to the judge, who read it and then handed it back. Linehan's expression revealed nothing. "Will the defendant please rise."

Ballard and his attorney stood.

"On the first count of the indictment, the charge of unlawful possession of a firearm, how does the jury find?"

The jury foreman looked down at the piece of paper in his hand. "We, the jury, find the defendant guilty."

Dawn didn't allow herself to relax. *That was the easy one. Proving he was carrying a concealed weapon even though he didn't have a permit was all it took.*

"On count two, possession of stolen property, how does the jury find?" Linehan asked.

"We find the defendant guilty."

"On count three, burglary, how do you find?"

"We find the defendant guilty," the foreman said again.

Another easy one. Dawn slid to the edge of her seat as her tension grew.

"On count four, resisting arrest, how do you find?"

"We find the defendant guilty."

"On count five, assaulting a public safety officer, how does the jury find?"

Dawn turned to look at Aiden, who sat with a neutral expression, as if she hadn't been the assaulted officer in question.

"We find the defendant guilty."

Yeah! Dawn breathed a sigh of relief but felt her muscles stiffen all the same. Her heart began to pound. The remaining charge was the only one that really mattered to her.

"Regarding three counts of rape in the first degree, what is your verdict?" Linehan asked.

"We find the defendant..." The jury foreman cleared his throat. "...guilty."

Dawn's whole body had been on edge from the moment Aiden had received Kade's text message, and now all the tension fled her body in a rush, leaving her dizzy. She slouched against the back of her seat. The bang of the gavel and Ballard's outraged protest sounded as if coming from a huge distance.

"You okay?" Aiden leaned over and looked at her with a concerned expression.

Dawn exhaled shakily. "Yeah, I think so."

"It's over now," Aiden said. "He's been found guilty, and he won't be out on the streets again for a long, long time. If I know Kade, she's going to push for the maximum."

Still a little numb, Dawn let herself be hugged by her mother, Del, and Ballard's two other victims, peering over their shoulders as a struggling and shouting Ballard was dragged from the room.

"We should celebrate," Grace said.

Dawn nodded, even though she didn't feel like celebrating. She was glad that she, and every other woman in Portland, would be safe from Ballard, but no punishment imposed on him could undo what he had done to her and the others.

"You and your partner are invited, of course, Detective," Grace said.

Dawn looked over at the prosecution table, where Kade was calmly gathering her things. "Should we ask Ms. Matheson if she wants to join us? She was the one who won the case, after all."

"Go and ask her." Grace gave her a gentle push.

Slowly, Dawn walked across the courtroom. She stopped right in front of the prosecution's table and waited until Kade looked up. "Hi." To her surprise, she found herself a little shy now that she was facing the object of Aiden's infatuation. Kadence Matheson was beautiful and confident, the way only a person whose feeling of personal safety had never been violated could be. Dawn could never hope to match up to that in Aiden's eyes. "My family is planning to go out and celebrate. Would you like to join us?"

Kade snapped her briefcase shut and started to shake her head.

"Oh, come on, Counselor," Ray Bennet shouted from the gallery. "Live a little!"

The DDA hesitated and glanced down at her watch.

"Come with us, Kade," Aiden called. "It's too late to get any real work done anyway."

"All right." Kade shouldered her briefcase as a soldier would his rifle. "But remember: I'm a woman with expensive tastes."

Aiden just laughed. "Who said this was an all-expenses-paid invitation?"

Kade didn't mind that they ended up in a cop bar. Being surrounded by beer-drinking, laughing, boasting cops didn't bother her in the least. She knew what horrors they had to face every day, so she didn't begrudge them this little celebration. Sipping her wine and leaning back in her chair at the head of the table, she watched her companions.

Ms. Matthews and Ms. Riggs were visibly relieved to have left the trial behind them. They laughed about the stories Ray was telling about his four daughters.

Mrs. Kinsley's silent friend, the intriguing Lieutenant Vasquez, smiled too, but half her attention remained on Dawn.

Kade followed her gaze and studied Dawn. Her key witness was deep in conversation with Aiden, their heads bent closely together because of the loudness of their surroundings.

Now that's interesting. Kade raised her brows. Everyone else at the table would probably think nothing of it, but years of examining witnesses on the stand and watching suspects through the one-way mirror had honed Kade's skills of observation. She also knew Aiden's body language. Like most cops, Aiden preferred to keep a certain distance between herself and whomever she was talking to—unless she happened to be attracted to her conversation partner. That was what had ultimately tipped Kade off about Aiden's crush on her.

Aiden and Dawn weren't touching, and the topic of their conversation was probably just small talk, but Kade could feel a connection between them anyway. Something was going on, something more than just the relationship of a victim and the detective working her case. *Well, well, well.* Kade took another sip of her wine. *I guess I'll have to do without the company of one Detective Aiden Carlisle in the courtroom during her lunch breaks from now on.*

It was common knowledge that Aiden was not immune to the charm of an attractive woman, and Dawn Kinsley was both charming and attractive. Away from the tense atmosphere of the courtroom and the presence of her rapist, Dawn's smile was warm and genuine, and her eyes shone when she looked at Aiden.

Kade watched the two women next to her with mixed feelings. *Come on. You're not jealous, are you?* Despite her awareness of Aiden's admiration, she had never considered a relationship with her or any other woman. Work had always come first.

Kade's thoughts and the conversation between Dawn and Aiden were interrupted when one of the men who'd sat drinking at the bar tapped Dawn on the shoulder. "Hey, beautiful lady. How about a dance?" He offered her his none-too-steady hand.

Dawn looked over her shoulder toward the dance floor, which was the general size of a postage stamp. No one was dancing. "No, thank you."

"A game of pool, then?" The man nodded at the pool tables.

"No, thanks."

"Oh, come on, just one—"

A low growl from Aiden interrupted him. She pressed her hands against the table and started to rise.

Del Vasquez was about to get up too.

Dawn's fingers on her forearm held Aiden back. Their gazes crossed for a second, and Dawn shook her head almost imperceptibly.

To Kade's surprise, Aiden sank back onto her chair without protesting.

Dawn turned toward the waiting man. Kade could see that she had to force herself to hold his stare without flinching back from the smell of beer on his breath. “I’m here with my friends and my family, so I don’t want to dance with you, play pool with you, or do anything else with you, okay?” Her voice was soft but firm.

For a second, the man stood frozen as if he couldn’t believe that he had been shot down until one of his buddies called from the bar, “C’mere, and leave her alone, Sim. I know these guys. They’re with the SAD.”

Finally, the half-drunk man grunted and stumbled back to his friends.

Dawn loosened her white-knuckled grip on the table and squeezed Aiden’s hand.

It had probably been her first confrontation with a man after her rape, and she had wanted—no, needed—to prove to herself and to Aiden that she could handle it on her own, without the help of her knights with shining badges. *Aiden, my friend, I think you’ve found your match.* Kade raised her wineglass in a silent toast to the courageous woman.

In twenty years on the job, Del had seen a lot of cases that never went to trial or were lost by a helpless DDA for lack of evidence. More times than she could count, she had dealt with victims who hadn’t been able to identify their attacker but couldn’t understand why he was acquitted. Her relief at not having to deal with any of those things in Dawn’s case was profound.

They had won, and Del fully intended to buy the victorious DDA a beer or two. She turned to look at Kade Matheson and found her talking and laughing with Carlisle, who sat between Kade and Dawn.

“And to think that you managed to win in Linehan’s court

without her holding you in contempt. Not even once!" Carlisle laughed, obviously familiar with Kade and her past courtroom experiences.

"Being held in contempt is not half as bad as losing the keys to your handcuffs," Kade answered haughtily, but a small, playful wink took the sting from her words.

"I didn't lose them," Carlisle said. "I just said that to scare the perp into confessing."

Kade gave her a sarcastic nod. "Oh, yes, of course."

"Yes," Carlisle said. "That's my story, and I'm sticking to it."

"Uh-huh. And do you lose the keys to your handcuffs very often, Detective?"

Del leaned back and watched them. *Are they flirting?* They were obviously at ease with each other, and Del wondered if Carlisle's reaction to her request to be "hooked up" with Kade Matheson had held a hint of jealousy. *I certainly couldn't blame her. Matheson's a looker, and she pulls off that arrogant, no-nonsense attitude better than any other woman I know. If even an old warhorse like me is impressed, there's no way in hell that Carlisle could be left cold. But where does that leave my little grasshopper?*

She turned her head to look at Dawn, who sat silently between Del and Carlisle and stared into her wineglass, not attempting to get involved in the conversation between Carlisle and Kade.

As if sensing Del's gaze on her, Dawn looked up and smiled.

Del raised a questioning brow. "You okay?"

"I'm fine," Dawn said.

Del looked back at Kade and Carlisle, who were still teasing and laughing. *I bet you're not fine with that.* Having known Dawn for almost all her life, she had sensed her interest in Aiden Carlisle from the start. "Dawn..." She had never interfered with any of Dawn's relationships before, even though she'd known that neither Caleb nor Maggie had been right for her. Now, though,

Dawn was so vulnerable that she couldn't help trying to warn her. "They seem to be pretty familiar with each other."

Without looking up, Dawn nodded. "They're colleagues and friends, so why shouldn't they be?" She glanced at Carlisle and Kade, then went back to studying her hands.

Del shrugged. "I don't know. I just got the impression that Carlisle wasn't just doing her job with you. That she might be—"

Dawn leaned over the table, making sure that no one could overhear them in the loud bar. "It doesn't matter. I'm not available for anything but a friendship right now."

For now, yes. But will Carlisle have the patience to wait until you're ready for more when she could have a woman like Kade Matheson right now? Del rubbed her chin and again watched Carlisle interact with Kade. "But—"

"Stop worrying about me, Del," Dawn said with her trademark kind smile.

"I can't," Del said. "It's my job to worry about you. I inherited it from your dad."

Dawn reached across the table and patted her hand. "And you do a great job, really. But in this case, it's not necessary. I'm well aware that Aiden likes Ms. Matheson."

Del eyed Kade Matheson's elegant lips, her aristocratic nose, and the slender legs. "Well, what's not to like?"

"I thought you had a thing for Latinas?" A teasing grin made Dawn's gray-green eyes sparkle.

Del returned the smile. "I'd make an exception for her." Dawn's laugh warmed her heart, and she watched as Carlisle turned her head at the sound of her laughter. The detective's gaze searched out Dawn's face, and she grinned when she saw that Dawn was smiling.

When Carlisle turned back to her own conversation, Dawn leaned toward Del again. "Aiden likes Kade. She admires her, but I'm not sure she would want to start a relationship with her. I think it's more like one of those worshipping from afar things—safe because you know that it will never become reality. Besides, Kadence Matheson doesn't swing that way."

"Ah." Del wasn't so sure. Kade Matheson may have never "swung that way" in the past, but she didn't strike Del as the type to vehemently oppose the possibility. "When you start to sound like a shrink, I know it's complicated."

Dawn laughed again. "There are some things that even the gold bar on your uniform couldn't change, hmm? You cops just love psychologists."

Del grinned. *Let's hope that a particular one of us will learn to.*

CHAPTER 23

"Good God!" Aiden groaned as she bent down to peer at the report on her desk more closely. "Is that a 'g' or a 'b'?" She turned the file and threw it onto the desk in front of hers.

Ray studied the words for a while. "Hmm. Could be an eight too." He tossed the file back to Aiden.

Frustrated, she gathered her files and emptied her cup of coffee.

When she stood, Ruben looked up from his own work. "You're not going to jump from the roof because you can't read the lieutenant's memo, are you?"

Aiden snorted. "Hardly. I think I'll go down and try to find someone from the hieroglyphics department to help me read this."

"Well, I have this theory." Okada ignored the groans of his colleagues at the word "theory." "It's not a coincidence that the guys and gals with the sloppiest handwriting always get promoted fastest. No one wants to spend hours trying to decipher their reports anymore."

"I'm sure the lieutenant would be very happy to hear what you think about the qualifications that got her this job," Aiden said.

Ray leaned back in his chair and crossed his arms behind his head. "You going to pay our friends from ballistics a visit?"

Moving toward the double doors, Aiden nodded. "We won't get any further on Powell until the lab confirms a ballistics match.

And it'll be good to get out and take a break from all this reading." She rubbed her burning eyes.

"Could you bring me back a salad?" Ray asked.

"Sure." As Aiden left, she heard the other detectives tease him about being put on diet by his wife. *At least he's got someone who cares about his health.* Aiden had dedicated her life to her job. It was the one thing that she could really be proud of. But sometimes, she wondered if there was more to life than the job. Ray had a beautiful wife and four kids; Ruben had a girlfriend and his whole life ahead of him, and even Okada had three or four ex-wives—Aiden had lost count a long time ago—to whom he paid alimony. She was the only one who didn't have a bond with any living human being. Thinking about significant others, relationships, and her lack thereof conjured up a mental picture of Dawn, and she shook her head to chase away these thoughts.

Once she had dropped their bullet off for analysis at the crime lab, she decided to use her lunch break for a little walk through Waterfront Park, just two blocks from the Justice Center. She strode along the Willamette River, breathing in the cold November air until she slowly felt her tension fade. She slowed her pace and took the time to look around. The wind was tugging at the flag that was flying over the Portland Police Memorial at the end of the park, and she mentally saluted the colleagues who had lost their lives in the line of duty. As she walked closer, she could make out a woman standing in front of the memorial wall, her blonde hair blowing in the wind. *She looks like Dawn.* She rolled her eyes at herself. *Oh, great! Now everyone you see reminds you of her. Cut it out, right this instant.*

Try as she might, she couldn't help herself. Her gaze wandered back to the Dawn look-alike, who had her back to her. She had the same blonde hair and the same petite, lithe body. *Stop it! Her hair isn't even as long as Dawn's.* She marched on.

The path circled around the memorial, and Aiden still found

herself sneaking glimpses at the solitary woman. Finally, she was able to see her in profile. "Dawn?"

The woman whirled around. It was Dawn. A smile lit up her features when she saw Aiden. "Hi!"

Aiden walked over to her. "You cut your hair." The blonde hair no longer fell most of the way down Dawn's back; the ends now just brushed her shoulders.

Dawn tugged the blonde strands back on one side, revealing a cute ear. "It was time for a change."

"It looks good," Aiden said and meant it.

"Thank you," Dawn answered with a hint of a blush. "What are you doing here?"

Aiden stuffed her hands into her coat pockets. "Um, I was dropping something off at the ballistics lab, and now I'm taking my lunch break. You?"

Dawn bit her lip. "Visiting my dad." She smiled sadly and touched one of the names on the memorial wall. *James Kinsley*. "I always come here on his birthday. I think he'd like it better than me going to visit his grave." She traced every letter on her father's plaque, one of twenty-nine that represented Portland police officers who had been killed in the line of duty.

Aiden watched the emotions play across Dawn's face. She could almost feel the connection between Dawn and her father, and it was painful to realize that she would never share a similar bond with either of her parents. "Sorry," she mumbled, taking a step back. "I didn't mean to interrupt."

"You didn't." Dawn stopped her retreat with a touch to Aiden's arm.

Aiden studied her. Dawn's face was flushed from the wind and the cold, and her eyes were red-rimmed from crying or from lack of sleep. Aiden found her beautiful nonetheless. *Maybe it's some kind of withdrawal symptoms.* She hadn't seen Dawn or heard from her since the trial had ended the week before—not because she hadn't wanted to, but because she was unsure how to behave around Dawn now that the familiar role of detective had been taken away. "How are you?" she finally asked, lacking another topic to introduce.

"Getting there." Dawn nodded almost to herself. "And how are you?"

"Same as always—up to my neck in cases."

"No vacation in sight, huh?"

"Vacation?" Aiden scratched her head. "Hmm, that sounds familiar. What was that again?"

Dawn smiled. "I think it's the very thing I'm getting too much of right now. It's getting really boring sitting at home and doing nothing, but I'm still not up to going back to work with rape victims."

"Don't force it." She hesitated. Now that Dawn had too much time on her hands, this could be her chance to ask her out. *I don't think she's ready to date anyone, least of all a woman who has as much baggage as I have. And I'm not even sure that I'm ready to be in a relationship.* She was still debating with herself and trying to work up enough courage to ask Dawn out when she remembered that she had promised to bring back lunch for Ray. She was still on duty and had work to do. This was not the right time to arrange dates. "Well, I think I'd better get back to the precinct."

Dawn said nothing; she just looked at her. For a moment, they both stood in silence. Finally, it was Dawn who spoke first, "Yeah, I'd better get going too. It's getting a little cold out here." She rubbed her arms.

Aiden nodded, unusually tongue-tied.

"See you." Dawn waited for a few seconds, but when Aiden just returned the good-bye, she turned and walked toward the path.

Idiot! Aiden watched her walk away. When Dawn had almost reached the path, she gave herself a mental kick. "Dawn! Wait!"

She jogged across the square to catch up with her. Stopping in front of Dawn, she licked her lips. "Do you...do you want to do something this weekend?"

Dawn studied her. "You mean...go out on a date?"

"If you'd prefer, we could make it just a friendly get-together." Aiden held her gaze. "There's this French restaurant Kade told me about, so...?"

Half a dozen different emotions flickered across Dawn's face too fast for Aiden to identify. Was that...disappointment? "It's really nice of you to ask, and normally I'd love to, but I can't."

"Oh, that's okay. It was just a spontaneous thought," Aiden said, trying to act indifferent. "Well, I guess I'll see you around." She turned, clenching her hands in her pockets, and strode away.

"Wait!" This time it was Dawn who was running to catch up with her. "It's not that I don't want to go out with you, it's just..."

Aiden stopped and looked at her. "You don't have to explain." Accepting a simple "no" from any woman under any circumstances was the most important rule in Aiden's book.

"Yes, I do."

"Okay. I'm listening."

"I'm still not working and..." Dawn looked down at the red cobblestones. "Money is getting a little tight. An expensive restaurant is just not within my budget right now."

Aiden stared at her for a moment and then smiled. "That's not a problem. I invited you, so of course I'm going to pay."

"No." Dawn shook her head. "I can't accept that."

Dismayed, Aiden folded her arms across her chest. "So, you're not going to go out with me because you're too proud?" She couldn't believe it. It seemed a very childish reason compared to Dawn's normally mature behavior.

Dawn didn't waver under Aiden's stare. "This has nothing to do with pride. Okay, maybe it has to do with pride, but that's just to a very small extent. Mostly, it's about equality."

"Equality?"

"Equality," Dawn said with a decisive nod. "We met at a very low point in my life. Until now, you were the strong detective, and I was the helpless victim—and those are not roles we can build a friendship on, much less anything else. I need to feel like I'm your equal, and we can't do that if we keep on adding other inequalities. I don't want to be a kept woman. Can you understand that?"

Aiden looked at her for a little longer. Not many women had stood up to her like that. Usually, she was the one to make the decisions, to start and end the affair when she got bored with the weaker partner. "Yes," she finally said with a grudging respect. "Yes, I can. So, you're not going out with me?"

"Not used to rejections, are you?" Dawn grinned.

"It doesn't happen often, that's for sure." Aiden studied the patterns of the cobblestones under her feet.

"Listen, why don't we do something else instead? I don't need you to spend half your paycheck to have a nice evening."

So, low-maintenance women really do exist. "Okay," Aiden said, in a much better mood. "What do you suggest?"

"How about an afternoon of ice-skating?" Dawn said.

Ice-skating? Aiden gave her a skeptical glance. Helplessly stumbling around at the edge of an ice-skating rink was not her idea of a fun afternoon, and she didn't think that falling on her ass was the best way to impress a woman. "You want to go ice-skating? With me?"

"Yeah! It's fun, it's not that expensive, and it's not your usual first-date activity, so it doesn't put as much pressure on us as a restaurant setting would."

Aiden had to admit that it sounded reasonable. "You're right, but there's still one problem. I, uh, don't know how to ice-skate."

Dawn raised both brows. "You've never been ice-skating?

Not even once? That's a sacrilege! But fortunately, we can remedy it—I could teach you."

"Hmm..." Aiden scratched her nose.

Dawn laughed, her eyes twinkling with delight. "You're not scared, are you, Detective? Don't worry. I'll catch you when you fall."

Are we still talking about ice-skating? Aiden gave in with a sigh. "Okay."

"Then it's a date?"

Aiden studied her. "Yes. That is...if you want it to be." She was well aware that it might take Dawn more time to be ready to begin dating again. "Or do you want to invite your niece to go with us?" Maybe Dawn would feel more comfortable with a chaperone.

Dawn blinked and then smiled. "It's nice of you to think of Jamie, but for now I want it to be just the two of us. Even a stellar teacher like me can't take on more than one student at a time."

"Yeah, you'll have your hands full with me. I mean..." Aiden blushed and glanced down at her watch. "I really do have to go now."

"Tomorrow, four p.m.?"

Aiden nodded without further hesitation. "I'll pick you up."

"Why don't I pick you up?" Dawn said, clearly in another attempt to establish equality.

"Because you drive a sardine can, and I need to have two functioning legs if I want to attempt ice-skating," Aiden said.

Dawn thought about it. "You can drive if I get to pay the admission at the ice-skating rink."

Aiden wondered if it would always be like this and then decided that she would like a partner who could stand up to her for a change. "You drive a hard bargain, Doctor Kinsley."

"Take it or leave it, Detective." Dawn held out her hand.

"Okay, okay, it's a deal." Aiden shook the offered hand. One last squeeze of her fingers and then Aiden departed. *I think I'm gonna join Ray and eat a salad today. I'll need the vitamins if I want to keep up with Dawn Kinsley.*

"Is this size okay?" Dawn knelt and looked down at the rented skates covering Aiden's feet.

"I think so."

"Okay, then let's get going." The indoor ice rink on the mall's first floor was beginning to get crowded, and Dawn didn't want to risk a collision between other skaters and her inexperienced skating partner. She finished strapping on her own pair of ice skates, stood, and offered her hand to help Aiden up.

Holding on to Dawn's hand, Aiden hobbled the few feet to the shiny surface of the ice. She stopped at the very edge of the rink. "Okay, how do I do this?"

Dawn held back a smile. Aiden was clearly uncomfortable now that she was the inexperienced, helpless one. The few dozen onlookers, watching the ice rink from the food court above, didn't help either. For Dawn, it was a perfect first-date situation, leaving her in control. "Hold on to my hand, distribute your weight evenly on both skates, and just try to glide. We're gonna stay near the rail on the outside, away from the more experienced skaters and the rowdies."

She stepped onto the ice, easily keeping her balance because she had done it hundreds of times before.

Aiden followed with more hesitation, one hand clutching Dawn's, the other holding on to the railing. As Dawn guided her around the rink, Aiden began a one-legged shuffle in an effort not to lose her tight grip on the railing.

"Let go of the railing," Dawn said.

Aiden shook her head. "I'll fall."

"Even if you do, you won't hurt yourself. Everyone falls."

Aiden still held on to the bar. "I don't see anyone in danger of falling, except for me."

Dawn laughed. "That's because you keep looking at your feet, so you can't see anyone else. You also can't keep your balance this way. Keep your head up. Trust me, I won't let you fall."

Slowly, Aiden loosened her grip on the railing and lifted her head while her other hand clutched Dawn's.

"Yes, that's it!" Dawn called, delighted that Aiden was starting to give up control.

Aiden slipped and slid around the ice.

"You're doing great! Now turn one foot sideways and use it to propel yourself forward on the other foot. Don't be afraid to take your foot off the ice."

They slowly made their way around the rink, once and then twice. "Want to try on your own?"

Aiden hesitated and then let go of Dawn's hand.

Grinning proudly, Dawn watched as her student skated away from her.

Aiden did well enough until, out of the corner of her eye, she detected two preteens who were doing effortless spins right next to her. Afraid of a collision, Aiden leaned to one side to correct her course and skate around them, but she overcompensated and fell.

Dawn dug the edge of one blade into the ice, raced toward her, and stopped in a tight spiral next to her. "Hey, you okay?"

"Yeah." Aiden looked up. "I fell on my butt. The only thing hurt is my pride."

"Want to try again?" Dawn loved ice-skating, but she knew that some people could never get up any real enthusiasm for it. She didn't want to force her hobby onto Aiden if she really didn't like it.

"You bet!" Aiden instantly got to her feet.

A few rounds and three falls later, she was gliding over the ice with much more grace and had even tried a few spiral turns. Dawn was skating backward so she could keep an eye on her. Aiden's cheeks were red from the cool air and the exertion; her short hair was disheveled, and her eyes were sparkling.

They were a little out of breath when they finally stopped, leaning next to each other against the railing. The ice-skating rink had gotten crowded, and loud voices drifted down to them from the food court—this was not the time or the place to hold a lengthy conversation.

As they trudged toward Aiden's car, snow was starting to fall. Aiden seemed as reluctant to end their afternoon as Dawn was.

"Come in for a minute to warm yourself up," Dawn said when they reached her apartment building.

To her satisfaction, Aiden followed her up and sank onto the couch without much hesitation. Groaning, Aiden stretched her legs and waggled her feet. "I think it'll take a while to get my land legs back."

"I hope you still had fun despite a few rather unfriendly encounters with the ice?" Dawn said when she pressed a cup of coffee into Aiden's cold hands.

"I had a lot of fun," Aiden answered. "Well," she added with a smile, "maybe not as much fun as all those preschoolers had, watching me hobble around the ice like a drunken penguin and fall on my ass while they did effortless pirouettes all around me."

Dawn laughed. "That's the advantage of youth, Detective."

Aiden set down her mug and studied her for a moment. "Why don't you call me by my first name? You can't call someone who spent an entire afternoon humiliating herself in your company by an honorable title like Detective."

Dawn had been waiting for this offer since the trial had ended. "Okay, Aiden." The name felt a little strange as it came over her lips, even though she had been calling her that in her mind for a while. "And for your information, you weren't that bad, and you certainly didn't humiliate yourself."

"Well, I won't give up my day job to train for the Olympics either, that's for sure." Aiden chuckled. "But it was fun and...I'd like to do it again."

Dawn shifted forward onto the edge of her seat. She had a hard time holding back her delighted grin. *Guess I didn't scare her off, huh?* "I'd like that too."

A few minutes later, Aiden swallowed her last sip of coffee and glanced out the window. "I'd better go now. The snow's still falling."

"Drive carefully," Dawn said, following her to the door.

"I always do." Aiden reached behind herself to open the door but still faced Dawn.

Dawn hesitated, unsure how to say good-bye. She had liked holding Aiden's hand during her ice-skating lessons, but no further touches had been exchanged. She stiffened without conscious thought as Aiden leaned down, knowing she wasn't ready for anything more than a quick peck on the cheek. Her worries eased when Aiden made no attempt to kiss her but just hugged her for a moment.

"Thanks for the lesson and the company," Aiden said when she let go.

"You're welcome."

Dawn stood by the door long after it had closed behind Aiden.

CHAPTER 24

Aiden paced next to the coffee table, where her phone lay. Finally, she plopped down on the couch and studied the device as if she could make it ring just by looking at it. No such luck. *Should I call her, or do I wait until she calls me? If I call too soon, she'll think I'm clingy. If I wait too long, she'll think I don't care.* Aiden groaned. *God, I really hate this dating stuff. It's more complicated than understanding the science behind DNA-testing.*

It had been a week since their ice-skating adventure—Aiden still wasn't sure if she should call it a date—and she hadn't heard from Dawn since then.

After another minute of internal debating, she gave herself a mental slap and reached for the phone. When it began to ring in her hand, she almost dropped it. *Jesus!* She fumbled for a bit until she found the right button. "Carlisle."

"Hi, it's Dawn." A short silence on the other end. "You sound a little breathless, did I interrupt anything?"

"Dawn! Hi! No, no, you're not interrupting anything. I was just about to call you." *Great! That sounds like the lamest excuse in the history of dating, even if it is the truth.*

"Yeah?"

Aiden curled her legs under her. "Yes. I wanted to hear how your week is going."

"It's been great so far," Dawn said. "I met an old friend from college. She's a child psychologist and a family therapist, and she suggested that I work as her co-therapist for a while. I'd mainly work with kids and with teens and young adults who have trouble coming to terms with their sexual orientation."

"Sounds wonderful." Aiden smiled. Going back to work would be another step toward healing for Dawn. "Do you think you'll do it?"

"Yes, I will. I have always wanted to try working with kids. Maybe I'll go back to counseling rape survivors in a few months, but for now, working with kids will pay the bills, and it'll give me a chance to expand my professional horizons. How's your week been?"

One dead body, two brutal rapes, and a five-year-old who's been molested by her own father. Dawn didn't need to hear that. "Oh, the usual. A lot of paperwork, a few search warrants, and a suspect puking all over my shoes."

"Ruined shoes? Then the suggestion I have comes at just the right time," Dawn said.

Aiden leaned back. "What suggestion is that?"

"Go shopping with me today."

Aiden scratched the back of her neck. She had been looking forward to spending more time with Dawn, but shopping?

"You already have other plans," Dawn said when Aiden failed to answer. The disappointment was clear in her voice.

"No! No, that's not it. It's just... Well, I'm not exactly Portland's shopping queen." She looked down at her blue jeans and the oversized T-shirt. "I don't have the patience for marathon shopping sprees. Before I'm even through the first clothing store, I always begin to wish that I had my service weapon with me to clear the crowd—or at least to put me out of my misery."

Dawn laughed. "Oh, now I understand. You're shopaphobic!"

Aiden chuckled into the receiver. "If that's your professional diagnosis."

"It is," Dawn said. "And it sounds like a severe case."

"Do you intend to cure my shopaphobia, Doctor?" Aiden smiled.

"Of course. Letting a disorder like that go untreated is against professional ethics, not to mention bad for our city's economy."

"So, what's the treatment plan?"

"I'd suggest you join a self-help group, but I fear you won't find another woman who hates shopping, so I think I'll try confrontation therapy with you," Dawn said.

Aiden lay back on the couch, taking the phone with her. "Confrontation therapy? What exactly does that entail?"

"The patient is confronted with the phobic stimulus until the fear disappears," Dawn explained, sounding like a textbook. "Or, in your case, until we reach the limit of your credit card—whichever comes first."

Aiden laughed.

"Come on, say yes. I'll even throw in an added incentive. You help me find the perfect dress for my cousin's wedding, and I'll help you pick out the rest of your Christmas presents that you haven't bought yet."

"The rest?" Aiden laughed. "In view of that generous offer, I should probably tell you that I haven't bought any Christmas presents yet."

"Not even one?" That concept was clearly foreign to Dawn.

"Let me guess. You're one of those people who start looking for Christmas presents in September." Christmas had never been big in the Carlisle household, and since her mother's death, Aiden had only bought small gifts for Ray and his family.

"No—I start looking in January."

Aiden smiled. She could see Dawn doing that. "Okay, when and where does my first therapy session start?"

"Right now?"

Aiden didn't hesitate. "Okay. Should I come pick you up?" She fully expected the offer to be rebuffed.

"I won't say no to that this time," Dawn said to her surprise. "We're gonna need the bigger trunk of your car."

"Want me to carry some of that?" Dawn nodded down at the shopping bags Aiden carried.

"No, that's okay." Aiden knew that the offer would be short-lived, anyway. All it would take was one more store and Dawn would pass the bags back to her because she'd need both hands to examine the goods on sale.

When they passed a store selling art and handicraft supplies, Aiden kept her eyes on Dawn.

As she had expected, Dawn looked back over her shoulder as they walked past. This was the third set of art supplies Dawn had looked at and then quickly walked on with one last, regretful glance at the price tag.

Aiden recognized the glances immediately. Her mother had never been able to walk past art supplies without stopping to take a closer look either. "Is that a hobby of yours? Painting and drawing?"

"Yes, it is...or rather it used to be," Dawn answered. "I haven't picked up a pencil or a brush since...the rape."

The word was like an electric shock to Aiden's system. She had to force herself not to flinch, not wanting Dawn to think that she had anything to be ashamed of. Sometimes it was hard to remember that Dawn had been raped just two months ago, because most of the time, she seemed so carefree and full of life. Aiden made a mental note to go back later and buy the art supplies for Dawn as a Christmas present.

"Is the shopping anxiety easing up some?" Dawn asked when they left the store and strolled side by side down the street.

"Well, Doc, all these heavy shopping bags have successfully held my flight reflex in check; that's for sure," Aiden said with a grin. To be honest, their shopping spree had been surprisingly painless for her. She hadn't felt the urge to turn around and head home as she usually did. From time to time, a crowded store would get to be too much for Dawn, who still couldn't stand to be bumped and jostled from all sides by strangers, and she would hold on to Aiden's arm until they reached the closest exit. Aiden found that she didn't mind those moments of closeness at all.

"That's good, because we still haven't found a dress for me." Dawn directed them into yet another clothing store. Strolling along the racks, she found two reasonably priced dresses that she liked. "I think I'll try these on."

Aiden didn't want to be left standing in the middle of the store, where the saleswomen would undoubtedly try to talk her into buying something, so she followed Dawn in the general direction of the dressing rooms.

With a small smile, Dawn closed the curtain between them.

Aiden waited with her back to the dressing room, giving Dawn some added privacy. That way, she could observe the other shoppers and direct anyone heading for the small room to another, unoccupied cubicle.

"Aiden?" Dawn's voice from behind the curtain made her turn around.

"Yes?"

"It seems I've lost a little weight. Could you please bring me the blue dress one size smaller?"

Aiden had noticed the weight loss. It worried her, but she had decided not to say anything for now. She knew it was important to let Dawn have complete control over her body, even in this. "Sure, I'll be right back."

Within a minute, she returned to the cubicle with the smaller dress. She lifted her hand and then hesitated, not sure if Dawn would be comfortable with being seen half-naked. "Uh, Dawn? Here's the dress you wanted."

The curtain moved back a little, and Aiden averted her eyes while she handed over the new dress and received the bigger one in exchange.

Fabric rustled, and then, a minute later, the curtain opened again.

Aiden had never seen Dawn in a dress before and couldn't help staring. "Wow, Dawn, that's..." She gesticulated, searching for a fitting adjective and finding none that could convey how she felt.

Dawn checked out her image in the full-length mirror and tugged at the hem of the dress that ended slightly above her knees. "You don't think it's a little too tight or maybe a bit too short?"

"No! It's really nice. It brings out the green in your eyes." Her eye color wasn't the only attribute that the dress accentuated nicely, but Aiden didn't think that she should comment on that.

Dawn eyed herself in the mirror when a woman ambled up to them.

For a moment, Aiden thought that it was the saleswoman wanting to encourage Dawn to buy the dress, but then the woman addressed her, not Dawn. "Well, well, well, if it isn't Aiden Carlisle out and about with her girlfriend. How domestic! And here I thought you didn't do relationships."

God, please, not now! Aiden groaned internally when she finally recognized the woman. She had picked up the blonde in a bar a few months ago and had promptly forgotten her the next day. Unfortunately, it was apparent that the woman, whose name she couldn't remember, hadn't forgotten her.

"Could you help me with the zipper, darling? You'll have to excuse her for a second. She's needed elsewhere." Dawn directed a sweet smile at the blonde before she tugged Aiden into the dressing room with her.

The second the curtain closed behind them, Aiden sank

onto the small stool. "God, I'm so sorry, Dawn!" She rubbed her forehead, where a dull throbbing had begun.

Dawn looked down at her. She didn't appear upset. "It's okay. We all have a past. I didn't expect you not to have had relationships before we started...whatever this is between us."

Aiden shook her head. "I haven't, not really."

"But what about...?" Dawn gestured to the other side of the curtain.

"I haven't been in a relationship for about five years, nothing long-term at least," Aiden said. "With my job and everything, it's easier to have one-night stands and short flings without the emotional entanglements."

When Dawn kept silent, Aiden looked up at her. "Dawn?"

Dawn nibbled on her lower lip. "I can't do that. I was never one for one-night stands, and I'm sure as hell not up for it now."

Aiden had known that from the start. "Good, because that's not what I want from you."

Dawn studied Aiden's face. "What do you want?"

For a moment, Aiden thought about answering with a joke that would lighten the mood, but then decided against it. Dawn needed her to be honest and express her feelings, even if it was hard for her. "Well, I want to get to know you for a start. Can we leave it at that for now?"

Dawn nodded, smiling once again. "Now, unless you want to watch me change, you should go and try to get rid of your stalker."

Heat shot through Aiden's cheeks at the thought of watching Dawn change. Surely, she hadn't blushed so much since puberty. "Okay, I should probably go and tell her that my girlfriend has anger issues, and she tends to take them out on my former...uh... romantic interests."

When Aiden opened the curtain and stepped out of the dressing room, the blonde had disappeared.

Half an hour later, Aiden navigated her car through heavy traffic. "Home now, or do you think I need more shopping therapy?"

Dawn laughed. "No more therapy...for now. But we should drop most of these bags off at my mother's. Otherwise Jamie will find her presents when she stays at my apartment. That girl is like a gift-seeking missile."

She unlocked the door of her mother's house while Aiden waited behind her, balancing half a dozen shopping bags in her arms.

When Grace came out of the kitchen, Aiden stopped in the doorway, unsure how Dawn's mother would react to her continued presence in her daughter's life.

"What's all this?" Grace pointed to the bags and parcels both of them were carrying. "Are you moving back in?"

Dawn chuckled. "No. I went out to buy a dress for Tommy's wedding and a few more Christmas presents, and I managed to con Aiden into helping me."

Grace's eyebrows arched at the use of her first name. "That was nice of you, Detective," she said, her tone carefully neutral.

Detective, huh? I guess she doesn't want me to be just "Aiden" to her daughter.

"Are you staying for dinner?" Grace asked, mainly in Dawn's direction. "It's almost ready."

"I'd love to." Dawn set her bags down and moved to take Aiden's from her. "I'm starving. You'll stay too, won't you?"

"You're welcome to eat with us," Grace offered with a little more warmth than before.

Aiden shook her head. She wasn't ready to deal with Dawn's mother yet, especially since she wasn't sure where she stood with her. "I think I'll head home now. I still have a few reports to go through." Then she remembered that running off now would leave Dawn stranded at her mother's. "Should I come back later to drive you home?"

"No, that's okay," Dawn said. "If I can still move after the tons of food I intend to consume, I'll wrap the Christmas presents and just stay here tonight. If you don't have other plans, maybe you could pick me up tomorrow and we could have breakfast or brunch?"

Aiden looked forward to spending more time with Dawn but felt awkward discussing their plans in front of Grace, so she just nodded.

Dawn climbed over the shopping bags blocking her way and stepped closer to Aiden. She softly touched her forearm. "I had fun today."

"Me too," Aiden said, looking back and forth between Dawn and her mother. She did not dare to hug her under Grace's watchful eyes. "So, I'll see you tomorrow?"

Dawn nodded. "Tomorrow."

Dawn could feel her mother's gaze resting on her as she carried the shopping bags to her old room, which now doubled as a guest room, and hid the presents in the closet. While she hung up the dress she had bought, her mother leaned in the doorway, watching her but not saying anything.

Finally, Grace stepped into the room and fingered the dress. "Very nice. You'll be the most beautiful woman at the wedding."

Dawn smiled. "You're biased, Mom."

Her mother said nothing. She studied Dawn for a few moments longer. "So Detective Carlisle helped you pick it out?"

"Yes, she did." Dawn knew what would be coming and squared her shoulders, ready to defend Aiden and her presence in her life.

"I wasn't aware that the Portland Police Bureau is offering fashion advice now."

Dawn folded the empty shopping bags, set them aside, and turned. "They aren't. Aiden didn't accompany me as a police officer. She went with me because she's...my friend." Neither she nor Aiden were ready to call it more—and certainly not in front of her mother.

Grace seemed to digest it for a few moments. "Well," she said. "I have to admit that she has good taste—in dresses and in friends." She picked up the empty shopping bags and returned to the kitchen, leaving Dawn staring after her.

With a satisfied sigh, Ray let the last report of the day sail into his outbox. "Hey, Aiden, want to come home with me?"

"If this is your subtle way of trying to pick up a woman, it's been too long for you, Bennet," Okada said from his own desk.

Ray grimaced but ignored him and continued to look at his partner, who was still bent over her work. "The girls told me to ask you. Susan is trying out a new recipe, and they don't want to suffer through it alone. So? You'll come?"

Aiden sat back and looked at him. "As promising as that sounds, I can't."

"You're not on call, are you?"

"No." Aiden signed her report and threw it into the outbox on her desk. "I have plans already."

This was the third time in the last two weeks that he'd heard that particular answer when he had asked her to join him for a drink or family dinner. "Do these plans include anyone I know?"

"Perhaps."

It was clear to Ray that she didn't want to lie to him but was equally uncomfortable discussing it. He would respect that. *For now.*

Okada knew no such restraint. "Please tell me it's not that thin brunette from the public defender's office."

"C'mon, get serious!" Ray rolled his eyes. "Aiden has better taste than you."

Okada smoothed back his hair. "I'll have you know that—"

"Cool down, guys!" Aiden said. "And please find something else to discuss other than my private life."

The fact that Aiden even had a private life was amazing enough to Ray, but he kept quiet and trusted that his partner would confide in him whenever she was ready to.

CHAPTER 25

THE SHRILL RINGING OF HER phone almost made Dawn fall from the couch. In her haste to reach the phone before it stopped ringing, she stumbled over her nephew's building blocks. "D..." She caught herself just in time as she remembered her underage company. "Dumb toys." She snatched up the receiver. "Hello."

"Hi, Dawn," Aiden said. "How's the kiddie shrink business?"

Dawn laughed and sank back onto the couch. They had talked on the phone at least every other day and as a result were much more at ease with each other. Dawn hoped that this easy, comfortable interaction would eventually transfer to their face-to-face meetings. "It's going really well, thank you. Are you done with playing the bad cop for today?"

"What makes you think that I haven't been the good cop?"

"Call it a hunch." Dawn grinned. "So, are you through with your shift?"

"That's why I'm calling," Aiden answered. "I'm about to go wall climbing at my gym, and I thought maybe you'd like to come with me and try it?"

Dawn let her forehead sink onto her pulled-up knee. *Shit. The first time she suggests an activity, without me prompting or asking her first, and I have to tell her no.* "I'd love to try it sometime, but right now isn't good for me. I'm babysitting Jamie and Tim."

"Oh."

For a few seconds, Dawn could hear only Aiden's breathing. She sighed. "Sorry, it's just bad timing."

"No. No, it's not. I mean, I don't want to intrude or anything, but if you still want the company—my company—I could come over and help with the babysitting."

Dawn stared at her nephew, who was busy rearranging every piece of living room furniture that he could reach. Her niece had just planted another sticker tattoo on her arm. Her ex, Maggie, had always preferred to flee the premises whenever Jamie and Tim were around. Either that or she acted as if she was making a huge sacrifice on behalf of world peace by spending half an hour in the company of two kids. Now here was Aiden Carlisle, offering to postpone her own plans and help her babysit after a stressful shift.

"Dawn?" Aiden asked when the silence grew between them. "Hey, it's okay if you don't want—"

"I do," Dawn said hastily. "I do want you to come over."

"Okay. Can I bring anything?"

Dawn looked around the living room. "A cleaning lady?"

Aiden laughed. "Sorry, can't help you there. Anything else?"

"No. Just yourself and a healthy appetite—we're ordering pizza," Dawn said.

"Yeah!" Jamie almost hit her in the face while pumping her fist in a victory gesture. "I want pepperoni and mushrooms."

"Me too," Aiden said and chuckled.

After hanging up, Dawn called her favorite pizza place, and then she and her niece spent the next thirty minutes out-fidgeting each other, waiting impatiently for the ringing of the doorbell. *I'm not waiting for a pimple-faced delivery boy, though.*

When the doorbell finally buzzed, Jamie jumped up.

"Ah, ah!" Dawn shook her head. "No running around in socks!" The way to the door was an obstacle course of toys, and she didn't want Jamie to hurt herself. When she peeked through the peephole, her smile grew brighter.

Standing in front of the door, bouncing on the balls of her feet, was Aiden.

Dawn directed a quick gaze down her own body, skeptically inspecting her baggy sweatpants and the results of Jamie's beauty contest: each and every finger- and toenail had been painted in a different color nail polish, and sticker tattoos of dragons, horses, and flowers covered both of her arms. *If this doesn't scare her off, nothing will.* She opened the door.

"Don't touch her!" Jamie screeched before they could even say hello.

Dawn stopped and turned, throwing an irritated glance back at her niece. When Jamie waved her hands, she finally understood and turned back around with a smile. "Don't worry, she's not homophobic or anything. She's just afraid that I'll smear the nail polish she so artfully applied."

Aiden inspected their nails. "Artistic talents seem to run in the family." She stepped past Dawn into the apartment.

Dawn wasn't sure whether she should be disappointed or relieved. She liked the warm, protective hugs Aiden gave, but their greetings and good-byes were often a little awkward, each of them unsure where the other's limits lay. "Come on in and make yourself comfortable. I'm not allowed to play hostess until my nail polish is dry." She returned to her place on the couch and watched Aiden step over the toys on the floor and take off her leather jacket. *I wonder if she suspects my secret—or maybe not so secret—addiction to her leather jacket?*

"I brought dessert." Aiden held up two boxes. "Ice cream for us and cookies for Tim since I wasn't sure if he could have ice cream."

As if recognizing his name, the ten-month-old crawled across the rug, grabbed one of Aiden's jeans legs, and pulled himself up into a half-standing position. "Mom-ma!"

Dawn laughed at Aiden's blush. "Don't worry, he doesn't want you to adopt him. He calls every woman 'Mom.' Sometimes, he even does it to men."

Aiden grinned. "And here I thought I was special."

"You are," Dawn said quietly.

Aiden looked up from the little boy holding on to her leg, and their gazes met and held.

The doorbell interrupted the moment.

"Pizza!" Jamie shouted and jumped up and down.

Aiden lifted an eyebrow. "Didn't you feed her today?"

"Feed her? Let me put it this way: every time Jamie leaves after a visit, my refrigerator looks like yours," Dawn said over her shoulder, looking for her wallet. Every time she had visited Aiden's apartment, the fridge had been empty except for yogurt, leftover takeout, and various beverages.

When she returned with the pizza and her niece in tow, Aiden had picked up Tim and was bouncing him up and down on her hip.

"I could put him in his high chair while we eat," Dawn said, even though her nephew didn't look as if he wanted to be taken away from this new, interesting person so soon.

"No, it's okay for the moment." Aiden sat down on the couch and settled the baby on her lap. "If you think it's okay, of course. I don't have much experience with babies."

Studying the smiling ten-month-old on Aiden's lap, Dawn found that hard to believe. "It certainly doesn't show." She began to put slices of pepperoni-and-mushroom pizza on plates for Jamie and Aiden, whose hands were busy with the bouncing baby.

"Are you Auntie Dawn's new girlfriend?" Jamie asked around a mouthful of pizza.

Aiden almost choked on a mushroom and directed a wide-eyed gaze at Dawn, who said nothing since she was very interested in what Aiden would answer. "Uh, well, I'm a girl, and I'm her friend, so I guess that makes me her girlfriend, doesn't it?"

"No, silly!" Jamie laughed at her. "I mean her real girlfriend, with kissing and everything."

Aiden stalled, taking a moment to rescue a slice of pizza from being grabbed by eager baby hands.

"Aiden is a really, really good friend," Dawn said. "But she's not my kissing buddy, so don't even think about starting with that annoying little song, rug rat." She poked her giggling niece in the side. *Not yet, at least.*

Later, with the pizza long gone, Dawn leaned back on the couch, an indulgent smile on her lips as she watched Aiden.

The tall woman had cleared some space and lay stretched out on the floor, letting Tim crawl all over her while she gently tickled him. The boy giggled and squealed as she lifted him up with both arms, making him fly above her head.

Jamie shook her leg to get Aiden's attention. "Me too, me too!"

Before Dawn could protest that Jamie was much too big to be picked up, Aiden set the baby down and stood, sweeping the girl up and around the living room in circles.

God, it would be a crime if this woman never raises a child. She's so good with them.

Finally, Aiden fell back on the couch next to her.

"You didn't have to do that," Dawn said. She tried not to notice the slight sheen of sweat above the two open buttons on Aiden's polo shirt and the way the shirt clung to her damp skin.

"I could paint your nails for you," Jamie said, gracing Aiden with a smile. "It's really pretty."

Dawn had to force herself not to laugh out loud at the expression on Aiden's face. She looked positively panicked.

"I never paint my nails," Aiden said. "They're too short for it."

Jamie didn't let that discourage her. "Then I'll paint your toenails." She tugged at Aiden's shoes.

Aiden looked down at her with rising alarm. "Uh..."

Dawn laughed. "What's the matter, Detective? Afraid that this could hurt your reputation? Rough, tough cops don't have purple toenails?"

"Well, it's not exactly part of our standard uniform, that's for sure." Despite her protests, she slipped off her shoes and socks and wiggled her toes at Jamie. "I surrender. Just no pink, please."

Dawn leaned down to help Tim crawl into her lap and took the opportunity to study Aiden's feet. *Cute.* She watched the bare toes curl into the carpet. *Somehow there's something almost intimate about sitting next to a barefoot woman.*

An hour later, Aiden put on her socks and shoes, covering her green, red, blue, and silver toenails. "I'll head out now. Thanks for the artful pedicure, Jamie." She nodded at the girl, scoring major points with Dawn's niece for not trying to tousle her hair as many adults did. After putting on her coat, she turned back to Dawn, who was still sitting on the couch.

This time, the sleeping baby in her arms prevented Dawn from hugging her. "If you want, we could go wall climbing tomorrow."

"Well, after that pizza, I could certainly use a little exercise." Aiden buttoned up her coat, and then there was nothing else to do but to say good-bye, turn around, and leave.

"Should I call you tomorrow morning?" Dawn asked in an attempt to stall a little.

"Around nine?"

Dawn grinned. "I'm not sure I'll be up by then. I tend to sleep in on Sundays." She could see Aiden as an early riser, someone who couldn't be kept in bed past eight, and she absentmindedly wondered if that would ever be of any importance between them beyond the planning of joint activities. "How about ten?"

"Ten, it is. See you tomorrow." Aiden leaned down, careful not to wake the sleeping boy.

Dawn's breath caught, very much aware of Aiden's closeness and the air of insecurity lingering between them. The warm but quick hug that had become their usual greeting was impossible since Dawn's arms were held captive by her nephew.

After a few seconds of hesitancy on both sides, Dawn decided that it was up to her to establish any form of contact between them. She leaned forward and quickly pressed her lips against Aiden's cheek for a fleeting peck before sinking back against the couch. "Thanks for keeping us company."

"Oh, you're welcome," Aiden answered with a smile, moving backward toward the door. "It's not every day I get my nails done." She winked at the giggling Jamie, and then she was gone.

A few minutes later, the doorbell rang again. Dawn cautiously slipped out from under the still sleeping baby and settled him onto the couch.

"Hi, Dawn." Eliza hugged her and then looked down at her fingers, arms, and toes. "What happened to you?"

"Your daughter," Dawn answered.

Jamie ran forward and wiggled her toes at her mother. "I did mine and Aiden's too!"

Dawn grimaced. She hadn't wanted to tell her family about her friendship—and certainly not the possibility of more—with Aiden just yet.

Luckily, Eliza just nodded, obviously assuming Aiden was one of Jamie's countless dolls or stuffed animals that she housed at Dawn's. "Okay, sweetie, why don't you start packing up your things. Your dad's waiting at home."

It was still a little strange for Dawn to hear Eliza referring to Rick, her husband of two years, as Jamie's dad, a title that would have been her brother's had he lived. But she pushed back her feelings, knowing that Rick was the only father Jamie would ever know—and a good one at that.

Jamie pouted a little but finally went to pick up her things from the bedroom.

"I could watch her again next weekend so you and Rick can have some time together," Dawn said.

Eliza looked up from her sleeping son and studied Dawn with a frown. "Not that I don't appreciate it, but I really don't want to impose. Don't you need a little time for yourself right now?"

"You think Jamie is just a distraction for me?" It hurt when other people reduced all her feelings to those related to the rape, as if she didn't have other things that were important in her life anymore.

"No, I don't think that at all," Eliza said. "I know that you love my kids. I'm sorry if—"

Dawn sighed. Her anger still stirred too easily whenever she felt she was treated like a victim. "It's all right, really. And I was serious about next weekend. We want to take Jamie ice-skating if it's okay with you." She bit her lip when she realized what she had let slip.

"Jamie would love that. Wait a minute! Did you just say 'we'? You didn't talk your mother or Del into ice-skating with you, did you?"

Dawn wasn't eager to discuss something that she wasn't too sure of herself, but she didn't want to lie either. "Um, no. I don't think they'd be interested in that."

"I know you psychologists are supposed to be a bit wacky yourselves, but you're not referring to yourself in the plural, are you? So, who else might that 'we' include?" Eliza's dark eyes glittered with curiosity.

There was no sense in trying to deny anything. She had no doubt that all Eliza would hear from her daughter on the drive home would be "Aiden did this" and "Aiden did that." "I've spent a little time with Aiden lately."

"Aiden?" Eliza's eyes widened. "You're dating Detective Carlisi?"

"Carlisle," Dawn said. "And I'm not dating her. Not really."

Eliza studied her through narrowed eyes. "She seems to be a nice woman, but starting a relationship with the detective who investigated your case... That could get really complicated."

Dawn couldn't deny that. *It's even more complicated than you realize.* After working with rape survivors for years, she knew how hard it could be to establish trust and intimacy in the first new relationship after facing such a trauma. Her reservations about being in a relationship with a cop didn't make it easier, and Aiden's own issues certainly didn't help either. *But I still think it could be worth it.* "I'm not trying to start a relationship with the detective. I'm trying to get to know the woman."

"And she's interested in getting to know you too?"

"I think so, yes." Dawn looked at her sister-in-law with pleading eyes. "We're taking it slow, though, so please keep it to yourself for now, okay? If my mom gets wind of it... What she'll put Aiden through would make the Spanish Inquisition look like a relaxation cure."

Eliza laughed. "Oh, come on, your mom's not that bad. She welcomed me into the family with open arms."

"Yeah, but you're not a cop, and you don't want to start a lesbian relationship with her only daughter."

Eliza's smile dimmed. "Okay, I'll keep quiet about it. But you could bring your sweetie over for dinner next Sunday. I want to get to know her."

"You will," Dawn said, ignoring the "sweetie" comment. "But not next Sunday. It's too soon." Aiden wasn't accustomed to big families. She had a feeling that under the right—or rather wrong—circumstances, it would be Aiden rather than she who would become overwhelmed by too much closeness and intimacy and run away scared.

"Then invite her to the house at Christmas," Eliza said. "There will be so many people around she won't feel like she's under a microscope."

Celebrating Christmas with Aiden. It wasn't the first time she had thought about it, but she hadn't found the courage to ask if it was what Aiden wanted too. "I'll ask her."

Dawn extended both arms to the sides and twirled around in circles, without caring that she got snow all over herself. "God, it's been a while since I've done this." She nodded down at the sled that Aiden dragged behind her. "When was the last time we got this much snow?"

Aiden shrugged. Even when they had gotten enough snow, she had gone sledding only once as a child. Despite bitter thoughts about her own childhood, she had to smile as she watched Dawn playing in the snow. Dawn had an almost childlike love of life, and her enthusiasm was contagious. During the last few weeks, she had spent a lot of time with Dawn—and that inevitably meant taking part in her Christmas preparations. She had bought more presents than ever before, had helped Dawn bake cookies, and had even agreed to put up a small, potted Christmas tree on a side table in her living room. For the first time in many, many years, the excitement of Christmas had come back to her.

This morning, she had even let herself be talked into going sledding with Dawn. She put her head down against the cold wind and the softly falling snow and stopped next to Dawn when they reached the top of the hill.

Dawn turned to her, and Aiden grinned at the blonde locks sticking out from under the bright red woolen cap. Dawn turned the sled around and straddled it. "I think it's better if you sit in the back since you're taller than me."

"Okay." Aiden took her place behind Dawn. Sitting this close to her, feeling Dawn's body pressed against her own, even through thick layers of clothing, made her heart jump. Carefully, she settled her gloved hands around Dawn's waist. "Is this okay?"

"Yes, of course." Dawn half turned to look at her, a slight smirk on her face. "I know it's not meant to be sexual."

Aiden bit her lip. She hadn't expected such openness. *Maybe I should have.* More often than not, Dawn was the one who was forcing herself to talk about the rape and its effects, while Aiden danced around the issue and tried to avoid anything that might remind Dawn of it.

"Hold on!" Dawn shouted. "Here we go!"

They pushed off and accelerated down the hill, leaning right or left or sticking out a leg to steer the sled around obstacles. Dawn hollered and cheered, making Aiden chuckle. When the sled bumped over a snow-covered molehill, she grabbed Aiden's knees for balance. All too soon, they glided to a stop at the bottom of the hill.

Dawn's eyes glittered, and her cheeks were red from the cold and the excitement. She grabbed the sled's rope to pull it back up the hill. "Again!"

A few rides later, Dawn stopped at the top of the hill. "You want to sit up front for a change? You have to steer, though. I can't see around you."

Aiden took the offered seat in the front. She sharply inhaled a lungful of the crisp winter air when she felt Dawn's arms snake around her and her hands settle against her stomach. Suppressing the impulse to cover the smaller hands with her own, she grabbed the sled's rope instead.

Dawn tucked her thighs behind Aiden's as she pushed off the edge. Soon, they were gliding down the hill again.

"I think we should stop for the day," Aiden said when they reached the bottom. Dawn's pants, like her own, were covered with snow up to the knees and were beginning to get wet as it thawed. The last thing she wanted was for Dawn to get sick during the holidays.

Dawn sighed and let her gaze wander over the snow-covered hills one more time. "I guess you're right, but it's just so peaceful out here, like we're a thousand miles away from the city and everything that happened there."

Aiden was not eager to leave either. She had enjoyed being close to Dawn and seeing her more carefree side. "We can come back here whenever you want to."

A little later, she parked her car next to Dawn's sardine can, which was waiting faithfully in front of Aiden's apartment building. They stomped their feet to relieve their boots of as much snow as possible before entering the building. Aiden's toes felt as if they were about to fall off, but it had been fun, and she decided that spending time with Dawn was worth a few lost toes. As soon as they entered her apartment, she made a beeline for the bedroom, changed, and searched for a pair of sweatpants and socks that Dawn could wear. When she returned with those articles of clothing, she found her guest in the kitchen.

The coffee machine was happily gurgling away, and water was heating on the stove while Dawn looked through the collection of teas that Aiden had bought for her. Dawn had turned on the CD player, and the Christmas CD that Dawn had insisted she buy was playing Christmas carols, with Dawn humming along.

Aiden watched her from the doorway, happy to see how obviously at home Dawn already felt in her apartment. It had never felt so much like home as right now to Aiden.

Dawn turned and stopped humming when she saw Aiden leaning in the doorway. A hint of a blush crept up her neck.

"I brought you something to change into," Aiden said.

"Thanks." Dawn took the sweats and socks and firmly closed the bathroom door behind her.

When she returned, they settled down on the couch and sipped their respective hot beverages.

"Will I see you again before Monday, or should I give you your present now?" Aiden asked.

Dawn put down her mug of tea and turned toward her. Their knees touched, sending a tingling sensation up Aiden's leg. "I thought it would be nice if we could exchange presents on Christmas Day."

"Are you sure that you'll have the time to come over?" Aiden asked. Dawn would spend Christmas with her mother, her sister-in-law, her niece and nephew, and a horde of other relatives while Aiden would treat herself to her favorite Chinese takeout and go over to Ray's house for a while if she wasn't called out to a crime scene.

Dawn reached for her mug and fiddled with the string of the teabag. "Well, actually... Why don't you come over? I would really like it if you spent just a little time with me and my family, maybe have dinner with us. Then we could come back here to exchange presents."

Aiden stared at her, not sure how to answer. "I'm on call."

"On Christmas Eve and on Christmas Day?"

Aiden nodded.

Dawn's brow furrowed. "Isn't it a little unusual that the same detective is on call for both days? My dad always had one of the days off."

"Your dad had a family—and I don't. I actually volunteered since I never really had anything worth celebrating anyway."

Dawn's delicate throat moved as she swallowed and looked down. "I understand."

Shit! Now she thinks that I don't want to spend time with her. "I suppose I could come over for a while anyway. I'll just bring my cell phone."

"Not if you don't want to." Dawn studied her intently. "I don't want you to do anything that you don't feel comfortable with."

Comfortable? Comfortable would be ordering Chinese takeout and praying for a call to rescue me from all the happy-family Christmas movies on TV. I think I'll opt for a little discomfort this year. Just thinking about sitting at the dinner table with Dawn's mother and the overprotective Del while a horde of strangers and a dozen kids were running around, spreading Christmas cheer, made Aiden's stomach clench. But if it made Dawn happy, she would at least try it for a while. "I'll come over," she said, not bothering to pretend she would be completely comfortable doing it. Dawn could see through her too easily.

"Okay. I'll call you with the exact time. I should head home now. It's still snowing." Dawn emptied her mug, stood, and grabbed her half-dry pants on her way to the bathroom.

Aiden slipped on her boots and leather jacket to accompany Dawn to her car. "Christ, look at that! I can't remember the last time we had this much snow." Another few inches of snow had fallen, and Aiden picked up her snow shovel to make a path to Dawn's car for her. She was leaning down to shift another shovelful of snow to the side when she felt a smack against her arm. Narrowing her eyes, she turned toward Dawn, who stood with an expression of innocence, quickly hiding another snowball behind her back. With a playful warning glance, Aiden went back to work.

Another snowball hit her in the middle of her back.

Aiden turned back around. "You're not by any chance trying to start a snowball fight with one of Portland's finest, are you?"

Dawn grinned brightly. She scooped up two handfuls of snow and fashioned them into a ball. "Is it working?"

Aiden gritted her teeth, forcing herself not to react to the challenging twinkle in Dawn's eyes. "No."

"No?" Dawn raised her hand and aimed a snowball at Aiden.

Aiden made no move to defend herself and lob a snowball of her own against Dawn. She tended to be very competitive, so she was afraid of what Dawn might see in her eyes if she responded with aggression, even if it was in a playful context. She wouldn't risk losing control and crossing a line. "No," she repeated firmly and then, with effort, formed a small smile. "Department rules don't allow me to shoot at civilians, not even snowballs. Plus I don't want you to get snow all over your clothes again."

Dawn looked at her for another few seconds before she relented and threw her last snowball into the tree next to Aiden, spraying her with snow from the branches.

"Hey!" Aiden shook herself. She squirmed as a load of melting snow slipped past her collar and began to glide down her back.

"C'mere, I'll help get it off, you big baby." Dawn slipped off her gloves and tugged Aiden down.

Aiden stiffened when she felt Dawn's warm fingers slide down her neck, slipping under her sweatshirt to fish out the snow.

Dawn stopped abruptly, her eyes widening as if she only now realized what she was doing. "Sorry, I..." She quickly stepped back.

Aiden closed her eyes for a moment as the rest of the snow slid down her back, melting against her skin. "It's all right." She stepped up to Dawn and handed her a glove that had fallen to the ground. She let her fingers linger on Dawn's for a moment to emphasize her point. "I want you to feel comfortable enough to touch me. Unless you don't want that?"

"I want it, but..." Dawn gesticulated, then let her hands dangle limply at her sides. "Sometimes I'm okay, and I don't think about it...about the rape...for hours or even days. But then there are times when I jump whenever someone comes near me. I think I'm getting better, and then I freeze when I'm touched, even in a perfectly innocent, friendly way. My body just can't always make that distinction, and I don't know when I'll be able to."

Aiden's own emotions reflected the helplessness and frustration she could clearly see on Dawn's face. "What can I do to make it easier for you?"

"You're already doing it," Dawn said. "You always let me be the one to establish any physical contact, and I want you to know how much I appreciate that. I know it's not easy for you to give up control either." Slowly, she stepped closer and played with the leather of Aiden's jacket.

Aiden looked down, watching the fingers that were tangled in her jacket. Somehow, she found the touch to her favorite jacket as intimate as an embrace. "So, I'll see you on Christmas?"

"Unless you want to come over tomorrow and help me pick out the perfect Christmas tree for my apartment?" Dawn asked, sounding tentative.

Aiden laughed. "Picking out the perfect Christmas tree... Is that as exhausting as finding the perfect shoes for you?"

Dawn slapped her on the arm and then let her fingers rest there. "More," she said. "I want a seven-foot tree."

"Well, then I'd better accompany you to make sure it'll fit into your living room," Aiden said. Except for the small potted tree that Dawn had convinced her to buy, she hadn't bothered to put up a tree for years, but she was determined that Dawn should have her perfect tree.

"Thanks. Uh, do you mind if we take your car?" Dawn indicated her tiny car.

Aiden smiled. *Do we ever take anything else?* "No problem. I'll pick you up at...ten?"

"You're learning," Dawn said with a grin.

Aiden bowed. "Never should it be said that you can't teach an old detective new tricks."

"Until tomorrow." Dawn hugged her. Her hands slipped

under the leather jacket and lingered on Aiden's waist for a few seconds.

Aiden gently squeezed back, careful not to use too much force or draw Dawn too close.

"I won't break, you know," Dawn whispered, close to Aiden's ear.

Maybe I'm afraid that I will. Aiden said nothing and just concentrated on the feeling of holding Dawn for a few more seconds.

Finally, Dawn stepped back and broke their embrace.

Aiden watched until the sardine can's taillights had disappeared in the distance. *God, what have I gotten myself into?*

Dawn took a deep breath when she saw how crowded the parking lot was getting and how many people were wandering around, picking out Christmas trees. Being around too many people made her feel helpless and out of control, but she was determined not to let her fears stop her from getting her perfect Christmas tree.

Just a few weeks ago, she couldn't imagine wanting to celebrate Christmas, but somehow she had found a new determination not to give up on life and all the little joys it had to offer. She turned her head to look at Aiden, knowing she had been a big part of it.

This was the third place where they had stopped in search of the perfect Christmas tree. Aiden had patiently followed her from tree to tree and only smiled whenever Dawn declared yet another tree "not perfect enough."

"Over there," Dawn said, pointing at a tree. "This one looks good."

"Don't you think it might be just a little too big?"

Dawn studied the tree through narrowed eyes. "You think so?"

Aiden stepped next to the tree and gripped it with both hands, getting it into a more upright position. She looked up to the treetop. "Seven-foot apartment, eight-foot tree—you do the math."

Dawn circled Aiden and the tree, studying both of them. "Darn," she muttered. "It really looks perfect otherwise."

"Doctor Kinsley?" someone called.

Dawn flinched at the sudden voice from behind her. She took a step back and whirled around.

Linda Harrison, bundled up in a bulky parka, stood in front of her, staring at Dawn with an expression that Dawn couldn't read right away, even after counseling her for six months.

"Hello, Linda," she said with a friendly smile, trying not to let her former patient know how unsettled she was by the sudden encounter. "How are you?"

"Fine," Linda answered. Dawn hadn't seen her so guarded and distrustful since their first session. "How are you?" There was no friendliness or concern in the question. Instead, something that looked almost like hostile reproach gleamed in Linda's eyes.

What's going on here? Linda had never been hostile toward her in any of her sessions. She had been depressed and afraid, but never anything but respectful toward Dawn. "I'm fine," Dawn said, very used to keeping her own issues from her interactions with patients.

Linda nodded stiffly. "That's what I thought." She turned and began to walk away.

Dawn looked at Aiden. "Sorry. I have to—"

"Go." Aiden gave her an understanding nod. "I'll wait here."

Dawn ran after Linda. "Linda! Wait up, please. What's going on?"

Linda stopped and whirled around. "Your secretary called and canceled our sessions, saying you couldn't see me anymore.

She implied that there was some health issue going on, but here you are, and you're obviously fine and..."

Dawn sighed. *And your abandonment issues kicked in at full force.* Linda's husband had left her after she had been raped, unable to handle the strain on their marriage, and Linda had struggled with self-worth and abandonment issues ever since. Dawn had never asked her secretary what reason she had given for having to cancel her sessions. *Damn. I should have handled it myself.*

But back then, she hadn't been up for it. Even if she had, she wasn't sure what she would have told Linda. She had never planned on telling her patients she had been raped. Maybe because she had thought it wasn't professional to bring up her own problems; maybe because she hadn't wanted to take away the safe setting of their sessions by revealing that even their therapist wasn't safe from rape, or maybe because she had wanted to hold on to her role as a therapist and didn't want to see herself as just another victim.

"Actually," Dawn said, taking a deep breath, "I'm not fine at all. I wouldn't have referred you to another psychologist without a good reason, Linda. I promise it had nothing to do with you."

Linda still looked guarded but not so hostile anymore. "Then why? Why did you cancel our sessions all of a sudden?"

Dawn knew there was only one answer now: the truth. "I was raped," she said quietly.

Linda gasped. "What?"

Dawn didn't repeat it. She pressed her lips together and looked Linda in the eyes.

"Oh, Jesus! I'm sorry. I didn't know. If I had known, I would never have—"

"It's all right." Dawn tried hard to reestablish her emotional equilibrium and find her way back into her role as a therapist. "There was no way for you to know, and I'm sorry if the way I handled it caused you any—"

"No. Don't apologize. You don't have to feel guilty about any of it—that's what you taught me, right?" Linda gave her a small, tentative smile.

"Right," Dawn said, returning the smile.

Linda shuffled her feet. "I don't know what to say."

"You don't have to say anything. Just promise me you'll continue with another therapist. You made so much progress, and I'd hate to have it all be destroyed just because I…I couldn't be your therapist any longer."

Linda nodded. "I promise." She bit her lip. "Do you…um, do you have any help…for yourself, I mean?"

Dawn half turned and looked back at Aiden, who was gesticulating and explaining something to the vendor while at the same time keeping an eye on her. "I do," Dawn said when she turned back around.

"Good. That's good."

A little awkwardly, they said their good-byes, and Dawn slowly made her way back to Aiden's side.

"Everything okay?" Aiden asked.

Dawn nodded. "I just had to clear up something with a former patient."

Aiden studied her. "You told her." It was a statement, not a question.

Dawn didn't ask how she knew. Aiden was a trained observer, and she knew Dawn well enough by now to guess what had happened. "Yes."

Slowly, Aiden reached out and took her hand. "That took a lot of courage. You're an amazing woman, Dawn Kinsley." She softly squeezed Dawn's hand before letting go.

Dawn had felt neither courageous nor amazing while talking to Linda, but under Aiden's admiring gaze, she began to feel better about her decision and herself. Absentmindedly, she rubbed her fingers over the hand Aiden had squeezed. "Why is your hand so sticky?"

"Oh. Sorry." Aiden wiped her hands on her jeans. "That's resin from the tree."

Dawn looked around. "Where is it?" Her perfect if too tall tree was gone.

"I got the vendor to take off a foot from the bottom so it would fit into your apartment," Aiden said. "I hope that's okay?"

"Okay?" Dawn grinned up at her. The way Aiden was there for her and tried to take care of her felt more than okay. "It's perfect."

"Well, that's what you wanted—the perfect tree, right?"

Dawn smiled. "Right."

CHAPTER 26

Aiden shuffled her feet and clutched the carefully wrapped presents. *Why on earth did I agree to come here? I've felt more at ease at the front door of serial killers.*

The door opened, and Aiden came face-to-face with the one person she had hoped to avoid for a little bit.

Grace didn't seem surprised to find Aiden on her doorstep. "Please come in. Dawn said you'd stop by."

Stop by? Is that wishful thinking on her part, or did Dawn forget to mention that she wants me to stay for dinner? With growing unease, Aiden followed Grace into the house.

"Aiden!" Jamie raced through the living room, barely giving Aiden enough time to put down the presents before throwing herself into her arms.

Grinning, Aiden picked her up and whirled her around. *Well, at least one Kinsley woman is happy to see me.*

"Hi," Dawn said over the head of her niece. Her eyes were twinkling with delight.

Okay, make it two Kinsley women. Aiden set the girl back down and stepped closer to Dawn to admire the formfitting corduroy pants and the soft woolen sweater she wore.

"I'm so glad you could make it. C'mon, I'll introduce you to everyone." Dawn grabbed her by the hand and then stared down at their joined hands for a second before dragging her to the living room.

Aiden took everything in with growing astonishment. Grace's

house looked like something she had thought existed only in picture books and movies. Her mother had never done a lot of decorating and, as far as Aiden could remember, had never even bought a tree.

The Kinsley family was the exact opposite. In one corner of the living room, a Christmas tree extended its branches to all sides, decorated with colorful lights and ornaments that must have been owned by the Kinsleys for generations. An angel with Dawn's clumsily scribbled name across its chest hung from one branch, next to a star with the carefully stenciled name of her brother, Brian, on it. More presents than Aiden had ever seen in one place rested under the tree, and half a dozen red stockings hung over the fireplace. The room smelled of hot chocolate, freshly baked cookies, and pine needles.

Dawn introduced her to uncles, cousins, friends, and colleagues, until the names and faces began to blur. Just when Aiden began to feel overwhelmed by the big family and all the Christmas cheer, Del appeared at her side. "Do you know anything about electronics?"

"Sure." Aiden would have said yes even if Del had asked if she knew anything about rocket science, just to escape the awkward situation.

"Sorry, grasshopper, I have to borrow her for a second," Del said and led Aiden out onto the deck, where half a dozen kids stood around a glowing reindeer. "We have a problem with Santa." Del pointed to the plastic figure next to the reindeer. "He refuses to shine."

Aiden fumbled with the wires for a minute before she stepped back from the now brightly glowing Santa. "Just a loose connection." She had a sneaking suspicion that Del could have fixed Santa on her own, but Aiden was too grateful for Del's intervention to call her on it. That she was now the hero of the assembled children didn't hurt her position in the Kinsley household either. Single-handedly rescuing Santa had to count for something.

"Hey." Dawn stepped out onto the deck, looking between Del and Aiden. "Problem solved?"

They nodded.

"Do you want eggnog or hot chocolate?" Dawn asked.

"Hot chocolate, please. I'm still on call."

"Coming right up." Dawn turned and headed back inside.

Del watched her retreat and then fixed Aiden with an intent stare. "You're on call on Christmas?"

To Aiden's ears, it sounded almost reproachful, as if she should have made sure that she would be able to spend the whole day with Dawn. Or maybe the accusation lay not so much in Del's words but in her own guilty conscience. "I'm always on call during the holidays. It's some kind of Christmas tradition with the SAD."

"The single, lesbian detective volunteers for duty because she doesn't have anywhere else to be anyway," Del said. "Been there, done that, and was stopped from doing it again by one determined Kinsley woman. So, you'd better prepare yourself for experiencing the same."

"Are you trying to warn her off?" Dawn reappeared and handed over the mug she carried to Aiden so she could bump Del with her shoulder.

Del pressed her palm against the left side of her chest. "Would I do something like that, grasshopper?"

"You would. The last cop who got on your bad side is probably still scrubbing the precinct bathroom with a toothbrush," Dawn said.

"I don't have a bad side. And now you'll have to excuse me—I'm thirsty and someone, who shall remain nameless, failed to bring me something to drink." With one last smile, Del herded the children inside and left them alone on the deck.

Aiden leaned against the railing that separated the deck from the backyard and looked down into the mug warming her hands. The hot chocolate was topped off by whipped cream and marshmallows. Aiden couldn't remember when someone had last taken the time to prepare cocoa with all the extras for her.

Dawn stepped next to her. "I know my family can be a bit much."

"No, no, they were all very friendly to me," Aiden said. "I just needed a minute out here. I'm not used to having a house full of people. It's always been just my mother and me. I needed a breather, but I'm okay. You don't have to stay with me. I'm sure there are a lot of relatives in there that you haven't seen all year." She nodded toward the living room.

Dawn leaned her hip against the railing next to Aiden. "Yeah, but I'll have time to talk to them later. I don't know how long I'll have you."

Is she talking about today, because I could be called away anytime? Or is she unsure whether I'll stick around long enough to give a relationship between us a chance? "You go on in. We'll have the time later too."

The glass door slid open. "Girls?" Dawn's mother stepped out onto the deck. "What are you doing out here in the cold?"

Girls? Aiden wasn't sure if she should be amused, flattered, or annoyed. *Does she want to believe that I'm just Dawn's kindergarten playmate?* She still didn't know how to take Dawn's mother.

"Come inside," Grace said when neither of them answered. "Dinner is served."

Aiden followed the two Kinsley women inside.

Some guests were already sitting around the large dining table while others were busy placing bowls, pots, and plates on the table or helping the kids into their chairs.

Aiden lingered behind, not sure where her place in the seating arrangements might be.

A small hand grabbed hers. "Aiden is sitting next to me," Jamie announced for everyone to hear.

"Jamie!" Her mother, Eliza, raised her voice to be heard above the commotion. "Maybe Detective Carlisle doesn't want to sit next to you? I'm sure she wants to sit next to your aunt."

"It's Aiden, and lucky for you I have two sides." Aiden winked at the girl and barely held herself back from calling her "grasshopper."

Jamie's mother nodded. "Then it's Eliza. And you probably remember my husband, Rick."

The slender man that Aiden had met during the trial looked up from his attempts to put his son into a high chair. "Hi. I don't suppose your child-whisperer skills extend to my youngest kid too?" He pointed to the ten-month-old who was kicking his legs, making it impossible to put him in the high chair.

"Oh, for God's sake, Rick!" Eliza took over the task.

Youngest kid. That means he considers Jamie his kid too.

Rick grinned apologetically at his wife.

Aiden allowed herself to be dragged into the chair next to Jamie. Over the girl's head, she studied Rick. His voice seemed familiar even though she hadn't talked to him during the trial. "Do I know you from somewhere?"

"I'm a dispatcher, so you probably—"

"No shop talk today," Grace said and handed Aiden a carving knife. "Would you be so kind?" She nodded at a giant turkey.

Aiden gripped the knife and blinked. *Me? She wants me to carve the turkey?*

Her face must have shown her surprise because Grace smiled at her. "You're part of the reason why my daughter is able to sit here today and celebrate Christmas with her family, safe in the knowledge that the monster who hurt her is behind bars. Therefore, you're our guest of honor and get to carve the turkey."

Aiden turned her head to look at Dawn, who gave her

a somewhat watery smile and a nod. She carefully started her appointed task.

Finally, everyone settled down at the table. Even the children were quiet as a circle was formed by joining hands. Jamie's small hand wrapped around Aiden's fingers on the left, and Dawn softly squeezed her right hand while Dawn's mother said grace.

As soon as she said "amen," the laughter, the chatter, and the clinking of plates and glasses started again. It was a family moment that Aiden had never experienced before, and she watched numbly as Grace heaped large amounts of turkey, ham, mashed potatoes, and gravy onto her plate. "Thank you, ma'am. I think that's enough."

"It's Grace," the older woman said while she added cranberry sauce to Aiden's dinner.

"Aiden." She nodded, much more at ease with Dawn's mother and the rest of the family now. She picked up her fork and tried a bite of turkey with gravy. "Wow, that's delicious!"

"Yeah," Del said, still chewing. "My mamá always told me that if I didn't bring home a Latina girl, I should at least pick someone who could cook. But alas, it was not to be—for some incomprehensible reason, she chose my partner over me." She blinked her lashes at Grace, who reached across the table to slap her arm.

"I was already married to Jim when he got partnered with your rookie Latina ass, Delicia Vasquez Montero. And your mother never told you to bring home any girl."

"She would have if she ever tasted the *arte culinario* of the charming Kinsley women," Del said with a bright grin.

"Dawn, no more wine for your aunt," Grace said, making everyone laugh.

By the time dessert was served—apple pie, Christmas pudding with brandy sauce, and pastries filled with dried fruit—Aiden's fear of being overwhelmed or not fitting in had all but vanished.

Jamie was chatting her ear off, half a dozen toddlers had tried to climb on her lap, and even Grace had gone out of her way to make her feel welcome.

Finally, she leaned back and pressed her hands against her stomach. "God, I'm stuffed."

Dawn patted her leg. "Want to come outside with us and build a snowwoman?"

"A snowwoman?" Aiden gave her a lopsided grin.

"Yep, it has to be a snowwoman, nothing else will do for me."

Aiden grinned and resisted the urge to look up and see if Grace had heard the comment. "All right. Let's build a snowwoman."

Half a dozen children, bundled up in warm jackets, scarves, and woolen hats, followed them outside and began to roll growing balls of snow along the driveway. Aiden helped the small hands lift the snowwoman's head onto the torso and watched as Dawn formed two smaller snowballs. "What's that going to be? A snowbaby?"

"We're building a snowwoman; you figure it out." Dawn attached the two snowballs to the figure's front.

"Ah, it's an anatomically correct version of a snowwoman—and a very nicely endowed one at that."

Dawn stepped back to study her work and then looked down at her own chest. "You think that's a life-size replica?"

Aiden's breath condensed in front of her as she barked out a surprised laugh. "Well, a woman can hope, can't she?" She winked at Dawn but didn't delve any deeper into a comparison of the snowwoman's endowments with that of anyone else around.

A snowball that pelted Dawn from behind interrupted the conversation before it could steer into that particular territory.

Dawn whirled around. "Jamie! You're throwing large, icy, hard snowballs at your favorite aunt?" She stared at the girl in exaggerated outrage.

Another snowball hit her on the shoulder, dusting her with

cold particles as it burst on impact. "My only aunt!" Jamie shouted back.

A few of the other giggling kids started to fling snowballs in Dawn's direction too.

"Aiden! Help me!" Dawn took cover behind her.

"Hey, hey, hey! Leave me out of this." Aiden bent to dodge snowballs and tried to step around Dawn, out of the line of fire, but Dawn held on to the back of her coat and followed each of her movements.

"I thought you're on call today?" Dawn panted behind her. "Well, there's a female citizen being attacked by a horde of hoodlums, so why don't you try to earn your paycheck and start protecting me? Now!" Dawn squeaked as one of the kids circled them, and another snowball hit her in the back.

Right at that moment, Aiden's cell phone chirped. She opened her coat and unhooked it from her belt to read the text message. *Shit.* She pressed her lips together. "I have to go." Being on call had been a safety line for her, a refuge should she become overwhelmed and feel uncomfortable with Dawn's family. She hadn't expected to feel regret when she was called away, but she did.

Dawn looked equally disappointed that their time together was coming to an end, but she didn't try to get Aiden to shirk her duties or even to keep her for a few more minutes. "Do you have time to say good-bye to everyone, or should I tell them you had to go?"

"No, I have the time to say good-bye." Two minutes more or less wouldn't matter.

Silently, they strolled back to the house side by side, some of the children following behind them. Dawn opened the front door for them.

"Aunt Dawn," Jamie cried.

They stopped and looked back at the gesticulating girl. "What?"

"You're under the mistletoe!" Jamie jumped up and down, pointing at the twig hanging above them in the doorway.

"So what?" Aiden tried to ignore the obvious meaning.

"You have to kiss."

Aiden tugged the girl closer and bent down to give her a kiss on the cheek while Dawn did the same to Jamie's other cheek. "There you go. One kiss. Can we enter now?"

"No!" The girl stomped her foot. "You have to kiss each other, not me. I'm not under the mistletoe."

Aiden's gaze flitted to Dawn's face and then back to the girl. Dawn looked as indecisive as she felt. Beyond a quick peck on the cheek, they hadn't exchanged kisses, and Aiden didn't want Dawn to feel pressured to take the next step in their relationship just because of a Christmas tradition. "Jamie, look, I'm in a bit of a hurry right now. Can't I kiss her later?"

"No, that's not allowed," Jamie said.

"How come a nine-year-old girl knows so much about the rules of kissing under the mistletoe?" Aiden asked.

Dawn rolled her eyes. "I think we have Del to thank for that particular pearl of wisdom. Del told her that if an unmarried woman is not kissed under the mistletoe, she'll remain single for the next year. But that doesn't help us now, so..." She rested one hand against Aiden's shoulder and lifted herself up on her tiptoes.

Aiden forgot to breathe as Dawn's face came closer to her own. In return, all of her other systems went into overdrive. She held still as Dawn's lips touched her own for one beat of her thudding heart. Then it was already over, and she had to blink a few times to break her rigor. *I thought a kiss was what woke Sleeping Beauty from her spell, not what put her under it.*

When Grace came out of the living room, Aiden stepped back.

Dawn stood rooted to the spot, breathing a little faster, her cheeks reddened by more than the cold.

Still dazed, Aiden thanked the hostess, said good-bye to the rest of the family, and then walked toward the door again, this time careful not to step through it at the same time as anyone else.

Dawn followed her to the car.

Their shoulders brushed as they walked, and Aiden wanted to reach out and take Dawn's hand but had a feeling Grace was watching them from the kitchen window.

They stopped in front of the car and stood in silence for a moment.

Snow crunched beneath Aiden's boots as she shuffled her feet, unsure what to say or do.

"If you want, you can come over to my place tomorrow so we can open presents," Dawn said.

"I'd like that."

Dawn raised a hand and tugged Aiden's scarf more tightly around her neck. The tender gesture warmed Aiden more than the scarf could. "Be careful, please."

Aiden cleared her throat. "I will." She wanted to kiss Dawn again but settled for a short hug. She got in, closed the door, and started the car.

Their gazes met one last time through the window on the driver's side before Aiden waved and backed out of the driveway. As she drove down the street, she looked in the rearview mirror.

Dawn was still standing in the driveway.

Del entered the kitchen, balancing a stack of dirty dishes in her hands.

The kitchen was empty except for Grace, who stood in front of the sink, her back to Del.

"Hey." Del set down the stack of dishes next to Grace. If

she hadn't known the woman for twenty years, she probably would have missed the slight jump and the tension in her slender shoulders. "You okay? You look a little tense."

"It's just all these dirty dishes." Grace busied herself with scrubbing cranberry sauce from another plate. "Remind me next year to accept all offers to help with cleaning up."

Del stepped closer. She sensed that the dirty dishes were not really what was upsetting her old friend. She picked up a dish towel and began to dry. "Do you need to talk?"

A plate sank into the soapy water as Grace let go of it and turned to look at her. "You know me so well," she said with a sigh.

Del smiled. "We had some of our best talks over piles of dirty dishes." It had been in the kitchen where Grace had cried endless tears in Del's arms over the loss of her husband; it had been the place where Grace had convinced Del that she should be the one to walk Dawn down the aisle; and here Del had patiently answered questions when Grace had first suspected that her daughter might be gay. "So, you'd better start talking before the last plate is clean."

Grace laughed but just for a second. "It's about Dawn."

She had expected it, but Del still felt a glimmer of concern. "Don't worry about her." She slung the dish towel across her shoulders and lifted her hands to Grace's tense neck. "Dawn is doing well, considering it hasn't even been three months since—"

"This is not about...what happened to her." Grace leaned into the touch of Del's gently kneading hands.

"What is it, then?" Del asked and ducked her head to look into the familiar face. It took her a few seconds to understand. "You've seen her with Carlisle."

"Why do you cops always pretend not to have first names?" Grace's complaint was two decades old.

"Probably because not all of our parents had such good taste in naming their offspring as yours did," Del answered with a grin.

Grace's head fell back onto Del's shoulder. "Charmer." She groaned when Del's hands worked on a particularly tense spot. "I've tried to ignore it for a while, but when I saw her saying good-bye to Aiden tonight..." Grace dried her hands on the towel and then tossed it on the counter before turning around to face Del. "Dawn told her to be careful, and I had a sudden déjà vu of me standing in the same place, telling Jim that very same thing."

Del closed her eyes, and for a moment, they shared their pain in silence.

"Dawn cares about her," Grace finally said.

"And that's a bad thing?"

Grace shrugged. "It could be. It would kill Dawn to lose another person she loves to the job."

"You can't choose who you love, Gracita," Del said. "You just...do."

A sigh came from Grace. "I know. I just wish..."

"That the object of your daughter's affections wouldn't be a cop." Del nodded in understanding. Both of them knew firsthand how difficult a relationship with a police officer could be.

"Yeah, and being male wouldn't hurt either," Grace said.

Del studied her stormy gray eyes. "And here I thought I had cured your homophobia."

"I'm not homophobic."

Del knew that to be the truth. Grace had never been uncomfortable with having a lesbian best friend.

"As far as I'm concerned, love is love. It's just that being with a woman has so much potential to hurt her." Grace sighed. "I don't want my daughter to go through life as an outsider...to be stared at, or spit on, or laughed at by total strangers, to be hurt simply because of who she loves. Dawn has already been raped just because some homophobe didn't like her sexual orientation. That's not the life a mother would choose for her daughter."

"That's just it—it's not your choice," Del said. "It's not even

Dawn's really. Being gay isn't a choice at all but a part of Dawn like the color of her eyes or her shoe size. The only choice is whether or not to have the courage to be open and honest about that part of her life. Living a lie, always hiding who she is, will hurt her too."

Grace's hand came up and tore at her still blonde locks. "I know, and if she's really gay, I don't want her to feel like she has to hide it from me."

"If she's really gay?" Del repeated with an incredulous laugh, reaching out to comb Grace's hair back into some semblance of order. "Darlin', I hate to point out the obvious, but she has lived in a lesbian relationship for over a year."

Grace stubbornly shook her head. "There was no real chemistry between Maggie and Dawn."

Del had to give her that. She had always suspected that the attraction between Dawn and the gallery owner had been more aesthetic than sexual, but that had more to do with Maggie's personality than with her gender. "The way she looks at Carlisle... at Aiden...doesn't leave much doubt about her sexual orientation either."

"Dawn is going through a very hard and emotionally confusing time. How can we be sure that she's not just clinging to the first person who's been there for her and protected her?" Grace looked up and searched Del's face for the answer.

Del shook her head. "I don't think so. Sure, the last few weeks may have changed the way Dawn looks at herself, at relationships, and at potential partners, and it intensifies every emotion, but I think whatever they have between them, it would have developed anyway. It happened despite Dawn being raped, not because of it."

Grace let her forehead rest against Del's shoulder for a second. "You're right. It's just... I find myself thinking about Jim, about what he always wanted for our daughter."

Through endless hours of patrol duty and surveillance,

Del had gotten to know her partner well, so she spoke without hesitation. "What he wanted first and foremost was for her to be happy—and I don't think she'll find that happiness with a man. He would have accepted any person Dawn wanted to spend her life with as long as he or she honestly loved and respected her."

Grace lifted her head off Del's shoulder to look into her eyes. "I know you're right, but he wanted her to experience motherhood too—and so do I. I've been looking forward to having grandkids from Dawn since the day she married Cal."

The picture of a lively little girl with blonde pigtails appeared before Del's mind's eye. Her lips curled into a wistful smile. "Yeah, I'd love to bounce a little grasshopper junior on my knees too. But Dawn being in a relationship with a woman doesn't have to mean that she won't have kids someday. Just because Maggie had a major panic attack at the thought of smelly diapers or a toddler with crayons anywhere near her white designer couch doesn't mean that other lesbians don't want children. It looks like Carlisle is really good with kids."

"That doesn't mean she wants to have her own. She seems like one of those cops who are really only married to their jobs."

Del winked at her. "Oh, I think she's about to get a divorce. Our daughter is not a woman who would let herself be kept as a mistress." Heat rose up her neck as she became aware of what she had just called Dawn. "I-I mean—"

Grace's hand on her arm stopped her. "It's okay, Del, really. In many regards, she's as much your daughter as she's mine. You were always there for her, even when I couldn't be because I was too caught up in my own grief. Have I ever thanked you for that?"

"You don't need to," Del said. A lump lodged in her throat. "I couldn't even be there for her when she needed me most."

"That's not true. You—"

"I shouldn't have left her that night." Del couldn't look at her old friend, but Grace reached out and lifted her chin.

"It's not your fault. You couldn't know."

During many sleepless nights, Del had tried to tell herself the same, but it was still hard to accept that she hadn't been able to protect Dawn.

"Come here." Grace pulled her into a tight embrace and repeated in a whisper, "It wasn't your fault."

Del exhaled shakily and rested her cheek against the side of Grace's head. For the first time in weeks, she started to believe it.

Just as they stepped back, both of them sniffling, Dawn's blonde head appeared in the doorway. "Are you sure that I can't help with the dishes?"

Del forced a smile. "Well, if you've finished pouting about your sweetie's absence, you're welcome to help."

Dawn's eyes widened, and her gaze flitted to her mother.

"It's all right," Grace said, handing her a dish towel. "I'm well aware that Aiden hasn't been slaving as your shopping Sherpa, Christmas tree advisor, and wall-climbing trainer because the police bureau is paying her to."

Dawn fiddled with the dish towel. "And you're okay with that?"

Grace's gaze flickered to Del for reassurance and then focused on her daughter. "If you're sure that it's what you want? I mean…a relationship with a woman—a woman who is a police officer at that."

"I've never been so sure of anything in my whole life, Mom."

"Then I'm okay with it," Grace said.

Visibly more relaxed now, Dawn picked up a washed plate and dried it. "What were you doing in here? Discussing my love life? Is that why you always decline any help in the kitchen except for Del's, so you can gossip without interruption?"

Her mother gently pinched Dawn's cheek. "I decline any help except for Del's because I learned the hard way that everyone else just wants to stay in the kitchen to sneak some more dessert."

"Yeah, and I concentrate on drying the dishes because I want to keep my girlish figure." Del patted her slender hips with a grin. "And just for your information, your mother and I are perfectly capable of conversing while doing the dishes without your name ever coming up, grasshopper." *That's not to say that it didn't this time.*

Dawn looked skeptical but nodded. "Hand me another plate to dry, Del. I have to work on my figure."

Aiden leaned her head against the back of Dawn's couch and tried to sit still. It wasn't an easy task because she could feel Dawn sitting close, so close that their knees sometimes brushed when one of them moved her leg. *That's progress. Last month she would have sat in the easy chair or left at least a foot of space between us.*

Her body wanted to reach out and establish more contact, but she forced herself to let Dawn be the one in control and distracted herself by looking at the Christmas tree. It was fully lit, making the decorations and tinsel hanging from its branches shine. *It's not quite seven feet, but it's perfect nonetheless.*

"In case you're wondering about that lonely present under the tree," Dawn said, interrupting the comfortable silence. "It's yours, so if you want to open it..."

Aiden reached down to pick up the bigger box resting next to the couch. "It just so happens that Santa left a little something for you too."

With a grin, Dawn studied the size of the present. "Seems like I've been really good this year."

"It's not the size that counts, Doc," Aiden said. She gently set the box down onto Dawn's lap. "Open it."

Dawn didn't have to be told twice. She ripped into the red-and-green-striped paper, tearing it from the box with childlike enthusiasm.

Aiden shifted her weight on the couch while she watched. She didn't have much experience with buying gifts, but she hoped Dawn would like it.

Dawn's impatient fingers stilled as she lifted the top off the box. She ran her hand along oil, watercolor, and acrylic painting brushes, over sketching chalks and tubes of color until her fingers finally closed around a drawing pencil. "Aiden! That's a complete set of art supplies! It must have cost—"

"Hush." Aiden touched her index finger to Dawn's lips but withdrew when Dawn flinched at the unexpected touch. "The price isn't important. Do you like it?"

"Yes, of course." Dawn caressed badger-hair bristles. "And what I like most of all is that you remembered how much drawing and painting means to me. I really missed it, and this will give me a reason to start again. Thank you." She leaned forward and placed a quick peck on Aiden's cheek.

Aiden relaxed a little. "Buying these..." She pointed to the contents of the box. "...was a rather confusing experience. I told the salesclerk that I wanted art supplies, brushes, and the like, and he asked me if I wanted hog hair, squirrel hair, badger hair, or a synthetic brush, and if it should be a 25-millimeter landscape brush or a 50-millimeter background brush." It had been embarrassing to realize how little she knew about something that had been her mother's biggest passion. She had never tried to learn more about it because she had felt that she would always fall short of her mother's expectations. Standing in the art supplies store, she had felt like an idiot, but the smile on Dawn's lips made everything worth it. "I didn't even know if you preferred oil, pastel, acrylic, or watercolors, so I bought a little bit of everything."

"I like a little bit of everything, so your present is just perfect," Dawn said. With one fingertip, she carefully tested the pointed end of a pencil. "I'll have to draw you sometime. And now, you open yours." She handed Aiden a light blue envelope.

Aiden pointed to the single present under the tree. "I thought that one was mine?"

"It is," Dawn said. "What's in the envelope is only partly from me. It's from Del and Mom too."

"They bought me a Christmas present?" Aiden felt herself blanch. "But I didn't buy them anything." She had never needed to buy more than a handful of presents at Christmas, and having to think of gifts for Dawn's family was a little scary.

"That doesn't matter. They wanted to give you this. Now open it!"

Hesitantly, Aiden slipped her index finger under the envelope and opened it. A gift certificate fell out. *A tandem skydive?* She arched a brow. "They want me to throw myself out of an airplane at ten thousand feet? Didn't you say that your mother approved of us?"

Dawn laughed. "She does. You'll have a parachute and an experienced tandem instructor. We thought that it was something that might interest you...?"

Now Dawn sounded insecure, and Aiden hastened to answer. "I am interested. I've wanted to try it ever since Okada told me about his parachuting experiences."

"Okada?" Dawn rubbed a finger over her chin. "Isn't that the Asian American detective with the dry sense of humor? He doesn't look like an adrenaline junkie."

Aiden smiled. "He claims that it's where he met his third ex-wife."

"The third?" Dawn's eyes widened. "How many ex-wives does he have?"

"Nobody really knows, except for Okada and his accountant." Aiden chuckled. She looked down at the gift certificate again. "It's great. Thank you."

Dawn crossed the room, reached under the Christmas tree, and returned with the second present. "Merry Christmas."

Aiden studied the present for a few seconds before loosening the ribbons and bows and removing the wrapping paper.

"It's much more fun if you just tear the paper," Dawn said.

Aiden loved seeing the childlike wonder and anticipation in Dawn's eyes, but she preferred a more controlled approach for herself. She folded the paper and set it to one side before she opened the small box. With trembling fingers, she lifted a silver necklace from the box. *She's buying me jewelry?* Aiden had never bought or received jewelry, and it made her a little anxious.

"Relax," Dawn said as if reading her thoughts. "It's not a ring or anything like that. It's just a lucky charm."

More relaxed now, Aiden studied the small, oval pendant. "Hey, that's Saint Michael, the patron saint of law enforcement, isn't it?"

Dawn nodded. "It was my father's."

Aiden's head jerked up. *She's giving me her father's good luck charm?* "I can't take this." She tried to press the necklace into Dawn's hand. "It should be yours."

"It was mine," Dawn said, refusing to take the necklace. "My father gave it to me a few weeks before he died. And now I want you to have it."

Aiden took a deep breath. She didn't know what to say. "Thank you," she finally whispered. She looked down at the necklace in her hand. She wasn't one to wear jewelry, but she would definitely wear the necklace, knowing how much it meant to Dawn. "Will you help me put it on?" She turned around and felt the couch dip behind her. Dawn's elbows came to rest on her shoulders for a moment, and the warm breath on her neck made Aiden shiver.

Then Dawn closed the necklace's clasp and moved back. "There." She touched the pendant resting on Aiden's chest with one gentle finger, making Aiden's breath catch even though she hadn't been touched at all. "It looks good on you."

"Thank you." Aiden knew that Dawn was still a little tight

financially, but this meant more to her than anything Dawn could have bought. Slowly, she leaned forward, making her intentions obvious to Dawn so she would have the opportunity to draw back.

Dawn didn't move away.

Aiden pressed a gentle kiss on Dawn's lips, allowing herself to enjoy the warm touch for a second before drawing back. Their eyes met. When Aiden couldn't read anything but trust and affection in Dawn's gray-green eyes, she gave in to the urge to lean in again and kiss her, this time a little longer. "Thank you," she whispered one last time. *For the pendant and for your trust in me.*

"You're welcome," Dawn answered quietly.

They settled back onto the couch. Half an hour later, Aiden watched with amusement as Dawn yawned for the third time in a row. "I hope it's not the company."

"What?" Dawn looked up and blinked, a hint of a blush staining her cheeks. "Oh, no, no, of course not. It's just... I didn't sleep so well last night."

God, she's adorable. "Couldn't sleep because you were waiting for Santa to come down the chimney and leave presents in your stocking?"

"Nothing quite as pleasant, I'm afraid." Dawn sighed. "I stayed in my mother's guest room last night, with Jamie and..."

"What happened?"

"Jamie tends to cuddle up to me, and I woke in the middle of the night with her weight pressing me down, unable to move." Dawn looked down to where her trembling fingers picked lint from the couch. "I came very close to having a full-fledged panic attack and stayed awake for the rest of the night."

Aiden fought the urge to enfold Dawn in a comforting embrace, not sure if any touch, innocent as it might be, would be welcome right now.

"So no, it's not the company," Dawn said, sounding more composed. "I'm just a little tired."

"Then I think I'll go now so that you can get some sleep," Aiden said, even though she was reluctant to leave.

Dawn shook her head. "No, I can get some sleep later. I want to spend a little more time with you." She couldn't hide another yawn, though.

"Then at least lie down for a while." She had been glad when she had seen the dark shadows under Dawn's eyes disappear during the last few weeks, and she didn't want to see them reappear.

"Only if you keep me company and promise not to leave," Dawn said.

"I promise." Aiden started to rise from the couch to make room for Dawn's whole body.

"No, no, stay." Dawn laid her hand on Aiden's thigh to press her back down. She licked her lips and stared down at her own hand. "I want to... I want to try..."

Aiden's eyes widened. A thousand assumptions and speculations about what Dawn might want to try raced through her mind, and she mentally slapped herself.

Dawn swallowed and finally looked up. "I want to try and be a little closer to you tonight."

Aiden's heartbeat picked up at these words. Her body was reacting to Dawn's suggestion of closeness even though she knew that it didn't imply anything sexual. "Okay." She fought to keep her voice calm. "How do you wanna go about it? Anything you want is okay with me."

"I thought, I could lie down right here," Dawn pointed to the couch, "and you could just stay where you are right now."

"Sounds nice." Aiden moved back to one end of the couch.

Dawn curled up on her side and settled her head on Aiden's thigh.

Aiden held still until she felt Dawn relax, and then she lifted her hand and rested it protectively along Dawn's shoulder. "Is this okay?"

"Mmm, very okay." Dawn brought one hand up and rested it on Aiden's thigh. Her index finger began to move, tracing lazy circles through the thick material of Aiden's jeans.

Aiden ignored the tingles shooting up and down her leg and let her head fall back against the couch. Keeping her gaze on Dawn's face, she slid her fingers through smooth, blonde strands.

After a few seconds, Dawn exhaled and closed her eyes.

Dawn woke with a start. Fingers tangled in her hair, and for a moment, she flashed back to Ballard grabbing her, but then she caught a whiff of Aiden's scent and relaxed. She realized she was still lying on the couch, using Aiden as her pillow.

Pain flared through her neck as she rolled around to lie on her back. "Ouch."

Aiden jerked beneath her and opened her eyes. She yawned and rubbed her eyes. "I must have fallen asleep sitting up." When she glanced at Dawn's face, her expression instantly became alert. "What's wrong?"

"Nothing." Dawn sat up and tried to massage the cramped muscles in her neck. "Just a crick in my neck or something."

"Let me." A pair of strong hands reached for Dawn's neck.

The unexpected touch made Dawn flinch.

Aiden pulled her hands back. "I'm sorry. I should have—"

"No, it's fine." Ignoring the pain in her neck, Dawn turned around and reached for Aiden's hand. "I need to get used to it."

"You don't need to do anything."

"Yes, I do." She traced the tendons in Aiden's wrist with her thumb. "I need to get used to you touching me if I want to have a relationship with you." When she realized what she had said, she froze and peeked up at Aiden, who stared back. "I mean, I...I don't want to assume that's where this is heading if you don't..."

Aiden silenced her with a quick touch to her lips. "What do you want?"

Dawn said the first thing that came to mind. "I want to be whole again," she whispered. "I want to be able to have a normal relationship—with you. But I'm not sure when...if I can..."

Again, Aiden touched her finger to Dawn's lips. "I want that too."

"I know you said you don't normally do relationships, and entering a relationship at this point in my life might not be the best idea," Dawn said, staring down at her knees. "We both have emotional baggage that won't make it any easier, but when I look at you, none of that matters."

She looked up, and their gazes met.

The warmth in Aiden's eyes made them seem to glow. "Yes, I told you I don't normally do relationships. None of the women I was involved with made me want to try—but you do. I know there'll be issues, yours and mine, that might come up, but we'll deal with them together. Okay?"

Dawn reached across the space between them, entwined their fingers, and leaned forward. Softly, she brushed their lips together. "Okay." She still wasn't sure it was fair to Aiden, but if Aiden was willing to try a serious relationship with her, she would grab that little piece of happiness and hold on to it as if for dear life.

CHAPTER 27

"HEY, AIDEN." RAY SHRUGGED OUT of his coat and perched on his partner's desk. He set a microwave container down next to a stack of files.

Aiden looked up. "What's that?"

"Since you missed Christmas dinner, Susan insisted that I bring you some leftovers. My wife is obviously afraid that you'll starve." Truth be told, he was a little concerned about his partner too. She had never celebrated Christmas, but at least he had always managed to convince her to stop by for dinner. But this year, she had refused to even take off her coat when she dropped off her presents for the kids.

Aiden snorted. "Hardly. I think I put on a pound or two over the holidays." She patted her flat stomach.

Ray settled down in his own chair, swung his legs up on the desk, and studied her. "You treated yourself to dinner in a fancy restaurant?" He tried to sound casual and hide his curiosity about what she might have been up to over Christmas.

"No." Aiden signed her report and threw it into the outbox. "I was invited to a home-cooked meal, with dessert and all."

Ray waited for her to say more. He had long since learned that Aiden refused to talk if he pressured her with too many questions.

Aiden sharpened a pencil and slowly raised it to her lips to blow away the wood chips from the point. Only then did she look up. "Dawn's mother is a really great cook," she said, trying for the same casual tone that Ray had used.

She spent Christmas with the Kinsley clan? To his knowledge, Aiden had never met the family of any of her dates before. "So it's really serious between the two of you?"

"Between Grace and me?" Aiden grinned. "No, don't worry. I don't get involved with older women. I only want her for her cooking skills."

Ray threw his eraser at her. "Smart-ass. You know who I'm talking about."

Aiden sobered. "I really like her, Ray."

A satisfied smile formed on his lips. He had waited for years for Aiden to find someone who held her interest beyond a few dates. "Why don't you bring her to our New Year's Eve party?"

"So you can interrogate her or tell her embarrassing stories about me?" Aiden shook her head. "I don't think so."

"Bring her," Ray said. "It'll be good for her to feel like a part of the group, and I'll even promise not to tell her the story about the search warrant, the bottle of tomato juice, and one Aiden Carlisle."

Aiden grabbed the next report. "We'll see."

Lieutenant Swenson's office door opened. "Carlisle, Bennet! They found the missing girl." Her grave expression told them all they needed to know.

Damn. All thoughts about New Year's Eve parties disappeared from Ray's mind as he rose and grabbed the car keys.

"Yeah, yeah, I'm coming," Dawn called to the ringing phone. She kicked the door closed with her heel, slid her grocery bags onto the couch, and snapped up the receiver. "Hello."

"It's me."

Dawn's smile broadened. "Hi, Aiden. If you want to, you can come over a little earlier. Dinner isn't ready yet, but you can keep me company while I cook." She regarded the ingredients of what would soon be a veggie lasagna.

Aiden cleared her throat. "Yeah, well, about that... I can't come over right now."

"Still at work?"

"No, I'm at home, but I'm just too tired." Aiden's voice sounded hoarse.

Sounds like she had a really tough day. "How about I come over and cook dinner at your place?" Dawn asked, ready to pamper her a little. "You don't have to move a finger, except for lifting the fork to your mouth."

"I'm not hungry," Aiden said.

Now Dawn was starting to worry. Aiden had always been eager to see her, no matter what. "You have to eat something, Aiden."

"Believe it or not, I didn't starve before I met you."

Dawn's legs started to tremble, and she plopped down onto the couch, not caring if she squashed the vegetables.

"Sorry! God, I'm...I'm really sorry, Dawn. I didn't want to..." Aiden inhaled and exhaled sharply. "That's exactly why I don't want to come over. I'm just not good company tonight."

Now that the first shock of Aiden talking to her in anything but soft tones was over, Dawn felt anger stir too. "I don't care. You don't have to entertain me. I just want to sit with you for a while."

"Not tonight, Dawn, okay?"

"Okay," Dawn mumbled even if it was anything but. She sat with the phone in her hand long after they had said good-bye and the call had been disconnected. Finally, she threw the cordless phone down next to the tomatoes that had escaped from their bag. *You should have known that it would come to this eventually. She's a cop, so what did you expect?* She had known from the start that a relationship between them would not be easy. Apart from her own intimacy issues that had developed after the rape, Aiden carried her own emotional baggage—including her fear of letting someone get close to her and getting hurt or hurting others in the process.

So what do I do? Do I allow her to distance herself from me and let her suffer in silence? Dawn looked down at the grocery bags. After eight hours of counseling upset teens, she was hungry, and cooking had always had a calming effect on her. *Let's cook lasagna.*

"Go away, Ray!" Aiden shouted when the doorbell rang again. "Leave me alone, goddammit!"

But the visitor at her door was as stubborn as she was.

Finally, Aiden marched over to the door and threw it wide open.

Instead of her partner, Dawn stood at her door, looking up at her towering form with an almost scared look in her eyes.

Immediately, Aiden was ashamed of her own behavior and hastened to make her stance more nonthreatening. "Dawn..." She was at a loss at what to say. "I didn't know it was you."

"I figured as much when you hurled obscenities at the door," Dawn said with a small smile.

"What are you doing here?" Aiden didn't want to sound harsh, but she wasn't equipped to deal with another person's emotions right now—it was more than enough to deal with her own.

Dawn lifted the ovenproof glass dish that she was holding in front of herself like a protective shield.

She made lasagna, just because I mentioned that it was my favorite dish. God, don't I feel like an ass now! Sighing, she stepped aside. "Come in."

Dawn moved past her, put the lasagna into the oven, and set the table for the two of them. After lighting a candle, she turned toward Aiden. "The lasagna will need at least half an hour, so why don't you sit down for a while and take that off?"

Aiden stared at her. She was wearing only jeans and a simple shirt, so there wasn't much to take off. "Uh...what?"

"That weight on your shoulders. You would feel better if you took it off."

Aiden rubbed her eyes. "It's not that easy."

"I know, but it's sure as hell not going to get any easier if you continue to keep everything to yourself," Dawn said.

Aiden sighed. She had always told Ray how wrong it was to exclude his wife from the job part of his life. She had never been in a relationship long enough for it to become a problem, but now she understood why he insisted on not bringing the job home with him. Dawn was the only good thing in her life, and she didn't want to taint their growing relationship by telling her about the gory stuff that went on at work.

"Don't you want to tell me what happened?"

Aiden bit her lip. "Nothing happened."

Dawn's eyes darkened like thunderclouds. "Don't lie to me, Aiden Carlisle!"

"Then don't ask me questions that I don't want to answer. I don't want to talk about it. Why can't you accept that? She's dead, and no amount of talking will change that!"

"But it might change how you feel about it." Dawn shook her head and sighed. "I don't know why police officers, who dedicate their lives to helping others, find it so difficult to accept help for themselves."

"I don't need any help." All Aiden wanted was to be left alone, but Dawn obviously had no intention of granting that wish.

"You're not invincible, Aiden. I know that you need to hide your feelings while you're on the job, but if you allow that to trickle into your private life, it'll hurt you—and it'll hurt our relationship."

Aiden started to pace. Why couldn't Dawn respect the protective barriers she had erected around herself? Dawn had managed to slip behind all her defenses from the start, and if she let her in now, they would crumble completely. "Stop trying to psychoanalyze me!"

Dawn threw her hands up. "Why do you have to make this about my job?"

"Why do you have to make it about mine?" Aiden looked around like a caged animal. She wanted to tell Dawn to shut up and leave, but she knew Dawn wouldn't go. A wave of intense fear rose—not of Dawn but of herself and what she might do to get Dawn to leave her alone. Without another word, she turned on her heel and stormed out, closing the apartment door between her and Dawn.

When she finally calmed down enough to think, she was out on the street, two blocks away from her apartment—where she had left Dawn. *She'll never talk to me again. Not that I could blame her. God, how did I fuck this up so fast?*

Slowly, she made her way back to the apartment, half hoping and half fearing that Dawn would be gone. The apartment was silent when she hesitantly unlocked and opened the front door. *Shit, she left.*

A delicious smell wafted up from the kitchen, where the lasagna was still sizzling away.

Aiden stepped into the kitchen and turned off the oven. The sight of the dish that Dawn had lovingly prepared for her almost brought Aiden to her knees.

"I'm sorry," said a small voice from the doorway.

Aiden whirled around.

The sight of Dawn standing in front of her was the most wonderful and the scariest thing Aiden had ever seen.

"I'm sorry," Dawn said again when Aiden just stared at her. "You've always been so patient with me, and here I am—pressuring you to do something you're obviously not ready for. I'm so sorry."

"I'm the one who needs to apologize." Cautiously, Aiden took a step toward Dawn, relieved when she didn't flinch back. "I know you're right. I have to talk about my feelings. It's just that... It's really hard for me."

"Come here." Dawn opened her arms in invitation, offering one of her warm hugs.

Aiden backed away. "I can't. I'm barely holding it together as it is. I can't fight this and you." Her voice was a hoarse whisper.

"You don't have to fight me. I need you to need me too."

Something about Dawn's honest words resonated with Aiden. She crossed the room in three long steps and engulfed Dawn in a crushing hug.

Dawn wrapped her arms around her without hesitation, pulling her even closer against her body.

Aiden rested her cheek against the blonde hair, closed her eyes, and exhaled shakily. "A little girl disappeared last week, kidnapped right out of her own backyard. They found her this morning. The medical examiner says she'd been abused and tortured for a week and then slowly strangled." Once she started talking, she couldn't stop. "She was just five years old, Dawn. Five! She'll never celebrate Christmas again, and her parents... We can't even tell them who did this to their daughter. He didn't leave a damn trace!"

"That's really awful, but it's not your fault. You did everything you could."

Aiden sighed. "Sometimes, it's just not enough."

"I know."

The simple answer and the fact that Dawn didn't try to invalidate her feelings took a part of the burden off Aiden's shoulders. She stood resting against Dawn until her legs stiffened. When she began to pull back, Dawn quickly brushed her lips against Aiden's before stepping back.

Dawn's lips tasted of salt, making Aiden realize that Dawn had been crying—and so had she. Still holding Dawn to her with one arm, she led her to the living room and sank onto the couch. Exhaustion set in. She didn't want to talk or to think, and most of all, she didn't want to fight anymore.

"Why did you run away?" Dawn asked, her voice soft.

"I was afraid." It was hard to admit, but if Dawn was willing to give her a second chance, Aiden was determined to learn how to trust and to share her feelings.

Dawn's eyes widened. "Of me?"

"Of myself. Of the anger I felt burning inside of me," Aiden said. "All the other people in my life know to leave me alone when I'm feeling like this, but you..."

Dawn rubbed the back of Aiden's hand. "When you walked out on me in the middle of our...discussion, it made me so mad that I almost threw out the lasagna. I'm a psychologist. I want to talk it out."

"And I'm a cop. I want to avoid talking about it."

Dawn smiled at her. "I guess we have to find a compromise, then. How about this: next time something upsets you, don't try to tell me that you're too tired or not hungry. Simply tell me that something happened, but that you're not ready to talk about it yet."

"Sounds like a deal," Aiden said.

"Good. Because I'm serious about wanting...needing to be there for you too," Dawn said. "If you're not willing to learn to trust me and to let me in, I can't be your partner. A relationship is not only about sharing the good things. Ray is your partner at work, and he watches your back while you're on the job. At home, I'm your partner, and I intend to do the same."

Aiden sighed. "I'd love to watch your back too, but I can't promise that I'll always be able to open up and talk to you."

"Can you promise to at least try?" Dawn asked.

"Yes," Aiden said. "I can promise you that."

Dawn sank against Aiden's shoulder. "Good."

That's it? That's all? Aiden peeked over at Dawn. She had always thought that the first time she lost her composure and showed any insecurity or anger toward Dawn, their relationship would be over. But here they were—just minutes after their first fight—in each other's arms, and the respect and affection she felt for Dawn were stronger than ever. "Is our first fight officially over?"

Dawn laughed. "Definitely."

"Then, if I read my copy of the relationship rulebook right, we have to take care of the 'kiss and make up' part now." She winked at Dawn, who lifted her brows.

"There's a rulebook?"

"Sure, didn't you receive a copy?"

Dawn grinned. "My secretary probably threw it out because she thought it was porn."

God, I love that sense of humor. "Okay, then I'll recite the relevant passage for you," Aiden said, adopting an official court clerk expression. "Said rulebook specifically states that, after a heated discussion, both parties involved are obligated to take part in a tradition called 'kiss and make up.'"

"Does this mysterious rulebook also state what happens if one or both parties fail to comply with that particular rule?" Dawn asked.

"Well, I didn't read that far, but it sounds like a really serious offense, so I imagine grave consequences."

Dawn inclined her head. "Then we better abide by the rules." She moved closer to Aiden.

"I was just joking," Aiden said quickly. "You're not obligated to do anything."

"I want to. I'm a law-abiding citizen, after all."

Aiden held her breath, never moving an inch, as Dawn drew closer. Only at the very last moment did she lower her head to meet Dawn's lips. Her eyes never left Dawn's until they fluttered closed at the soft contact. The kiss was as gentle as Aiden could possibly make it. She didn't try to escalate the kiss or to touch any part of Dawn's body except for holding her hand.

When they finally broke apart, Aiden was breathless, not so much from the physical exertion of the kiss—for she had kissed her dates with much more passion than this—but because of the emotions the gentle kiss had evoked. "Was that okay?" She lifted her head so she could see Dawn's face.

"It was nice," Dawn said.

"Nice?" Aiden lifted a brow. "Just nice?"

Dawn tapped Aiden's nose. "Do women usually use other vocabulary to describe your kisses?"

"Usually, they're too breathless to use any vocabulary at all."

Dawn smiled wistfully. "I think we should leave the breathless part for another time. I'm just not ready for—"

"I know." Aiden lifted their still entangled fingers to her lips and kissed Dawn's knuckles. "It really was a nice kiss. I'm not asking for anything more."

Dawn studied her for a while, but before Aiden could ask what was on her mind, she spoke again. "So, now that we've complied with that rulebook of yours, are you hungry?"

To her own surprise, Aiden found that she was. "You didn't poison the lasagna because I snapped at you on the phone, did you?"

Dawn stood and tugged her up from the couch. "Let's find out."

CHAPTER 28

"ARE YOU SURE THAT YOU want to go?" Aiden asked her for the third time.

"We're standing in the Bennets' driveway, so it's a little late for these doubts." *That's not to say that I don't have them.* It was the first party hosted by strangers that Dawn was going to attend after her rape.

Aiden rounded the car to stand at her side. "You didn't want to go with Del and your mom to the New Year's Eve cruise on the Willamette?"

"With five hundred people rushing on deck at midnight, pushing against me from all sides?" Dawn shuddered. She still couldn't stand the thought of strangers touching her. "No, thank you. I'd rather ring in the new year with you."

Aiden smiled and extended her hand. "Okay, then let's go, or we'll ring it in still standing in the driveway."

Holding Aiden's hand had become an almost automatic gesture for Dawn during the last week, so she entangled their fingers but then paused. "Is this okay?" She lifted Aiden's hand. "Are you out on the job?" There was still so much they had never talked about.

Aiden stopped next to the front door. "Out and proud, so don't worry."

"And you're not going to get into trouble if you show up at your annual New Year's Eve party with a former witness in one of your cases?"

"Ray told me to bring you. As for the rest of them..." Aiden shrugged. "I don't know how they'll react, but I'm not going to hide you, no matter what. I'm proud of you."

Dawn blinked away the tears stinging her eyes. It felt so good to hear Aiden say that, especially since at times she still wasn't sure she could be the partner that Aiden needed.

The door in front of them opened. Ray Bennet leaned in the doorway and grinned down at them. "Are you going to come in, or is there something fascinating about my front door?"

"It could use a new coat of paint," Aiden answered without missing a beat.

Ray waved them in. "Tell it to Susan. You know she wears the pants in this family."

Dawn entered after Aiden, hanging back when she saw all the people milling around the living room.

"Hey, guys." Aiden wrapped one arm around Dawn and tugged her forward. "For all of you who don't know her yet, this is Dawn Kinsley."

Relying heavily on the social skills that were second nature to a psychologist, Dawn smiled and exchanged greetings with Aiden's friends and colleagues.

"Hi, Aiden." A slender black woman engulfed Aiden in a hug. When they separated, Dawn found herself the object of the woman's close scrutiny. "I'm Susan, Ray's wife. Welcome to the most chaotic New Year's Eve party you'll ever see."

Dawn readily shook her hand. "Thanks for inviting me."

"Don't thank me until you've seen the piles of dirty dishes and pans that you'll have to help me with later on," Susan said with a laugh.

"Yeah," a girl who Dawn guessed to be Ray's eldest daughter said. "No thanks necessary, hard labor will do."

Kade Matheson, a wineglass in one elegant hand, strolled

toward them. "Hi, Aiden. I'm glad to see you—I'm reasonably sure that you'll have to arrest someone before the night is over."

Aiden smiled but didn't hug this particular colleague. "And who might that be?"

"I'm not sure yet," Kade answered. "Either me for murder or Okada and Ruben for sexual misconduct."

Aiden laughed. "Ray's punch is that good, huh? What have they done now?"

"They're following me around with a piece of broccoli." Kade rolled her eyes.

A lopsided grin formed on Aiden's lips. "I didn't know that broccoli is considered to be a dangerous weapon under Oregon's penal code."

"They're not trying to assault me with it. They're trying to kiss me under it."

"I had Ray take away every piece of mistletoe in the house before the party started," Susan said, "so they settled for the closest thing they could find—a piece of broccoli from the buffet."

At the sound of Dawn's laughter, Kade seemed to notice her for the first time and turned toward her. "Hello, Dr. Kinsley." If Kade was surprised to see her at the party, she was too polite to show it.

"Hello, Ms. Matheson," was all Dawn could think of to say. While she admired the deputy district attorney, knowing Aiden's infatuation with her made her a little tongue-tied in Kade's presence. She had often wondered what Kade's feelings toward Aiden might be, but the attorney was much too adept at hiding her emotions for Dawn to even guess.

"Do you want to have a glass of punch?" Aiden asked Dawn, nodding in the direction of a giant punch bowl.

"No, thank you," Dawn said. "I don't want to go around chasing people with a vegetable."

Aiden grinned and stepped a little closer. "Do you mind if I have a glass?"

Dawn had noticed months ago that Aiden avoided drinking alcohol in her presence. "No, of course not, go ahead." She watched Aiden weave her way through the small crowd of her coworkers.

Aiden hadn't even reached the punch bowl when Ray's two youngest daughters intercepted her. "Aiden! You have to come upstairs and look at our presents."

"How about you show me a little later? I have to find something to drink for me and my friend first."

The kids ran off in search of a more willing victim.

Aiden continued her way across the room. She ladled punch into a glass and then looked around until she found some apple juice for Dawn.

"Aiden, my friend." Okada stepped next to her and refilled his glass of punch.

Aiden eyed him cautiously. "Do I have to frisk you for a piece of broccoli?"

Okada smirked, and Aiden realized that she had never heard him laugh out loud. "Are you that hungry, or is this your subtle way of asking me for advice concerning your love life?" He turned to look at Dawn, who was engaged in a lively conversation with Susan and her oldest daughter. "I see Santa brought you something really interesting this year."

Aiden smiled for a moment, but then pierced him with a serious stare. "You can tease all you want when it's just me, but please no jokes in front of her, okay?"

"My, my..." Okada studied her. "I never thought I would see this—Aiden Carlisle head over heels in love!"

Aiden wasn't ready to call it love just yet, but she didn't try to deny that she was hopelessly stuck on Dawn. "You're not shocked that it's a former witness?"

"Shocked?" Okada bit into a piece of broccoli. "If you've been on the job for as long as I have, there's not much that can still shock you. If you want shock, you have to watch my partner's ugly mug when he realizes how futile his attempts to flirt with your sweetheart are."

Punch splashed over her hand as Aiden whirled around. Sure enough: Ruben, in his best suit, was showing his pearly whites while he grinned at Dawn.

"Come on, my friend." Okada nudged her with his elbow. "Let's go rescue your damsel in distress."

When Susan and her daughter excused themselves and disappeared into the kitchen, Dawn leaned back against the wall, watching Aiden's colleagues talk and laugh with each other. She didn't know most of the guests, so she was content to stay where she was and just observe.

"Hello," someone said right next to her.

Dawn tried to hide her flinch and turned around with a polite smile.

Aiden's young colleague stood in front of her, offering her a boyish grin and a glass of champagne. "I noticed you don't have anything to drink." He gave a charming little bow. "Ruben Cartwright."

Dawn took the offered glass, even though she had no intention of drinking the champagne. With so many people around, she wanted to be in full control of her senses. "Dawn Kinsley," she said, "but you probably already knew that."

He grinned at her. "Of course. I never forget a beautiful woman."

Dawn stared at him. She had expected him to refer to her

case and not answer with a compliment. *Is he flirting with me? He has to know I'm gay, right?* For a few seconds, she felt completely overwhelmed, unequipped to handle it.

Then, after he just continued to smile at her without hitting on her more aggressively, she started to feel flattered too. This was probably the way he treated all women, gay or straight, and it felt good to have him treat her like any other woman, not like a rape victim.

"Can I get you something to eat?" Ruben asked.

"Don't bother, my friend," another male voice said. "She's here with someone else."

They turned to see Jeff Okada approach, Aiden right behind him.

Ruben groaned. "You're not trying to tell me that she's your date?"

Dawn felt Aiden's familiar presence move in behind her. "She's mine," Aiden said, handing her a glass of apple juice and taking the champagne from her.

"Aw, come on." Ruben stuck out his lower lip. "Why do you always get the hottest dates?"

"How about I show you where our esteemed hostess stores the edibles while the two of them are busy butting heads?" Okada offered Dawn his arm.

Dawn didn't hesitate for more than a second. Despite her now instinctive caution when meeting strangers, she couldn't help liking Aiden's colleagues. "Lead on," she said, resting her hand lightly on Okada's arm, "but please stay away from the broccoli."

"I think someone's spreading ugly rumors about me." He led her away, handed her a plate, and watched as she picked a few tidbits from the buffet. "Has Aiden already introduced you to the other wives?"

Dawn looked up from the prawn cocktail and grinned. "The

other wives? So, I'm a wife now? I wasn't aware of any recent changes in my marital status."

If she had hoped to see the experienced detective flustered, she was disappointed. "You may not wear a ring yet, but the simple fact that you're here tells me a lot about your relationship with our favorite female detective."

Dawn nibbled on a pickled gherkin. "Why's that? From what I've seen so far, most of your colleagues brought a date."

"Sure, everyone brings his or her squeeze of the month, just to have someone to kiss at midnight, but I never make much of an effort to learn their names." Okada shrugged. "They won't last until the next party."

"So what makes you think that I belong in the 'wife' and not the 'squeeze of the month' category?" Dawn asked. She wasn't sure why, but out of all of Aiden's colleagues that she had talked to so far, she liked this man best. She sensed that he was hiding a soft heart behind his mask of sarcasm.

Okada snagged another piece of broccoli from the buffet. "Aiden's never brought anyone to any of the parties before. She wouldn't have bothered to risk showing up with a former key witness if she thought that she would attend the next party alone again."

Dawn was stunned—and happy—at that insight. *I really hope he's right about that.* "You said your name is Okada, right? You're not the unit's forensic psychiatrist, are you?"

The corner of Okada's mouth lifted into a half smile. "I've been married four times, so I guess you could say that I hold an honorary degree in crisis psychology."

"Is he giving you a hard time, Dawn?" Ray Bennet sidled up to her, taking on a protective stance. "Okada is infamous for driving psychologists mad. In his last psych evaluation, he answered the question about the 'most disturbing experience during his career' with 'my second marriage.'"

Dawn smiled at Ray, then at Okada. "I'm divorced too, so I can relate."

"Well, on that positive note, I think I'll go and rescue my partner from Aiden's wrath," Okada said and walked away.

Suddenly alone with her girlfriend's work partner, Dawn fidgeted with her glass of apple juice. *Is this how Aiden felt when I took her home for Christmas dinner with my family?* She had watched the interaction between Aiden and Ray, and it reminded her very much of her relationship with her brother. Now she felt as if she was trying to win the approval of a big brother.

"Thanks for talking to Rebecca earlier," Ray finally broke the silence, "and for offering to get her in contact with your friends in the university's art department."

"No problem," Dawn answered. "Your daughter is a really nice young woman."

"Don't remind me." Ray shuddered. "It's hard to believe that she's almost grown and will soon move out."

When Ray reached for a carafe of juice to refill her glass, Dawn used the pause in conversation to look around in search of Aiden.

It took a moment to find her, for she was sitting in a quiet corner—with Kade Matheson. They were deep in conversation, leaning close to each other to be able to hear over the increasingly loud party. The DDA had set her wineglass down and touched Aiden's forearm whenever she made a point.

Ray handed Dawn her glass and followed the direction of her gaze. For a few seconds, he observed Kade and Aiden before turning back to Dawn. "Don't worry," he said. "Kade is not a threat to you."

Dawn bit her lip. She hadn't intended to reveal her stupid insecurities to Aiden's partner. But now that he had brought up the topic, she didn't want to let the opportunity to learn more about the relationship between Aiden and Kade pass her by. "Because she's straight?"

Ray shrugged. "I assume that she is, but no one ever had the balls to ask her to her face, and Kade likes to maintain an air of mystery. But even if she was gay, it wouldn't matter. Aiden is the most loyal person I know."

Dawn didn't doubt it for a second. She trusted Aiden, but sometimes she wondered whether Aiden would be happier with a woman like Kade Matheson at her side—a woman who shared a part of her work life, whom she could hug or kiss without her flinching back. Someone without the emotional baggage of a rape victim.

As if feeling Dawn's gaze on her, Aiden looked up and made eye contact. She smiled and arched one eyebrow as if to ask, "Everything okay?"

Dawn gave her a smile and a nod.

Aiden's other brow joined the first one, forming an, "Are you sure?"

With a quick glance at Kade, who was leaning back and observing their silent interaction, Dawn nodded again. She was feeling a lot better now that she had seen how readily Aiden had directed her attention away from Kade and toward her.

Their eye contact was broken when Susan Bennet waved for Aiden to follow her into the kitchen. Kade stood too, and for a second, Dawn thought that she would follow Aiden, but the DDA strode toward her instead.

"Ray." Kade's nod could have been a greeting as well as a dismissal.

"You'll have to excuse me now," Ray said. "I think my presence is required in the kitchen. Leaving my wife and my partner alone to gossip about me is usually not a bright idea."

For the first time since she was more than a witness to Aiden, Dawn found herself alone with Kade Matheson. She suppressed the urge to fill the awkward silence with small talk, curious to see what topic of conversation the attorney would choose.

"I hear you're back at work," Kade said.

Dawn furrowed her brow. *Did Aiden tell her that? Does she talk about me...about our relationship? Does Kade even know that we're in a relationship?* She had a feeling there wasn't much that escaped Kade Matheson's attention.

"The Matheson clan has more informants than the Mafia," Kade said as if reading her thoughts.

She's a prosecutor, used to reading body language, so you'd better be careful if you don't want her to read you like a book. "Yes, I'm back at work. Not at my old job, though. I decided to work with families and kids, with a few teens and young adults thrown in, who have problems coming to terms with their sexual orientation."

"That's important work." Kade's face revealed no emotions.

Is that the politically correct Matheson way of telling me that she's okay with my own sexual orientation...and my relationship with Aiden? Dawn wondered. "It's a nice change of pace from working with rape survivors."

"I can definitely understand that," Kade said with a decisive nod. "After prosecuting white-collar crimes, transferring to the sex crimes unit was... Well, let's just say it's been a challenge."

Dawn studied her. What had made an ambitious woman from a wealthy family choose a job with a frustratingly low conviction rate and little media attention? *Why did she become a prosecutor? I'm sure her family wanted to see her as a partner in a big shot law firm.* "The detectives that I know always tell me that working with living victims is the hardest."

Kade swirled the wine in her glass. "Yes, but some of them wouldn't trade it for anything else."

She's talking about Aiden. "For some, it's the only thing they know how to do—and the one thing they feel they have to do."

"The only thing they feel they have." Kade sipped from her wine like a lady of noble birth.

"That's not true, though. They are and they have so much more than just the job." Dawn let her gaze wander around the room, taking in all the laughing people. "These people are almost like a family."

Kade turned so she could look at the same things that Dawn did. "A family, complete with a strict but softhearted mother, an eager younger brother, and a weird uncle."

Dawn had to chuckle as she looked at Lieutenant Swenson, Ruben, and Okada.

"And what's your role in that nice little family analogy?" Aiden asked as she came up behind them.

"That's easy—I'm the utterly brilliant but completely underappreciated sister," Kade answered, still looking at Dawn.

Sister. Was that a message for her?

Aiden chuckled. "You forgot painfully shy and modest sister. So, what part does that leave for me?"

Kade nonchalantly turned to her. "The protective family dog."

Juice dribbled down Dawn's chin and drenched her blouse as she laughed. Grimacing, she looked down at her blouse that was almost transparent now. "Damn."

"It's not that bad." Aiden reached out with one finger and flicked a drop of juice from Dawn's chin. "At least you didn't drink red wine."

Dawn pinched the wet, cold fabric between thumb and index finger and pulled it away from her skin.

Aiden was heroically trying not to look anywhere but into her face. "Come on." She lightly gripped Dawn's elbow. "Let's find Susan and ask her if she has something you can wear."

Susan readily gave them access to her wardrobe. "What's it gonna be?" She lifted a see-through blouse from its hanger and grinned back at Dawn. "Something sexy?"

"Don't tease her, Susan," Aiden said from somewhere behind them.

"Her?" Susan winked. "It's you I want to tease."

"Something less transparent than what I'm already wearing would be nice, thank you," Dawn said.

Susan handed her an elegant, dark red blouse. "Aiden, please show her where the bathroom is."

Aiden led her down the hall and opened a door. "Are you okay?"

"Why wouldn't I be?" Dawn turned to look up at her, aware that they were alone for the first time since arriving at the party. "It was just a little juice."

"That's not what I meant." Aiden reached out a hand and, after a second of hesitation, let it rest against Dawn's cheek. "Are you okay with being at the party? I'm sorry that I keep abandoning you."

Dawn covered the hand on her cheek with her own. "Abandoning? Aiden, we're not joined at the hip. You're allowed to leave me for a while to talk to your friends."

The guilty expression on Aiden's face faded. "I hope no one tried to hold a piece of broccoli above you while I wasn't looking."

"No. Okada has been very nice to me. He's a real sweetheart."

Aiden's fingers tickled under her chin. "He has a soft spot for you. And Ruben's still pouting because he's no longer allowed to try and charm you with his lame one-liners."

Dawn leaned back against the doorjamb. "You mean one-liners like 'would you like to have coffee with us?'" she quoted one of the first things Aiden had said to her.

"That wasn't a line," Aiden said. "And you shot me down pretty fast."

"Not because I wanted to, but I couldn't very well cancel a patient's session because I wanted to go out with a cute detective that I had just met."

For a second, Aiden's amber eyes narrowed at the teasing "cute," as Dawn had known they would, but then she asked with a more serious expression, "Would you have agreed to go out with me if we had met again under different circumstances?"

Dawn's own thoughts had circled around those what-ifs for months now. What if she had accepted Aiden's offer to go out for coffee the first time they met? What if she hadn't made Aiden run away by asking her to speak to her group of pregnant rape victims? And, most of all, what if she had never been raped? "I would have hesitated because you're a cop and I promised myself to never again get involved with one of the boys—or girls—in blue."

"But?"

"But if you'd been persistent, I would have finally said yes." She studied Aiden's face. "Would you have been persistent?"

Aiden looked down at her boots.

"Please, tell me."

"I can't see myself going out of my way to get close to a shrink," Aiden said, one corner of her mouth lifting into an apologetic half smile. "At least not emotionally close."

There was something that Aiden was holding back. "But...?"

Aiden rubbed her neck, head down, looking up through her lashes with a mixture of childlike innocence and full-blown seduction. "Well, if I met you in a bar, after a stressful week, I'd have tried to get you into bed."

Dawn had long since known that Aiden normally was the one-night stand type, preferring sex without emotional entanglements, but to think that she would have gotten the "love 'em, leave 'em" treatment from her hurt nonetheless. She knew that Aiden was a woman with intense emotions and passions. From time to time, she would need to let go of her tight self-control. Dawn suspected that sex was that kind of release for Aiden, but she was no longer in a position to give her that. "Where does that leave us now?"

"Hey, you two!" Susan called from the living room. "What's taking so long? Hurry up. The one-minute countdown has started!"

One minute till the new year! Dawn's eyes widened. It wasn't enough time to go into the bathroom to clean up and change. She didn't want to begin the new year alone in a strange bathroom, separated from Aiden by solid walls. She also didn't plan on ringing in the new year in a stained, wet blouse that made Aiden politely look away from her. "Hold this and turn around."

"What?"

Dawn handed her Susan's blouse. "Turn around."

Aiden hastily followed the command when Dawn tugged the wet blouse from her slacks and began to unbutton it. Without looking, Aiden handed the new blouse back over her shoulder when Dawn told her to.

Dawn had just closed the last button when the guests in the living room shouted, "Five, four, three, two, one! Happy New Year!"

She turned Aiden back around and met her eyes. "We don't have champagne."

"We don't need any." Aiden stepped closer and wrapped her in a full-body embrace.

Dawn's eyes fluttered shut. She slid her arms around Aiden and breathed in her scent—leather, cinnamon from one of Susan's pastries she had eaten, and something that was the scent of Aiden Carlisle alone.

"Happy New Year," Aiden whispered, her breath warming Dawn's ear. "I hope you have a wonderful year."

"Happy New Year." Dawn pulled back a little.

From the living room, she could hear shouts and laughter, the popping of champagne corks, and Ruben's enthusiastic voice as he butchered the words to "Auld Lang Syne." Outside, fireworks started going off in the sky.

Dawn ignored the noise, concentrating only on Aiden's eyes and the warm, golden flecks in them. "What does that relationship rulebook of yours prescribe for a situation like this?"

Aiden chuckled. "The rulebook predicts a year of bad luck for anyone who fails to smooch their significant other at the stroke of midnight."

Fine hairs tickled Dawn's palm as she slid her hand up Aiden's neck. "Oh, I wouldn't want that on my conscience."

"No, we can't have that." Aiden's body pressed against hers more fully as she leaned forward and brushed her lips against Dawn's before pulling back an inch to study Dawn's reaction.

This time it was Dawn who closed the remaining distance between them. Aiden's lips caressed hers slowly and gently, not trying to deepen the kiss. Dawn could feel her holding back, could sense the passion slumbering just beneath the surface. She wanted Aiden to enjoy their intimate contact and not have her planning her every action and analyzing Dawn's reactions, watching for any signs that she wanted her to stop. She tightened her arms around Aiden's waist and nibbled on her lips until she had teased them open.

Aiden moaned into her mouth.

"Hey, Aiden, Happy New Year!" Ray stepped from the living room.

They pulled back enough for Dawn to rest her forehead against Aiden's shoulder. "God," she whispered. "I hope he has better timing when he's on the job."

The assembled party guests followed behind Ray, heading for the front door.

Aiden broke their embrace. "Did you run out of alcohol?"

Ray rolled his eyes. "We're going outside to watch the fireworks. Come with us." He pressed champagne flutes into their hands.

Dawn would have preferred to stay inside and continue her

conversation—and other oral activities—with Aiden, but she followed them outside nonetheless.

A ball of light burst overhead, streaking the night sky with purple sparks that drooped down to the ground. Golden and red fireworks launched high in the sky and divided into spirals. Dawn flinched when they finally exploded with a sudden "boom." Just a faint glitter remained after they burst.

She touched her flute to Aiden's and those of the other guests before taking a sip of the bubbly liquid.

"So, what New Year's resolutions did you make?" Susan asked no one in particular.

Okada shook his head. "I've given up on resolutions. The changes I'd like to make are beyond the control of a mere mortal."

"I could suggest a resolution or two for all of you." Lieutenant Swenson looked at each of her detectives in turn. "Always following my orders, for example."

Ruben shook his head. "Sorry, Lieutenant, that'll have to wait till next year. I've got another resolution already. I'm gonna quit smoking."

"What about you, Aiden?" Susan asked. "Do you have any resolutions?"

Aiden paused a moment to contemplate the golden lights that were falling down from fireworks like branches of a willow. "Well, I guess now that I'm trying my hand at this relationship thing, I'll have to give up the strippers."

Dawn had expected Aiden to answer with a joke. Or was it a serious answer after all? Was this her way of telling Dawn that she no longer wanted to be the one-night-stand type?

"Strippers?" Susan asked. "Is that what's really going on when my dear husband tells me you have another all-night surveillance?"

"Hey, we are watching very closely," Ray said. "That's what surveillance is all about."

Susan rolled her eyes, then looked up to watch what looked

like hundreds of shiny jewels falling from the sky. Finally, her gaze came to rest on Dawn. "Have you made any resolutions?"

For a few seconds, Dawn contemplated answering with a joke of her own, but then she felt Aiden's gaze on her, almost like a touch. "I resolved that I'm going to bid the last year farewell tonight. I want to take my life back and live it to its fullest."

Exploding fireworks sounded unbearably loud in the sudden silence. Then Aiden stepped forward and raised her champagne flute. "To living life to its fullest."

CHAPTER 29

RAY SET THE PHONE DOWN. "We've got a witness." He made quotation marks in the air at the word "witness."

Aiden furrowed her brow. "What's that supposed to mean?"

"A nearsighted granny claims that Robert Danton just moved into the apartment next door from her."

When she read the address on the piece of paper he handed her, she snorted. "Philadelphia Street? That's practically in the lap of the North Precinct. Even Danton couldn't be that stupid. If you ask me, he's not even in Portland anymore."

"Yeah, he's probably breathing fresh Canadian air by now. But we have to check it out anyway. Your lieutenant buddy from the North Precinct said she'd meet us there." Ray grinned.

"Lieutenant Vasquez is not my buddy." Aiden clipped on her holster and checked the magazine. "She's Dawn's friend, not mine." At the mention of Dawn, her gaze fell onto the good luck charm that had escaped from the confines of her V-neck shirt. She opened her locker. "Let's wear the vests today."

Ray watched as she fastened the Velcro straps of the dark blue bullet-resistant vest. "You have a premonition or something?"

"No, nothing like that. It's just that..." Aiden hesitated. "I promised myself that I wouldn't take any unnecessary risks." *It's not only me that I have to think of anymore.*

Ray grabbed his own vest. "Ah, so you did make New Year's resolutions."

"I'm just not eager to be the next dead cop Dawn has to cry over." Aiden closed her locker. "Let's go."

The detectives left their car one block from the targeted address. On the remote chance that Danton, who had brutally raped and murdered three women, was really in the area, they didn't want to alert him to their presence.

Two uniformed officers from the North Precinct were already waiting for them—and they weren't alone. Del leaned against the hood of her unmarked car, also wearing a vest and her service weapon. "Carlisle." Del gave her a curt nod. She was all business now, a tough, competent cop, not the charming aunt that Dawn knew.

Aiden returned the greeting in the same professional manner.

With a quick glance toward the uniformed officers who had taken cover positions around the block, they entered the building. Del jammed a ballpoint pen under the front door to hold it open in case they needed backup. The officer behind Aiden lowered the volume of his portable radio to a whisper.

Aiden drew her weapon from its holster and held it alongside her thigh, the index finger resting next to the trigger, as they climbed the stairs.

Somewhere above them, a door banged and a man shouted at someone.

They stopped before turning around the last corner, communicating with quick hand gestures.

Aiden's heart began to pound. Adrenaline pulsed through her veins. All her senses were focused on the landing before her as she rounded the corner.

The landing was empty. The number on the door revealed that it was the apartment they were looking for.

Aiden tensed when the door next to it opened, but it was only a silver-haired lady peeking out. "Get back into your apartment, ma'am."

As the old woman moved back, they took positions on each side of Danton's door.

Aiden listened for a second, trying to hear what was going on behind the door, and shook her head. Nothing.

She and Ray exchanged one last, silent glance, and then Ray raised his fist to knock.

Another door behind them opened.

"Get back into your apartment," Ray said without looking away from the door in front of them.

Aiden turned to make sure the neighbor had moved back. Instead of looking into a curious tenant's eyes, she was staring down the barrel of Robert Danton's gun.

Apparently, their elderly witness wasn't only nearsighted, she had a bad memory for numbers too—they were standing in front of the wrong apartment.

"Weapon!" Aiden shouted. "Police! Drop it!"

Danton's index finger moved, and she squeezed the trigger.

Shots echoed through the stairwell.

Aiden wanted to fire again, but pain exploded in her chest, and she found herself staring up at the gray ceiling.

Ray spun around, his pistol trained on the man who had appeared behind them. One quick glance told him that he didn't need to worry about Robert Danton anymore. A bullet from Aiden's weapon had killed him instantly.

Just to make sure, he kicked Danton's weapon out of his limp grasp before turning back around toward his partner. "That wa—Aiden!"

Aiden was lying flat on her back, one hand pressed against her chest, gasping and wheezing. To his half-trained ear, it sounded like a collapsed lung. A pool of blood was spreading under her head.

Oh, shit, shit, shit! God, no, please, let her be okay. He fell onto his knees next to her.

Somewhere behind him, Del Vasquez had taken over the portable radio. "10-74! Officer down! We need the EMTs at 7017 North Philadelphia Street—now!"

Aiden stared up at him with wild, unfocused eyes. For a few moments, Ray wasn't even sure if she could see him until she groaned, "Ray..."

"Lie still."

It seemed as if Aiden was unable to move anyway.

Del sank on her knees on the other side of the wheezing woman. "Carlisle, if you dare to die, I swear I'll—"

"She's not going to die!" Ray didn't care that he was shouting at a lieutenant. Frantically, he ripped open Aiden's pierced shirt. Smoke rose from a hole in the vest, and for a few scary moments, he couldn't see if the bullet had penetrated or not. Then his trembling fingers felt the deformed lump of hot metal that was imbedded in the Kevlar layers directly over Aiden's heart.

Together, he and Del struggled to loosen the Velcro straps, and Del tugged up the white T-shirt underneath.

No blood. Relief almost made him collapse on top of his fallen partner. An extensive bruise was already spreading, but the Kevlar had protected her from more serious injuries or even death.

"Your vest caught it. You'll be fine." He almost sang it out to Aiden.

Aiden stared up at him, her amber eyes glowing against her pale face and lips. She was still fighting for breath, and blood was spreading from what he hoped was just a laceration but could just as well be a cracked skull. "D-don't—"

"Shh, don't try to talk." Ray slid out of his jacket, gently lifted her head, and pressed the jacket against the source of the bleeding. Approaching sirens had never sounded so good. "The ambulance will be here any second."

"D-don't...call...Dawn." Aiden wheezed.

The EMTs came trampling up the stairs. Ray and Del stepped back to let them work. He looked back and forth between Aiden and the uniformed officer who picked up Aiden's gun and placed it into an evidence bag. As much as he wanted to follow his partner to the hospital, he had to stay and wait for the Internal Affairs Shooting Team.

"Go," Del said. "The Internal Affairs guys can talk to me first. There'll be time for your interview later."

Ray breathed a sigh of relief. He moved to follow the EMTs down the stairs, but then turned back around. "You're going to call Dawn anyway, aren't you?"

"Wouldn't you want your wife to know if you had been shot?" Del asked.

"No." Ray could understand the impulse to protect the woman you loved. "But she'd want to."

"Doctor Kinsley?" Dawn's new secretary stuck her head into the office. "There's a police officer here who wants to see you."

Dawn held back a grin. *Aiden Carlisle, you're not using that gold shield of yours to scare my secretary, are you?* "Is she tall, dark-haired, and attractive?"

"Yes, she is," Del answered as she entered despite the secretary's protests.

"Del!" It was not the tall, dark-haired, attractive detective she had wanted to see but not a bad second choice either. "It's okay, Mrs. Phillips. She's a friend of mine."

The secretary closed the door behind her, but Del still didn't move closer.

"Del? Is everything all right?"

Del trudged across the room and slumped into a visitor chair. "Sit down." Her voice was without any trace of her usual humor.

A clump of ice formed in Dawn's stomach. She had heard those words and had seen that look on a cop's face before. "No. I don't want to sit."

"Dawn, please..."

Dawn, not grasshopper. This is serious. A part of her didn't want to hear what Del had to say, but another part couldn't stand the dreadful silence any longer. "Just tell me."

"There's been a shooting."

"God, no! Aiden!" Dawn stumbled back. Her stomach heaved when she detected the blood on Del's sleeve. "Is it...? Is she...?" The world around her seemed to fade out, and she swayed.

Del leaped from her chair and enfolded her in protective arms. "No, no, I don't think it's anything serious. Her bulletproof vest caught it. The EMTs said she should be fine."

Dawn closed her eyes and waited until she was sure that she could speak without throwing up. "Yes, this time. But how long until..." She swallowed and fell silent. The words hurt too much to say them out loud. "I can't stand it, Del. Not again."

Del's familiar dark eyes studied her. "So, what are you gonna do? Ask her to resign?"

"No." Dawn shook her head. That had never been an option. "The job is so much a part of who she is. I would never ask her to give that up."

"Then what else can you do? Break up with her?"

Dawn bit her lip until she tasted blood.

Del smiled softly. "Didn't think so. You're way past the point where it would hurt any less if you ended it now, grasshopper."

"I...I think I love her, Del."

"I know." Del's hand drew comforting circles across her back.

Dawn could remember her doing the same when she had skinned her knees over twenty years ago. *I don't think a Band-Aid and ice cream will make it better now.* She blinked away her tears. When she moved back a few inches, she was surprised to discover that Del's eyes were a little misty too. Anger gripped her. "Damn you!" She hit Del in the chest, but Del made no move to defend herself. "Why do you cops have to be so...so..."

Again, Del caught her in an embrace.

Dawn closed her eyes and rested her forehead against Del's shoulder. "When Dad and Brian died, I swore I would stay away from cops and never go through what Mom did, and now... It's just not fair."

"I know," Del whispered. "But despite all the pain, your mother never regretted marrying your dad."

Dawn nodded and sighed. "Take me to Aiden, please."

When Dawn hurried through the double doors with Del at her heels, Ray was pacing the hospital hallway. He was looking as worn out as Dawn felt—his shirt wrinkled and bloodstained, his jacket missing, the tie hanging loosely around his neck, and his eyes haunted.

He was no longer a stranger that she hardly knew, but an anxiously waiting family member. She wrapped her arms around his tense shoulders for a quick hug, ignoring Aiden's blood on his shirt as best as she could. "How is she?"

"I haven't heard anything yet." Ray shoved his hands in his pockets and shuffled his feet.

Dawn sank into an uncomfortable plastic chair and fell into some sort of trance while waiting for news about Aiden. She barely noticed Del and Ray taking seats to either side of her, yet was immediately fully alert when a doctor in scrubs stopped in front of them.

"Anyone here for Detective Carlisle?"

"Yes!" They jumped up.

The physician looked from Ray to Del and finally to Dawn. "Are you family?"

Ray and Dawn spoke at the same time, "I'm her partner."

The doctor's brows lowered in silent reproach. "I would recommend you get your stories straight if you want information about the patient."

Clearly not in the mood for debates, Ray shoved his gold shield under the doctor's nose. "I'm her work partner, and she's her life partner. Now tell us how she is."

"She's lucky to be alive," the doctor answered. "The vest prevented the bullet from entering her body, but she still absorbed the bullet's energy, which caused blunt force trauma."

Dawn swallowed and gripped Del's hand. The word "trauma" wasn't part of her favorite vocabulary at the moment.

"And that means...?" Ray asked.

"She has a chest contusion—a fist-sized hematoma, a few bruised ribs, some swelling and discoloration," the doctor said. "She'll be very sore for a week or so."

Dawn stared up at him. "But she'll be fine?"

"Well, she also has a laceration on the back of her head and a possible concussion, so we're doing a CAT scan and we're admitting her overnight for observation." The doctor shrugged. "But if there aren't any complications, she should be fine."

"Can we see her?" Dawn had to see with her own eyes that Aiden was okay.

"If she's up for seeing visitors and wants to see you. The nurses will let you know when she's back in her room." The doctor held up a finger. "Don't stay too long, though. Detective Carlisle needs her rest."

Time seemed to crawl, but finally a nurse arrived. "You can see her now."

"You go in," Del said to Dawn. "We can see her after you speak to her."

Thankful for the opportunity to be alone with Aiden, Dawn followed the nurse toward one of the rooms. She opened the door and peeked in.

Aiden was slumped against the pillows of a hospital bed, her face as pale as the linens. She had been stripped of her clothes and her gold shield and was wearing a hospital gown. An intravenous line was taped to her hand. She was looking at the wall, so Dawn could see the white patch of gauze covering the back of her head.

"Hi." Dawn's voice was a mere whisper. The sight of a wounded Aiden shook her to her core.

At the sound of her voice, Aiden tried to straighten and take on a more casual pose, but then sank back with a groan.

"Don't get up." Careful not to jostle her, Dawn perched on the edge of the hospital bed. She took Aiden's hand in her own and stared down at her, trying to catch up with her whirling thoughts and comprehend what had happened.

"Don't look at me like that." Aiden nudged her under the chin to make her smile. "I'm fine, really."

Dawn didn't smile. "You have to stay overnight in a hospital. That's not 'fine' in my book."

"It's just standard procedure." Aiden waved a hand. "A formality."

"Of course!" Dawn's voice was dripping with sarcasm. "It's not like you have any reason to be here, like a concussion or massive bruising."

Aiden struggled to sit up. "I'll be fine. I've had worse. They shouldn't have called you."

"Oh, yes, they should!" Dawn didn't want to argue, but her emotions were running high. The thought of how close Aiden had come to dying was making her dizzy. She wanted to hug Aiden and hold on to her for a long time; she wanted to shout and to cry and to laugh with relief, but Aiden didn't seem to want any displays of emotion. It took all her self-discipline to imitate Aiden's matter-of-fact behavior. "What happened?"

"I can't talk about that."

"You can't or you don't want to?"

Aiden shrugged. "It's an ongoing investigation—"

"An investigation that almost cost you your life and I'm not allowed to ask you about it?" Dawn knew that she would see every possible scenario of what might have happened in her nightmares.

Aiden closed her eyes.

Sighing, Dawn decided that this was not the time for an argument. Aiden was exhausted and in pain even if she tried to hide it. *Give her a little time and space. Aiden is a woman who needs it, and you have to accept that.* "Do you have a headache?" Her fingertips touched the fine hairs on Aiden's temple.

"It's not too bad."

A soft knock sounded at the door before Ray and Del entered.

Ray stopped at the foot of the hospital bed and wrapped his hands around the railing surrounding it, his gaze never leaving Aiden's face. "You okay?"

Aiden grinned up at him and tried for a casual shrug but then flinched. "I would be better if I didn't have to wear this flimsy sheet of paper and stay here overnight to enjoy three low-cal, low-taste meals."

Del crossed the room and rested one hand on Dawn's shoulder as she looked down at Aiden. "Hey, Carlisle. The first time you work with me and you pull a stunt like this. You just couldn't stand the thought of letting a lieutenant with the North Precinct have all the attention, could you?"

Aiden chuckled, clearly more comfortable with Del's teasing than with Dawn's questions about her well-being. Her nostrils flared in an attempt to suppress a yawn.

"We should go and let you get some rest," Dawn said, even though letting Aiden out of her sight was the last thing she wanted to do. A little uncomfortable under Ray's and Del's watchful eyes and not sure if Aiden was up for the public display of affection, she leaned down and pecked Aiden's cheek instead of wrapping her arms around her for a longer good-bye.

Aiden gazed up at her, her eyes cloudy with pain and emotion. "Dawn?"

She stopped in mid-turn. "Hmm?"

"I… We'll talk tomorrow, okay?"

Relief trickled through Dawn. *She's not shutting me out.* For the first time since Del had appeared in her office, she could breathe freely. "Okay."

Another figure in scrubs entered Aiden's hospital room with a tray.

Aiden barely glanced up. "Thanks, but I'm not hungry."

"Well, I guess then I'll just take this delicious Chinese food that my daughter prepared for you and—"

A wave of pain shot through Aiden as her head jerked up, stretching the sore muscles of her chest and shoulder. Dawn's mother stood in front of her, wearing blue scrubs. "Grace? What are you doing here?"

"I work here at the hospital. I'm a nurse upstairs in the pediatrics unit." Grace glanced down at her scrubs. "Or did you think this was a fashion statement?"

Aiden didn't know how to answer the gentle teasing. Never in her life had she been concerned with making a good impression, but now she wanted Grace to like her. She knew how important Grace was to Dawn, so if she wanted a serious long-term relationship with Dawn, she'd better try to establish some sort of mutual acceptance with her mother. "No, I…I guess I'm not thinking clearly right now."

Grace moved closer and set the tray down on the bedside

table. With the trained eye of a nurse, she checked the dressing on Aiden's head and the bruise peeking out from under the thin hospital gown. "You're lucky to be alive." Her voice was a whisper.

"I know."

"If you hadn't worn a vest..."

Aiden pressed her lips together. It had been a routine visit, following the tip of an elderly witness. She had been sure it would turn out to be a dead end. Before, she had never worn a bullet-resistant vest in situations that she didn't expect to end in a confrontation. Only a coincidental glance down at the Saint Michael good luck charm had made her stop to get a vest this time. *I really had a guardian angel today.* She lifted a hand to touch the pendant—only to find the place on her upper chest empty. *God, no! I must have lost it when they ripped the vest and shirt off me!*

"Are you looking for this?" The silver pendant dangled from Grace's fingers.

"How...?"

"Del found it at the scene after the EMTs had carried you off," Grace said. "She recognized it immediately because it's one of a kind. My mother-in-law had it made for Jim's father, who was a cop too." She looked down at the good luck charm, her thumb caressing the metal.

It's an old family heirloom. Did she know that Dawn gave it to me?

Grace reached out to hand Aiden the necklace.

"No." Aiden pulled her hand away and shook her head. "It belongs to your family."

Grace studied the silver pendant for a second. "Yes, it does." She stepped forward and pressed it into Aiden's hand, closing her fingers around Aiden's to prevent her from letting go. "And if my daughter has anything to say about it, you're a part of it now."

Aiden looked down at the hand resting over hers. Did Dawn's mother really want her to have something that was so valuable to her family? "And if you had anything to say about it?"

"Then it would be Jim who gave the pendant to you," Grace said, her gray eyes misty. "But if you have it, I can at least imagine that he's there, watching over you and making sure that his daughter's heart won't be broken again by losing a cop."

Aiden tightened her grip, finally accepting the necklace. She liked the thought of having Dawn's father watching over her. *Although I hope that he won't be watching in certain situations when I'm off-duty and spending quality time with his daughter.*

CHAPTER 30

THE NEXT DAY, DAWN WAS in her mother's kitchen. She looked up when a key rattled in the lock.

Her mother's footfalls came down the hall. "Dawn?"

"I'm in the kitchen, Mom."

Grace cracked the door open and peeked into her kitchen.

Dawn turned away from the stove. "I hope you don't mind that I used your kitchen. Mine is just too small."

"It's certainly too small for all of this." Grace gestured with both hands, pointing at the lasagna, the Caesar salad, the chocolate mousse, and the cookies that were baking in the oven. She wandered closer and touched Dawn's back. "Are you okay, sweetie?"

Dawn nodded. "I'm not the one who got shot."

"You're the one who looks more upset, though," her mother said. "I always know that something's bothering you when you're cooking up a storm. Is Aiden still pulling that stoic warrior routine that they seem to teach at the law enforcement academy?"

A tired smile crept onto Dawn's face. "I think she was the top pupil in the class."

"Your father was the all-time champion, though," Grace said.

Dawn leaned against the kitchen counter. When her father had been alive, she had been a teenager without much interest in the dynamic of relationships, and now she tried to think back and remember how her parents had interacted. "Was Dad communicative as a partner?"

Grace laughed. "Are you kidding? He came from a family of Irish cops who thought that 'pass the potatoes, please' constituted sufficient marital conversation. It's not that he wasn't concerned about me and my feelings; he just didn't like to talk about his own."

"What did you do when he tried to shut you out?"

"It took a few years, but I eventually figured out when to push and when to let him be." Grace smiled. "And I cooked a lot."

Dawn snorted. "Great. Nice to know that I'll be frustrated and fat."

"Talk to her," Grace said. "I have a feeling that Aiden wants to talk to you but is just not used to having someone be there for her. She doesn't have family, does she?"

Dawn didn't want to delve into that topic. That was something that only Aiden could decide to share. "I don't think she has any connection to people outside of her job."

"Except for you," Grace said.

"If she wants me."

Grace pinched her arm. "Of course she does. What's not to want?"

"You're biased, Mom." Could she really be an equal partner for Aiden, despite her emotional wounds?

"I don't think so," Grace said. "She'd be lucky to have you. You're intelligent, beautiful, and honest, and seeing as how I can't stand lasagna, I guess you just spent a few hours in the kitchen to make her favorite dishes for her."

Dawn felt a blush crawl up her neck and color her cheeks. "Aiden is not much of a cook."

"See?" Grace patted her shoulder. "You're perfect for each other. If she were the type to cook when she's upset too, I'd never get to use my kitchen again. Now go and feed that detective of yours."

Loaded with half a dozen containers of food, Dawn drove across town. She pressed the familiar buzzer to be let in, but no one answered. *Hmm, either she's asleep or she doesn't want company.*

One of Aiden's neighbors moved past her, turned his key in the lock, and entered. With one hand on the door to prevent it from closing, he looked back at Dawn, probably recognizing her from a previous visit to Aiden's apartment.

After a second's hesitation, Dawn followed him into the apartment building. If Aiden still didn't open the door, she would at least leave the food on her doorstep. To her surprise, the door was opened after the first knock.

Aiden leaned in the doorway in jeans and a loose shirt. Her feet were bare and her hair tousled. "Sorry I couldn't let you in when you rang the bell. I was in the shower. Took me forever to get this shirt on." She was breathing hard, and sweat was forming on her brow even though she was just out of the shower.

Dawn resisted the urge to kiss a drop of water from the tip of Aiden's ear. "You didn't hurt yourself, did you?" She checked the bandage on the back of Aiden's head. "Why didn't you choose a button-down shirt? It would have been much easier than trying to get into this shirt."

"Yeah, I realize that now," Aiden said with a rueful smile. "But by the time I came to that conclusion, I heard the doorbell and I knew it was most likely you, so..."

"So you didn't take the time to go into the bedroom and pick another shirt." Dawn shook her head, not sure if she should be annoyed that Aiden had been so careless with her own health or flattered that she was so eager to see her. Deeply breathing in her scent, she slipped past Aiden into the apartment. "How are you?"

"Much better now that I escaped those sterile hospital walls." Aiden followed her into the living room and watched as Dawn spread out the food she had brought on the coffee table. "What's all this?"

"I made you dinner."

"You didn't have to."

Dawn pressed her lips together. "I know I didn't have to. I wanted to."

"Thank you. It smells great."

They strolled into the kitchen, where Aiden opened the cupboard and reached up to take out two plates. A groan escaped her lips when she stretched to reach the upper shelf.

Dawn raced around the kitchen island and urged Aiden away from the cupboard. "Sit down and rest. Did they prescribe pain meds for you?"

"I have some pain pills."

"Then take them. You don't have to play the hero with me." With a loud clink, Dawn set a glass of water down in front of Aiden.

Aiden made no move to get the pills. "I don't—"

Dawn closed her eyes and took a deep breath before she opened them again. "Please. I don't like seeing you in pain." In fact, she hated it.

Aiden's gaze met hers, and without further discussion, she rose and returned with two white pills, which she swallowed.

Heaving a sigh of relief, Dawn began to set the table.

"I'm sorry." Aiden stepped behind her and covered Dawn's hand, which had just laid a fork on the table, with her own. "I know I'm a terrible patient, but I'm not used to being fussed over."

Dawn turned and wrapped her arms around Aiden's waist, careful not to exert any pressure on her chest. "I'm sorry for fussing."

"No, no, I like it." Aiden's hands, warm against her back, squeezed her gently.

Dawn laughed. "It makes you crazy."

Aiden pressed a kiss to the crown of Dawn's head. "Hmm, maybe I like crazy?"

Dawn closed her eyes and relaxed into the embrace. Being so close to Aiden, feeling her breath warm her neck, and inhaling her scent made it difficult to think about how easily Aiden could have been taken away from her. After another minute, she forced herself to move back. "Come on. Let's warm up the lasagna and eat."

After dinner, Dawn busied herself with the dishes and directed Aiden to the couch. The lack of protest told her how groggy Aiden was. After putting away the last plate, Dawn tiptoed into the living room.

Aiden was lying on the couch, her eyes closed.

Intent on not waking her, Dawn snuck across the room to retrieve her coat.

"Are you trying to steal my TV?" Aiden's voice made her jerk, and Aiden chuckled. "I'm not asleep, just resting like you told me to. Do you have to get back to the office?"

Is that her way of asking me to stay a little longer? Dawn hoped it was, for she had no intention of leaving Aiden without addressing the shooting and the emotions it had caused in both of them. "No, I'm done for the day. I just wanted to let you sleep without interrupting."

"I haven't done anything but laze around for the last three days, so how could I be sleepy?" Aiden sat up with a groan and patted the space she had just cleared on the couch next to her. "Let's see if anything interesting is on."

Dawn settled down at the end of the couch, curling one leg under her. She watched in silence as Aiden turned on the TV and flicked through various channels. A passionate kiss between two soap characters flashed across the screen, rapidly followed by a single cop chasing down a suspect.

"Ha! If I'd done that, I wouldn't have made it out of the academy." Aiden finally settled on a documentary about a team that was trying to climb Mount Everest.

Not calm enough to settle down and get lost in other people's lives, Dawn shifted her legs.

"Why don't you make yourself comfortable?" Aiden reached out a hand to draw Dawn toward her. "Come on, lean back against me. I promise I won't bite."

"That's not a good idea. You're in enough pain as it is. Why don't you lean back against me?"

Aiden's hand froze on Dawn's arm. For a moment, she just stared at her. "Uh, okay. I guess that works too."

Dawn slipped behind Aiden and leaned back against the arm of the couch. She rested one leg along the back of the couch and set the other foot on the floor. With an inviting smile, she patted the empty space in between her legs.

Inch by inch, Aiden moved toward her and stopped when her back was barely touching Dawn's body.

The stiff, upright position couldn't be comfortable, so Dawn wrapped an arm around Aiden's waist and drew her back.

"I'm too heavy." Aiden tried to resist.

"Nonsense. I'm not made of glass. I can take it." Dawn tugged again, and Aiden finally allowed herself to sink back against her body. Tension vibrated in the muscles under Dawn's hand. Clearly, Aiden was not used to being held, more comfortable with the protective stance of the "holder" than with the more vulnerable position of the "holdee."

The team in the documentary had almost made it to the summit when Dawn finally felt Aiden relax. Her head came to rest against Dawn's shoulder, and the white dressing brushed against her cheek whenever Aiden moved. Dawn hastily directed her gaze away from the reminder of Aiden's injury. She didn't want to bring up that particular subject now that she had gotten Aiden to relax. Following the contours of Aiden's ear with her eyes, she then lifted a finger and traced the rim of the ear. "Your ears are really cute."

They were. The small ears, left free by Aiden's short hair, somehow reminded her of Aiden's softer, more vulnerable side.

"What?"

"Your ears," Dawn said, "they're cute."

"My ears?" Aiden craned her neck to look back at Dawn but then sank back with a groan.

Dawn's shrug moved the body that was lying half on top of her. "Yeah, I like them. They're very...kissable." She enjoyed the shiver that raced through Aiden as her lips graced one of the cute ears. Her own body was virtually vibrating with Aiden's closeness. "Hasn't anybody ever complimented you on your ears?"

"No." Aiden laughed, her voice a little rough. "Most of my dates told me they like my smile or my eyes, and the more daring ones commented on my breasts or my ass. I remember one woman who had an obsession with my arms, but no one ever paid any attention to my ears."

Dawn grazed the almost microscopic hairs on the earlobe with her fingernail, sending another shudder through Aiden. "Well, then it's high time that someone made up for that neglect." She looked down at the woman in her arms, mentally debating whether she should voice the thoughts going through her head. "That's not to say that I don't like your eyes and your smile and the way your arms feel when they hold me or that I don't think what I've seen of your ass and your breasts is awe-inspiring. I do. But still, your ears are cute."

Aiden tilted her head to the side to smile up at Dawn. "While you're already lying down on a couch, please tell me, Doctor, when did your ear fetish start?"

Dawn chuckled. "Well, I guess that would be around the time that I met you."

They lay without talking for a while. Another documentary started, but neither of them paid it any attention. Aiden flicked the remote and turned off the TV.

"I want to stay the night," Dawn said.

Aiden's stunned silence matched her own. Dawn hadn't planned to invite herself.

"Um, you want to...?" Aiden pointed in the direction of the bedroom.

Dawn was thankful that Aiden was in front of her and couldn't see her blush. "I want to sleep with you...next to you. Just sleep, if that's okay with you."

"Of course it is. I don't feel very adventurous right now," Aiden said. "But my bed is not exactly king-sized. Will you be comfortable sleeping so close?"

Dawn's shoulders moved like the wings of a wounded bird. "I don't know. I haven't slept...stayed with anyone since... since I was raped." She forced the words from her lips. "Just Jamie, and that attempt didn't work out too well."

Moving slowly so she wouldn't aggravate her ribs, Aiden rose and turned to face her. "If you're uncomfortable at any time, tell me and I'll sleep on the couch."

"If anyone sleeps on the couch, it'll be me." Dawn made her voice firm. "But let's try the bed first. Do you need help in the bathroom?"

Aiden blinked a few times. "No, thanks, I've been able to manage that on my own since I was three."

The urge to slap Aiden on the head rose, but knowing she was hurt there too, Dawn held herself back. "You weren't bruised and battered when you were three."

"Thanks, I can manage." Aiden disappeared into the bathroom.

Soon after, the water started, and after a few minutes, a toothbrush clanked as it was placed back into its glass. The water was turned off, but Aiden didn't return. Dawn was just about to knock when Aiden called through the closed door, "Dawn?"

"Yes?" She cracked the door open just enough to peek in.

Aiden had changed out of her jeans and into a pair of pajama pants but was still wearing her shirt. With a defeated gesture, she held her sleep shirt out to Dawn. "Raising my arms over my head hurts like hell. I barely managed earlier."

Without a word, Dawn directed her to sit on the closed toilet and lean forward. She grabbed the hem of the shirt and carefully raised it higher on Aiden's back. With gentle fingers, she pushed the fabric past the dressing on Aiden's head until the shirt fell free and she could pull it off by its sleeves.

When she reached for the sleep shirt that she had placed over Aiden's knees, her gaze was directed downward. From the upper edge of the bra that she forced herself not to linger on, a dark bruise extended up to the collarbone. Before she was aware of it, her fingertips touched the swollen, purple skin. The knowledge that a bullet could have pierced that skin made her breath catch.

"Um, Dawn?" Aiden's voice was husky, and goose bumps covered her chest and arms.

Another blush heated Dawn's skin. She stilled her hand on Aiden's chest. "The bra...um...do you want it on or off?"

Aiden looked up, her amber eyes glowing. "Off, please."

Quickly, before she could lose her composure, Dawn reached around her and unfastened the clasp. She tried not to watch as the bra straps slipped off strong shoulders, knowing she wasn't ready to act on the sensual images racing through her mind. When she finally had Aiden dressed again, she was as breathless as Aiden. "There. That wasn't so bad, was it?"

"Bad?" Aiden smirked. "It was torture—and I don't mean the damn bruise. That was not how I imagined the first time you saw me naked."

Dawn leaned back against the sink, letting the porcelain cool her overheated skin. "Ah, so you imagined that, huh?"

Aiden shot her a glance. "Let's not go into details right now."

"All right. And just for your information: I didn't really look."

"I know. Your parents raised a real gentlewoman." Aiden stood and slipped past her, placing a kiss on her cheek as their bodies brushed against each other in the narrow space in front of the sink. "There should be towels and a toothbrush in the cupboard, and I'll go get you something to sleep in."

Ten minutes later, Dawn entered the bedroom and stopped in front of the bed, tugging on the T-shirt that hung loosely and reached almost to her knees on her smaller frame.

"Cute," Aiden said from the bed.

Dawn glanced down at the image on the front of the shirt. "I didn't peg you for a *Finding Nemo* girl, Detective."

"It was a present from Ray's daughters."

Dawn slipped under the covers that Aiden held up for her. She fiddled with the blanket, trying to tuck her bare feet in, and then pounded her pillow into submission.

"You know, you actually have to lie still to fall asleep," Aiden said.

Dawn rolled around and wrapped her arms around the pillow. "I don't want to go to sleep. Not yet."

Aiden flashed a grin at her. "Let's see... What other things are there to do in bed when you're not alone but with a wildly attractive woman?"

"Talking," Dawn said.

"Has anyone ever told you that you have a one-track mind?" Aiden tried to sit up but sank back down with a groan. "Okay, okay, I know I promised you we would talk about what happened."

Dawn rolled around and let her head come to rest against Aiden's uninjured shoulder. "So, what did happen?"

"We tried to chase down a murderer, but a witness gave us the wrong address and we knocked on the door of the wrong apartment. The perp must have heard us and panicked. When I turned around, he was right behind me."

Aiden's tone was matter-of-fact, but Dawn could hear the underlying tension. "You shot him?"

"Yes. There was no time for—"

"You don't have to explain. I know you would never hurt, much less kill anyone, if it wasn't a matter of him or you." Dawn knew that Aiden was hypersensitive to anything that would make her appear violent or aggressive. Aiden was neither, but sometimes she needed to be reminded of that. "Just for the record, I'm glad it was him."

Aiden gave a curt nod.

Dawn interlaced her fingers with Aiden's, their palms pressed together. "Were you scared?"

"No, it all happened too fast. Ray was panicking more than me." Aiden laughed.

Dawn just looked at her, silently raising an eyebrow.

Aiden sighed. "Okay, so it was a little scary there for a minute while I was lying there, hurting like hell and gasping for breath, not knowing if the bullet had penetrated the vest or not."

"Why didn't you have someone call me?"

"It was pure chaos, nobody thought—"

"Nobody thought I'd want to know that my...my girlfriend had been shot?" Dawn struggled to sit up without pulling her hand away from Aiden's.

"I wasn't shot; the vest caught it."

Dawn knocked her pillow off the bed. "Don't get technical with me. Why didn't you call me?"

Aiden stared at the ceiling for a moment before she sighed and looked back to Dawn. "I didn't want to scare you after all you've been through with your dad and your brother."

"I understand that, and I appreciate that you want to protect me, but can we make a deal?"

"A deal?" Aiden's fingernails teased the inside of Dawn's wrist, and Dawn squirmed in an attempt not to giggle. "I confess all my sins to you, and you're gonna put in a good word with your boss for me?" She pointed their entwined hands upward.

Dawn pinched her thigh with her free hand. "I'm a psychologist, not a priest."

"Ah, yes, of course. So, what's the deal?"

"I want you to share yourself with me—and no, this is not a come-on." Dawn watched Aiden's face for any reaction. She was laying down the ground rules for their relationship, and if Aiden didn't accept them, there wasn't much hope for them. "I know your job requires emotional distance. I know you have to erect barriers to protect yourself from all the evil you see as a detective. But I need something else from you to make this...to make us work."

Aiden's nod urged her to continue.

"I need to know you—the whole you, not just the parts you allow your colleagues to see. I want to share your pain and your fears as well as the good things in your life."

Aiden closed her other hand around Dawn's fingers. "You already have enough pain and fears of your own. You don't need to carry my burdens too."

"Yes! Yes, I do." Dawn squeezed as hard as she could. "A relationship can't be one-sided. I want to be an equal partner for you. Don't you understand?" She shook Aiden's hand. "You have to trust me enough to be vulnerable with me. If you can't sleep because some bastard hurt a child, I want to know. If the precinct's coffeemaker bit the dust and you had a crappy day, I want to know. If Kade lost a case that meant something to you, I want to know. If you get a paper cut while writing reports, I want to know. If you need a hug or a kiss or a bowl of chicken broth—"

"You want to know," Aiden said with a smile.

"Yes, and then I want to be the one to hug you and kiss you and cook chicken soup for you."

Aiden looked stunned, and then, after a minute of silence, she smiled. "Did you just propose to me?"

Dawn's lips automatically echoed the smile, but hers was a little sad. "No. I'm not in a position to do that. It wouldn't be fair to you if I made promises I'm not sure I can keep."

"Promises you can't keep?" Aiden sat up with a groan. "What promises are we talking about?"

"I know that your other relationships—"

"I told you I didn't do relationships—at least not successful ones. There's no reason to compare yourself to anyone who has been in my life before. You win, hands down."

Okay. Dawn could see that she would have to be more direct than that. She took a deep breath. "I'm talking about your...our sex life—or the lack thereof." She gestured to their fully clothed bodies that were not touching anywhere but at their fingers.

"So, you think just because you don't sleep with me at the drop of a hat means that it would be unfair to expect a full commitment on my part?"

For someone who usually avoided talking about intimacy issues, Aiden had paraphrased her thoughts with amazing accuracy. Dawn nodded.

"I admit it has been a while since I've been invited to a wedding, but did they change the vows in the meantime?" Aiden asked.

"Change the vows?"

"Yeah." Aiden tapped Dawn's foot with her big toe. "You seem to know a different version than I do. In my version there's something mentioned about 'in sickness and in health, through the good times and the bad, till death do us part.' I don't remember a 'for as long as you don't get migraines and provide me with daily toe-curling sex.'"

Hot tears burned behind Dawn's eyes, but she refused to let

them fall. "Now, did you just propose to me?" Her voice was rough with emotion.

Aiden shrugged. "Well, that depends."

"On?"

"On whether or not you'd say yes." Aiden sounded casual, as if she were just teasing, but the look in her eyes spoke another language—she was unsure about what Dawn's answer would be.

Dawn wasn't. In all her life, she had never wanted to say "yes" to anything with such intensity. But still... "What about...?"

"What?"

"Well, you know, marriage is traditionally followed by the wedding night." Dawn studied her over the rim of her glasses.

Aiden shrugged. "I'm not in a rush. Sex is not important."

"Aiden Carlisle, you're a terrible liar." They had never talked about their attitudes toward sex before, but Dawn knew that Aiden had been no wallflower. Her good looks in combination with her commanding presence and the leather jacket had to be a chick magnet. A passionate woman like Aiden wasn't used to living a celibate life. "Of course sex is important in a new relationship. It's a nonverbal expression of our caring for each other."

"Okay, it may be important, but it's not the most important thing in our relationship," Aiden said. "I've had enough one-night stands and short-term flings in my life to know that a mature relationship is not about jumping into bed."

This was getting really interesting. Aiden Carlisle's philosophy about relationships—she had to hear this. "What's it about, then?"

"Ah, you know..."

"Tell me."

Aiden shrugged away her embarrassment. "It's about the little things," she said, echoing something that Dawn had once told her about her relationship with Maggie. "It's about volunteering to take out the trash on a freezing cold evening. It's about figuring out how to pay the mortgage when money is tight. It's about holding you close after we fight. It's about caring, respect, and yes, even passion—when the time and the place are right for both of us. There's no hurry. I'm not going anywhere."

Dawn blinked. "Wow," she said, overwhelmed by emotion. "I didn't know you were such a poet."

"I'm not." Short hair tickled Dawn's cheek when Aiden shook her head. "It's just that I let sex cloud my judgment before, and it always ended up hurting the relationship, so I think a little restraint might actually be a good thing."

More self-restraint? Dawn doubted that it was what Aiden really needed. With a sigh, she picked up her pillow that she had knocked to the floor, helped Aiden to lie down again, and then settled down too. She turned off the light, closed her eyes, and listened to Aiden's breathing, hoping that it would lull her into a nightmareless sleep.

"Dawn?"

She opened her eyes. "Hmm?"

"Do you want me to put you down on the 'notify in case of emergency' form?" Aiden asked.

There was no doubt in Dawn's mind. "Yes—if it's not going to get you into trouble with anyone in the precinct."

"Trouble?"

"Yeah. It's a pretty big announcement of our relationship, and I'd understand if you—"

Aiden laughed. "Dawn, I think by now even the precinct's cleaning lady knows that I'm involved with you. Cops are the worst gossips in the world, present company excluded, of course."

"Of course. In that case, yes, I'd like for you to put me down on the 'notify in case of emergency' form. I want to be as fully involved in your life as possible." In the gentle glow of the night-light Aiden had left on for her, their gazes met.

"I want that too."

Dawn watched Aiden's eyelids droop, and she pressed a kiss to her palm. "Let's get some sleep now. We can talk more about this tomorrow."

Aiden nodded and yawned.

"Goodnight, Aiden." Dawn leaned over and kissed her cheek. "And thanks for participating in this little sensitive chat."

"Anytime. Well, maybe not anytime, but I'll work on it." Aiden touched Dawn's hand one last time. "Night, Dawn."

Aiden was on administrative leave for the rest of the week, but someone had apparently forgotten to inform her body of that fact. She woke five minutes before her alarm clock would have normally announced the start of a new day. Careful not to rock the mattress or hurt her ribs, she turned to look at her companion.

Dawn was still asleep, lying in a position that reminded Aiden of a cat—rolled into a ball, with her head resting more on her arm than on the pillow. The honey-blonde lashes of the one eye that Aiden could see fluttered in her sleep but didn't open. Her nose twitched once, perfecting the feline image she presented.

God, how cute is that? Aiden smiled at the woman in her bed.

Despite the tossing and turning Dawn had done when she had first slipped under the covers, she hadn't moved from her position near the edge of the bed all night. Either she was not a restless sleeper, or she hadn't really relaxed, uncomfortable with Aiden's physical presence so near. Aiden hoped it was the former.

She settled down on her side to watch the sleeping woman. Being tempted to stay in bed because she wanted to be near her bed partner was a new and unfamiliar feeling. Normally, Aiden couldn't grab her clothes and run away from her one-night stands fast enough. Even in her few relationships, she had never been a cuddler. Now she wanted to draw Dawn into her arms, breathe in her scent, and kiss her neck until the gray-green eyes opened. But, of course, she didn't, knowing it would scare Dawn.

Aiden inched out of bed and tiptoed to the bathroom. Wrestling the sleep shirt over her head without the help of her protesting muscles took some maneuvering. Tight tops were taboo for the foreseeable future, she decided when she stepped under the shower. Being able to dress on her own was more important than trying to impress Dawn.

Dawn was still asleep when she returned to the bedroom. Watching her, Aiden tiptoed across the room and bent to pick up her socks from the floor next to the bed. Pain flared through her ribs. "Ow. Shit."

A crash from the bed made Aiden forget her pain. Dawn sat up, rubbing her head that she had bumped against the headboard. She stared at Aiden with wide, panicked eyes for a second before she recognized where she was.

"Sorry." Aiden dropped the socks and knelt on the bed. "I didn't want to wake you." *Or scare you.*

Dawn took a few deep breaths and forced a smile. "It's okay. I would have had to wake up anyway to eat the delicious breakfast you'll make me."

Aiden sat next to her and stuck her bare feet under the covers. "Does Casa Carlisle look like a bed-and-breakfast to you? What makes you think I'm gonna cook you breakfast?" She teasingly touched her cold feet to Dawn's warm ones.

"It's only breakfast—not much cooking involved." Dawn paused to tuck a few damp strands from Aiden's forehead. "I'm sure a gentlewoman like you would never think of letting her guest leave without breakfast after spending the night with her, would you?"

"I don't know..." Aiden carefully leaned back against the headboard, resting her head next to Dawn's. "Seeing as how I'm gravely injured, I thought I'd let you make breakfast for me."

Dawn snorted. "Gravely injured? Didn't you tell me it was just a scratch? But if you insist on having a grave injury, I can help you with that." Raising herself up on her knees, Dawn grabbed a pillow and drew back her arm.

"You wouldn't...!"

"Oh, you think so?" Dawn raised the pillow even higher.

Aiden tried to wriggle back, but the headboard stopped her retreat. "You wouldn't dare."

That had been the wrong thing to say. The pillow hit her on her uninjured shoulder.

"Hey!"

Dawn grinned and hit her again.

Aiden directed her most threatening glare at Dawn—without much success. The pillow thumped against her shoulder. "Don't force me to—"

"To do what, hmm, Detective?" One corner of the pillow poked Aiden in her chin. "You going to cuff me and read me my rights?" Dawn's eyes twinkled, the challenge in them clear.

Aiden sighed. Dawn wanted to play—and she couldn't. With Ray or one of her male colleagues, she would have grabbed the second pillow and hit him left and right until he begged for mercy. But in her interaction with women—and especially this woman—she was too conscious of her own strength, too afraid that she would slip and lose control. She was very aware of Dawn's body, pressed against her own in a gesture of playful intimidation. The oversized Dori-and-Nemo shirt had slipped off her shoulder on one side, and Aiden could feel the heat radiating off the exposed skin. A few freckles tempted her to kiss them. Gritting her teeth, she held back, afraid that roughhousing would ignite her passion and turn into something that would scare Dawn. "I think I'll go and try my hand at making breakfast." As fast as her protesting ribs allowed, she scrambled from the bed.

Dawn stared at Aiden's retreating back. *What's wrong now?* Something had upset Aiden, but she had not the slightest idea what. After their sensitive chat last night, Aiden had once again retreated behind her gold shield and the emotional barriers that came with it.

Now that she was alone in bed, the warm nest around her had lost its appeal. With a sigh, she swung her legs out of bed, slipped into her jeans, and padded to the bathroom.

When she entered the kitchen ten minutes later, Aiden stood in front of the stove, her back to Dawn, who paused in the doorway to take in her form.

One lean hip was resting against the counter, and the sleeves of Aiden's unbuttoned blouse had been pushed up, as was her habit, revealing strong forearms. Dawn found her incredibly sexy in her worn jeans and the old T-shirt she wore under the blouse. For the first time since the rape, she felt an almost physical pull of attraction and was surprised by its strength.

Without allowing herself time to censor her actions, Dawn crossed the room and hooked her finger into the back pocket of Aiden's jeans to tug her closer. When Aiden resisted, she wrapped both arms around her waist. Her hands brushed back the open blouse and slipped under the T-shirt to feel Aiden's skin. The taut muscles under her hands vibrated with tension.

"What's going on?" Dawn asked.

Aiden tried to step away again. "Just waiting for the water to boil. You want tea, right?"

"Later." Dawn reached around her to turn off the stove.

Aiden turned around in Dawn's arms that still held her captive. She said nothing.

"Do we have to have the same conversation over and over again? Trust is one of the cornerstones of a relationship, Aiden, and I can't do this if you don't trust me and—"

"I do trust you."

Dawn looked down at her hands resting on Aiden's hips, and then her gaze wandered to Aiden's arms. They were hanging down like immovable statues, making no attempt to hug back. *She doesn't trust herself.* All the times when Aiden had refused to start a snowball fight with her now made sense. "Tell me why you're holding back." Dawn caressed tiny circles on Aiden's bare forearms. The touch made both of them shiver.

For a few seconds, Aiden looked as if she wanted to deny it, change the topic, or make a joke out of it, but then she sighed and her shoulders slumped. "I have to."

"Why? Did I—?"

"No," Aiden said. "This is not about you. It's my problem and my problem alone. You don't have to concern yourself with it."

Dawn held her gaze. She refused to back off. "You were the one that quoted 'through the good times and the bad' to me, remember? There's no such thing as 'your' problem. What are you so afraid of?"

With gentle hands, Aiden broke the embrace and took a step to the side. Her amber eyes looked haunted. "There are times when I'm not sure if I'm the right one for you. I don't want you to get hurt."

Dawn had to grip the counter for balance. Did Aiden think about ending their relationship? "Aiden, if you invest all your emotions in a relationship and really, really care for another person, you're gonna get hurt sometimes. That's normal."

Aiden shook her head. "I'm not talking about hurting because we fight about your habit of squeezing the toothpaste from the wrong end or because I cancel a date to work overtime."

"What kind of hurt are you talking about, then?"

Aiden rubbed her neck, a sign that Dawn had learned meant that emotions were swirling just beneath the surface. Her voice was hollow when she finally said, "A rape victim and a woman conceived by rape... Do you really think that's a healthy relationship, Doctor?"

Dawn tightened her already white-knuckled grip around the edge of the counter. "It's going to be as healthy as we make it. Just because we're victims of—"

"I'm not a victim!"

"Yes, you are. You're a victim of rape too—even if you haven't been raped."

Eyeing the front door, Aiden began to pace. "I investigate sex crimes for a living and, yes, my mother was raped, but I'm not a victim of anything." Her voice was like grinding gravel.

"Oh, you're not?" She blocked Aiden's pacing route and forced her to look into her eyes. "Then why do you have all the typical symptoms, hmm? Guilt, self-blame, anger, shame, fear..." She ticked each word off on her fingers. "It's all there."

"Bullshit!" Aiden trembled, and her hands were clenched into fists.

Dawn continued nonetheless. She knew she had to get through to Aiden now, or she would repeat the same conversation, the same fight about Aiden's reluctance to let her get close over and over again. "You feel guilty because of what your mother had to go through. You blame yourself for something that you had no control over. You're angry and full of hate against the man who raped your mother. You're ashamed of the way you were conceived. You live in constant fear that you could turn out like your father and hurt other people." Each sentence made Aiden flinch, but she couldn't stop. "And now tell me, Detective, doesn't that sound like a textbook victim?"

Aiden squeezed her eyes shut. The trembling became a swaying.

Dawn rushed forward and wrapped her arms around her, squeezing until she felt Aiden wince. "I know you would never hurt me purposely. You couldn't," she whispered in her ear.

The body in her arms was stiff. "How could I not?" The words tumbled roughly from Aiden's lips. "I was conceived in violence. Violence is the sole reason why I even exist."

"No!" She gripped Aiden's face in both hands and directed her head around. "Look at me and listen. If there is a single reason for your existence, it's love."

"Love?" Aiden's snort sounded almost like a sob.

"Love," Dawn repeated, her voice firm. "If your mother hadn't loved you, she would have had an abortion. She was a strong and caring woman—and so are you. You're nothing like the man who fathered you."

"How can you know that? How can you be sure that there's not something..." Her rough voice trailed off, and she spread her hand over her chest as if to hold back the evil that might lurk there.

Dawn took the tense hand and lifted it away to press a kiss to the warm fabric over Aiden's chest. "I can be sure because I know you. Just look at you: you're standing there, trembling and agonizing over the thought that you might hurt me. Do you think the man who raped your mother gave a single thought to her feelings? You're nothing like him."

Finally, Aiden raised her arms and positioned them around Dawn. She lowered her head to press her cheek against Dawn's. "I think..." Her voice gave out, and she had to clear her throat. "I think this relationship might be the healthiest thing that could have happened to me. I swore to myself that I would be there for you and help you through the aftermath of everything that happened—and now you're the one who's helping me."

"We're helping each other—and that's exactly the kind of relationship I want."

"I want that too," Aiden whispered.

Dawn hugged her closer, careful not to hurt Aiden in the process. Every inch of their bodies touched. It was intoxicating—

and a little overwhelming. With one final kiss to the collarbone that peeked out from under the blouse and T-shirt combination, she released her. "Can we go back to bed now?"

She dragged Aiden back into the bedroom and slipped under the covers, suddenly exhausted. Maybe they could sleep for a while longer and start this day anew when they woke up.

"Dawn?"

Aiden's voice made her open her eyes again. "Yes?"

"You still haven't answered my question from last night, and I know with our laws it's just not possible and it would be much too soon anyway, but...if I were to propose one day, would you accept?"

Instead of an answer, Dawn inched across the bed. Supporting herself with her hands on either side of Aiden, she leaned down until she felt their breaths mingle. Aiden's body heat and her scent engulfed her. For a moment, she wanted to abandon all reason and throw herself at Aiden, but the fear of hurting Aiden or experiencing a flashback held her back. She carefully pressed her lips to Aiden's, but when Aiden wrapped her arms around her and returned the kiss, passion threatened to escalate. Dawn drew back with a gasp that was half arousal, half fear.

Aiden withdrew her arms from around Dawn but kept one hand resting on the small of her back. "Was that a yes or a consolation kiss?"

With a laugh and one last, small kiss Dawn rolled back to her side of the bed. "It's definitely a yes. And now settle down and let me sleep in, or you'll have your first marital fight on your hands."

"All right. Sleep tight, Mrs. Carlisle."

"Oh, no, no, no! I said yes to your hypothetical marriage proposal, not to carrying your name, Detective." Dawn nudged Aiden's uninjured shoulder.

"What's wrong with Carlisle?"

"Nothing. What's wrong with Kinsley?"

Aiden stared at the ceiling. "Aiden Kinsley? I don't think so. Dawn Carlisle, now that has a nice ring to it."

"Now that I think about it..." Dawn said. "Maybe it was a consolation kiss."

"Oh, you!" Aiden reached over and began to tickle her.

Dawn was glad that Aiden finally allowed herself to show a little playful aggression, but at the same time, she couldn't stand to be tickled. "Aiden!" she squeaked. "Stop if you don't want me to wet the bed!"

Aiden's hands retreated. She snorted. "God, you're really a romantic at heart, aren't you?"

"But of course. Anything for you, Mrs. Kinsley."

Aiden groaned. "Go to sleep, Dawn."

CHAPTER 31

THREE WEEKS LATER, AIDEN WAS finally back on active duty. Files of unsolved cases were piling up on her desk, and she sighed at the thought of working late and not getting to see Dawn tonight.

Ruben entered the squad room and held up a piece of paper. "I've got Marcinowski's phone records."

Aiden looked up from her desk. "And?"

"He had four outgoing calls from his house on the eighteenth."

Okada paused in his two-fingered report typing. "Were any of them to our victim?"

"Nope."

"What about his cell phone?" Aiden asked.

Ruben waved a second piece of paper. "Another dead end. We should pull the LUDs for his girlfriend's cell."

"Hey, Carlisle!" A uniformed officer called across the squad room. "Did you know that your girlfriend is down at the Central Precinct headquarters?" He pointed downward, indicating the first floor of the Justice Center.

A few other officers hooted and whistled, and Aiden had to shout to be heard over the commotion. "What? McFadden, if that's one of your silly jokes, I swear I'm gonna—"

"No, really. I saw her," Officer McFadden said. "She's that hot strawberry blonde, right?"

Aiden nodded, not bothering to reprimand him for calling

Dawn "hot." "What was she doing there? Was she accompanying a client?"

"Don't know. She looked pretty upset, though."

With gritted teeth, Aiden clipped on her shield and gun. "Ray..."

"It's all right. I'll take care of Marcinowski." Ray waved at her to go.

Two frantic minutes later, Aiden jogged through the door of the Central Precinct headquarters. Her gaze flew from face to face until she finally found Dawn, sitting in a plastic chair against one wall of the busy squad room, waiting for someone to take notice of her. Aiden breathed a sigh of relief when she saw that Dawn seemed uninjured. She crossed the room and touched Dawn's shoulder. "Dawn?"

Dawn flinched at the touch but then smiled when she recognized Aiden. "Hey, what are you doing here? Aren't you on duty?"

"I came when someone told me you were here. What's going on?"

Dawn nibbled on her bottom lip. "My car..."

"You were in an accident?" Aiden's gaze flew over her body again.

"No. When I wanted to go to work this morning, someone had smashed in the window on the passenger side, stolen my car radio, and destroyed everything that was destroyable—the seats, the seat belts, the indicator switch. He even turned on the light so that the battery would be dead by the time I found the car." Dawn sighed. "It was a mess."

Aiden sat in the uncomfortable seat next to Dawn. "I'm sorry. I know you love that little sardine can."

"It's my first car. I've had it for eleven years now. My dad bought it for me."

Now Aiden understood why the tiny car meant so much to

Dawn. She reached for Dawn's hand, not caring who saw it. "I'm sorry. Do you think it can be repaired?"

Dawn bit her lip. "I'm not sure. The spare parts are gonna be hard to find because they don't make the car anymore."

"Why didn't you call me?" Aiden asked.

"Last time I looked, sex crimes detectives didn't investigate larceny offenses."

Aiden squeezed her hand to get Dawn's attention. "This sex crimes detective does—if it's an offense against you. So next time, please call me."

Dawn nodded.

"You already talked to the police?"

"Yes. An officer came to look at the car. He snapped a few photographs but didn't give me much hope that they'll ever arrest someone." Dawn's voice was full of frustration.

"They didn't leave any evidence?" Aiden asked.

Dawn shivered. "The officer said it looked almost personal. Whoever did it didn't just steal the radio; he practically went berserk on my car. The officer suggested it might have been someone who has something against me."

Shit. Aiden fought hard against the anger she felt rising. Just when Dawn was in the process of reestablishing her inner balance, someone hurt that trust in her personal security again.

An officer appeared to take Dawn's statement against the unknown thief. As soon as he led Dawn to his desk, Aiden pulled her cell phone from her pocket and pressed one of her speed dials. "Ruben? It's Aiden. Listen, I need you to do me a favor." She stuck a finger into her other ear and listened. "Yes, the 'little doc' is okay. Her car is not, though. Are you still friends with that miracle-working mechanic you told me about? Good. Yes, exactly. It's 7 Carlisle Street. Yeah, yeah, yeah, laugh it up. Tell him the costs don't matter. I'll pay whatever it costs to get the car into top condition again. Thanks."

Once Dawn returned, she led her to the parking lot. "I'll drive you to wherever you want to go."

Dawn stopped in front of Aiden's car. "I'll take a cab. I know you have to work."

"It's okay. I've got enough overtime racked up to take the rest of the year off." Aiden opened the passenger side door for her. "Your chariot awaits, Madame." She waited for Dawn to settle in and closed the door. "Where to? Home?" she asked when she started the car.

Dawn fiddled with the seat belt and nodded reluctantly. "I need to get back to the car and find someone who is willing to work on it."

"Don't worry about it," Aiden said. "I'll take care of it for you. Ruben knows someone who will do a good job."

"I really shouldn't dump all this on you, but to tell you the truth, I'm not eager to get back home," Dawn said. "I think it's gonna take me a few days to feel comfortable there again. Knowing that someone broke into my car, right in front of my home... It just doesn't feel safe anymore."

"Move in with me." Aiden's eyes widened when her brain realized what her mouth had just offered. Hastily, she added, "Just for a few days until you feel safe again."

Dawn turned to look at her. "I don't know. What about Kia? I don't know any of my neighbors well enough to trust them with my cat and a key to my apartment."

"Just put her in that pet carrier she loves so much and bring her with you," Aiden said. "She can enjoy a holiday at Casa Carlisle too."

"Are you sure that you want a cat in your apartment?" Dawn asked.

Aiden wasn't, but she nodded anyway.

"Okay, Detective, you've got yourself two roommates." Dawn shook the hand that wasn't resting on the steering wheel. "I promise that at least one of them won't drink your orange juice straight from the container. You should think about getting a bulletproof vest for your couch, though."

Aiden groaned.

"Honey, I'm home."

Dawn almost dropped her book at Aiden's sudden entry. "You're late. Did something happen?" She had started to worry when Aiden hadn't been home on time. *God, listen to yourself. It's been one day, and you're already calling her apartment "home."*

"No, I just stopped to pick up a few things after work." Aiden lifted the large shopping bag in her hand.

"Takeout?" Dawn asked. "I thought I could cook something for us."

"It's not takeout."

"What is it, then?"

When Aiden leaned down to brush her lips against Dawn's, she seized the moment to peek into the bag.

Aiden chuckled and quickly stepped back, moving the shopping bag out of her line of sight. "You're not curious at all, are you?"

"Me?" Dawn pointed a finger at herself. "No, I just have an investigative mindset."

Aiden chuckled but still held the bag out of Dawn's reach. "Sorry, it's not for you. You're not the only female in my life, you know."

By now, Dawn felt secure enough in their relationship to laugh about that comment. "Oh, is that a confession, Detective?"

Kia strode in and circled Aiden's legs, leaving a tuft of hairs behind on her black pants.

"God, is she molting or something?" Aiden tried to brush

the hairs from her clothes without much success. "Should I have bought something for that too?"

"Bought? You bought presents for my cat?"

Aiden finally allowed her to open the bag.

Dawn settled down cross-legged on the floor and lifted one thing after another from the bag.

"Just a little something," Aiden said when Dawn had emptied the bag and stared up at her.

"A kitty blanket, a rubber mouse, a yarn ball, a scratch board, and a dozen different cat snacks. Is that a 'little something' in your book?"

Aiden shrugged. "I want her to feel at home in my apartment."

You want me to feel at home. And I do. "You're a mushball, Detective."

Kia stalked closer to her pile of presents.

Aiden watched to see which toy the cat would prefer.

The feline extended one paw and nudged the bill from the pet supply store, which Aiden had crumbled into a ball so Dawn wouldn't see it. A few moments later, she was chasing the paper ball through the apartment, ignoring all the fancy cat toys Aiden had bought.

Dawn laughed at the expression on Aiden's face.

"Cats." Aiden shook her head.

"Yeah. They never do what you expect or want them to," Dawn said. "I like that."

Aiden watched as paper ball and cat disappeared under the couch. "Typical psychologists' pets, huh?"

"Actually, there's this theory that says they're typical lesbians' pets," Dawn said with a smile.

Aiden arched one dark eyebrow. "Is that a quantitative theory? The more cats you have, the higher the probability that you might be gay? I wonder what that says about Judge Linehan and her seven cats."

"She has seven cats?" Dawn couldn't imagine being bossed around by seven feline roommates.

"There's this rumor that says she won them in a poker game," Aiden said.

Dawn chuckled. "Portland's honorable judges are betting cats in poker games? Maybe the previous owner is a reformed lesbian?"

"No, Judge Yates is still firmly interested in women." Aiden packed away the cat toys. "He's practically drooling every time Kade walks into his courtroom."

Dawn nudged her with an elbow. "And he's not the only one."

"Me? No, I don't drool over Kade." Aiden shook her head but then said, "Well, I might look a little—just to confirm that she's seriously lacking in comparison to you, of course."

"Has anyone ever told you that lying is a sin? I seriously doubt that Kade is lacking in any department."

"I'm not lying. I told you, as far as I'm concerned, you don't need to fear any comparison. You're the one I want to be with." Aiden's eyes held no hint of the previous teasing anymore.

The beeping of Aiden's cell phone interrupted before Dawn could answer. Aiden looked at the display. "Shit. I have to go. I'm sorry."

Dawn had known from the start that being in a relationship with a cop would mean a lot of interrupted moments and canceled dates. Sighing, she wrapped her arms around Aiden and reattached the gold shield to her belt. "Be careful and wake me when you get in."

Aiden hesitated. "It could get really late."

"I don't care. Wake me."

"Okay." Aiden wrapped her arms around her and leaned down slowly, giving Dawn every opportunity to withdraw.

Not that Dawn wanted to. She slid her arms more firmly around Aiden and pulled her into a deep kiss. She could feel the pulse in Aiden's neck begin to race along with her own.

Only when her cell phone began to ring did Aiden break away. She left small kisses on Dawn's upper and lower lip as she pulled away.

As the door closed behind her, Dawn threw her body down onto the couch. "God, I could learn to hate modern technology."

When Dawn heard the key turn in the door, she laid down the sketch pad and wiped her stained fingers on a rag.

"Hi," Aiden called from the hallway.

Dawn had noticed that she took care not to walk up behind her unexpectedly, and she appreciated it. "Hi," she called back. "I didn't expect you home so early."

"Well, after the late night yesterday, the lieutenant sent most of us home early." Aiden went into the bedroom, and when she returned, her gun and badge were gone. She always locked them away in a safe place, leaving behind her job before she greeted Dawn. When she saw what Dawn was doing, she stopped in the middle of the living room and smiled. "You're drawing."

"Nothing big, just a few drawings of Kia. I haven't done it in a while, and I need to get the hang of it back." Dawn critically eyed her work.

Aiden stepped next to her. Instead of gazing at the drawing, she stared at Dawn, though.

"What?" Dawn rubbed her hands over her cheeks. "Do I have pastel dust on my face?"

Aiden laughed. "Well, not before, but you do now." She gently rubbed her thumb over Dawn's cheek. "There. It's gone."

"Thanks." Dawn resisted the urge to touch her face again. "Why were you looking at me if there wasn't anything on my face?"

"Maybe I just like looking at you?" Aiden said with a smile.

Dawn gave her a doubtful gaze.

"No, really, I do," Aiden said, now completely serious. "As a kid, I often wished I had my mother's artistic talent, but never because of any honest desire to draw. It was always about meeting my mother's expectations and proving that I was like her—and not like my father. But now I'd really love to be able to capture what I see when I look at you."

A blush heated Dawn's cheeks. She longed to reach out and touch Aiden but didn't want to get the powdered pigment of the pastels all over her clothes, so she leaned up on her tiptoes and brushed her lips against Aiden's cheek.

Aiden touched her own cheek.

Dawn grinned and leaned up again, this time to kiss Aiden's lips. She loved Aiden's patient, unhurried kisses.

When the kiss ended, Aiden loosely slung her arms around Dawn and held her while she gazed over her shoulder at the sketch pad on the table. "Wow! You're good."

"I'm good at drawing cats—and I should be because I've done about a thousand sketches of Kia. She's the only model who's willing to lie still long enough for me to draw her."

"What about me?" Aiden asked. "When I gave you the set of art supplies for Christmas, you said you'd have to draw me sometime. So if you still want to..."

Dawn studied her. "Is that something that you'd like to do? I mean, with your mother being an artist, I wasn't sure how you'd feel about it."

"I didn't have a lot of patience sitting for my mother when I was a teenager, but I'm no longer a teenager—and you are not my mother." She grinned at Dawn. "So, where do you want me? Do you want me to just sit on the couch or...?"

Dawn fidgeted with her sketch pad as she trailed her gaze over Aiden's face and down her shirt-covered upper body. Part of her screamed that this might not be a good idea, but she answered before she could stop herself, "I'd like to draw you. All of you."

Aiden stared at her. "You mean...?" She tugged at her button-down shirt. "Naked?"

Dawn cleared her throat. "Yes. If you're comfortable with it."

"Sure," Aiden said without hesitation. "I'm not the shy type. But are you comfortable with it?"

Dawn hadn't allowed herself to think about it when she had told Aiden she wanted to draw her naked. Now she realized that it would give her an opportunity to share some kind of physical intimacy that seemed limited and controllable. "I'm fine with it."

"All right. Then let's do this." Aiden began to undo the buttons of her shirt.

Dawn busied herself with preparing a blank page on the sketch pad and getting her pastels ready. Then there was nothing else to do, and she silently watched Aiden undress.

Aiden smiled and held her gaze as she slipped the shirt off her shoulders. "Have you done this before?" She reached back to unhook her bra, clearly a little too nervous now to just let Dawn watch her undress in silence.

"Uh, what?" Dawn asked as the bra fell away and revealed Aiden's breasts.

Aiden kicked off her shoes and unzipped her pants. "Drawn a nude model?"

Dawn tore her gaze away from Aiden's body and looked up into her face. "Once."

"Cal?"

"No. I never felt the urge to draw him." She had never found her ex-husband's body as inspiring as she found Aiden's. "Maybe that should have told me something, huh?"

Aiden slowly slid her pants over her hips, revealing long, smoothly muscled legs. "Then it was Maggie?"

Again, Dawn shook her head. "She drew me once, but I never drew her. I didn't do a lot of drawing or painting when we were together."

"No?" Aiden finally stood before her fully naked, fidgeting just a little, and Dawn had trouble focusing on the conversation. "Why not? She's an artist too, right? I would have thought you'd have been doing a lot of artsy stuff together."

Dawn had to swallow before she could answer. She was very aware of Aiden's gaze resting on her, observing her reactions. "We did. We went to a lot of art exhibitions, but I focused on other people's art, on Maggie's, not my own. I felt like an amateur next to her. When I draw, I do it for myself, not to share it with the world or to produce a great piece of art. I was more comfortable letting her be the famous artist." She realized how much of herself she had held back in that relationship, and she vowed not to repeat that mistake with Aiden.

Aiden gave her an understanding nod. "So, who was your nude model, then?"

"I took an art class a few years ago. Our teacher had a nude model come in and pose for us." That model hadn't made her hands shake as Aiden did now, though.

"Then let's see if I can do as well as that professional model. Where do you want me?"

Dawn licked her lips and looked around the room. "Could you lie down on the couch?" She watched Aiden move around the room, admiring her naked body. Then a sudden thought came to her. "You're not cold, are you?"

"Cold?" Aiden chuckled. "Quite the opposite. It's getting a little hot in here."

Dawn silently agreed as she watched Aiden recline on the couch and stretch her long body. "Could you move one arm behind your head and bend your left leg a little?"

"Like this?"

"No, a little more..." Dawn gestured. "No, no, that's a little too far." She stepped closer to the couch and reached out a hand to position Aiden's arm exactly the way she wanted it. Aiden's skin was warm and soft, and Dawn found herself lingering a few seconds longer than strictly necessary.

Aiden lay still but sucked in a breath. The muscles under Dawn's hand started to vibrate.

"Like this," Dawn finally said and stepped back. She sat down in the easy chair across from Aiden and picked up her sketch pad. For a few seconds, she just looked at Aiden's body, overwhelmed and sure that she could never do it justice.

Aiden didn't say anything. She lay still, a hint of a smile on her face.

Come on. You can do this. Just focus on one little detail after another. Dawn lifted her pastel stick to the sketch pad, her gaze still on Aiden. She traced the shape of a strong shoulder on the paper, then sketched the well-defined muscles of her arm. She worked silently, focusing on one body part after another and trying to portray it in loving detail.

During the last few months, she had mainly seen Aiden as a person she admired—a competent detective, a strong woman, a loyal friend, a supportive girlfriend. She had been aware of the attraction she felt toward Aiden since she had first seen her, but it had faded into the background after her rape. Now she allowed herself to really see the desirable woman and to let herself react to what she saw, channeling her thoughts and feelings into the drawing that slowly emerged under her hands.

She smudged the curve of a small, firm breast with her thumb to give it a softer look. Finally, when everything else was done, she sketched in the details of Aiden's face. She looked back and forth between Aiden and the sketch pad, smiling when their gazes met and Aiden's lips curled into a smile before she resumed her "professional model" expression.

Dawn bent over the sketch pad. She traced a stubborn jaw with the pastel stick, moved her hand in small, quick half-circles to sketch in the black, ruffled locks, and softly rubbed her fingers over the paper to hint at the shadows under proud cheekbones. Finally, she tried to achieve the exact hue of the amber eyes that calmly looked back at her.

When Dawn finally exhaled and straightened, she realized that some time must have passed. The muscles in her back protested from being bent over the sketch pad for so long, and the natural light in the living room was almost gone.

"Done?" Aiden asked, still holding her pose.

Dawn nodded.

Aiden stretched languidly and shook her arm that had been behind her head the whole time. "Can I see?"

"Sure."

Aiden slipped her pants and shirt back on, not bothering with the buttons or her bra. She moved across the room and looked over Dawn's shoulder, so close to her that Dawn could feel the warmth of her bare skin. "Wow."

"Yes," Dawn said, her voice a little hoarse. "Wow." She looked down at the drawing, then at its model. "You're beautiful."

"No, I mean, wow, you're really talented," Aiden said.

Dawn looked down at the sketch pad and ran a finger over the drawing. "It turned out better than I thought it would." She smiled at Aiden. "Having a beautiful model does make it easier."

Aiden shook her head. "It's not me who created this drawing. You're very talented." Finally, she looked up from the drawing and grinned at Dawn. "Models usually get paid for this, right?"

"Sure, but I don't think you're gonna be as happy as my usual model with a can of tuna. What do you want as a reward?"

"What are you offering?"

It would have been natural for Aiden to playfully demand a kiss as a payment, but Aiden always let her take the lead and initiate any contact. She always took care not to tease Dawn in any way about their physical intimacy.

"Whatever you want," Dawn answered, firmly placing her trust in Aiden.

"I'd love to have a picture of you." Aiden pointed at the sketch pad.

Dawn hadn't expected that. "I..."

"It doesn't have to be a nude one," Aiden added quickly.

"It's not that. It's just... I can't draw myself. I've tried it before, but for some reason I never get it right." She looked at Aiden with an apologetic shrug. "Sorry."

Aiden answered the shrug with one of her own and grinned. "Then I guess I'll take that can of tuna after all."

"How about a kiss instead?" Dawn felt comfortable with offering it.

"I'll never say no to that," Aiden answered, ducking her head a little to look into Dawn's eyes.

Dawn stepped closer and wrapped her arms around Aiden. She slid her hands over Aiden's sides and up her back, directing her closer.

Aiden went willingly, lowering her lips to meet Dawn's.

Heat shot through Dawn as their lips and bodies touched. Aiden's unbuttoned shirt parted, and Dawn pressed against the naked upper body she had drawn a few minutes ago. Aiden's body heat skyrocketed her own. The firm muscles of Aiden's stomach and the softness of her breasts pressed against her body, separated only by the thin layer of Dawn's shirt.

Dawn started to pant. She tore her lips away from Aiden's and pressed her face against Aiden's shoulder instead. The kiss and her feelings were quickly getting out of control, and it scared her a little, but at the same time, she didn't want to end this contact. She turned her head, resting her cheek against the bare skin of Aiden's upper chest, and deeply inhaled her scent.

Aiden hummed and combed her fingers through Dawn's hair. "You're very talented at this too."

Dawn felt Aiden's heart pound under her ear. At the same time, Aiden's willingness to rein herself in and her reassuring compliment were calming her own wild heartbeat. She brushed her lips against Aiden's collarbone and then quickly stepped back. "Come on," she said, grasping Aiden's hand. "Let's get you something to eat."

Aiden followed her to the kitchen. "Not a can of tuna, I hope?"

Dawn laughed. "You'll just have to wait and see."

CHAPTER 32

AIDEN LAY AWAKE AND STARED into the darkness, listening to Dawn's soft breathing next to her. Dawn had fallen asleep over an hour ago, but for some reason, Aiden was wide-awake. It wasn't Dawn's presence in her bed. While she had never liked sharing her home or her bed, she found that she actually liked having Dawn around.

Dawn's body didn't touch hers while they slept, but her breathing in the otherwise quiet, dark room was soothing after a hard day at work.

A long moan interrupted the peaceful silence. The covers rustled as Dawn began to toss and turn in her sleep.

Shit! Another nightmare! Aiden sat up and tried to make out Dawn's face in the darkness. "Dawn?"

No answer, just another moan.

Aiden reached out to turn on the light. Initially, she had hesitated to wake Dawn from her nightmares, not wanting to scare her, but Dawn had assured her that nothing could be more frightening than her nightmares.

When she turned on the light, Dawn didn't wake. She moaned again.

Aiden froze.

Dawn wasn't tossing and turning like someone in the throes of a nightmare. She moved and sounded like a woman writhing under her lover's passionate touches.

Aiden grinned, glad to see that Dawn still had some

sexual impulses. During their more passionate kisses, she often wondered whether Dawn was in any position to feel real desire or just going along with what she thought was expected of her. *Guess this answers that question.*

Dawn's hand slid over the sheet as if reaching for something—or someone.

Is she dreaming about me?

Dawn threw back her head, baring her neck to the kisses of her dream lover.

Aiden drank in the sight of her. She felt a little guilty for watching Dawn like a voyeur, but she couldn't look away.

Another sound came from Dawn, and this time it wasn't a sensual moan or a breathless gasp of passion. This time, it was a whimper of distress. Her sensual writhing turned into a desperate struggle against an unseen attacker.

"Dawn! Sweetheart, wake up!"

Gasping, Dawn woke, shot upright, and clutched the sheet to her chest. Her gaze darted around the room.

"You were dreaming," Aiden said, careful not to touch her in any way.

Dawn buried her face in her hands. "Oh, God."

"It was a bad one, wasn't it?" She longed to reach out and comfort Dawn but knew it would only make things worse.

"Yes. No. It wasn't worse than usual, but this time, it started out as..." Dawn trailed off and rubbed her face without looking at Aiden.

"I know," Aiden said.

Slowly, Dawn took her hands away from her face and glanced at her. "You...you know? You know...what?"

"I know you were having a sexy dream." Aiden grinned to ease Dawn's tension.

A blush crept up Dawn's face. "What did I do?"

"Nothing. You just sounded like you were enjoying yourself."

Aiden reached out and softly touched Dawn's shoulder. "That's nothing to be embarrassed about. It means that you're starting to think about having sex and sharing intimacy again—and that's a good thing, right?"

"Yeah," Dawn said, not sounding very convinced, "but then you turned into... I mean... Suddenly it was Garret Ballard's body on top of me and his hands that were touching me and..." She shuddered.

Aiden squeezed her eyes shut. She had turned into Garret Ballard in Dawn's dream. Her loving touches had turned into something hurtful. Did Dawn's subconscious think Aiden capable of hurting her?

Dawn reached over and touched her forearm. "My dream had nothing to do with you. Well, the first one featured you in a prominent role," she added with an embarrassed half smile, "but the second one was about my own fears and issues and about nothing else."

Aiden took in the trembling hand on her arm. "Wanna tell me about those fears and issues? Maybe it would help to talk about it."

"It's just so hard to realize that everything has changed," Dawn said, her voice so low that Aiden had to strain to understand. "Making love has always been something special, almost sacred to me. It was beautiful and unmarred, but that night changed all of that. Suddenly, violence and sexual stimulation are no longer separate. Sex feels like something uncontrollable that could easily hurt me."

Aiden swallowed. "I hope you know that I would never hurt you, especially not in that way."

"This is not about what you're doing—it's about what I'm feeling."

For a moment, Dawn's pain paralyzed her. Then Aiden

asked, "What can I do to help make physical intimacy feel like something beautiful and positive again?"

"You're already doing everything within your power." Dawn reached out and entangled her fingers with Aiden's. "It just takes some time."

Aiden stroked her thumb over the back of Dawn's hand. "I know." She studied Dawn's worried expression. "And we have all the time in the world. You never have to worry about me getting impatient or hooking up with someone else because I was sick of waiting for you."

"I didn't..."

"Yes, you did."

Dawn sighed. "I just feel like this isn't fair to you."

"Fair? You being raped, that's what wasn't fair. You didn't choose that, but I chose being with you out of my own free will. Please don't feel like I'm getting the short end of the stick."

Dawn sighed again, but this time, it sounded almost blissful. "You're so good for me. You should be a recognized therapy."

"No, thanks. I come with too many side effects." She tucked a strand of blonde hair behind one of Dawn's ears. "Want to try to go to sleep again?"

Dawn nodded. With her hand still resting in Aiden's, she closed her eyes.

"Dawn?" Aiden called through the closed bathroom door.

The shower was shut off, and Dawn answered, "Yes?"

"Can I come in for a second? Your cat coughed up a hairball, and I need the cleaning rag that I keep in the bathroom." Aiden expected a teasing answer about her emphasis of "your cat" whenever the litter box or a soiled carpet needed to be cleaned. Instead, momentary silence answered her.

"Uh. Um, could you wait a minute?" Dawn finally called. "I'll come out as soon as I'm dressed."

Aiden stayed in front of the door and tried not to feel hurt. *Do you really want to make her uncomfortable just because the cat upchucked all over your carpet? You're not that desperate to see her naked, are you?*

The truth was that the sexual tension between them was increasing. Every time she was near Dawn, she longed to touch her and be close to her. Even though every glance from Dawn made her breath catch and her heart thump, she tried to fight the physical attraction and hold back. She was determined to let Dawn set the pace, but it was getting harder and harder to stop.

The bathroom door opened, and Dawn stepped out, fully clothed. The top buttons of her blouse were unfastened, and her shirt clung to her hastily dried skin.

Aiden snatched the cleaning rag from her hand and turned on her heel, hoping that cleaning up cat puke would have a calming effect on her libido.

It seemed to work. After cleaning Kia's mess, she settled on the couch with the cat on her lap and read through the reports she had brought home from work. Aiden thumbed through the first report one-handed while scratching Kia under the chin with her left hand.

After a few minutes, Dawn joined her on the couch. She curled up next to her, so close that their bodies were touching from knee to shoulder.

Kia jumped down from the couch and stalked to the kitchen.

Aiden quickly turned the page in her report, not wanting Dawn to see the photos of their latest crime scene. She would have to reread that page later anyway, because right now she was too distracted by the warm body resting against her side.

Dawn turned on the TV, leaned against Aiden, and threw one arm around her waist. While she flicked through the channels, she slid one hand into the sleeve of Aiden's T-shirt and caressed her arm and shoulder.

The curious fingertips were driving Aiden crazy, but she couldn't find the strength to stop them. The report in her hands slipped lower and lower. She sucked in a breath when Dawn's finger brushed the sensitive inside of her arm. "I can't read like this."

"Is it important that you read it now?" Dawn asked, peering at the report without reading.

"Not really. I'm reviewing it for court on Monday." She set down the report and slipped her arms around Dawn.

Dawn snuggled closer. "This is nice."

"Yeah." Aiden bent her head to catch a look at Dawn's face. Was Dawn as affected by their physical closeness as she was, or was she just going through the motions of kissing and cuddling without feeling any real desire?

There were times when Dawn couldn't stand to be touched or have any physical contact. On other days, Dawn searched her out and cuddled so close as if she was desperate to absorb her body heat. Sometimes she even initiated passionate kisses that didn't help Aiden's attempts to hold back.

She tried to divert herself from Dawn's lingering touch by watching the news on TV and had almost succeeded when the fingers that had been stroking her shoulder dipped lower and brushed against the side of her breast. A wave of heat shot down her body, followed by goose bumps. "Uh, Dawn!" She stilled Dawn's hand with her own.

Dawn pulled her hand out from under the T-shirt and rested it on Aiden's shoulder. Leaning over her, she touched her nose to Aiden's in an Eskimo kiss.

Aiden's eyes wanted to close as she felt Dawn's breath on her lips, but she forced them to remain open. She held still as Dawn slowly lowered herself. Their lips brushed and then separated for a second before meeting again in a firmer contact. Aiden moaned at the warmth of Dawn's lips and the softness of the breasts that were pressing against her. She caressed Dawn's back as she deepened the kiss, careful not to move her hands any lower than the small of her back.

Dawn pressed closer and moaned against Aiden's lips.

Aiden fought desperately not to roll over and press her hips against Dawn's. Finally, her body felt as if it had reached its boiling point. She drew back with a gasp. "Dawn, please, we've got to stop."

"Mmm..." Dawn followed her to nibble on her lips. "Why?" Her voice sounded dazed.

"Because you're not ready, and I'm only human."

Dawn squeezed her eyes shut and buried her face against Aiden's shoulder, still breathing hard. "Sorry," she mumbled against Aiden's shirt. "I'm sorry. I want to make love to you. I really, really want to, but..."

"No. You've got nothing to be sorry for. There's nothing wrong with just making out, without going any further right now." Aiden tightened her arms around Dawn once more, enjoying the feel of the small body against her own for a few extra seconds before releasing her. "Hey, wanna go on an ice cream run with me?"

"Ice cream? Now?"

"Yeah." Aiden gave a rueful smile. "It's either that or a cold shower."

Dawn forced her body up from the couch and Aiden. "Ice cream it is."

Dawn raced up the stairs, taking two at a time, and slid to a stop in front of Aiden's apartment door. Trembling with excitement, she fumbled with the key that Aiden had given her for the time she stayed in the apartment.

Finally, the door opened, and Dawn tumbled into the apartment. “Aiden?”

Instead of an answer, rhythmic thumps and muffled groans came from the bedroom.

Dawn reined in her excitement and went to investigate.

Aiden was in the bedroom, agilely dancing around the punching bag that hung from the ceiling. Chains rattled and leather groaned as she hit it again and again.

Sweatpants, cut off at the knees, and a tank top clung to her sweat-drenched frame. A light sheen of perspiration glistened on well-muscled calves and arms. Her short hair had the tousled look that always made Dawn want to run her fingers through it, and her amber eyes glowed against the flushed face that was wild and focused at the same time.

Dawn had never seen anything so primal—and so sexy. Without allowing herself time to think, she crossed the room and wrapped her arms around the swaying bag to stop its movement.

Aiden stumbled as her punch missed its target. She grabbed the bag for balance and looked up sharply when her bare skin touched Dawn, as if she hadn’t been aware of her presence before.

“Hi.” Despite Aiden’s physical exertion, Dawn was the one who was too breathless to say more.

“Dawn...” Aiden moved back, the punching bag now between them. “What are you doing here?”

“I live here at the moment, remember?”

“Yeah, but...”

Dawn stepped around the bag and touched one of the gloved hands. Her body demanded closeness even though Aiden was moving back. “I wanted to get home early to thank the good fairy who waved her magic wand over my car and made it whole again.”

Aiden took another step back and tried to open the boxing gloves with her teeth. “This is not a good time.”

Now, up close, Dawn could see the wariness in Aiden’s

eyes. She had vented her rage about something that must have happened at work on the punching bag—and that rage was still there, glowing in the depths of her eyes. "I'm not afraid."

Aiden's head jerked up, and their gazes met. "Maybe you should be," she whispered.

Dawn held out her arms. "Come here."

"No." Aiden moved back.

"Come here."

A few droplets fell from her face as Aiden shook her head. "I don't want to get you all sweaty."

"Maybe I've just been waiting for an opportunity to get all sweaty with you?" Dawn winked at her.

Aiden looked stunned for a second, and then her laughter broke the tension.

Dawn drew the finally unresisting woman into her arms.

The boxing gloves gently came to rest on her back.

For a few seconds, Dawn was tempted to forget about talking and to kiss Aiden senseless instead, but she knew that Aiden needed to talk. "What happened?"

This time, Aiden didn't even try to lie or avoid the topic. "We had to let a child molester walk because the whole family refuses to talk."

"No other witnesses? No evidence?"

Aiden sighed. "Nothing that would hold up in court."

"I'm sorry." Dawn wrapped her arms more tightly around her, not caring what the contact did to her elegant pantsuit. Aiden's body fit perfectly against her own. She stepped back only when she felt Aiden begin to shudder as her bare legs and arms cooled. "Go shower."

"I could use a little help," Aiden said, her voice hoarse.

Dawn swallowed. "You want me to help you...in the shower?"

"Get your mind out of the gutter." Aiden laughed. "The only things that you get to take off my body are these boxing gloves."

"For now," Dawn said with a daring grin.

"My, my, you certainly are in a mood, hmm?"

Dawn smiled while she helped Aiden take off the gloves. "Having my sardine can delivered to me as good as new, complete with car keys and a big red bow wrapped around it, does that to me." Even though Aiden had promised to have one of Ruben's friends take care of it, Dawn had secretly feared that the old car was beyond repair. Now, after less than a week, the car looked better than it had in years.

"So, cars are an aphrodisiac for you? And here I thought it was all the bare skin that I'm displaying," Aiden said, turning to resume her way to the bathroom.

Dawn wrapped her arms around her from behind and kissed a droplet of sweat from her neck. "There's that too. Don't think that it'll make me forget that you paid for having the car repaired, though. I told you I don't want to be a kept woman."

"It was an exception." Aiden turned in the embrace and gently kissed her. Even her lips tasted salty. Her movements were slow, and her arms hung down as if they were still weighted down by the heavy gloves.

Dawn frowned. *She must've tried to punch the bag into submission for quite a while.* "Take a shower and then come to the bedroom."

"I think I'll just crash on the couch tonight."

When she tried to walk away, Dawn grabbed her sweaty arm. "No. You're trying to protect me from something that I need no protection from. Take a shower and then come to the bedroom."

Aiden stared into her eyes as if searching for confirmation that Dawn didn't need her to be in control of herself, that she would be able to hold her own against Aiden's demons. Finally, she nodded and closed the bathroom door behind her.

The apartment lay in silence when Aiden left the bathroom. She felt refreshed, not only from the shower, but also because she finally believed that she could let go of her iron self-control. If she stumbled, Dawn would take over.

She padded through the empty living room in search of her temporary roommate. She opened the bedroom door quietly, just in case Dawn had fallen asleep.

Dawn wasn't sleeping—and suddenly, Aiden was wide-awake too. Dawn sat on the bed, surrounded by flickering candles. She had changed out of her pantsuit and was wearing only the knee-length *Nemo* sleep shirt that Aiden secretly loved because it frequently slipped off one shoulder. The room smelled of vanilla and sandalwood. A bottle of Aiden's favorite red wine was resting on the bedside table.

Dawn turned back the covers and patted the bed. "Lie down."

"Uh, what's the meaning of all this?" Aiden asked when she had taken in every lovingly prepared detail. The whole scene resembled attempts at seduction from her younger days.

"Does it have to mean anything?"

Aiden raised her brows.

"It means that I care about you and that I want you to relax for one evening," Dawn said, again patting the mattress.

Half relieved and half disappointed that this was not a seduction, Aiden crawled onto the bed and lay down on her belly. She turned her head to see what Dawn would do.

"Close your eyes and relax," Dawn said.

Aiden closed her eyes.

The mattress dipped as Dawn moved closer, her warmth now resting lightly against Aiden's side.

She fought the impulse to open her eyes and held her breath when she felt Dawn lean over her. Dawn's hair brushed the back of her neck, and it took all of Aiden's self-control not to roll over and capture her lips in a passionate kiss.

Then Dawn's warm hands came to rest on her shoulders and squeezed experimentally.

A groan wrenched from Aiden's lips.

"Sounds like you could use a massage." Dawn's hands slipped under the T-shirt and began to knead Aiden's shoulders.

Aiden groaned again as her muscles, tense from the day's frustrations and her workout with the punching bag, finally relaxed. "You don't have to pamper me like this. You just came home from work yourself."

Dawn's small but strong hands began to work on a large knot between her shoulder blades. "I want to." The fingers moved down on both sides of her spine.

Aiden turned her head to peer up at Dawn. "I can take the shirt off if it's in the way." When Dawn nodded, she slipped it over her head and lay back down. The scent of sandalwood filled the air again, and Aiden reopened her eyes to see Dawn pour massage oil into her hands, warming it up. "Mmm, I get to enjoy the full R & R program."

Dawn didn't answer, too focused on her task. She kneaded Aiden's upper back again and worked on her shoulders. Gentle fingertips slid up her neck and played with the short hair there for a while.

A shiver raced down Aiden's body as Dawn dragged her nails down her spine. At the small of her back, Dawn's fingertips stopped and traced the birthmark that Aiden knew was located there. Dawn took her time, circling every birthmark, every freckle, and every scar. Her fingers splayed over Aiden's back as if measuring its length and breadth.

It occurred to Aiden that Dawn needed this massage just as much as she did. For Dawn, it was a nonthreatening way to be physically close, to experiment with closeness and touching, and to get to know her body without feeling the pressure to go any further. She tried to lie still and take calming breaths even though Dawn's touches weren't soothing so much as exciting her body.

Dawn's fingers followed the contours of her shoulder blades and brushed, maybe by accident, against the outer curve of one breast, making Aiden gasp. Dawn seemed to be completely unaware of the effect her touch was having. Finally, Aiden couldn't take the sweet torture anymore. She raised herself up on her knees and slipped her T-shirt back on. "Your turn." She nodded down at the mattress.

Dawn knelt on the bed without moving.

"Come on. I haven't broken anyone's spine yet." Aiden busied herself with the massage oil, making a point of looking away from Dawn as she slipped the sleep shirt over her head and lay down.

Aiden decided not to straddle Dawn for the massage. It would have given her the best angle, but she wasn't sure if Dawn would be able to relax with her weight pressing her down. She knelt next to Dawn and lowered her hands onto small, but lightly muscled shoulders. Her fingers were trembling. Carefully, she began to smooth the oil over the pale skin, staying well away from the sensitive sides. She kneaded and caressed until she felt the tension ebb from the body under her hands. Dawn kept her eyes open the whole time, but she didn't tell her to close them, knowing that unexpected touches in the dark often scared her. When she reached the small of her back, she moved farther down the bed and lifted one small foot into her lap.

Dawn moaned as Aiden rubbed each toe.

Aiden ignored the sensual sound and let her fingers swirl up her instep and past the ankle. She kneaded the strong muscles of her calf with a little more pressure. The massage continued up the leg until she reached the knee. Hyperaware of Dawn's reactions, she felt the slight tensing when her fingers strayed higher, so she let go of the leg, picked up the other foot, and started the same treatment.

When she finally stopped, Dawn half turned to look up at her with now smoky-gray eyes.

Aiden caressed her face with a single finger. She leaned in, careful not to touch her half-naked body, and brushed her lips against Dawn's.

Dawn rolled around and wrapped her arms around Aiden's neck to pull her more firmly into the kiss.

Aiden moaned when she felt the naked torso press against her T-shirt-clad body. Her hips shifted against Dawn's, and she supported herself on her elbows so she wouldn't crush Dawn beneath her. Her fingers flexed, fighting against the urge to wander over the bare skin. She let them tangle in the golden-blonde strands instead. She nibbled on Dawn's lips, and when they opened in response, she leaned over her more fully to have a better angle.

Dawn gasped and shifted under her. Her grip on Aiden's shoulders tightened.

It took a few moments for Aiden's passion-clouded mind to realize that those were not signs of desire but an attempt to stop her. She immediately moved back, breaking the contact between their bodies.

Dawn lay flat on her back, looking up at Aiden with wild eyes. Her breathing came in gasps.

Aiden wasn't sure if it was more a sign of arousal or of fear.

"I'm sorry. I just... It..."

"It's okay." Aiden rubbed both hands over her face. She closed her eyes to control herself and to give Dawn an opportunity to slip her shirt back on. "Tell me what I did wrong. What can trigger a flashback? I need to know so that I don't accidentally..."

Dawn sank against the headboard. "I don't know either, Aiden. I haven't even thought about sharing physical...sexual intimacy with anyone since that night, so how would I know?"

Aiden blew out a shuddery breath. "We'll figure it out

together." She moved closer and, never taking her gaze off Dawn's face, wrapped her arms around her, relieved when Dawn pressed closer.

"I think it was... Your fingers were in my hair and..."

"You don't like that?"

"I do. I did." Dawn burrowed her face against Aiden's shoulder. "I enjoyed what we did. Very much so. But I also felt a little out of control, and that scared me. And then your fingers in my hair and your body on top of mine... He...Ballard, he grabbed my hair when he forced me to kiss him."

Aiden bit her lip. It hurt to think that she had triggered memories of that awful night. "I'll be more careful next time."

Dawn wrapped her arms around her waist and squeezed. "You're already the gentlest and most patient lover I could wish for."

"And the most talented?" Aiden tried a grin and was glad to see Dawn smile in return.

"But of course."

"Want to go to sleep now?"

When Dawn nodded, Aiden reached out an arm and extinguished the candles even though she knew that she wouldn't be able to fall asleep anytime soon.

Someone was in her bedroom.

She tried to turn on the light but couldn't move. He had her arms pinned to the bed, holding her down with his body on top of hers. His breath washed over her face as he bent down. Screaming, she tried to dislodge him.

"Dawn! Dawn!"

It wasn't his voice. Someone else was there, in her bedroom. *Help!* Dawn struggled again. Her arms came free, and she swung them around.

"Ow! Dawn! Dawn, sweetheart, you're dreaming. C'mon, wake up. It's just a dream."

Dawn shot up. Her eyes flew open. She pressed a hand over her hammering heart and looked around. She wasn't in her bedroom, and Ballard wasn't there. She was with Aiden. She was safe. Dawn shook her head to fight off the remnants of her nightmare.

"Hey." Aiden's voice was gentle. "Are you all right?"

She took a deep breath. "Yeah, just a nightmare."

Aiden reached out a hand but hesitated to touch her until Dawn nodded her agreement. Dawn loved her for her intuitive understanding of how difficult it was for her to be touched right now. Her eyes fluttered closed when Aiden rubbed the tears from her cheeks. "Do you want to talk about it?"

Dawn sighed. "It was just the usual. I dreamed that I was back in my old bedroom and couldn't move because he held me down." She didn't want to go into too much detail, fearing that it would trigger another flashback.

"Shit!" Aiden slapped her own forehead. "I'm sorry. I think that was me."

"What do you mean?"

"I woke up when you started tossing and turning and screaming. I had moved toward your side of the bed and wrapped an arm around you in my sleep—I practically held you down." Aiden groaned, her expression guilty.

Dawn shook her head. "It's not your fault. I had the same nightmare a hundred times when I slept alone."

"But you haven't had one in a while, have you? Is there something that caused it now?"

"Maybe it has something to do with my work. I saw a patient today whose story hit a little too close to home."

"You treated a rape victim?" Aiden's brow furrowed. "Why didn't someone else take that patient? I thought your colleagues agreed to see all rape and abuse cases?"

Dawn sighed. "Well, it's not like all of them come in and reveal to the secretary that they're here because they were raped. It was a teenage girl whose parents sent her because of her 'behavioral problems.' It wasn't until the eighth session that she trusted me enough to tell me that she was raped."

"Will you refer her to one of your colleagues?"

Dawn appreciated the concern, but she shook her head. "I can't do that. It took a lot of trust and courage on her part to tell me. If I refuse to see her again, she might not continue her therapy. I can't destroy our progress just because it's hard for me."

"Dawn..."

She touched Aiden's cheek. "Don't worry. I'll talk it over with my supervisor. I really think I can do it. I can help this girl."

"Okay," Aiden said. "You're the expert."

The simple words of trust made Dawn smile.

"Do you want to try and go to sleep again?" Aiden asked.

Dawn knew that there would be no more sleep for her this night. "I think I'll stay up for a while, maybe watch some *Xena* reruns or something. I'll turn down the volume. Don't worry."

"Why don't you stay right here instead? Let's talk for a while."

"I don't want to keep you up. You have to work tomorrow."

Aiden gently pinched her nose. "I've been up all night before. I'm used to it. But maybe you want to be left alone to ogle your Warrior Princess?"

Dawn laughed. "No, thanks, I have my very own warrior; that's enough for me. Or do you want to go and drool over Gabrielle again?"

"I never drooled over that bard," Aiden said. "I have my own drool-worthy strawberry blonde."

"Drool-worthy, hmm?" Dawn grinned. Hearing how she affected Aiden as a woman was like a healing balm for her battered perception of her own attractiveness. She leaned forward to touch her lips to Aiden's. "Hey, what's that?" She rubbed her thumb over the dark smudge on Aiden's jaw but jerked back when Aiden flinched. "Is that a bruise?"

Aiden turned her head away so that the light from the bedside table couldn't reach that side of her face anymore. "It's nothing."

"That's cop speak for 'It hurts like hell,' right?" An icy ball formed in her stomach when she remembered the desperate kicks and punches she had thrown at her nightmare attacker. She vaguely remembered hitting flesh. "Oh, God! Was that me?"

"Let's just say that those self-defense classes are starting to pay off. You pack quite a punch, girl." Aiden grinned proudly.

Dawn was anything but proud, though. "I'm so sorry." She reached out to lightly touch Aiden's jaw again. "I didn't want to..."

"It's okay, really." Aiden took Dawn's hand off her jaw and pressed a kiss to every single finger. "It's good to see that you know how to hit someone hard enough to hurt."

Dawn still couldn't see anything positive about her hitting Aiden. She slipped out of bed and returned with a ziplock bag full of ice. "Lie down." She directed Aiden down until her head rested in Dawn's lap. With one hand, she held the bag to Aiden's jaw while the other gently combed through her hair.

"Hmmm, you can hit me anytime." Aiden closed her eyes with a hedonistic grin, her limbs sprawled across the bed like a puppy that was getting its belly rubbed.

"That's not funny."

"Okay, okay." Aiden turned her head to press a kiss to Dawn's knee. "So, what do we talk about?"

Dawn thought about the million things she wanted to know about Aiden. She supposed she would just begin at the beginning. "Tell me about your childhood."

The body resting in her lap tensed.

"What were you like in kindergarten?" Dawn quickly added.

"What?" Aiden's laughter broke the tension.

Dawn smoothed a finger over a dark eyebrow. "Come on, don't be shy. Tell me. I bet you were cute as hell."

Aiden snorted. "Cute is not the word my kindergarten teachers would have used to describe me. I drove them crazy, always climbing on trees and skinning my knees."

Dawn would have loved to see that. "Do you have photos?"

"No. My mom was never big on family photos."

Silence spread. The shadow of Aiden's father lurked in the room. "Tell me about your mother. What was she like?" She left the question vague enough that Aiden wouldn't feel backed into a corner.

"I imagine you already know as much about her as I do."

Dawn shook her head. "I know a lot about her as an artist, but not about her as a mother and a human being. What did she like to do when she wasn't painting?"

"Drinking," Aiden said.

Dawn caressed the bruised jaw. "Are there really no positive things that you remember about her?"

Aiden sighed. "She loved teaching," she finally answered. "She taught art at the university."

"So you do have some things in common with her," Dawn said.

Aiden peered up at her with a skeptical gaze. "I know nothing about art. You know that."

"Maybe not about art, but you are a good teacher." Dawn nodded when she saw Aiden start to shake her head. "I couldn't have asked for a better teacher when you taught me how to wall-climb. And you have the patience of a saint with Jamie."

"My mother was nothing like me. She wasn't into sports at all. She liked languages, literature, and expensive wine."

Dawn let her fingertips caress the slight dimple in Aiden's chin. She was aware of the implied self-criticism, but she let it go. "Sounds like a woman I would have liked."

"She would have liked you," Aiden said. "She would have dragged you out of my arms and into her studio, discussing art for hours."

"Was she aware that you might bring home a woman someday?"

"I don't think so. I never told her."

"She wouldn't have been overjoyed to hear that you live in a lesbian relationship?"

"Probably not," Aiden said. "I never had the courage to find out. Our relationship was damaged enough as it was, and I didn't want to disappoint her more than I already had."

Dawn stroked the bitter lines from Aiden's face. "Disappoint? Why do you think you were a disappointment to your mother?"

"From the moment of my conception, nothing about me was like the daughter she wanted to have."

"Did she tell you that?" Dawn asked.

"She didn't need to. It was obvious. She was an artist; I'm barely able to draw crime-scene sketches. She loved architecture and literature; I'm a jock. She didn't like my choice of careers, and she probably wouldn't have liked my sexual orientation."

"She loved you," Dawn said, cradling Aiden's face between both palms and looking deeply into her eyes.

Aiden sighed. "Yeah. I guess so."

"She loved you and was proud of you," Dawn said with more determination. "I don't have to guess to know that." She pointed at the wall and the two portraits hanging above the bed.

Aiden looked up too. "She was an artist. Of course she would draw me sometime. That proves nothing."

"Maybe not the fact that she painted a portrait of you—but the way she did it. Look at this." Dawn pointed at the older portrait. It showed a tiny baby being cradled in her mother's arms. "What do you see?"

Aiden shrugged. "Me as a baby."

"You look beautiful and innocent," Dawn said, studying the portrait.

"All babies look beautiful and innocent."

Dawn shook her head. "Your mother made you look beautiful and innocent in the portrait because that was the way she saw you."

"I was just a baby," Aiden said again. "Everyone thinks babies are beautiful and innocent."

"What about this?" Dawn pointed to the second portrait. "How old were you when your mother painted that?"

The portrait showed Aiden as a teenager, her lanky frame sprawled on a couch in a posture of typical teenage rebellion. Her honey-colored eyes held a hint of warmth, though, not the careless disrespect Dawn had expected.

"It was her present for my sixteenth birthday. We fought about it for days—I had wanted a car instead," Aiden said with a chuckle.

Dawn stroked the bruised jaw. "She loved you. She knew you were basically a good girl and would become a wonderful woman. It's obvious in every little detail." She pointed at the familiar golden flecks in the eyes of the teenager in the portrait and at the way the long hands were wrapped around a can of pop, carefully keeping any drips from falling onto the couch. "Just because it wasn't always easy between the two of you doesn't mean she loved you any less."

Aiden lifted her hand and caressed the fingers that held the ice bag to her jaw. "You're right. I sometimes forget all the happy moments and the good things about her."

"How old were you when you learned...about your father?" Dawn lifted the ice bag from Aiden's jaw so that she could see the emotions playing over her face.

"Seven," Aiden said, her mouth a grim line.

For a moment, Dawn thought she hadn't heard right. "Seven?"

"My mother shouted it at me when she was drunk one night," Aiden said. "I didn't really understand what it meant until I was older, but I knew that he was a bad man who had done terrible things to my mother." She grimaced. "That did wonders for my self-esteem during puberty."

Dawn bent down to kiss her, knowing that nothing she said could take away the pain of a lonely childhood.

"So, tell me, what kind of trouble did you get into when you were in kindergarten?" Aiden asked when their kiss ended.

By the time the alarm clock went off, Dawn knew all about Aiden's first crush on a woman, about her adventures at the law enforcement academy, her childhood, and her dislike of green beans. She had told Aiden about the difficult year after her father's and brother's deaths, her short marriage, and her secret—or not so secret—addiction to cookies.

They finally found themselves lingering in bed, reluctant to get up and leave each other, even though they had talked for hours. "I really enjoyed this," Dawn said when she sat up.

Aiden yawned. "What? Staying up all night to keep the nightmares at bay and listening to the sad story of my life?"

"Your life is not a sad story." Dawn lovingly combed her fingers through a few tangled curls. "I enjoyed staying with you for a few days, getting to know you better. Still, I think it's time to move back into my apartment before Kia can consolidate her reign over your place."

Aiden looked up. She studied Dawn and then said, "Whatever you want."

Want? Dawn wasn't sure that she ever wanted to spend another minute without Aiden, but she suspected that moving in together at this point in the relationship wouldn't be the best idea. She still had a lot of issues to resolve, and Aiden needed more time to get used to the idea that her independent bachelor life was over.

"Will I see you tonight?" Aiden asked when they both moved out of bed.

Dawn nodded. "We're having dinner with my mom and Del, remember?"

"Oh, right. Spanish Inquisition for the advanced." Aiden gave her a crooked grin.

Dawn swatted her behind. "They're not that bad."

Aiden laughed. "Right."

CHAPTER 33

RAY THREW A STACK OF crime-scene photos across his desk and onto Aiden's. "So, what are you doing tonight?" He leaned back in his chair, arms crossed behind his head, and studied her.

Aiden spread the photos out on her desk. "Doing? Why do I have to do anything?"

"It's Valentine's Day."

"I repeat: why do I have to do anything?" Aiden looked up and began to twirl a pen between her fingers. "I never celebrated Valentine's Day."

Ray leaned forward, folding his hands in a schoolmasterly way. "It's just the thing you do when you're in a committed relationship and want to show her that you care—and you do care, don't you?"

Aiden met his curious gaze. She normally didn't discuss her relationships at work, but then again, there had never been much to discuss. "Sure I do. But I don't know... Buying the obligatory card, chocolate, and flowers for Valentine's... Isn't that awfully cheesy?"

"It's romantic," Ray said. "At least that's what Susan says. So, take my advice and send her flowers or chocolate or something. I haven't been exiled to the couch for a couple of years."

"Dawn doesn't even like chocolate." She didn't need a silly day to prove that she cared for Dawn; she wanted to show her every single day.

"Every woman likes that V-Day stuff," Ray said. "Even Okada ordered flowers for someone."

Okada looked up from his paperwork. "That had nothing to do with Valentine's Day. I always send my divorce lawyer flowers on her birthday—you never know when I'll need her again. Don't succumb to the pressures of rampant consumerism, Aiden."

Aiden smirked at Ray.

Ruben returned with a tray full of coffee-to-go cups for them. "Hey, Aiden, what are you doing for Valentine's?"

Groaning, she rose and collected the photographs. "I'll run these over to Kade, see if she wants to use them in court." At least their single, career-oriented deputy DA wouldn't ask about her plans for Valentine's Day. Aiden would bet her paycheck that Kade wasn't even aware of the date.

Kade was all business as she thumbed through the crime-scene photos, picking out those that she wanted to present in court. Only when she had seen the last picture did she look up at Aiden. "I haven't seen you all week. Were you busy preparing for Valentine's Day, Detective?"

Aiden groaned. "Not you too!"

Kade sent her a confused gaze.

"Everyone and their brother asked me about my plans for tonight—I don't have any, okay?"

"Okay," Kade said. "I just thought..."

"What are your plans?" Aiden asked, her tone challenging. Most likely, Kade would spend the evening working as she always did right before a trial started. That would prove her point that not everyone had to have something special planned on Valentine's Day.

Kade laid down the photos. A smile played around her lips. "I have a date."

What? So much for her theory. "Not that used-car salesman

again?" She realized that she felt protective toward Kade, but she was no longer jealous of her dates.

"He's the Vice President of an international car manufacturer, but no, it's not Wayne."

"It's not Judge Yates, is it?" Aiden asked.

"Yates?" Kade's eyes widened. "Why would you think that?"

Aiden leaned her elbows on Kade's desk. "Come on, Counselor, don't tell me you didn't notice how he almost fell from his bench last week because he was too busy staring at your legs."

Kade directed a confident Matheson smirk at her. "Well, my old law school professor used to say that sometimes long legs are better than long legal arguments. But no, I would never go out with a judge."

"So, who's this mystery date of yours? Do I know him?"

"Actually," Kade paused to make sure her office door was closed, "you know her."

The pen Aiden had been playing with clattered to the floor. "Her? You're dating a woman?" She leaned down and picked up the pen, just to have a second to collect herself. Of all the things she had expected Kade to say, this was the last on a list of a thousand possibilities.

"Don't tell me you of all people have something against that." Kade crossed her arms and stared her down.

"No! It's just..." Aiden shook her head to clear it. "I'm surprised as hell. I didn't know you were into dating women."

"Woman, singular," Kade said in her precise lawyer tone. "It's a rather recent development and, well, it's just one date and we'll see where it goes."

Aiden still didn't know what to say. All those months of secret admiration and longing glances when she thought Kade wasn't looking—and now she discovered that there was at least a theoretical possibility that Kade could have returned her interest. "You said I know her...your date? It's not Stacy, is it?"

"Stacy? Stacy Ford?" Kade laughed. "God, no! She's a very nice woman, but dating another DDA? Really, really, really bad idea."

"Not a DDA and not a judge—a cop, then?"

Kade nodded. Her eyes shone.

"Someone with the SAD or Central Precinct?" Aiden asked.

"No."

Aiden furrowed her brow. "No? Then where do you know her from?"

"Actually, you were the one that introduced us."

"Me?" Aiden couldn't believe it. As far as she knew, she hadn't introduced Kade to any lesbian cops. *Except for...* She stared at Kade. "You're not dating Lieutenant Vasquez, are you?"

Kade's smile widened.

"God!" Chaotic thoughts ping-ponged through Aiden's mind. Kade dating a woman was mind-boggling enough, but the thought of her with Dawn's adopted aunt... That would definitely take some getting used to. "Why did it have to be Del Vasquez? This practically makes you my aunt-in-law!"

Kade laughed. Her good mood seemed indestructible. "She's really sweet."

Aiden arched an eyebrow. "Kade Matheson wants sweet?" She had always imagined that Kade was a woman who would want to be conquered.

"I want sweet, honest, reliable, and passionate. Del is all that."

"She's also old enough to be your mother," Aiden said.

Kade rolled her eyes. "Maybe if she'd had me when she was ten. Besides, not that I've ever been in a relationship with one, but maybe I like older women?" She winked at Aiden, who almost swallowed her tongue.

"I'm older than you," she said and then wanted to slap herself.

"Oh, you don't say? Is that an offer, Detective?" Kade peered at her over the rim of her glasses.

This conversation came a few months too late. At this point in her life, not even Kade could make her forget about Dawn. "No! I'm happily partnered already, thank you very much."

"Relax, Detective. I'm just teasing you."

Aiden frowned. Kade was enjoying this a little too much. "Oh? So you wouldn't have gone out on a date with me?"

"You never asked."

The teasing turned serious. "Were you waiting for me to ask?"

Kade regarded her with a steady gaze. "No. The only question I've been waiting for since I passed the bar is 'Do you want to run for DA?' For the last few years, I took case files and law books to bed, not lovers."

Aiden nodded. Kade had never made a secret of how career-oriented she was. "So, what made you risk all that for a date with a woman?"

"She sent me flowers."

"You agreed to go out with her just because she gave you a bunch of flowers?" Aiden laughed. "Counselor, you're cheap."

"She sent me flowers every day since the trial ended. Every single day," Kade said. "Handpicked and grown in her own greenhouse."

Aiden whistled. "Since the trial ended? Wow, she must have a pretty big greenhouse." She hadn't known that Del was a gardener or that she had a romantic streak, but there was one thing she did know and it made her worry about Kade. "Kade, seriously, I don't want to spoil this for you, but I'm not sure Del is emotionally available. I had the impression that she's a bit in love with Dawn's mother."

Instead of reacting with concern or outrage as Aiden had expected, Kade leaned back in her chair, the picture of calmness. Her high-heeled shoes thumped to the floor when she slipped them off. "Del already told me."

"She told you she's in love with another woman?" Clearly,

Aiden had been absent from the world of dating for too long if that was the new way of winning over a woman. She had been convinced that the proud Kade Matheson would never play second fiddle to anyone.

"It's not like that. Not really. It's complicated." Kade fidgeted. For the first time since the conversation had started, she looked uncomfortable. "When Del met her, Grace was married to her partner and best friend. She liked her, and she admired the kind of relationship Grace and Jim had, but that was all. After Jim's death, she kind of took over a parental role for Dawn. Del has always wanted to have a big family, but hers didn't take too kindly to her coming out, so she fell into the comfortable role of playing house with Grace. Yes, she said that she was half in love with Grace for a lot of years, but she recently discovered that what she was in love with was really just the idea of having a family, someone she belonged to."

"If she hurts you, I'm gonna kill her," Aiden said, clenching her fists.

Kade reached across the desk and squeezed her arm. "I bet Del said the same thing about you and Dawn."

"That's not the same thing."

"Of course not." Kade grinned.

Aiden scowled until the grin dimmed. "So, what are you and your Latin lover doing for Valentine's Day?"

Kade pointed a sharpened pencil at her. "Refer to her like that again, and I'll let some slimy defense lawyer grill you next time you're on the stand. I'll catch up on my beauty sleep while you sweat during the cross-exam."

"All right, all right." Aiden held up her hands. "I'd better get back to work. Seems I'll have to leave early to plan my Valentine's Day activities. I don't want it told that some old lieutenant with the North Precinct outclassed me in that department." Kade's chuckle followed her to the door. "Bye, Auntie Kade."

Dawn had slaved in the kitchen for hours, but now she found herself ignoring the delicious food on her plate. The woman at the table across from her took her complete attention. Aiden filled all of her senses: the subtle fragrance of her perfume, the sound of her voice, the candlelight that made her eyes glow, the way she lifted the wineglass and then licked a drop of red wine from her sensual lips.

She had rarely seen Aiden dressed up. While she found her spectacular in faded jeans and her leather jacket, in a pair of black dress pants and a formfitting powder blue shirt with the top two buttons open, she took Dawn's breath away.

Aiden was equally busy staring at Dawn's dress, not eating much even though she had told her three times how delicious everything tasted.

Finally, they carried half-full plates to the kitchen, and Dawn tugged Aiden with her to the couch. She wanted to cuddle up to Aiden, throw her arms around her and a leg over her thighs, but her snug-fitting dress made that impossible.

Aiden reached behind her and handed Dawn the gift she had placed on the coffee table earlier. "Happy Valentine's Day."

Dawn chuckled as she looked down at a giant box of her favorite cookies and various potted herbs that had been missing in her new kitchen. "Herbs?"

"You told me that you were not a big fan of cut flowers," Aiden said.

Dawn nodded. She hated to see them wither and die after just a few days. "Thank you." Her ex-husband and Maggie had never given her anything but generic gifts like roses and chocolate, and she loved Aiden's unconventional but thoughtful gifts. She leaned over to reward Aiden for her creativity with a kiss. Her hands slid over the smooth material of Aiden's shirt, then slipped beneath and touched the bare skin of her back, where they began to wander without conscious thought. She caught a full lower lip between her teeth and deepened the kiss.

Aiden's warm hands came to rest on her waist, pulling her closer.

Only the need for air and the vague memory of the gift she still had to give Aiden finally made her break the kiss. She took the small box from the coffee table and handed it to Aiden.

Aiden's eyes widened as she took in the jewelry box. Her thumb caressed the velvet. She lifted the lid, but instead of looking down, she stared at Dawn. "Uh, this isn't...?"

Dawn smiled at the mix of fear and hope in Aiden's eyes. She fully intended to buy a ring for next Valentine's at the latest, but for now, something else lay in the small box. "Take a look. I promise it won't bite."

Aiden finally looked down and lifted the object from its box. "A key? You didn't buy me a car, did you?"

Dawn laughed and shook her head. "Nope, sorry, no car. It's a key to my apartment. It's very close to the courthouse and your precinct, so if you don't feel like driving across town during rush hour to your own apartment, I want you to come here, even when I'm at work. Mi casa es su casa." She took a deep breath. "And, maybe in a few months, if you decide that you want to move in, that would be okay with me. Very okay."

Aiden rose and moved to the door.

"W-where are you going?"

Aiden picked up her keys that she had left on a sideboard by the door. "I'm adding your key to my key chain. The idea of someday living with you is very okay with me too." She moved back to the couch and bent down to kiss Dawn. Once again, Dawn's tight-fitting dress prevented full-body contact. "As stunning as you look in that dress, it's really starting to annoy me."

"Then let's take it off and get more comfortable." Dawn rose with sudden determination, grabbed Aiden's hand, and led her to her bedroom. She handed Aiden one of her larger T-shirts and chose one for herself.

T-shirts in hand, they stood and looked at each other. Neither of them moved to the bathroom to change.

"Your zipper is on the back," Aiden said, her voice low. "Do you want me to...?"

Dawn stared at the triangle of smooth, tan skin revealed by the open buttons of Aiden's shirt. "In a moment. But first, let me help you." She lifted her hands to unbutton the shirt, but instead, her fingers traced a trail down Aiden's neck to the hollow at the base of her throat and then across the contours of her collarbone. She closed her eyes when she felt the heat radiating from Aiden's skin and inhaled deeply. Her lips touched Aiden's neck and wandered downward. The buttons were momentarily forgotten and only remembered when they hindered her path. With trembling fingers, she opened the first button, then the next. The shirt began to fall open, and her lips followed its way down.

"Dawn..." Aiden groaned. It was a warning, an attempt to slow her down.

"No." Dawn was determined not to stop. "I want this. I'm sick of being a rape victim without a normal love life."

"I know, but—"

Dawn shook her head. "Don't try to protect me. I know your intentions are honorable, but protection is not what I need. Let me make my own decision about whether I'm ready or not."

Aiden looked into her eyes, still holding the shirt closed with one hand. "I don't want to scare you." Her voice trembled with barely suppressed emotions.

"You seem to be more frightened than I am." Dawn stepped closer again, drawn to Aiden's heat and scent.

Aiden smiled ruefully. Her intense gaze, which still rested on

Dawn's face, felt almost like a touch. "Stop me anytime you want to, okay?"

Dawn nodded, determined not to stop this time. She watched as Aiden let the shirt slide down her arms and stepped out of her pants. When they fell to the floor, Aiden stood in front of her in just a simple bra and a pair of panties.

"Can we..." Dawn licked her dry lips and pointed at the bra. "Can we take that off too?"

Aiden reached behind herself and unhooked the bra. In just her panties, she stood motionless and with a confidence that was as breathtaking as her body.

Dawn couldn't help staring. She wanted to reach out a hand, eager to touch and taste Aiden's skin, but Aiden's hoarse voice stopped her.

"I want to see you too." Aiden's hands shook as she directed Dawn to turn around so she could reach the zipper.

Dawn gripped the dresser in front of her when she felt the length of Aiden's almost naked body come to rest against her back. Heat shot through her as hard nipples brushed against her upper back and Aiden's breath washed over her neck. "Aiden," she groaned, desperate to turn around, to see her and kiss her.

But Aiden was in no hurry to give up her position. Instead of unzipping the dress, she laid her hands over Dawn's, pressing even closer and pinning Dawn against the dresser. Her lips nuzzled the sensitive spot under Dawn's ear and then trailed upward to capture her earlobe.

"Aiden!" Dawn was trembling, no longer sure how much of it was desire and how much was rising panic. She had known that Aiden would be an intense and passionate lover and that she would unconsciously try to take over and control their lovemaking. Usually, it would be a turn on for her, but right now it was beginning to overwhelm her.

Aiden immediately dropped her arms and turned her around. "We don't have to do this."

Dawn had no intention of having this discussion again. She didn't want to talk at all. She crushed her lips to Aiden's, swallowing any further words. When she had to break away to breathe, she leaned up on her tiptoes to nibble on one of the ears she loved so much. The movement pressed Aiden's bare breasts against her and made both of them gasp.

Aiden's low growl sent a shiver down her body. She breathed in Aiden's musky scent and pressed her lips to the hollow at the base of her throat.

"Your dress has to go. Is that okay?" Aiden asked, moving back a little to look into Dawn's eyes.

Dawn nodded.

Warm hands directed the zipper down her back. The sound of the zipper's metal teeth giving way one by one made Dawn hold her breath in nervous anticipation. Aiden's hands followed the falling dress down her body and pushed the pantyhose down Dawn's hips.

The cool air in the bedroom barely had time to touch her before Aiden's hot skin covered her own. Aiden trailed kisses down her throat and traced the lacy edge of her bra with her lips. "This too?" Aiden's husky voice, her breath on Dawn's chest, created a trail of goose bumps.

"Please."

With gentle fingers, Aiden undid the clasp of her bra and then touched the underside of one breast. "You're beautiful."

Dawn sucked in a sharp breath.

"Let's move this to the bed." Aiden began to direct her backward.

The dress and pantyhose that pooled forgotten around her feet tightened around her ankles, trapping her for a moment. Without warning, Dawn's vision dimmed and she started to hyperventilate. The dress morphed into Ballard's hands and feet that were manacling her helpless limbs to the bed. Aiden's breath caressing her cheek became his scratching beard stubbles. The smell of beer and smoke seemed to linger in the air.

"Dawn!"

She could barely hear Aiden's voice over the roaring in her ears.

"Dawn, it's okay. It's only me, Aiden."

With a choked gasp like a diver breaking through the water's surface, Dawn found her way back into the present.

Aiden enclosed her in an embrace that was now trying to be soothing rather than arousing.

"God damn it!" Dawn let her head drop against Aiden's shoulder. Tears of frustration burned her eyes.

Aiden kissed her temple. "Shhh, it's okay."

"No, it's not okay!" She wanted to make love with Aiden. She wanted to lose herself in the passion she felt, but Garett Ballard had taken that away from her.

"Dawn, we have all the time in the world—"

"I don't want time," Dawn said. "I want you. Don't tell me that this isn't driving you crazy too." She could feel Aiden tremble with suppressed desire. Passion simmered in the honey-colored eyes.

Aiden sighed. "Come to bed and just let me hold you, okay?"

Dawn struggled out of the dress and pantyhose, trudged across the room, and sat down heavily on the edge of the bed. This was not how she had planned this evening.

"Hey." The warmth of Aiden's hand on her back reminded her that she was still mostly naked.

Her breath quickened, and her body reacted to the touch even though her mind was not yet ready to take the last step. Sighing, Dawn slipped under the covers. Aiden's skin touched hers, and she forgot her frustration as she started to caress her shoulders, then her collarbone and—

"Dawn!" Aiden took hold of the hand that was about to touch her breast. "Are you trying to kill me?"

"No." Dawn brushed her lips against the hand that held her own. "I'm trying to love you."

Aiden shook her head. "You're not ready to make love. My poor body just couldn't take it if we had to stop again."

Dawn looked down at her and traced the forced half grin on Aiden's lips with her fingertips. "Just because my body refuses to be touched right now doesn't mean that I can't make love to you."

Aiden tightened her grip on Dawn's hand. "No. This is not about physical satisfaction. I want to make love with you and give you the same pleasure you give me."

"You do. It would please me very much to make love to you," Dawn said. "I want to share this with you as much as I'm able to right now. You don't help me by being a martyr. Please, let me have this." She knew that Aiden had never liked giving up control and letting her partner direct their lovemaking, so she just looked into her eyes without further attempts to convince her, prepared to accept her decision, whatever it might be.

Aiden exhaled. "All right. Consider me your willing sex slave." She sprawled her arms and legs to both sides, injecting some much-needed humor into a situation that was weighted down by fears and frustrations.

With trembling limbs, Dawn lingered over her, bracing herself with her hands on either side of Aiden.

Aiden raised both hands to caress her face, then laid them on Dawn's hips and gently tugged her down.

Dawn gasped when their nearly naked bodies pressed together all along their lengths, belly to belly, thigh to thigh, breast to breast, separated just by their panties. Aiden's skin burned against her own. She closed her eyes for a moment, overwhelmed with sensation. When she opened them again, she looked directly into Aiden's darkened eyes. Never breaking eye contact, she began to trace the contours of Aiden's face.

Aiden lay still as Dawn's fingertips explored arched eyebrows and well-defined cheekbones.

Leaning down, Dawn stifled a gasp when their breasts brushed against each other. Heat raced up and down her body. She pressed her lips to Aiden's cheek and watched as dark lashes fluttered when she teased them with her breath before she moved down to kiss the faint laugh lines around Aiden's full lips.

When she trailed kisses downward, eager to press her lips to the firm jaw line, Aiden arched forward and drew her into a deep kiss.

Dawn collapsed onto her and let the heat and softness envelop her. When Aiden shifted under her and began to roll over, she drew back and pressed one hand against Aiden's chest, gently pushing her back down. "Patience, patience."

Aiden groaned but flopped back down.

Dawn knelt over her, slowly lowering herself. She let her hair trail over Aiden's skin before nibbling on a tempting earlobe. Aiden's shiver sent an answering rush of goose bumps down her body. She rained soft kisses down Aiden's neck, tasting the pulse pounding under her lips, and then nibbled on her collarbone.

With her fingertips, she traced the necklace around Aiden's neck and kissed the good luck charm, the metal cool against her lips before they returned to the heat of Aiden's skin. Nuzzling the soft spot at the base of her throat, she inhaled Aiden's scent. "Hmm, I love the way you smell."

A moan escaped Aiden's throat as Dawn grazed her teeth over her neck and sucked lightly on her skin. "God..." Aiden lifted her head to gaze at Dawn and then let it drop back on the pillow. "You're driving me crazy."

Dawn smiled. Discovering that she had this kind of power

over Aiden gave her back the sense of control that had been taken from her.

She kissed the slope of Aiden's breast just over her heart. The skin under her lips was salty and trembled with the thudding beat of Aiden's heart. Cradling one breast in her palm, she bent down to kiss it.

Aiden tightened her arms around her but resisted the urge to draw her back to her breast as Dawn continued her path down her body. She caressed the defined muscles of Aiden's abdomen with her lips. Aiden's hips twitched restlessly as Dawn smoothed her hand down the flat belly, stopping when she encountered her panties. "Let me take these off," she said in a voice she almost didn't recognize as her own.

The muscles of Aiden's thighs stretched under her as Aiden lifted her hips, allowing Dawn to push the panties down long legs.

"Yours too?" Aiden asked hoarsely.

Dawn nestled her body between Aiden's thighs. "Not yet," she mumbled before her mouth was on Aiden's breast.

Aiden gasped as she pressed closer. She was panting, clearly struggling not to take control of their lovemaking. One strong hand clutched Dawn to her; the other grasped the sheets to anchor herself as her hips surged upward. "Dawn!" Her skin was flushed and covered in a light sheen of perspiration. "This will be over in two seconds if you don't slow down."

Dawn had wanted to take her time and to slowly explore every inch of Aiden's body, but Aiden's legs tightening around her thigh and the pressure growing in her own belly urged her on. "Don't hold back," she whispered, staring into amber eyes burning with passion. "I love how you react to my touch." She trailed her trembling fingers over Aiden's trim waist, over the gentle curve of her hip and down to the hollow where her abdomen met her thigh. Her fingertips danced over the soft skin on the inside of her thigh.

Aiden's muscles quivered and twitched under her touch.

She pressed her face against Aiden's neck and closed her eyes as she stroked across her clit with one gentle finger.

"Dawn!" Aiden sucked in a sharp breath. Her head lolled to the side, giving Dawn's wandering lips more access to her neck.

Warm fingers splayed across Dawn's lower back, drawing their bodies even closer. Aiden's movements grew more frantic, and Dawn felt her body answer, surging against Aiden's. She moved her finger faster. Hot breath washed over her cheek as Aiden panted against her.

Aiden's hips rose and fell. Her eyes fluttered shut.

"Look at me! Look at me, Aiden." Dawn needed that contact, needed Aiden to be fully present and with her until the very last second.

Immediately, Aiden opened her heavy-lidded eyes. Their gazes locked, and their mouths collided in desperate passion as Dawn slid two fingers inside Aiden.

Aiden's legs began to tremble, and with another thrust from Dawn, they stiffened. Her hips arched off the bed, and she wrapped her arm more tightly around Dawn while her other hand clutched at the sheet. When Dawn's thumb brushed against her clit, Aiden broke the kiss with a gasp and threw her head back, the fine muscles in her neck tensing. Her mouth opened in a silent cry. She stopped breathing. Her body shuddered, then collapsed back onto the pillows.

Dawn stilled her hand and curled into Aiden's side, resting her cheek against her sweat-dampened chest to listen to the pounding of her heart. A feeling of peace settled over her. After a few minutes, she touched her lips to Aiden's and whispered, "Thank you."

"You're thanking me?" Aiden rasped. "It's me who—"

Dawn interrupted her with another kiss. "No. You did this for me. You trusted me enough to make yourself vulnerable and gave me full control even though that's not what you'd normally do. So, thank you. It may not have been 'let's tear each other's clothes off and break the bed' sex, but—"

Aiden lifted her head. "Who says it wasn't?"

Giving her an embarrassed grin, Dawn shrugged. "I know that it wasn't what you're used to."

"Maybe not, but that's not a bad thing. It may have been out of my comfort zone with anyone else, but I trust you enough to give up control." Aiden pulled her even closer. "Do you want to...?" She raised her eyebrows, still out of breath.

"No." Dawn brushed her thumb over Aiden's deep red, swollen lips. Making love to Aiden hadn't left her unaffected, but she didn't want to spoil this wonderful experience by trying for too much. She reached down and drew the crumpled sheet over them both.

"Are you sure?" Aiden entwined their fingers and rested them against her still quivering belly. "I feel a little selfish—"

"Selfish? God no, that was the most beautiful gift that I've ever gotten for Valentine's."

Aiden nuzzled her throat. "Mmm, me too. Happy Valentine's Day, Dawn."

"Happy Valentine's." Dawn burrowed deeper into the embrace and closed her eyes.

Dawn blinked and opened her eyes. It was still dark in the bedroom, and for a few moments, she wasn't sure what had woken her. She searched for her glasses and discovered that she still had two hours before she had to get up. When she shifted a little, soft skin brushed against her thigh.

Aiden was cuddled up behind her, one arm providing Dawn

with a pillow while her other hand rested just an inch under her breasts. Their legs were entwined. By now, Dawn was familiar with Aiden's presence in her bed, but this intimate skin-on-skin contact was new and made her breath quicken.

Her mind presented her with snapshots of Aiden, her head thrown back in ecstasy, trembling in her arms. She licked her lips and shifted in Aiden's embrace, gasping when Aiden's thigh, entwined with her own, pressed against her.

"Mmm?" Aiden clutched her even closer as she woke. She groped for the switch of the lamp on the bedside table and blinked into the light. "Dawn? You okay?" She gently turned Dawn around so she could see her face.

Their bare torsos pressed together, and Dawn suppressed another gasp. "Yeah."

"Sure?" Aiden cupped her cheek and traced the rim of her ear. "You sound a little breathless. You didn't have a nightmare, did you?"

At the tender touches, Dawn's eyes fluttered shut. "No nightmare. If I sound breathless, it's entirely your fault."

"My fault? Oh!" Aiden grinned. After a few moments, her grin dimmed and was replaced with a look of concern. "I could get up and put on a sleep shirt if this makes you uncomfortable."

"Or you could stay in bed and help me undress," Dawn said, even though a voice in the back of her head whispered, *What if I can't do this?*

Aiden studied her as if she was about to tell her again that they had all the time in the world and should wait, but instead, she finally nodded. "Okay. Keep talking to me. Tell me if I'm going too fast or you want to stop."

Dawn swallowed and nodded.

Slowly, Aiden reached out to remove the turquoise-rimmed glasses, but Dawn stopped her with a quick touch. "Leave them on. I need to see you."

Aiden moved back a little and waited until Dawn had slipped off her underwear, still covered by the sheet, before she drew her closer.

Both of them sighed when skin touched skin. Dawn's gentle curves fit perfectly against Aiden's taller, leaner form.

Dawn instantly began to kiss her, and Aiden closed her eyes as if fighting to control her emotions and let her set the pace. Keeping her gaze on Dawn's face, she trailed a path of kisses and light nips down her throat. Her lips caressed each of the freckles dusting Dawn's shoulders and then wandered lower, sending trails of fire down Dawn's body. Aiden tugged at the sheet covering both of them. "Is it okay if I take that away? I want to see you."

Dawn threw the covers back. Naked, she struggled not to fidget under Aiden's gaze. Would Aiden really like what she saw?

Aiden breathed a kiss onto her chest, just over her left breast. "You're so beautiful."

"I like your body better." Dawn glanced down at her own body, taking in her broader hips and softer thighs. "You have that really defined, flat abdomen, and I—"

"You're beautiful, exactly like you are." Aiden caressed the curve of Dawn's belly and looked up at her with a challenging grin. "Now, do you want to continue this discussion about our different aesthetic standards, or do you want to make love?"

Dawn grinned. "Make love."

"Very good. Right answer." Leaning over her on one elbow, Aiden bent down and pressed her lips to Dawn's collarbone, then continued down her sternum. Simultaneously, her fingers followed the arch of Dawn's ribs inward until they came to rest along the curve of her breasts. Slowly, she lowered her head.

Dawn's breath caught. She shuddered and moaned when warm breath teased her nipple.

Aiden nipped on the outer curve of one breast, playfully

kissing away the goose bumps. After a few seconds, she lifted her head and locked gazes with Dawn. "Is this okay?"

"Oh, I think it'll do," Dawn answered, struggling to catch her breath. She tangled her fingers in Aiden's hair, drawing her back down.

Aiden's chuckle ended when her lips touched Dawn's breast and began worshipping it.

Dawn fought to keep her eyes open, but she continued to watch Aiden. Never had she felt so connected to anyone.

"Hmm. Nice." Aiden kissed in smaller and smaller circles until she lightly captured a nipple between her lips and grazed it with the tip of her tongue.

A wave of pleasure shot down Dawn's body. "God, Aiden!" She gasped and clutched Aiden's hair.

"Mmm, I love touching you. And kissing you." With one last kiss to the hardened nipple, Aiden continued her path downward. She nuzzled the skin between Dawn's breasts and then planted kisses down her sternum, tasting her skin with gentle flicks of her tongue. She paused and pressed her cheek against the slight curve of her belly for a moment.

Dawn lay almost paralyzed. Her limbs felt molten; only her fingers alternately stroked and flexed in Aiden's hair.

Aiden trailed her hands down the outside of Dawn's thighs as she moved lower.

Dawn squirmed as Aiden tickled the almost microscopic hairs under her navel with her tongue and then followed them downward. For a moment, the feelings and sensations coursing through her grew so intense that they were almost a little overwhelming. A strangled moan escaped from her throat.

Aiden hastily looked up. "Is this too fast? Should I stop?"

Looking into Aiden's anxious eyes, Dawn tried to catch her breath. "No, no. I'm sorry. It was just a little overwhelming for a second."

Aiden scrambled up the bed, and Dawn willingly let herself be held. She took a deep breath, trying to catch up with the onslaught of sensations and emotions. "I felt like I was going to explode or something."

"I thought that was our goal?"

Dawn laughed and kissed her, keeping her eyes open to reestablish their connection. The feeling of Aiden's smooth skin sliding against her own soon made her forget her momentary trace of panic. She squirmed when Aiden's tongue flickered over the crook of her elbow and then traced imaginary patterns down to her pulse point. Their gazes met when Aiden kissed each knuckle. Gentle teeth captured her index finger, and Dawn couldn't keep her eyes open any longer. She settled back onto the bed and gave herself over to Aiden's touches. Only when she felt openmouthed kisses wander up her thigh did she reach out to stop her. "No."

Aiden froze and looked up at Dawn with an expression that almost reminded her of a kicked puppy.

"Not this time." Dawn entwined their fingers and drew Aiden up to rest next to her. "This time, I need you up here with me. I want to look into your eyes and know that this is you, you and me, making love."

Aiden gazed intently into Dawn's eyes. "Help me, please."

"What?"

"Help me to make love to you," Aiden said. "Show me how you want to be touched."

Dawn stared at her. "Believe me, you don't need any help. You did a fantastic job all on your own."

"I don't doubt my skills as a lover," Aiden said with her famous Carlisle grin, buffing her nails on an imaginary shirt. "I just think that it'll be easier for you to let go if you can control what happens."

Dawn took a deep breath. "Okay, then. I just didn't want you to get an inferiority complex."

Aiden kissed her. "No danger of that." She lifted their entwined fingers. "So, give me a tour, please."

"All right. No stops to take photos without my permission, though." A lot more relaxed now, Dawn took the larger hand in her own and placed it on her breast. "First stop, enjoy your stay."

Aiden's fingers began to move under hers. "Hmm, nice view."

Dawn gazed down too, studying the contrast of Aiden's tan hand against her own pale skin. "Uh-huh." Stifling a moan, she closed her fingers over Aiden's and pressed them harder against her.

Aiden didn't try to hurry her along. She seemed content to explore first one, then the other breast under Dawn's direction.

The double sensation of feeling Aiden's strong but gentle hand move under her fingers and gliding over her skin made her entire body tingle. Being able to direct the attention of a woman as intense and confident as Aiden was intoxicating. Panting, Dawn guided their linked hands down her body.

Aiden's fingertips drew a sensual line from her breastbone to her navel, gently circling it until Dawn shuddered. "Where to now?" she whispered, her breath washing hot over Dawn's ear.

This time, Dawn had to struggle and catch her breath to formulate an answer fitting their road trip analogy. Thinking and talking were no longer a priority. "I think our trip's destination lies southward."

Aiden kissed her, gazing into her eyes from just a few inches away. "Lead the way, sweetheart."

Dawn eased their hands down her belly. Heat followed the combined touch until their hands came to rest on Dawn's hip.

"Still all right?" Aiden asked, her lips almost touching Dawn's. Her thumb drew circles over Dawn's hip bone.

With a nod, Dawn guided Aiden's hand down the outside of her thigh.

Halfway down her thigh, Aiden stopped and gaze her leg a gentle squeeze.

Maintaining eye contact, Dawn trailed their fingers up the inside of her thigh. She was gasping for breath, her vision was becoming hazy, and her pounding heartbeat almost drowned out the soothing sound of Aiden's voice. For a second, she mistook the symptoms of arousal for those of fear, and panic threatened to rise.

"Easy." Aiden kissed the glimmer of panic away. "It's me—Aiden. I won't touch you anywhere until you tell me to."

Dawn pulled her closer, pressing their upper bodies together with the strength of her embrace. She breathed in Aiden's unmistakable scent as she brought their hands back to the inside of her thigh, slowly moving them up. When Aiden's fingers hesitated under hers, she guided them the rest of the way.

Two of Aiden's fingers combed through damp curls and slid on either side of her clit, making Dawn jerk and suck in a shaky breath. Aiden kept her strokes light, never breaking eye contact as she circled Dawn's clit with a featherlight touch.

Staring into Aiden's eyes, Dawn started to rock her hips. She let go of Aiden's hand and instead gripped her forearm, where she felt the muscles flex with each movement. Warmth flooded her body, matching the heat radiating from Aiden. Drops of sweat pooled behind her knees and ran down the back of her calves. She could already feel the pressure in her stomach build. Her legs started to tremble.

"Does that feel good?" Aiden searched her face.

Dawn moaned her answer. Her hips surged against Aiden in a faster rhythm. Her gaze never leaving Aiden's face, she closed her fingers tightly around her forearm, guiding her again.

"Dawn..." Aiden hesitated. The muscles under Dawn's hand tensed. "Are you sure you want me to—?"

"Yes." Dawn gasped. "I want you...there. Only you."

Cautiously, Aiden dipped one finger inside of Dawn and then paused to watch her face. "All right?"

Dawn exhaled slowly. "Yeah." She clutched Aiden's neck and pulled her down into an urgent kiss, moaning into Aiden's mouth when she felt her finger slide deeper into her. "Aiden!"

A ball of hot tension began to build in her belly, spreading in all directions, making her breath catch until lights exploded behind her now closed eyelids. Every muscle in her body stiffened and then went limp. She slumped against Aiden, trusting the strong arms around her to keep her safe.

Aiden curled her body protectively around Dawn, holding her close while kissing her flushed cheek.

Dawn gradually became aware of soothing words that were whispered in her ear and Aiden stroking her back as aftershocks rippled through her. She lay quietly, clinging to Aiden and listening to the urgent pounding of their hearts until she could breathe again. She moaned as Aiden withdrew her fingers. Finally, she lifted her head a few inches off Aiden's shoulder.

Their gazes met and locked.

"God, Aiden, I..." She buried her face into the crook of Aiden's neck, snuggling deeper into her embrace. Emotions burned behind her eyes, and she had to press her lips to Aiden's skin to hold back a sob.

"Hey, hey!" Aiden wrapped both arms around her and pulled her up to look into her eyes. "You okay? Did I hurt—?"

"No!" Dawn dabbed at her eyes. "Of course you didn't. It's just... I never thought that I would have this...feel this again."

Aiden's lips curled into a soft smile. "I never thought that I would have something like this, either."

Dawn touched the smiling lips with one reverent finger. "Somehow, I find that hard to believe. You're so good at this. The way you made me feel... God!"

"Thanks, I aim to please." For a second, a teasing smile flitted across Aiden's face, but then her expression grew serious. "What I'm used to and what I've always been good at is having sex—making love is a new experience for me too."

They had always called it "making love" when they had talked about the physical part of their relationship, mainly because "having sex" had seemed much too clinical an expression for something that was so emotional for Dawn after her rape. But now, she sensed a deeper meaning behind Aiden's words. "You mean...?"

Aiden nodded.

Dawn restlessly played with the short hairs on Aiden's neck. "Can you...tell me?"

The muscles in Aiden's throat moved as she swallowed. "I love you," she whispered.

Dawn closed her eyes for a second. She hadn't known how much hearing the words meant to her until Aiden had spoken them. Wordlessly, she dipped her head and set out to kiss Aiden breathless. When they finally drew apart, she looked into Aiden's eyes. "In case there are any doubts left—I love you too."

They snuggled down together, never breaking eye contact until their eyes fluttered closed.

An hour later, the buzzing of the alarm clock woke Dawn. She reached out for Aiden, only to find the other side of the bed cold. Sitting up, she clutched the sheet to her naked body and looked around for her missing partner. Aiden was nowhere to be seen. *God, how could I have been so out of it that I didn't hear her get up?*

Then she heard the sound of clanging plates and metal scraping over metal from the kitchen, followed by a crash and a curse.

Smiling, she swung her legs out of bed to join her lover and rescue her kitchen utensils from further abuse.

The door opened, and Aiden entered the bedroom, wearing

just a bathrobe. “Hey, you’re supposed to be in bed.” Balancing a tray with coffee, tea, toast, bacon, and eggs, she settled down on the edge of the bed.

Dawn chuckled and slipped back under the covers. “One night and already all you can think about is to keep me in bed? Damn, I must be good.”

“You are.” Aiden kissed her gently.

“Thank you. You are not so bad yourself.” Dawn glanced at the lovingly prepared breakfast, picked up the mug, and inhaled the scent of her favorite tea. Her nose twitched as it detected something else that didn’t smell nearly as pleasant. She turned over the piece of toast. The unbuttered side was almost black.

“Well...” Aiden leaned over the tray to kiss her again. “You can’t have everything.”

Dawn closed her eyes as their lips met. *I don’t know—I think I do.*

###

ABOUT JAE

Jae grew up amidst the vineyards of southern Germany. She spent her childhood with her nose buried in a book, earning her the nickname "professor." The writing bug bit her at the age of eleven. For the last eight years, she has been writing mostly in English.

She used to work as a psychologist but gave up her day job in December 2013 to become a full-time writer and a part-time editor. When she's not writing, she likes to spend her time reading, indulging her ice cream and office supply addictions, and watching way too many crime shows.

CONNECT WITH JAE ONLINE

Jae loves hearing from readers!

E-mail her at: jae_s1978@yahoo.de
Visit her website: jae-fiction.com
Visit her blog: jae-fiction.com/blog
Like her on Facebook: facebook.com/JaeAuthor
Follow her on Twitter: @jaefiction

EXCERPT FROM *HIDDEN TRUTHS*

BY JAE

Stage Depot
Baker Prairie, Oregon
April 20, 1868

THE STAGECOACH SWAYED TO A halt, and Rika braced herself so she wouldn't be thrown onto the laps of her fellow travelers.

She drew in a breath. This was it, her new home. The stage's leather curtains were drawn shut to protect them from the mud flung up by the horses' hooves, so she hadn't yet caught a glimpse of the town. The two passengers opened the door and climbed down, but Rika was almost afraid to step outside and see what she had gotten herself into.

One of the men offered his hand to help her out of the stagecoach.

With one step, Rika sank ankle-deep into the mud on the main street. She shook out her wrinkled, sooty skirts and stepped onto the boardwalk.

A few dozen buildings dotted the rutted main street. Wooden signs announced the presence of a barbershop, a doctor's office, a blacksmith, and a saddle maker's shop in the little town. In front of the dry-goods store, a brown horse stood hitched to a buckboard.

One of Rika's fellow travelers disappeared into the barbershop; the other climbed onto a buckboard, tipped his hat, and drove off. Now only Rika stood waiting on the boardwalk.

She scanned the faces of the townspeople milling about Main Street, going into and coming out of buildings. The man with the handlebar mustache, her future husband, was nowhere to be seen.

The stage had come in late. Had he gotten tired of waiting and left? What if he changed his mind and no longer wanted a wife? Rika clutched her carpetbag to her chest.

Her gaze darted up and down the street, but no wagon came to pick her up. People hurried across the boardwalk, trying to get out of the rain that had started falling again. Some threw curious glances her way, but no one talked to her. Shivering, she slung her arms more tightly around the carpetbag.

A few young men wandered over from the livery stable. One of them doffed his battered hat. "Can we help you, ma'am?"

"No, thank you." Rika drew her bag against her chest. "I am waiting for Mr. Phineas Sharpe, my betrothed."

"Ah, then you're plumb out of luck, ma'am, 'cause Phin left to drive a few horses up to Fort Boise and won't be back for two months."

The blood rushed from her face, and she swayed. "Two months?"

"Or more." The man shrugged.

Oh, Jo. Good thing her friend would never find out that her beloved Phineas didn't intend to keep his promises. *Riding off to Boise when he knew his betrothed was coming...* She was stranded in an unfamiliar town, forsaken by a future husband who had apparently changed his mind. *What now?*

"I'm sorry I'm late," someone said behind her.

Rika turned.

A young woman stopped midstep.

Rika took in the woman's mud-spattered bodice and the bonnet hanging off to one side, revealing disheveled fiery red hair. Under a skirt that was ripped up to midthigh, flashes of long drawers startled her. Behind the woman, a sweat-covered gray horse pranced around.

What did she do to the poor horse?

When the wild-looking woman reached for the carpetbag, Rika flinched away. "Who are you?"

"Oh." A flush colored the stranger's golden skin. She wiped her hand on her skirt, probably not getting it any cleaner. "I'm Amy Hamilton, a friend of Phin Sharpe's. And who on God's green earth are you?"

The young woman stared at her.

Amy stared back.

"I'm Johanna Bruggeman," the stranger said.

Amy put her hands on her hips. "No, you're not. I've seen the tintype. You're not her."

The fragile beauty of Phin's bride had burned itself into her memory. The stranger, however, was neither fragile nor beautiful. While the tintype hadn't provided colors, Amy could tell that Phin's bride had fair hair. The stranger's brown hair, though, shone with the same coppery gleam as the mahogany coat of Nattie's mare. Her wide brown eyes reminded Amy of a spooked horse.

The woman's gaze flitted around, and she hid behind her carpetbag as if it were a shield. But then she tilted her head and composed her stern features.

Like a mustang. Spooked but unbroken in spirit.

"Of course I am Johanna Bruggeman." Her slight accent made the name sound exotic.

Right. She's Dutch. So was she Phin's bride after all? "Then how come you don't look like the woman in the tintype?"

A muscle in the stranger's face twitched. "Phineas showed you the tintype?"

Amy nodded and dug her teeth into her bottom lip. She hoped she wasn't blushing. Why did she feel like a boy who'd been caught with the picture of a dance-hall girl? It wasn't as if she had ogled the young woman's picture. She raised her chin. "You still owe me an explanation."

The stranger lowered her gaze. "I was too embarrassed to have my picture taken. I know men don't find me all that appealing, so a friend allowed me to send her picture instead."

Amy slid her gaze over her. *She is a bit on the plain side. All the better.* She had been afraid of how a woman who was every bit as beautiful as Hannah might make her react.

"I know it's vain," the young woman said. "But I hope you won't judge me for it."

"None of my business," Amy said. Just to be on the safe side, she didn't plan on having much to do with Phin's bride. Easy to do, since she would be busy with the ranch. "All right, then let's go. I'll take you to the ranch. My family will take care of you until Phin returns." She kept her movements gentle but firm, as if dealing with a young horse, and again reached for the carpetbag.

Finally, the woman handed over her baggage.

"Do you have any other bags?" Amy asked.

A flush stained the young woman's pale skin. "No, just this one."

As far as Amy was concerned, there was no shame in being poor. At least she wouldn't have to drag half a dozen suitcases, bags, and hatboxes to the buckboard and could get back to the ranch sooner.

The ranch and Mama. No doubt Mama would have something interesting to say about Amy's skirt and the mare.

Hidden Truths is available as a paperback and in various e-book formats at many online bookstores.

OTHER BOOKS FROM YLVA PUBLISHING

http://www.ylva-publishing.com

TRUE NATURE

Jae

ISBN: 978-3-95533-034-7
Length: 480 pages

When wolf-shifter Kelsey Yates discovers that fourteen-year-old shape-shifter Danny Harding is living with a human adoptive mother, she is sent on a secret mission to protect the pup and get him away from the human.

Successful CEO Rue Harding has no idea that the private teacher she hires for her deaf son isn't really there to teach him history and algebra—or that Danny and Kelsey are not what they seem to be.

But when Danny runs away from home and gets lost in New York City, Kelsey and Rue have to work together to find him before his first transformation sets in and reveals the shape-shifter's secret existence to the world.

HIDDEN TRUTHS

(revised edition)

Jae

ISBN: 978-3-95533-119-1
Length: 476 pages

"Luke" Hamilton has been living as a husband and father for the past seventeen years. No one but her wife, Nora, knows she is not the man she appears to be. They have raised their daughters to become honest and hard-working young women, but even with their loving foundation, Amy and Nattie are hiding their own secrets.

Just as Luke sets out on a dangerous trip to Fort Boise, a newcomer arrives on the ranch—Rika Aaldenberg, who traveled to Oregon as a mail-order bride, hiding that she's not the woman in the letters.

When hidden truths are revealed, will their lives and their family fall apart or will love keep them together?

SOMETHING IN THE WINE

Jae

ISBN: 978-3-95533-005-7
Length: 393 pages

All her life, Annie Prideaux has suffered through her brother's constant practical jokes only he thinks are funny. But Jake's last joke is one too many, she decides when he sets her up on a blind date with his friend Drew Corbin—neglecting to tell his straight sister one tiny detail: her date is not a man, but a lesbian.

Annie and Drew decide it's time to turn the tables on Jake by pretending to fall in love with each other.

At first glance, they have nothing in common. Disillusioned with love, Annie focuses on books, her cat, and her work as an accountant while Drew, more confident and outgoing, owns a dog and spends most of her time working in her beloved vineyard.

Only their common goal to take revenge on Jake unites them. But what starts as a table-turning game soon turns Annie's and Drew's lives upside down as the lines between pretending and reality begin to blur.

Something in the Wine is a story about love, friendship, and coming to terms with what it means to be yourself.

COMING HOME

(revised edition)

Lois Cloarec Hart

ISBN: 978-3-95533-064-4
Length: 371 pages

A triangle with a twist, *Coming Home* is the story of three good people caught up in an impossible situation.

Rob, a charismatic ex-fighter pilot severely disabled with MS, has been steadfastly cared for by his wife, Jan, for many years. Quite by accident one day, Terry, a young writer/postal carrier, enters their lives and turns it upside down.

Injecting joy and turbulence into their quiet existence, Terry draws Rob and Jan into her lively circle of family and friends until the growing attachment between the two women begins to strain the bonds of love and loyalty, to Rob and each other.

HEARTS AND FLOWERS BORDER

(revised edition)

L.T. Smith

ISBN: 978-3-95533-179-5
Length: 318 pages

A visitor from her past jolts Laura Stewart into memories—some funny, some heart-wrenching. Thirteen years ago, Laura buried those memories so deeply she never believed they would resurface. Still, the pain of first love mars Laura's present life and might even destroy her chance of happiness with the beautiful, yet seemingly unobtainable Emma Jenkins.

Can Laura let go of the past, or will she make the same mistakes all over again?

Hearts and Flowers Border is a simple tale of the uncertainty of youth and the first flush of love—love that may have a chance after all.

COMING FROM YLVA PUBLISHING IN 2014

http://www.ylva-publishing.com

IN A HEARTBEAT

RJ Nolan

Veteran police officer Sam McKenna has no trouble facing down criminals on a daily basis but breaks out in a sweat at the mere mention of commitment. A recent failed relationship strengthens her resolve to stick with her trademark no-strings-attached affairs.

Dr. Riley Connolly, a successful trauma surgeon, has spent her whole life trying to measure up to her family's expectations. And that includes hiding her sexuality from them.

When a routine call sends Sam to the hospital where Riley works, the two women are hurtled into a life-and-death situation. The incident binds them together. But can there be any future for a commitment-phobic cop and a closeted, workaholic doctor?

HEART'S SURRENDER

Emma Weimann

Neither Samantha Freedman nor Gillian Jennings are looking for a relationship when they begin a no-strings-attached affair. But soon simple attraction turns into something more.

What happens when the worlds of a handywoman and a pampered housewife collide? Can nights of hot, erotic fun lead to love, or will these two very different women go their separate ways?

Conflict of Interest
© by Jae

ISBN: 978-3-95533-109-2

Also available as e-book.

Published by Ylva Publishing, legal entity of Ylva Verlag, e.Kfr.

Ylva Verlag, e.Kfr.
Owner: Astrid Ohletz
Am Kirschgarten 2
65830 Kriftel
Germany

http://www.ylva-publishing.com

First edition: September 2008 (L-Book ePublisher)
Revised second edition: April 2014 (Ylva Publishing)

Credits
Edited by Judy Underwood and Nikki Busch
Cover Design by Streetlight Graphics

Lightning Source UK Ltd.
Milton Keynes UK
UKOW02f2128140814

236979UK00001B/26/P